Praise for
## *All I Want for Christmas*

"All *you'll* want for Christmas is [this] thoroughly de-lightful story. Cuddle up by the fire with a glass of eggnog and get ready to be immersed in the joy of the season with Suzi Christmas and Nicholas Claus."
—*New York Times* bestselling author Debbie Macomber

"A real dickens of a story."
—Susan Andersen, author of *Be My Baby*

"All the warmth and cheer of Christmas wrapped up in a heartfelt package."
—Jill Barnett

# Be My Valentine

## Sheila Rabe

JOVE BOOKS, NEW YORK

BE MY VALENTINE

A Jove Book / published by arrangement with
the author

PRINTING HISTORY
Jove edition / January 2001

ISBN: 0-515-12995-X

A JOVE BOOK®
Jove Books are published by The Berkley Publishing Group,
a division of Penguin Putnam Inc.
375 Hudson Street, New York, New York 10014.
JOVE and the "J" design
are trademarks belonging to Penguin Putnam Inc.

PRINTED IN THE UNITED STATES OF AMERICA

10  9  8  7  6  5  4  3  2  1

*For Kim,*
*cause you loved Shelby so much*

# Acknowledgments

Writing a book is a solitary occupation, except when it comes to research. Then a writer can always find someone to bug, which means that there is always a someone or two who should be thanked. So, here are mine.

Thanks, first of all, to the wonderful staff at the Fifth Avenue Theater in Seattle, who not only gave me a tour of this beautiful, historic building, but also allowed me to observe some of the rehearsals for *Camelot*. Thanks to Norb Joerder for taking a few moments to chat with me, and graciously allowing me to drop his name. Special thanks to Diane Sweeney, Miss Golden Throat, for introducing me to the fascinating people and exciting world that is the theater. Thanks to my nephew Clay, for the football info. (Aside from ogling the players, I still don't get the attraction of this game. But maybe my editor will explain it to me someday.) Thanks, also, to John Burrows, who let a perfect stranger tour his Greenlake house for inspiration.

So, John, let's have a book-signing there. Oops. Somebody pick John up off the floor, I think he fainted. I was just kidding John, honest.

Thanks again all, and a happily ever after to each of you.

# *One*

*Just a kiss?* That was all she was getting for New Year's? Shelby Barrett stared through the swirling confetti at the face of the man to whom she had given her heart and soul, not to mention her body.

Matt was looking back at her, smiling as if nothing were wrong. He looked like a movie star with that perfect, square chin, those blue eyes and that tousled, blond—bleached, what a phony!—hair. She would have to save for months to buy herself anything as expensive as the suit he was wearing. He could certainly afford a ring.

And, after his professions of love, their recent talk of their glowing future together, she had expected him to pull a small, velvet box from one of his pockets and wave it under her nose. Instead, he had only given her a long, searing kiss. And a kiss was not a diamond.

The words of the famous song from the classic movie, *Casablanca,* came floating into her mind, reminding her that a kiss is just a kiss. How true! Tonight, with no proof of his love to go with it, that touching of the lips was

*1*

nothing more than a small electric shock to be shaken off and forgotten.

"Come on, baby, let's dance in the new year," said Matt, tugging her into the frenzied crowd of generation X'ers.

All around her, bodies boogied and writhed. The sequins on the women's dresses fought the shattered laser lights for attention. The music shrieked. The balloons that had just dropped from the ceiling popped underfoot and several of her sister revelers squealed with each new pop.

Everyone was having fun, even Matt, who seemed unaware of the fact that a sinewy brunette in a tight, black dress had just danced in between them. There he was, her hero, slinking around the dance floor like he thought he was the second coming of John Travolta, while she stood here with a broken heart.

*The quality of mercy is not strained*, she quoted to herself. But she wasn't playing Portia now, and her quality of mercy was being strained to the breaking point. The brunette threw an arm out in wild abandon, narrowly missing Shelby's nose. That did it. No more mercy!

Shelby left the floor, snatching up her coat and purse on her way past their table. She shouldered by a group of laughing revelers, and someone blew one of those stupid paper snakes at her. The thing curled out and popped her in the eye and she grabbed it from the man and tossed it on the floor as she marched on, ignoring his startled, "Hey!"

Outside, Seattle's Pioneer Square was dotted with people. When her mother was young, the historic part of the city had been relinquished to street people and thugs, but other Seattleites were now staking a claim with shops and hot dance clubs. Under a myriad of tiny, golden Christmas lights, yuppies in slick suits, long, sleek coats, and expensive faux furs strolled, unseeing, past men in twenty-year-old jackets with beards to match. Music from the various clubs hung faintly on the air like stale perfume. The night was frosted and heavy drops of snow danced down to skate on half-frozen puddles.

Shelby pulled on her gloves and stepped to the edge of the sidewalk, looking for a cab. Cars zipped by. One zipped a little too close to the curb and threw up a rooster tail of dirty slush, splashing her coat. She let out a startled screech, then looked to see a wet stain drizzling down her front.

"Oh, lovely," she growled, brushing at it.

Like a knight to the rescue, a turbaned cabdriver pulled carefully up to the curb in front of her, and with tears of self-pity leaking out the corner of her eyes, she opened the door.

A hand on her shoulder stopped her from getting in. "Shelby."

She turned and saw Matt, his expression a demand to know what on earth she thought she was doing. As if she couldn't read his every expression by now, he added words. "What the hell are you doing?"

"Don't swear at me," she snarled. "I'm going home."

He grabbed her arm. "Are you nuts? I was looking everywhere for you."

"Well, now you found me. Let go," she added, jerking away.

Matt obliged, and the force of her movement sent her stumbling backward to land with a yelp in a mess of dirty, old snow piled up against the curb. Contact with the icy stuff fanned the flames of her anger to a blaze.

"Oh, geez," he muttered. He reached down and hauled her up. "I'm sorry, baby. Come on back inside and let's get you out of that wet coat."

"No, thanks. I'm not in a party mood anymore."

Matt scowled. "So I see. Do you think you could rein in that redheaded temper of yours long enough to tell me why?"

"You just don't know, do you? Well, Matt Armstrong, that speaks volumes about our relationship." She yanked the glove off her left hand and held it up for his inspection. "Do you see anything there?"

"No."

"Well, there's your answer: that's why the party's over." While he stood there, looking stunned and stupid, she climbed into the cab and shut the door on him, muttering, "Happy New Year."

Her roommate, Leeza, awakened Shelby on New Year's Day by banging out *The Anvil Chorus* with the pots and pans. Shelby buried her head under her pillow, but it was no use. The cacophony followed her. So did the memory of her obnoxious behavior the night before. She finally gave up trying to blot out both, and got up, crossing the few feet of living room to see what Leeza was concocting in the limited rectangle their landlord tried to pass off as a kitchen.

"Hey, how was your New Year's Eve?" Leeza greeted her.

"Rotten," said Shelby. She shuffled into the kitchen, drawn by the smell of freshly made coffee, grabbed a mug from the cupboard and filled it. "Let me just get some caffeine in me and I'll help you," she mumbled.

"No need for help," said Leeza. "I'm far too efficient. That's my New Year's resolution, in fact, to be more efficient."

"Oh, please," moaned Shelby. "It's too early to be talking about New Year's resolutions. There must be something I can do."

"If you want to feel helpful you can get out the knives and forks."

Shelby complied, then wandered back into the kitchen to hover over the stove. "If you don't turn those pancakes now they're going to burn."

Leeza made a face and surrendered the spatula. "Okay, Betty Crocker, you win."

"Now, don't pout just because you're a lesser woman in the kitchen," teased Shelby, flipping the pancakes. "What you lack in culinary skill you make up for in glamor."

"Yeah, right. Even Audrey Hepburn couldn't have looked glamorous at ten in the morning on New Year's Day."

Shelby surveyed her friend. Leeza's brown mane was barely contained in a scrunchy, and her generous chest made its presence known from under the ratty, turquoise bathrobe she favored.

"You make me sick," said Shelby, shaking her head. "Even looking bad you look good. If boobs were removable, I'd put yours in the dryer and shrink 'em."

"Now, now, boobs aren't everything. And you've got . . . some."

"Fried eggs."

"Oh, they're not that small."

"No, that's what I want for breakfast," said Shelby, slipping the first batch of pancakes onto a plate and pouring more batter. "And croissants and grapes and chocolate-dipped strawberries. That's the only thing that will make this day bearable."

"Yeah, and I wanted to wake up next to Brad Pitt this morning," said Leeza. "All we've got until one of us goes to the store is pancake mix. By the way, Matt's left five messages on the answering machine."

Shelby groaned. "I don't want to talk to him."

"Shel, you didn't . . ."

"Do something stupid? No. I did something smart. Well, I did it stupidly." Shelby sighed. "If we're going to make New Year's resolutions, mine better be to get control of my temper and quit acting like a thirteen-year-old every time I'm ticked."

"Never mind your temper. What did you do?"

"I told Matt to take a hike," said Shelby. And even though she knew she'd done the right thing, just the thought of not seeing him again made her voice shake and her eyes tear up. She filled a second plate and slipped by Leeza, settling herself on one of the wobbly chairs of their garage-sale dinette set.

Leeza followed her to the table, scolding, "I told you not to do anything rash, you little goon!"

"After all the time we've been together, nothing I could do would be rash. I'm beginning to feel like Adelaide in *Guys and Dolls*."

"Oh, well," said Leeza. "Whatever happened, it doesn't matter. He wants to make up. By the time that Rose Bowl party starts . . ." Shelby was shaking her head. Leeza frowned. "What do you mean, no?"

"What's the sense in continuing this relationship? He's never going to marry me," Shelby moaned and laid her head on the table. "What am I going to do?"

"First, get your hair out of your pancakes," advised Leeza. "Then, cancel your subscription to *Bride* magazine. Oh, that's right, you don't have one."

Shelby sat up and examined a long, thick strand of hair for damage. "At this rate, I'll never need one."

"Well, the course of true love never ran straight, or however that saying goes. You do love him, right?"

"Of course, I love him. What's not to love about Matt? He's fun, he's smart, he's gorgeous."

"Then what on earth is the problem?" demanded Leeza.

"The problem is he's selfish and stubborn!"

"Congratulations. You have just described practically every man on planet earth. They're all spoiled little boys. But then, who are we to talk? Women can be selfish and stubborn, too."

"You think it's selfish and stubborn of me to want an

engagement ring after three years? I gave up Broadway to be with him. All I want in return is commitment."

"Just because Matt hasn't given you a ring yet doesn't mean he isn't committed to you," said Leeza. "I'm not sure he's the right man for you, but you sure can't dump him on the grounds of lack of commitment. He never so much as looks at another woman when he's with you."

Shelby sighed. "I know. But after all this time, and from the way we talked just a couple of weeks ago, I really expected a ring for Christmas."

"You didn't exactly suffer at Christmas," said Leeza. "I only dream about owning perfume that expensive."

"Well, perfume stinks when you're expecting a ring," Shelby retorted. "And when he didn't give me one, I figured he was planning to surprise me New Year's Eve. Then, last night, nothing."

Leeza loaded a forkful of pancakes into her mouth. "You shouldn't be thinking of marriage right now, anyway. You have your career. We have callbacks this Sunday, and you're going to lose your focus."

"I am not going to lose my focus," said Shelby. "I've waited too long for a chance to be in a production at the Fifth Avenue. Anyway, that has nothing to do with Matt and me getting engaged. Most actresses manage to find time for a private life. Look at Julia Roberts."

"Oh, there's a great example," scoffed Leeza. "How many men has she been through?" She pointed her fork at Shelby. "When women are starting out like us they don't get tied down, especially to men who aren't actors."

"I met Matt in a play, remember?"

"A bit part in one college play does not an actor make," said Leeza. "And Mr. Business Major hasn't treaded the boards since. He's a civilian, and you know it. And people in the arts should never get seriously involved with civilians. They don't understand."

"Lots of people support the arts who aren't in them," argued Shelby.

"They support 'em, but they don't marry 'em."

"If you marry someone who isn't an actor, you don't have that competition thing. Anyway, Matt does support me, and he wants me to get on at the Fifth Avenue. And once that's in the bag, there's no reason why we shouldn't be married."

Leeza rolled her eyes. "You don't have to marry anyone at twenty-three. What kind of a free spirit are you, anyway?"

"A rotten one. When you love someone, you should marry them."

"Not necessarily," said Leeza. She shook her head in disgust. "You are so conventional."

"How else could you expect me to turn out with the mother I had?"

Leeza shook her head. "You need help."

Shelby tapped her chin thoughtfully. "You know, I think you're right." She jumped out of her chair and hurried back to her bedroom.

"Hey," called Leeza. "You haven't finished your pancakes. Where are you going?"

"To talk to an expert."

Diana Barrett, a.k.a. Diana Valentine, bestselling romance writer, lounged in her silk pajamas against the sofa cushions, sipping her second cup of cappuccino and watching the fire. The fireplace didn't do much to heat the room, but who cared? She could afford to run the furnace as much as she wanted. The fire was for her soul; nothing more, nothing less. A blustery wind pushed against the picture windows. The outside sky was a dirty gray, and the waters of Puget Sound beneath it pocked with whitecaps, but here inside her beautiful home, seated in her French Country-style living room and nestled among sofa pillows, Diana was cozy as a butterfly in a cocoon. She smiled and took another sip of her cappuccino.

Diana had been widowed three and a half years now. Thanks to her husband's good management, she had no financial worries, and what she earned these days she spent as she pleased. And living well, in this house in Edmonds, with the Olympic Peninsula and her new summer home a ferry ride away, pleased her just fine.

So did her manless existence and the freedom it allowed. Last night she had entertained a few select friends. Only women. They had enjoyed a catered dinner, watched chick flicks on her big screen TV in the game room, and then toasted in the new year with champagne expensive enough to make poor, cheap John turn in his grave. And the party hadn't ended with the televised fireworks over Seattle's Space Needle. The women had lingered on, chatting about their plans for the new year. Why not? None of them had husbands whining to go home and hit the sack. Today Diana would celebrate the new year, not chained to a house full of men and a television blatting the play-by-play of a football game, but by shopping the New Year's sales at the nearby mall. And she'd follow it with dinner at the kind of pricey restaurant to which John had never taken her. Her mother kept telling her that life was not good without a man. Diana had to agree. It wasn't good. It was better.

Except for sometimes at night, when, unexpectedly, the king-sized bed would feel too big, the room too empty, and the memories too piercing. But when that perception clouded Diana's vision of her perfect present, she would remind herself that sometimes she had felt just as unhappy with John, like unmatched bookends trying desperately to hold something together. She'd stretch across the bed and tell herself how pleasant life was with only herself to consider, and those sentiment-induced feelings would scuttle back into the dark corners from which they came.

By morning there would be no sign of them, and Diana would know it was really true: she no longer needed a hero, either between the covers of a book or under the covers of her bed. Which was why she was just about to launch her new career as mystery writer, Amy Stery. Clever little anagram. She hoped some of her readers would puzzle it out.

New readers, that is. She wasn't sure many of her current fans would follow her to this brave new world, she, a traitor abandoning the dream of perfect men and great sex that had brought her such success. But it was time to leave. She had been a disillusioned passenger on the *Love Boat* far too long.

The doorbell jarred her out of her thoughts and she looked at the clock. Who on earth was dropping in on her at eleven o'clock on New Year's morning? The last of her company hadn't gone home until two, and her mother was in Arizona.

She opened the door, and in blew her daughter, the tempest, carrying a small, plastic grocery bag. "I need help," cried Shelby, sweeping past Diana to fling herself on the couch.

Diana took a deep breath and followed her into the living room. She loved her daughter beyond reason, but life had been so calm since Shelby had moved out that Diana was beginning to think she, perhaps, loved Shelby best in small doses. High drama was exhausting.

"Don't tell me," said Diana, trying not to sound hopeful. "You've broken up with Matt."

Shelby slumped against the cushions. "He didn't give me a ring."

The sober expression on her daughter's face, the glint of weak tears fighting against a strong will pulled at Diana's heart, and she felt the familiar tide of feelings rising in her chest. Fear for her daughter, anger, a need to protect: the whole mother bear with a cub thing.

Diana believed in the were-bears of Viking and Native American mythology. She was one. She'd first transformed when that bully had terrorized Shelby in the second grade. Diana had gone to the school and walked her daughter home, but not before looming over the little monster and telling him a pant-wetting tale of what happened to bullies that sent him running away like a frightened hyena.

She'd often felt similar transformations coming over her when Shelby was in middle school and high school. But with the exception of being allowed to go to battle against an unfair teacher, both her daughter and her husband had insisted she remain human, sit on the sidelines and let Shelby fight her own battles. In her heart, Diana had known she had to, but she'd sat grudgingly, grinding her teeth and longing to rip the hair off the head of the girl who dared gossip about her darling, fantasizing over depriving that first boyfriend of a vital body part when he broke Shelby's teenage heart.

Now, here it was again, the same near-overpowering surge of protectiveness. Her daughter was unhappy, being used by a selfish, young man who thought marriage was a dirty word. She could almost feel her fingernails morphing into claws, and coarse, brown fur rising on her arms. Matt Armstrong should be glad he wasn't in this room right now.

She was still irked over his behavior Christmas Eve. Shelby had brought him for dinner and he'd been his usual polite self, using the old suck-up ploy, asking about Diana's writing, saying how delicious everything was, even offering to help with the dishes. But when the conversation came to the subject of one of Shelby's friends, who was getting married, he had turned them to another subject so fast Diana got whiplash. And now, this.

Well, what had Shelby expected? Matt was callow, more interested in sports and sex than mortgages and children. And even if he settled down tomorrow, would he turn out to be the kind of man who could give Shelby the life her artistic little soul needed? Would her dreams matter at all? Diana strongly doubted it.

But she knew her daughter would answer these questions with an emphatic yes. Shelby seemed unable to see that Matt's character bore a strong resemblance to his hair: pretty on the surface, but with questionable roots. Charm, it had a way of deceiving.

Even after all these years, Diana could still feel pain from the wound inflicted by the charmer who broke her heart before John came along. She knew from experience: a man who couldn't commit was misery in the making. She'd told Shelby that over a year ago, and her daughter had refused to listen. Perhaps Shelby's hearing had improved.

Diana sat down next to her daughter and smoothed her hair back from her forehead. "I'm sorry, darling, but maybe it wasn't a bad idea to break up."

These consoling words did comfort Shelby. "But I really don't want to dump him. I want him to commit. I just need some suggestions for how I can handle this."

Wait a minute, cautioned Diana's saner self. We've been down this road before. First Shelby will ask for advice, then she'll go and do exactly as she pleases. And when things don't work out, she'll be back, more miserable than before. *Don't get involved.*

"Shelby, I'm your mother, not your fairy godmother. I can't wave a magic wand over Matt and make him propose."

"Come on, Mom. You were married for twenty-some years."

"Twenty-four."

"Okay, twenty-four. You write romance novels. Love is your specialty. You've got to have some ideas."

Diana had all kinds of ideas these days, none of them having anything to do with love. Her saner self spoke up again, reminding her that no intelligent woman meddled in another woman's love life.

What did her saner self know, anyway? How could Diana turn down a request for help from her own child? But she had a feeling she'd wind up sorry she hadn't. Not for the first time since Shelby moved out, Diana found herself wishing she could make life easier for them both by bringing her daughter back home and locking her safely in her room.

She sighed and rose from the couch. "I need another cup of coffee. Come on out to the kitchen and let's see what we can do."

"Coffee works for me," said Shelby, following suit. She held up the bag. "I brought croissants to go with it. Wish the darned strawberries were in season," she added, leaving her mother to puzzle out that cryptic remark as best she could.

She trailed Diana to the kitchen and set the croissants out on a plate and got some jam. Then she laid them on the whitewashed oak table in the corner, sat down and ignored them, gazing out the window at the moody sky.

Diana studied her daughter's face. When it came to looks, the gene pool had splashed Shelby generously. She was what the young men her age called hot, a real babe-a-licious. She'd inherited Diana's fiery curls, and let them fly to her shoulders, long and wavy. Diana remembered sporting that look herself a decade ago, before she decided she preferred easy maintenance to a sexy look. Shelby had inherited her father's round face, and Diana's small nose and large, brown eyes. The dark eyebrows over them contrasted with Shelby's porcelain skin and made her face even more lovely. She was the same height as her mother, but smaller, a size eight. Today that perfect, little body was outfitted casual chic, in jeans, a knit top, and a blazer. Shelby knew how to dress.

She also knew how to decorate on a shoestring, and she was a gourmet cook. She could dance like a feather on the wind and out-sing Streisand. Yes, Shelby was a very accomplished young woman, who knew a lot about many things.

Except life. And at barely twenty-three, she was too young to know all there was to know about that. Even if Diana could pour the knowledge gained from forty-seven—actually, almost forty-eight now—years of existence on planet earth into her daughter, it probably would make little difference in how Shelby charted her course. She was impetuous, and because of it, frequently landed herself in rough waters.

"I yelled at him last night," Shelby confessed. "Got in a cab and left him. Probably not a good way to start the new year. What do you think?"

Diana slid a mug of coffee in front of her daughter and sat down opposite her. "I think that was last night and you have the whole rest of the year to mend your wicked ways."

Shelby gave a half smile, then took a sip. "You know, he really is wonderful," she said. "He's so fun, so easygoing."

*Easygoing. Maybe not a selfish user; just a young man who needed to learn to think ahead.* The possibility that she might have misjudged Matt made Diana's bear claws retract a little. Perhaps her daughter's heart wouldn't get broken after all.

"Maybe that's part of your problem," she said thoughtfully. "Maybe Matt's really not much of a planner."

"Like Daddy?"

Diana shrugged, pretending the sarcastic words had rolled off her, unfelt.

"I didn't mean that the way it sounded," Shelby apologized. "I loved Daddy a lot, and I still miss him so much. But he was a control freak, and that's not what I want in a husband."

"He wasn't that bad," protested Diana, feeling somehow responsible for her husband's faults, and therefore in need of defending them.

The look Shelby gave her mother said, Yeah, right. "Didn't you ever get tired of always doing what he wanted to do?"

*Yes.* "It's called compromise," said Diana. "And how is that different than your relationship with Matt?" she countered.

Shelby opened her mouth to speak, then closed it. "I don't know," she said at last.

"Darling, any good relationship involves compromise. Anyway, in the end, they're all like Daddy. They all like to get their own way. Think about it. How many times have you given in to what Matt's wanted since you've been together? Think about the big things and the little things, the farthest back and the most recent."

Shelby chewed her lip. Diana knew when the light had dawned. Her daughter looked like a math student who had just mastered a difficult concept.

"Movies," she said. "We always end up going to see something with tons of violence. Every time I suggest seeing something where the actors actually talk he says, 'That sounds like a chick movie. Why don't you go see it with Leeza?'"

"In all fairness to Matt, you probably let him do that right from the beginning," said Diana. "I'll bet on one of your first dates he asked, 'Do you want to go see a movie?' And you said, 'Sure.' Then he said, 'What would you like to see?' and you probably said something like, 'Oh, I don't care.' And so he figured you didn't. The pattern was started, and once you start a pattern with a man, it's almost impossible to change it. To them it's like making up new rules in the middle of a football game. It doesn't make sense."

"I don't see how that applies to getting engaged," said Shelby.

"Well, perhaps after three years, you've established a certain unspoken agreement."

"Yes, that we'd get married. That's why I thought he was going to give me an engagement ring."

"Oh, so you've actually talked about when you'd get married."

"No. But we've talked about wanting to."

"Wanting to when?"

Shelby was frowning now. "We hadn't set a date or anything. We'd just talked about getting married in the future."

Diana had heard that line. Right before she lost her virginity, in fact.

She nodded sagely. "In the far-off, distant future."

"No, after I got my career going."

"What, exactly, does that mean?" asked Diana.

"It means after I get in the chorus at the Fifth Avenue," said Shelby.

"He said that?"

Shelby was silent a moment. "Well, not in so many words."

"So, you said that."

"I can't remember exactly who said what," replied Shelby testily. "But we did have an understanding."

"I think, perhaps, your understanding is different than Matt's," suggested Diana.

"Okay, what's his understanding?"

"His understanding is that he's got all the time in the

world. You're a couple, and someday, if and when the mood strikes, you'll legitimize it."

"We could go on like that forever," protested Shelby.

"Yes, you could."

"So what do you think I should do?"

Diana shrugged. "I suppose you have a couple of choices. Keep playing the game by his rules and hope something happens."

"I don't like that one," said Shelby.

"Or start a whole new game," finished Diana as if she hadn't been interrupted.

Shelby stared at her. "With someone else? What kind of a suggestion is that? I love him."

*Just what every woman whose hormones have switched off her brain says.* "Well, darling, you asked for advice. I'm just telling you your options," said Diana. "What else do you want me to do?"

"I want you to help me . . ." Shelby's sentence faded into silence.

"Manipulate him?" guessed Diana.

"That sounds crass," said Shelby, the picture of offended innocence.

"But true, right?"

Shelby turned her head to gaze out the window.

Diana knew that ploy. She'd seen it enough when her daughter was growing up and trying to hide an expression that was bound to betray her. Sure enough, when Shelby turned her face back to her mother's scrutiny, it still held traces of a very wicked smile.

"It's not as if I'd be forcing him to do something he doesn't want to do," she said. "He really does want to marry me. I just have to get him on the same timetable."

Diana couldn't help smiling. "There's got to be a way" was Shelby's motto. Like Scarlett O'Hara, the girl was never long without a plan.

"All right, my darling daughter," she said. "But let me

warn you, you're about to start a battle that's been going on since Adam and Eve, and I can't guarantee you'll win it. You might even lose Matt." *One could always hope.* "Are you prepared to risk that?"

Shelby nodded. "Absolutely, because I know I won't lose him. So, let's make a plan. What should I do first?"

"Talk with him and be very specific about what you want; make sure you're both communicating."

Shelby rolled her eyes. "Of course we're communicating. It's not as if we never talk."

Diana forced back the cynical laugh begging to come out. "But are you using the same language?" she asked. "You need to sit down with Matt and be specific about what you envision for this relationship. You both need to be clear, not only on what you want out of it, but when. If you want an engagement ring and a specific wedding date, you have to tell him."

"That makes sense," said Shelby. "I guess I should have come right out and said I wanted a ring for Christmas. Although you'd think he could have figured that out."

"You'd think so," Diana agreed.

Shelby brightened. "Well, there's still Valentine's Day." She jumped up from the table. "Thanks, Mom! I knew you'd come through." She hugged her mother, then rushed out of the room, saying, "I'm going to go home and call him right now."

Diana sighed. When Shelby was a child, it had been easy to blow the clouds from her horizon. It still was. But whether or not they'd stay gone was another matter.

All Shelby got when she called Matt was his answering service. He was probably already on his way to the party they had planned to attend together, she thought wistfully. Not that she liked football. But she liked parties, and she enjoyed visiting with the other girlfriends who came.

*Never mind*, she told herself. *You can have your own party later.* "Matt, it's Shel. Call me. I love you."

There. That should do it. He'd call and she'd tell him to come over. They'd talk, set a date, make plans. And once those plans were made, she'd be well on her way to having everything she wanted: marriage to the perfect man, and a fulfilling career. Granted, it wouldn't be Broadway, but she really didn't need to be a star on Broadway to be fulfilled. A stage was a stage on any coast.

Meanwhile, she'd hurry home, make a cheesecake, take a bubble bath, and think about exactly what she wanted to say.

Matt didn't call. Instead, he showed up at her door with a huge bouquet of carnations. He held them out to her. "Truce?"

There he stood, so earnest, so sincere. Geez, he was gorgeous! "Oh, Matt," she cried, and rushed into his arms.

He grabbed her in a hug that brought her feet off the floor and she threw her arms around his neck. Everything was going to be all right now. There was nothing Matt wouldn't do for her.

He finally set her down and gave her a kiss that sent a jolt clear down to her toes. "Happy New Year, Shel," he whispered, and handed over the flowers.

She would have preferred roses, but, hey, it was the thought that counted, and she did love the smell of carnations. She buried her nose in the bouquet and sniffed, catching only the faintest hint of fragrance. Abandoning the effort, she laid them on the kitchen counter.

"I made cheesecake," she offered.

"I'm not too hungry," he said. "I ate a lot at the party.

Which," he added with a frown, "you were supposed to be at with me."

"I know." Shelby walked to the corner of the apartment she and Leeza had labeled as the living room and settled on the love seat. She patted the cushion next to her, saying, "We need to talk."

He joined her, sliding an arm around her midriff. "About last night," he began.

"I want to get engaged."

Matt's features froze in an expression that looked very much like panic. He pulled back, saying, "You know I love you, Shel, but where's the fire?"

"We've been together three years. I wouldn't call getting engaged rushing things. Don't you think it's time for the next step?"

Matt shot off the love seat like she'd just threatened to break his legs. "Baby, that's not a step. That's a jump, and I'm not ready for it yet."

Shelby felt like he had just thrown ice water on her. "You just said you love me."

"I do. I haven't so much as looked at another woman since we've been together!"

"Well, if you're so in love, why does the subject of marriage make you act like someone's threatening to torture you?"

Matt's brows shot together. "Because we don't have enough money to get married. Weddings are expensive. So are honeymoons and houses and kids."

"I wasn't suggesting we get married tomorrow," said Shelby impatiently. "And I don't want to have kids for another ten years."

"Then what's the rush? Wait a minute. What brought all this on?" His eyes narrowed suspiciously. "Your mom said something about weddings when we were over there Christmas Eve. Have you been talking to your mom?"

Shelby blushed as if she'd just been accused of cheating on a diet. "This is not about my mom."

Now he was smirking. "Oh, isn't it?" he retorted. He crossed his arms over his chest and leaned against the wall. "Your mom writes those romance novels where everybody gets married, doesn't she? How many of those things did you read growing up?"

"That has nothing to do with anything!" protested Shelby.

"Shel," he said, his voice softening. "I'm not saying I never want to get married. I'm just trying to be practical here. Marriage is a big, expensive step, and I'm not ready to be tied down."

Shelby felt her pulse rate quickening. "Tied down? What are you, a kite? You make it sound like I'm going to put you in jail."

"I didn't say that."

"Well, you may as well have."

Matt started to pace. "It's not what I meant. Quit putting words in my mouth, will ya?"

"Okay. Choose your own words and tell me what you meant by that remark."

"I meant I'm not ready, that's all. I still have things I want to do."

"So do I," said Shelby in a quiet voice. "But I thought we were going to do them together. As a team."

Matt let out his breath and dragged his fingers through his hair. Shelby remained on the love seat, trying to decide which she wanted to do most, cry or hit him.

"Hey, what are we doing?" He returned to her side and put a finger under her chin. "Why are we fighting like this? It's not like we're not going to get married."

A bubble of hope rose in Shelby. "When?"

"When the timing's right."

Matt's patronizing tone of voice irritated her. So did his placating arm around her shoulders. She'd given up moving to New York for him and now he was balking at committing to her. She jerked away and crossed the room to glare out the window at the leaden sky and the shoddy gray buildings of her downtown fringe neighborhood squatting under it. The monochrome scene matched her mood, and the long-suffering sigh Matt gave didn't do anything to improve it. She heard his approaching footfall on the cheap, cream-colored carpet, felt his hands rest on her shoulders, and shrugged them off.

"Come on, Shel," he protested. "Be reasonable. You know I love you. But I want to make sure I'm ready. Do you want to end up a divorce statistic?"

"Of course not."

"Well, then, let's take our time. We're not in a hurry to have kids, so where's the rush? We've got our careers, we've each got our friends. We've got the best of everything. Let's not be in such a hurry to turn into our parents. Let's just . . ." He ran a hand up her arm and kissed her shoulder. ". . . enjoy . . ." His mouth moved to her neck and he slipped his arms around her midriff. Her chest tightened in response. ". . . being . . ." He caught her earlobe between his lips, then whispered, ". . . together."

He turned her into his embrace, ran a finger along her lips, starting a delicious tingle. "And you know there's no one else I want to be with, nobody like you, baby." He kissed her, sending her body temperature soaring, and melting her knees to jelly. She should stop this right now, before his kiss got any deeper, before his hands roved any farther. Oooh.

It was too late to fight the fire he was building. She'd already died from smoke inhalation.

Smoke screen, she thought an hour after he'd left. She was no closer to an engagement ring than she'd been the night before, and no happier about it. Time for more expert advice. She grabbed the phone and dialed her mother.

Mom was out.

Shelby ground her teeth and waited for the tone, then said, "Mom, this isn't working. Call me as soon as you get in. I think I need a new game plan."

# Two

♡

"Why are men so difficult?" Shelby groaned, pushing away her half-eaten quiche.

Diana downed the last of her tea. Buying Shelby lunch at her favorite cafe in downtown Seattle's historic Pike Place Market hadn't done much to lift her spirits.

"Men are difficult because they're different from the rest of us," she said. "It's just that simple."

"Well, I'm not finding it simple handling Matt."

"At least you know where he stands on the subject of marriage now," said Diana.

"Yeah, as far away as possible."

"That should tell you something."

"He's just afraid of the responsibility."

"So why are you trying to force him to shoulder it?"

"Because it's time. I'm done with my Master's."

"And the next step after a Master's degree in drama is into marriage with a reluctant man? Does that make sense?"

"It's not that he doesn't want to marry me," protested Shelby. "It's just that he's concerned about things that don't matter. He thinks the day after we get engaged he'll have to cough up money for a honeymoon, a house, six kids, and a dog." She shook her head. "He needs to see that we're drifting here, that we need to take the next logical step." Diana must have been looking dubious as to whether an engagement to an unenthusiastic man was logical, for Shelby hurried to add, "I mean, you, yourself, said that most people get married when they're finished with college."

Diana remembered the day she made that remark. It had been meant to prod Shelby into a more stable lifestyle. But Shelby and Matt had showed no signs of wanting a marriage license to prop beside the bed. Until the end of spring quarter, when she had finished her schooling and suddenly decided she needed that piece of paper after all. She'd been pricing wedding dresses ever since.

Diana wasn't sure why her daughter should suddenly feel the burning need to abandon all hope of Broadway and marry, but she was pretty sure she understood Matt's reason for not wanting to.

Why should he be in a hurry to march down the aisle? He had everything he wanted without the big, church wedding. Including her daughter's heart, the beast! A man who wouldn't fight dragons for a woman, move heaven and earth for her, and, most importantly, give up his so-called freedom for her, was not a man in love. Matt Armstrong was probably in like with her daughter, definitely in lust with her daughter, but not in love with her. Someone was going to get hurt, and judging from the look on Shelby's face, it wasn't hard to predict whom.

But there was no sense telling Shelby that. An out-and-out lecture wouldn't get through to her. Shelby had her own learning style—the hard way—and Diana would have to let Matt's behavior open her daughter's eyes.

"Most people get married because both of them want

to," Diana said. "You're trying to force something Matt's not ready for."

"How on earth do I make him ready?"

"By giving him a chance to see what life without you would be like. Perhaps you two need some time apart to consider how important your relationship really is."

The panic on Shelby's face made Diana's heart ache. And the neediness and stupidity behind the panic made her want to reach across the table and shake her silly daughter. "It's up to you," she said, keeping her voice neutral. "You said yesterday you wouldn't lose him. Are you afraid to put your conviction to the test by putting on the brakes?"

Shelby's chin jutted out. "No."

"Well, then, that's what I suggest you do."

"I guess it's worth a try," said Shelby dubiously. "He's coming over for dinner tonight. We can talk then." She looked out the window at the Seattle waterfront and gnawed her lower lip.

"Don't look so worried," said Diana, reaching across the table to pat her daughter's hand. "You haven't lost the war, just the first skirmish. Come on, let's hit the flower stalls. I want some dried lavender."

They spent the next half hour prowling the Market's produce stalls and watching the famous Pike Place fish merchants in action. Situated under the Market's big clock, this particular vendor was a favorite with both tourists and locals. Every time a customer picked out a fish, the clerk on the floor would toss the thing football style to the man behind the counter to be wrapped. The ceremony was always rewarded by applause from the shoppers.

Shelby, normally an enthusiastic appreciator of the show, was underanimated today, and Diana felt irrationally responsible for her daughter's melancholy. Maybe she shouldn't have suggested Shelby cool things. But if Matt wasn't going to love and cherish her, it was better to weed him out of her heart right now. Diana would have given the same advice to any woman in similar circumstances. So why did she feel so guilty? She wasn't sure, but she paid for her guilt with a pair of silver-and-turquoise earrings made by a local artisan.

By the time they parted, Shelby was smiling bravely, determined not to let whatever happened in her personal life distract her from her callback the following day at the Fifth Avenue Theater, Seattle's home for lavish musical productions and touring Broadway shows. For every Seattle starlet, the next best thing to Broadway was to get hired for the chorus at the Fifth Avenue.

"After all," Shelby said. "Matt is a big part of my life, but he's not all of it. And I won't let what's happening with him make me lose my focus."

Both the speech and the smile would have fooled an audience, but not a mother. Diana drove home feeling depressed, and wondering why no one warned women that parenting didn't stop when the kid moved out.

Matt arrived at Shelby's place with his stomach growling. She opened the door, and the aroma of beef wafted out to tickle his nose. "Something smells good," he said, strolling into the apartment. He bent to kiss her just as she turned back to the kitchen and found himself kissing air.

"Pot roast with mashed potatoes and gravy," she said, "and homemade biscuits."

Meat and potatoes. Yeah. A good, filling meal. And Shelby for dessert.

"And cherry pie for dessert," she added.

"Oh, man, that sounds good. How soon till we eat? I'm starving."

"Just a few more minutes," said Shelby.

Matt wandered into the tiny living room space and sprawled across the love seat. "Where's your roommate?"

"Flying. She won't be back until late tonight."

He grinned. Having a girlfriend whose actress roommate moonlighted as a flight attendant had its pluses.

In fact, he and Shel had the perfect setup. Between Leeza's regular absences and his bachelor pad, they already had plenty of privacy. There was no need to live together and clutter up his place with panty hose dangling on the shower stall and hair in the drain. They each got a bed to themselves when it was time to end the fun and games, and Shel didn't have to lose beauty sleep when he snored. This was the best of all possible worlds, and he was glad she'd come to realize it.

Now the smell of beef was so strong it invaded Matt's mouth and sat on his tongue, making him salivate. This was his kind of meal, a real cut above some of the stuff Shel normally concocted when she felt the urge to eat in. Just the memory of that squash soup she had forced on him a couple weeks back was enough to make Matt shudder.

She emerged from the kitchen, bearing a platter with a thick slab of meat topped with cooked carrots and onions. The sight and smell grabbed Matt by the stomach and pulled him to the table.

"Boy, Shel. No one can cook like you. What's the occasion?"

She cocked an eyebrow. "Occasion?"

"I mean, this is a pretty fancy-looking meal."

"This is not fancy," she corrected him. "And there's no occasion." Then she returned to the kitchen.

Matt sat down in front of the meat platter. Was he imagining it or was Shel not quite as chatty as usual? When she hadn't stopped to let him kiss her, he had thought she was just getting into her Martha Stewart role. Now he began to wonder. Was she being a little distant? And what about that tone of voice?

Don't go looking for trouble, he told himself. Pretend nothing's wrong. "Need some help?" he called.

"No," her voice came back lightly. No anger there. Good. He'd been imagining things.

She returned with a plate of biscuits. Laying them next to the meat, she commanded, "Butter them while they're still hot," then left again.

He broke off a piece of one and tested it. The thing dissolved in his mouth and his stomach rumbled in anticipation.

Now Shelby appeared, bearing a casserole dish. She set it next to his plate and lifted the lid, and cream of mushroom soup–scented steam escaped to play further havoc with his excited taste buds. He peered into the dish and saw his favorite green-bean casserole.

Matt looked up at her. "I'm not forgetting the anniversary of our first date or something, am I?"

"Why would you think that? Haven't I ever cooked nice meals for you?"

*Uh-oh.* That tone of voice was not playful. Something was definitely up.

"Did you remember the wine?" she asked.

"Oh, man. I forgot."

"Never mind. I've got some sparkling cider in the fridge," said Shelby, sounding like a long-suffering saint. She started toward the kitchen.

Okay. Enough was enough. Matt grabbed her arm. "All right, Shel, spit it out. What's bugging you?"

She raised both eyebrows. "Should something be bugging me?"

"No, but something is. Look, if it's about the wine, I'm sorry. You know what it was like today." Even though she was just a temp, she'd been working at Mutual Care long enough now to know when it was crazy there.

"Of course I know what it was like," she said. "And it's not the wine."

"But it is something," Matt persisted. Out of the corner of his eye he could see steam curling off the meat and vegetables. They'd be cold by the time he got any. He leaned back in his chair and folded his arms. "Let's get whatever is bugging you out in the open so we can eat."

Her eyebrows dipped and her mouth puckered like she'd just bitten into a lemon. "That's the only reason you want to find out what's wrong, so you can eat?"

This was ridiculous. "I don't get it. You make me this great dinner and then you try to start a fight so I can't enjoy it. All that work for nothing. What's the sense?"

Shelby's cheeks flamed. "I am not starting a fight!"

"Well, it sure looks like it to me. What are you mad about? You're mad and I don't even know why."

"I'm not mad. I just think we need to have a talk."

They had just talked. What new problem could have come up in one day?

Matt forced himself not to look at the food. "Okay. Tell me what's bothering you."

She turned suddenly shy, sitting down opposite him and lowering her gaze to her empty plate. "I think we need to cool things off a little."

Just last night they were Romeo and Juliet. Now they were cooling things off a little? "What?"

She looked up at him, and her expression was sad, as if she regretted her words. "I'm not sure we have the same goals for this relationship, and until we do . . ."

"Of course we have the same goals," Matt interrupted. "Maybe not quite the same timetable, but the same goals." *Who kept putting these goofy ideas into her head, anyway?* "Have you been talking to your mother again?"

The color in her cheeks spread. Bull's-eye.

"Why do you keep bringing my mother into this?" she demanded.

Tactical error. That had made her mad. Well, he was getting mad, too, damn it! They had this marriage thing all settled and now here it was again like some kind of monster that wouldn't die.

"Because I think she put you up to this," he said.

Oh, boy, another blunder. She looked like she could reheat their dinner just by blowing on it. Her eyes almost glowed red.

"Put me up to this? I can't think for myself?"

This was too much. Shel was trying to escalate a simple misunderstanding into a full-fledged war. Well, he didn't want to fight. He wanted to eat, and by God, they were going to end this once and for all and enjoy their dinner!

Matt shot up from the table. "We had this whole marriage thing settled," he informed her, pointing his finger at her. "So what's this really all about, Shel? You're not getting your way and so you're going to make my life miserable until you do? Is that it? I spend practically my every waking minute with you, I take you out, I buy you things, but that's not enough."

Now she was on her feet too, and glaring at him. "Are you saying I haven't done any giving in this relationship? My God, Matt, I gave up Broadway for you!"

"Oh, come on. You weren't giving up anything. You decided all on your own that you'd be just as happy staying in Seattle. And, frankly, that was probably a smart decision. You'll have a hard enough time making it here."

"What kind of thing is that to say?" she snarled.

He held up a hand to ward off the sparks shooting from her eyes. "Hey, I wasn't trying to insult you. I was just stating a fact. You know how few people ever make it in show business."

Oh, great. Now she was looking around the room like she was trying to remember where she'd hidden her gun.

The flowers he'd brought her on New Year's sat in a glass vase at the center of the table. She reached for it and Matt backed up warily. "Now, Shel, don't lose your temper."

She didn't pick up the vase and throw it, but she did

yank out the carnations, shove them at him and bulldoze him toward the door, saying, "Get out."

"Okay, fine!" He didn't need to stick around here to be yelled at and humiliated. Shel was already scouring the room for a new weapon. It was definitely time to take off. "Call me when you're sane." He turned and tried to leave with some dignity. A sofa pillow hit him on the back of the head, speeding him on his way.

Lance Gregory had a date. He had shed his Armani suit in favor of a more casual look.

Adele was the casual type. And she was one of those women who adored sports, so he was taking her to a Son- ics basketball game. After the game, they would hit a bistro downtown before he took her home and the real games began.

He checked his reflection in the mirror and smiled. The hair was graying a little at the temples, but all the women he dated insisted it made him look distinguished. And at forty-eight, the chin was still holding firm. With his good skin and well-toned body he could still easily pass for early forties.

The sound of the doorbell made him frown. He needed to leave soon.

When he opened the door, he was surprised to see his nephew on his doorstep.

"I need help," said Matt.

The kid was a mess, with his hair mussed and his tie loose. His eyebrows were shooting every which way, as if he'd run his hand over his face several times. From his ex- pression, he'd either been fired or dumped by his girl- friend. Matt was too good a worker to get fired.

"Woman troubles?" asked Lance, swinging the door wide.

"How'd you guess?" said Matt. He stepped inside,

driving his fingers through his hair and making his fastidious uncle cringe.

"Come on in," said Lance. "I'm going out, but I have time for a drink."

"Thanks," said Matt and followed him through the big house to the library. "I really appreciate you taking time to talk to me. I don't know what to do. She's acting crazy."

Lance flipped on the lights, bringing out the patina so carefully cultivated on the room's mahogany furnishings by his housekeeper. This was Lance's favorite retreat. The furniture in the room was masculine-looking and comfortable, the art modern and expensive. Its long wall, lined with glass bookcases filled with leather-bound books on history and economics and first edition literary fiction offered him the perfect companionship on those evenings when he chose to be solitary. And the impressive view his custom-built, contemporary house offered of the east side's Lake Sammamish never failed to impress visitors. Actually, it never failed to impress Lance, either, and reminded him what a lucky devil he was.

"You're talking about Shelby?" Lance asked.

"Who else," said Matt. "She's driving me crazy."

Lance went to the bar and poured two glasses of Scotch, handed one to Matt, then settled himself in his favorite brown leather, wing-backed chair. Matt took the matching one opposite.

"So," said Lance. "She wanted a ring for Christmas and didn't get it and now she's not happy."

Matt stared at Lance in amazement. "How did you know?"

Lance smiled. "This isn't rocket science. You two have been going out for a while now, right?"

"Three years."

"And you're seeing a lot of each other?"

"Yeah, especially since she came to work as a temp at Mutual Care this fall."

Lance nodded like a doctor who had just had his diagnosis confirmed by the lab. "You're lucky you've been able to get by as long as you have. You see, women have this hidden agenda. They never date a man without considering him as a potential husband. If you go out with a woman long enough, she starts thinking you might be The One, Mr. Right, the father of her children. After a certain point, her timetable says, time for this guy to commit."

"I hate that word!" Matt exploded. "I *am* committed to Shelby. I stopped seeing anyone else practically the day I met her."

"That's not good enough. She wants proof. She wants a ring. You don't produce proof, she starts getting antsy. Christmas looked like the perfect time for you to surprise her with a diamond, and you didn't. Big letdown."

Matt sighed and drained his Scotch. He sank back against the chair, looking like a man who had just been told he had one week to live.

"Hey kid, buck up. Nobody's sending you to prison."

"I feel like it," said Matt. "Geez, Uncle Lance. I love Dad and Mom, but I don't want to be like them. All they ever talked about when I was growing up was the mortgage and what bill they were going to pay off next. They never went anywhere but to my ball games or Debbie' and Laurie's piano recitals. They're great people, but they're about as exciting as rocks."

"I don't think it was marriage that made them dull," said Lance. "Just timing. Your dad shouldn't have taken on a wife until he was on his feet financially."

"Like you." Matt looked around the room, wearing the first smile Lance had seen since he arrived. "This place must be worth a million bucks. A Mercedes, money, and stocks up the wazoo. That's what I want."

"Well, you won't get it by marrying at your age."

"Shit," muttered Matt.

"That's what you're in, all right," agreed Lance.

"You know, she wouldn't be acting like this if it wasn't for her mom," Matt grumbled.

"So, she's being coached?"

"Yes," said Matt, his voice bristling umbrage. "It was her mom who brought up the subject of weddings at Christmas."

"In regards to you two?"

Matt shook his head. "No. Nothing that obvious. Just one of those guess-who's-getting-married remarks. She's been coaching Shel to cool things with me. I know it."

Mama's meddling made the sides uneven, thought Lance. "Sounds like you need someone in your corner," he said.

"I can't really go to Dad," said Matt. "He'd just say marry her."

Lance nodded. Yes, stepbrother Danny Armstrong was very conventional. He and Lance had been the best of buds when their folks first married, but once puberty hit, things changed. Old Dan completely lost his sense of humor the Thanksgiving he brought his new girlfriend home from college and little high school senior Lance stole her right out from under his nose. Said nose had gotten pretty out of joint over the incident and, although they eventually patched things up, Lance was sure it still bugged Danny boy. Over the years, looking down from his high mountain of morality, Dan had often pronounced Lance's lifestyle selfish. The hypocrite. If it hadn't been for his stepbrother's selfish lifestyle, Dan's kids wouldn't have gotten a college education. Now here was his son coming to bad, old Uncle Lance for advice. Ah, sweet irony.

"What's the mom like?" he asked.

"She's a fox."

"Does she work?"

Matt nodded. "Yeah. She writes those paperback romances. Not as Diana Barrett, though. For those she's Diana Valentine," he sneered.

"The happily-ever-after kind of woman," said Lance, and took a sip of Scotch.

"She's a widow," continued Matt, "so she doesn't have anything else to do but poke her nose into her daughter's business."

Widow: lonely, frustrated, middle-aged, sexually deprived? Hmmm.

I'm not saying she's not nice or anything," said Matt. "I just wish she'd stay out of Shel's life."

"Well, she'd have to be pretty heartless not to care what happens to her daughter," pointed out Lance.

"I'm not a serial killer, for Pete's sake. Nothing's going to happen to Shel."

"That's what she's afraid of."

Matt didn't catch the joke. He was staring at some unpleasant vision only he could see. "I don't know why Mrs. Barrett isn't out looking for a man, herself," he muttered. "It's not like she's that old."

"Just how old is she?"

Matt shook his head. "I'm not sure. She must have gotten married really young, because she looks great, more like Shel's older sister than her mom."

Shelby was a cute kid with lots of curls and a baby doll face. So, Mama looked like her. The girl was in her early twenties. If mom had married at nineteen and had a kid at twenty or twenty-one, she'd be about forty-one or -two, just the time of life when a woman was hitting her stride in confidence and personal strength. And flexing those muscles, making sure everyone around her danced to her tune. Lance had seen women that age in action before. In a battle of the sexes with such an Amazon, a younger man would leave the field limping and bloodied.

"There's gotta be something I can do to distract her mom long enough for me and Shel to get our life back on track," said Matt. "Can you help me think of something?"

The wheels began to turn, the ideas to whirl around

Lance's head. He didn't like the one that made the most sense: he preferred his women younger and more malleable. Only for his favorite nephew would he even consider it.

Matt was looking at him hopefully. Well, what the hell.

"Maybe," he said thoughtfully, "Mama needs someone to distract her so she won't have time to run her daughter's love life."

"You got an idea?"

"I might. Where does this Diana Barrett live?"

"Edmonds. She's got one of those houses up on the hill with a view."

So, Mama was living comfortably-ever-after on her late husband's life insurance. The more Lance heard about Shelby's mom, the less he liked her. She needed to quit meddling in his nephew's love life and pick on someone her own size.

"I can get you the address," offered Matt.

"All right, I tell you what. I'll see what I can do to take the woman's mind off her daughter's business."

Matt grinned. "You're the man who can do it." His grin faded. "But what do I do about Shel? She's not speaking to me. She wants to refrigerate our relationship."

Lance shrugged. "Sublimate."

His nephew stared at him as if he'd said castrate.

"You do remember your psychology from college, don't you?"

"Yeah, I remember. Substitution."

"Work out longer at the gym and hit the cold showers. And don't go near the girl."

Matt was looking dubious.

"That is what she's asked you to do. Right?"

"Well, yeah, but . . ."

"Listen," said Lance. "The only place women like carpet is on their floor. If you crawl to Shelby, promising to do whatever she wants, she'll walk all over you. And I can guarantee she won't value you. You've got to take a lesson from their book and play hard to get. If she wants to cool things off, let her. Back away. It's not really what she wants, and if she thinks she's losing you, she'll beg you to come back, and on your terms."

A slow smile spread across Matt's face and he nodded. "Yeah."

"And when she approaches you—and she will—you tell her that you don't think she really cares for you. She won't be able to resist the challenge of showing you that she does, too, care."

"Man, you're great," said Matt, his voice filled with awe. "Is there anything you don't know about women?"

Lance smiled. "Only enough to fill a book. Any man who claims he knows everything there is to know about women is a fool." He checked his watch. "Speaking of which, I have a date with a very beautiful one. Woman, that is, and I'd be a fool to keep her waiting."

Matt took the hint and rose, and Lance clapped a hand on his back and walked him out of the room.

"Thanks again, Uncle Lance," said Matt. "I'll E-mail you that address for Diana's mom."

"No problem," said Lance, and he knew it wouldn't be. He didn't know everything there was to know about women, but it had been years since he'd met one he couldn't handle.

# *Three*

*Shelby had to* make this audition work to prove to Matt, and more important, to herself, that she could. She entered the huge audition room and the stage manager introduced her to the people seated at a long table. Here were the people who held her future in their hands. Three other human beings to impress, including the executive director. But the one Shelby most wanted to shine for was Norb Joerder, the New York Director/Choreographer, who had been imported to direct this production of *Camelot* with Noel Harrison.

Everything in her was shaking. She was going to pass out. Or embarrass herself. She had just gone to the bathroom five minutes before, but now she had to go again.

*Stop it! Focus. Prove your prof wrong. You have the determination to make it and you can do this.* She visualized the blown-up picture of her drama professor that hung on a piece of corkboard in the kitchen and mentally threw another dart at it. Then she recited her mantra. *I am dedicated to my art, and determined, and the Fifth Avenue will want me.* She took a deep breath, like a gymnast preparing to mount the balance beam. Reaching down into the deepest depths of her soul, she pulled up a mind-shattering smile for Norb.

He was a small, fine-boned man, with blond curls, and blue, sensitive eyes that made him look like an angel.

He smiled back.

*Give it to him.*

She didn't announce what she was going to sing. Instead, she handed the music to the accompanist, then marched to the table, slammed her palms down on it, making Norb flinch, and glared at him. "Do you know what you're doing to me?" she growled, drawing on the frustration with which Matt had so conveniently supplied her the night before. "Do you have any idea how very much you are frustrating me?" She took a step back. "Didn't your mama ever tell you that talk is cheap?" With a quick flick of the wrist, she motioned for the pianist to start the introduction to the song she'd given him, then launched into Eliza Doolittle's famous vocal diatribe, demanding he not talk about love, but show her.

Norb was grinning. She superimposed Matt's face over his and became even more impassioned. She paced, she threw out her arms, carving circles in the air. Then she advanced on the table, making the executive director's eyes widen in apprehension. Now she had reached the sentence where Eliza threatened to scream, but she didn't sing the word "scream" like Audrey Hepburn had in the movie. This audition demanded more. She shut her eyes and, clutching fistfuls of hair, let out a blood-curdling screech that brought an answering yelp from someone at the table. She had them now and they all knew it. She wanted to smile, laugh for the joy of it, but she stayed in character and sang on.

Finally, she came to the final words of the song. She raised her arms, threw back her head and turned loose her voice, releasing enough volume to rattle the windows.

"My God," said someone.

"Thank you," said Norb politely, smiling at her. "Do you know the song 'Follow Me'?"

That song belonged to Nimue, the wood nymph, Merlin's seducer. It represented an actual part. Shelby had listened to the music from *Camelot* over and over in preparation for this moment, and she knew every nuance, every vocal inflection of that song. "I think so," she said modestly.

She refused the proferred sheet music, knowing she wouldn't need it, then nodded to the pianist that she was ready. He began to play and Shelby lost herself in the haunting melody of the piece.

The intro ended and it was time to sing. She kept her voice in check at first, making it light and lilting, then letting it soar to the high notes. This time she didn't march up to the table. Instead, she held out both hands and glided backward, step by step, away from the table, a siren, beckoning the mortals to follow her to an uncertain future. Her voice had never sounded better. She was all the way to the door when the song ended.

On her last note, she opened it, then slipped outside, shutting it behind her and giving the poor mortals in the other room a moment to stay under the spell she had woven. She let out her breath and realized she didn't have to visit the bathroom anymore. Her heart was pounding from the adrenaline rush and she felt like cartwheeling down the hall.

Another woman was waiting there, clearing her throat and pacing. She stared at Shelby as if she were nuts.

Shelby smiled at her, then turned and went back inside. The people at the long table were consulting in soft voices. She stayed by the door. "Is there anything else you'd like to hear?" she asked.

"No, thank you," said Norb. "That was very impressive, Ms. Barrett. Would you mind reading something?"

Would she!

She sailed through the scene they gave her, loving every minute of it.

"Thank you," said Norb when she had finished. "You'll be hearing from us."

She flashed him a grin. "I hope so." She left the room, forcing herself not to skip, and blessing Matt for helping her find the emotion she had needed to give her performance that extra oomph.

She thought of waiting around for Leeza, who was in another part of the building, getting ready for her dance audition, but decided against it. She was too hyped to just hang around. Instead, she went home and called her mom to report on her success.

"That's wonderful!" Mom exclaimed. "So, should I go out and get tickets tomorrow?"

"No. Wait until I'm in the show. I should be able to get you a discount. Gosh, I wish you could have seen me. I was fabulous."

"I'll bet you were," said Mom. "I'm so glad you didn't lose your focus."

"I can thank Matt for that."

"Oh, does that mean you worked things out?"

"No," said Shelby, and the thought of their previous night's argument freshened her anger with him. "Nothing's worked out. We had a fight. In fact, I'm still so mad at him I could strangle him, so I'm keeping my distance."

"Well, that's one way of cooling things off," said Mom. "Not quite what I was thinking of when I suggested it."

"I know," said Shelby. "I'd planned for us to have a rational, calm conversation. Somewhere along the way we lost that. It seems like lately I'm not very calm or rational when I'm with Matt."

"It's because you're getting frustrated. That is not a good sign."

"I know," said Shelby, "but don't worry. I've got things under control."

That was a lie, and they both knew it.

Monday morning Lance was at the computer early, checking on his various stocks. He did a little business, then read his E-mail. True to his word, Matt had sent Mama's address.

"I think she usually knocks off work around four," Matt had written. "If you want to see a picture of her, you can visit her web site: DianaValentine.com."

Why not? Lance got back on the net and brought up Diana Valentine's web site. He thought he would be greeted by a hot pink page with red heart's swimming all over it, but her home page was a tasteful taupe color, patterned in a field of embossed flowers laying like a whisper of lace on the page. Her name, printed in gold script, marched across it. Under it, the words "bestselling author" proclaimed her success.

Beneath that he saw a picture of a small, svelte woman with big, brown eyes and short, coppery curls. She wore a cream-colored, satin blouse tucked into dressy black slacks, and diamonds sparkled at her ears.

The picture wasn't one of those blowsy glamor things that were a dime a dozen these days. It was still glamorous, but more subdued, classy. Like her expression. She sat perched on the edge of her desk with her lips set in a Mona Lisa smirk, as if she had a naughty secret she was keeping from the rest of the world.

The picture intrigued him. He normally wasn't a fan of short hair—not enough to play with in bed—but he rather liked Diana's. It was tousled enough on top to still look halfway sexy.

He stared at the picture for some time, examining the play of light on the curls of her hair, the curve of her cheek, the swell of her breasts under her blouse. He suddenly realized he was giving this picture the same rapt attention he might have given a *Playboy* centerfold when he was fifteen, which made him frown in disgust and move on.

He opted to see Diana's latest book, and a million pixels swirled to form a book cover showing her name in big letters, and under it, a painting of a bedroom with an old-fashioned brass bed decorated with a floral spread and frilly pillowcases. On the nightstand next to it sat what looked like a journal. It lay open, and an old-fashioned quill pen fanned out over its pages. Under it, the title *Dreams* flowed in elegant script.

Beneath the book cover, several lines of hype declared how fabulous the novel was. Lance read the synopsis and thought it sounded sappy. He opted not to take advantage of the offer to show him the first chapter. He also passed on the opportunity to win a dream vacation from the publisher.

Instead, he went back to the home page and chose the section entitled "Scrapbook." It brought up a couple of pictures. The first one was a Christmas shot, and showed Diana caught in mid-laugh, looking warm and vibrant. Her gaze was directed toward Shelby, who was standing next to her, trying to hang on to an enormous, struggling, white cat with battered, gray ears and a matching tail.

The Christmas tree behind them was a woman's tree. No big, multi-colored lights here, no messy tinsel. Instead the poor thing had been smothered with mauve ribbons, little gold trumpets, and blown-glass ornaments, then strung with tiny, white lights.

Lance hated those little, white lights. You saw them everywhere and they had become trite. The ones on that tree were probably symbolic of Diana Valentine's writing.

"Diana, daughter Shelby, and Barrymore, the main man in their life," read the caption.

No picture or mention of Matt. Of course, he wouldn't

rate any mention until he had proved himself worthy by slipping a ring on the daughter's finger.

Diana was a little more casually dressed here than in her promo shot, but still elegant in caramel-colored slacks and a matching sweater. The gold chain around her neck was simple, but Lance could tell at a glance that it wasn't cheap.

He moved his attention to the next picture, this one of Diana and another middle-aged woman in a restaurant, which he immediately recognized as Canlis, one of Seattle's better dining establishments. "Writer's night out" proclaimed the caption. "Diana with pal Suzanne Goodman."

Lance supposed the other woman was a romance writer, too, and that the mere mention of her name meant something to readers visiting this web site. The name was probably phony, just like Diana's.

He took in the women's expensive-looking clothes, and the bottle of champagne perched in the ice bucket by their table. Mama obviously liked the good life.

He'd dealt with more than enough middle-aged women like that when he was young and working on the *Caribbean Queen*. He'd have no problem distracting Ms. Valentine from her daughter's love life.

He left Diana's web site and logged off. It was time to shift gears and think again about the business half of his life. With three jewelry stores to run, he had more than enough to keep himself busy, and more than one Valentine to think about. February, the jeweler's favorite month, would soon be here.

Mutual Care was a large insurance company that occupied the entire eleventh floor of the Puget Building in downtown Seattle. The office where Shelby and Matt worked was one big sprawl of desks and cubicles, richly deserving of mention in a *Dilbert* cartoon.

Shelby looked across the huge room to Matt's desk. He

was on the phone, investigating a claim, not even glancing her way. It had been like this since they came in. Matt had managed to dissolve her euphoria over her triumphant Sunday afternoon callback simply by walking past her desk with only a polite nod and a "Morning, Shel."

The weasel. He should be begging her to forgive him. She should have a bouquet sitting on her desk right now.

Her co-workers had noticed the cooling trend, and two of them had already dropped by on pretend errands to find out what was going on. Shelby had insisted nothing was wrong, which, of course, no one believed. Not because she wasn't a good enough actress to convince them, but because Matt was behaving like King Worm.

She looked at the clock. It was almost noon. Finally, lunch hour was here. The morning had limped by and it had seemed as if lunch break would never come.

Shelby pulled her purse out of her bottom desk drawer and fished out her lipstick. She shot a quick glance across the room to make sure Matt wasn't looking, then applied it generously, and shot herself a double spritz of Obsession. That would get him when he walked by.

She turned to her computer and pretended to be busy. Slowly, bodies began parading past her desk. "Want to go to Palomino's with us?" called one of her co-workers.

"No thanks," she said. "I've still got some work I need to get done."

"Good luck," said another in a low voice. "Here he comes."

Shelby's heart rate picked up. Now was the moment. What, exactly, was she going to say to him when he apologized?

But he didn't apologize. Instead, he walked past her without so much as turning his head. The slime!

Shelby didn't stay steaming at her desk for long. Deciding it was time to bring the issue to a head once and for all, she grabbed her purse and stormed out of the office.

She found Matt right where she'd expected. He was *sooo* predictable. There he sat in the tacky little sandwich shop favored by the male population of Mutual Care. As usual, the TV bracketed to the wall was tuned to ESPN, and Matt and his work buddies were lounging at a table that gave them the best view, idly watching some stupid sports show, talking and . . . laughing! Matt Armstrong, who claimed to love her, had surrounded himself with a whole army of co-workers and was laughing as if he hadn't a care in the world.

Shelby turned and stalked back to the office. She yanked open her desk drawer, threw in her purse, kicked the drawer shut, fell onto her chair and brought up her E-mail.

Matt had watched Shelby's retreating backside with a smug smile. Uncle Lance was right. Beat 'em at their own game. Another day of this and Shel would be calling him in tears, begging to get back together.

His smile faded just a little. He felt like a jerk pulling this stunt.

But, no, Uncle Lance was right. Only a wuss would let his girlfriend lead him around by the nose. And Matt wasn't going to have his friends telling him he was whipped. No way.

The thought that he might really lose her knocked at the back of his mind, but he firmly barred the door. Shelby loved him, adored him. She'd come around.

Sure enough. He got back to his desk to find he had an E-mail waiting for him. Good old Uncle Lance sure knew what he was talking about. Matt opened it.

"HOW DARE YOU!"

The words hit him like a winter wind, pushing him back against his desk chair. He glared at the screen, then began to type, "Listen here, you little . . ."

Wait a minute. How would Uncle Lance handle this?

He'd say to beat Shelby at her own game. *Think like a woman, Matt. What would a woman say?* Something cryptic and totally illogical.

Inspiration hit. He deleted his near misstep and typed back, "I don't know what you mean." Ha! That was a good one. He clicked SEND.

She fired back: "You know perfectly well what I mean. How dare you not speak to me when you should be apologizing and you know it!"

*Okay, think.* He sat, chewing his lip.

Fresh mail popped up on his screen. "Well?"

Oh, she was pissed. He had her right in the palm of his hand. "I don't think there is much to talk about at this point," he typed. "You were the one who wanted to cool things off. It's obvious you don't really appreciate me, so what's there to talk about?"

One last E-mail came through for him. "You are the king of the bottom feeders!!"

"Thank you," he murmured. "Now, you just sit over there and stew for a while."

After a long meeting with Lars Larson from the agency about the Valentine's Day ad campaign for Gregory's Fine Jewelry, Lance tooled up I-5, toward Edmonds and Diana Barrett's house, anticipating the profits the upcoming season of sentiment would bring him. With the possible exception of the Tiffany's in downtown Seattle, probably no other jewelry store would do as well as his. His stores provided what successful middle-class people wanted most: affordable jewelry served up with luxurious ambience. Walking on thick carpets under crystal chandeliers, sitting on elegant furniture and drinking champagne, (which was always poured after the engaged couple had made the last payment on their rings), his customers could imagine themselves as moving in the same circles as the Rockefellers or the Vanderbilts. Even his new web site had class, and customers ordering via it received a complimentary box of Godiva chocolates to give their sweetheart along with whatever bauble they bought.

Not only was his business growing, so was the value of his other investments. He'd make a good interviewee for Thomas Stanley and William Danko, authors of *The Millionaire Next Door*. Only he lived better than the tightwads they wrote about. Lance wasn't the millionaire next door, he was the millionaire at the top of the hill—ruler of an ever-growing financial empire.

There was still one thing lacking, though: an heir. Lance liked kids, and he was just about ready for one of his own. But to get one, he needed a wife, and he had yet to find someone who could hold his interest for longer than six months. Which was why he wasn't going to rush into anything. Better to be safe than sorry. There was no sense in leaping before he looked and winding up with a shattered ego and a depleted bank account. Anyway, he still had time, and lots of applicants to interview for the position of Mrs. Lance Gregory.

When they were young, his sister, Bett, had called him "the Bee." "Every woman on the planet was not made just for you, Lance Romance," she'd tease.

And he would shoot back, "Then why do they act like it?"

"Because you're cute, and you're slick, like something out of a movie," she'd say. "I should take pictures of you when you first get up in the morning and wave your gym socks under their noses. That'd cure 'em."

Ah, Bett. She'd always made him smile. She had always been his defender, always found good in him.

His smile turned bitter. Dear God, how he missed her! It wasn't right that she should die before even seeing her fiftieth birthday. They'd tried everything, but the cancer had gotten her in the end, leaving her husband and daughters stunned. Not to mention her siblings.

There was just no guarantee after a certain age. Good reason for a man to find himself a young woman who would live long enough to raise their child.

But these days the young women Lance dated seemed so immature. Most were more interested in fashion than world events, and if you mentioned Watergate, they looked at you as if you were talking ancient history. He couldn't imagine trusting any one of them to raise a kid. And he was beginning to feel slightly lecherous, with most of them nearly young enough to be his daughter. Well, a woman in her mid-thirties would be okay, maybe even late thirties, if they had a child right away. A boy. Much as he appreciated women, he didn't want to have to raise and worry over one.

Adele was thirty-something. Lance thought of her horse laugh and tried to imagine her at a business dinner party or fund-raiser, wearing an evening gown. He couldn't. It was time to send Adele a tennis bracelet and move on.

And time to turn his mind to the challenge at hand. Lance took the Edmonds exit off I-5 and headed toward the water. He found the Diana Barrett, a.k.a. Valentine, place easily, and pulled his black Mercedes up alongside the opposite curb.

Nice house. It was redbrick and looked like it had been built in the early sixties. Nothing he would pick, but a good piece of real estate. It would probably fetch a quarter of a million. The view alone was worth that.

Lance checked his watch. Ten till four. The widow Barrett was probably still at her computer, writing some new piece of romantic propaganda. If Matt was correct, she should be knocking off work soon. Lance had a hunch that, after being cooped up inside all day, the lady would be going through shopping withdrawal and anxious to get out of the house. If she surfaced, he'd follow her and see what happened.

Meanwhile, there was no sense wasting time. He grabbed his cell phone and made some business calls.

At ten after four there was still no sign of her. Lance decided to give her another five minutes, then move on.

He was just about to pull away from the curb when he saw her garage door open and a nearly new Lexus pull out. He followed at a discreet distance.

The Lexus drove to a nearby shopping center, turned in at the supermarket, and began circling, looking for a parking space.

By now it was almost five, the twilight was yielding to winter darkness, and the after-work shopping rush hour was beginning. Every parking space had been taken, except one. Looking at it, Lance saw why. The Bronco to the right of it had parked at an odd angle, and its back fender hung over the line, daring other cars to just try and get in.

Diana Barrett took the dare. She whipped her car around and began jockeying. Lance found a parking spot at the far end of the lot with a view and watched in fascination as she maneuvered her car by degrees until she had claimed the parking space, leaving the hog next to it with a severe challenge to get free. Lance chuckled.

*Chancy, though,* he thought. She could end up with a dented fender or a scraped paint job.

He watched as she got out of her car and walked to the rear of the neighboring vehicle. She was wearing jeans and an olive drab parka. A brown leather purse hung from her shoulder. She pulled a small tablet from it and a pen, and began to write. It wasn't hard to guess what she was noting.

Lance was impressed. Here was a woman who rose to a challenge, but took no chances. Unless the bozo next to her had no insurance. Then his license number would do Ms. Hearts and Flowers no good.

She tucked the tablet back into her purse and headed into the grocery store, giving him a tempting glimpse of the region just below the parka. But he didn't give in to the temptation to follow her. Instead, he remained in his car, waiting to see if the owner of the Bronco would show.

A few minutes later he was rewarded with the appearance of the parking space hog, a chunky man with a receding hairline toting a case of beer.

The guy looked first at Diana's car, then his, then back at hers. He shook his head, then gesticulated as if the nervy driver who had wedged him in were standing there in front of him. Now his mouth was moving, and Lance could just imagine what he was saying. The guy tossed his beer in the back of the vehicle, then went around the front to the driver's side, opened the door and squeezed in. Lance chuckled, watching the man inch forward and backward, trying to escape the tight spot Diana Barrett had created for him. Finally, the vehicle was free, and its owner squealed off in a snit.

Lance pulled out his wallet and removed a business card. It was white, with his company name embossed on it in gold block print, his own underneath. He turned it over and wrote on it. Then he walked to Diana's Lexus and inserted the card under her windshield wiper, and sauntered away.

There. Let the games begin.

Diana didn't feel like cooking, so she visited the store's Chinese take-out section and purchased a carton of Almond Chicken, along with some Peking Pork and a carton of noodles. She stocked up on some sale items, then picked up an intriguing-looking book by a new author. She'd start it tonight. Sparkling apple cider caught her eye as she headed for the checkout, and she added that to her cart as well. A good book, a cozy fire, and some sparkling cider should make for a nice, relaxing evening.

The clerk rang up her purchases and she pulled out a fifty to pay. Even though she had been enjoying good fortune now for several years, the satisfaction of having an abundant supply of cash in her wallet still hadn't diminished. She remembered what Joe E. Lewis said: "I've been rich and I've been poor, and believe me, rich is better." *Amen to that,* she thought. Not that she'd ever been poor, but she'd lived on some pretty tight budgets, and that was as close as she ever wanted to come.

She took her bags and headed for her car. The cretin next to her had gone, and Diana hoped he'd worked up a major sweat getting free. When she got close enough to see the small card on her windshield, she cringed. Of course, no man could find himself thwarted and not retaliate. She could just imagine the threats she'd find on that little card.

She plucked it off, telling herself not to even dignify such childish behavior by reading it, but her curiosity would not be denied. She held the card at arm's length and slanted it toward the parking lot light. Gregory's Fine Jewelry? That creep was the owner of one of Seattle's most popular jewelry store chains?

She turned the card over to read the hand-scrawled note. The letters were cramped, as if the writer were a man of large gestures, who had had to force himself to fit his handwriting to the small space allowed. She had to squint to make them out.

"I couldn't help observing your creative parking job," he wrote. "Do you conquer all obstacles as easily? If you're not married, would you join me for drinks at Canlis some night? Lance Gregory."

Diana smiled. She looked around the parking lot, hoping for a glimpse of the mysterious Mr. Gregory, and, of course, saw no one. Intriguing. It was like something out of one of her own books.

She set her grocery bag on the backseat and got in the car. Lance Gregory. Great name. What did he look like?

Probably not as good as his name, she decided. Anyway, she didn't want to be bothered with men anymore.

She was perfectly happy with this new phase of her life, with no commitments, no responsibilities, no one fighting her for control of the thermostat, the checkbook, the TV or the vacation itinerary. Her life was hers and hers alone.

She tossed the card on the dashboard and backed her car out of the parking spot, then turned on the radio to the oldies rock station. Aretha Franklin was singing about feeling like a natural woman. You didn't need a man to feel that way. Diane punched the radio back into silence.

And into that silence crept thoughts of the mysterious Lance Gregory and drinks at Canlis. It did sound temptingly romantic.

And romance had been seriously lacking in her marriage. In marrying John, she had picked sensibly, finding a man who knew the meaning of the word "responsibility." Unfortunately, "romance" was not one he had ever gotten a good handle on, and the sizzle had cooled to lukewarm early on. That was hardly surprising. They'd both been so busy, especially Diana, with her writing career and raising Shelby, that it had been easier to settle for—what had they settled for? Habit, she supposed—John because he liked it that way, and Diana because she was too proud to ask him to break the mold and do something unexpected once in a while.

She didn't need a man to have romance in her life, anyway. She could buy her own flowers now, and any diamond trinket that caught her eye. She could book her own cruises and lean on the deck rail and enjoy the swoosh of the water against the bow of the boat as it plowed through turquoise waters to exotic destinations.

Alone.

Alone was just fine, she reminded herself. It was better than irritation. And as for romance, well, no man was really romantic, which was why women read fiction. God knew, they had to feed their souls somehow.

She pulled her car into the garage and got out, leaving

the card on the dashboard. On second thought, she reached in and snatched it out. She'd throw the thing in the garbage.

Shelby watched through tear-blurred eyes as Matt's broad back exited through the glass office doors of Mutual Care. The E-mail war had only made matters worse, and at quitting time he had walked right past her desk without saying a word. He could have left by another route, but he had chosen to deliberately pass her and say nothing.

She felt rejected, and angry with him for making her feel that way. She looked down the corridor of time and saw herself, a lonely old woman, running her lines on the stage of some small community theater, while backstage pretty, young women gossiped about her. *"They say she loved someone once, but he broke her heart, and she's been alone ever since."*

"Shelby, are you all right?"

Shelby knew that voice. It was Greta Amundson. Greedy Greta, the other women called her, because she flirted with every man in the office. No male was safe from her grasping, acrylic-tipped hands, even ones who everyone knew were taken. Greta had been chasing Matt off and on for the last three months, whenever she thought Shelby wasn't looking. And now here she was, pretending concern, the fake-blonde hypocrite. Well, she and Matt would have a lot in common. They could compare colorists.

"I'm fine, but I'm a little busy right now," said Shelby, keeping her gaze firmly pinned on the cats on her screen saver.

"Counting cats?" taunted Greta.

"It's more interesting than counting fake blonde hairs," replied Shelby sweetly.

"Well," huffed Greta. "Excuse me for caring."

"Yeah, right," muttered Shelby.

She shut down her computer, gathered her things, and

slowly headed for the door, where her coworker Jackie was waiting.

"What did Greta say to you?" demanded Jackie, the light of battle glowing in her eyes.

"She just wanted to console me."

"Oh, I believe that," said Jackie.

"Me. too. Just like I believe in the tooth fairy."

"So, how are you doing? Want to go to Red Robin and have a drink?"

Shelby shook her head. "No, I think I'll just go home and swallow poison."

"Men are pigs," said Jackie.

Shelby nodded and headed out the door.

Once home, she wished she had gone to Red Robin. Leeza was flying the friendly skies, building up hours in anticipation of soon being able to abandon sky for stage, and the solitary apartment felt as comforting as a newly dug grave. Appropriate metaphor, thought Shelby miserably. She looked over at the love seat where she and Matt had kissed so passionately on New Year's Day and burst into stormy sobs. She was going to lose him, she knew it.

No, she wasn't! She just needed to get a grip and get control of the situation.

She grabbed the phone and called her mother. Mom answered on the fourth ring, just as Shelby was resigning herself to leaving a desperate message on the answering machine.

Shelby didn't waste time on pleasantries. "Now he's not speaking to me."

"That doesn't surprise me," said Mom. "I'm sorry, darling."

"And he deliberately humiliated me in front of the whole office by not speaking to me," continued Shelby, fresh anger rising.

"It looks like he beat you to the punch on that strategy," said Mom.

"Yeah, well, he's just full of clever strategies," said Shelby bitterly. "Do you know he had the nerve to tell me I didn't appreciate him?"

"I thought you said he wasn't speaking to you."

"I E-mailed him. He E-mailed back and told me I didn't really appreciate him. Talk about manipulative!"

"Um-hmm," said Mom.

"He thinks I'm going to come crawling, begging him to go back to the way things were."

"And are you?"

"No way," sneered Shelby. A vision of Greedy Greta in a tight sweater sprang to mind. "But there must be something I can do."

"There is," said Mom. "You can find someone else."

"But I don't want anybody else," protested Shelby.

Her mother's sigh spoke volumes. "You enjoy being taken for granted?"

"Absolutely not, but Matt doesn't realize he's taking me for granted," explained Shelby. "He's just being dense."

"Well, then, I guess you need to un-dense him," said Mom.

"Yeah?" prompted Shelby.

"Show him that he's not the only man at the party."

"Of course!" exclaimed Shelby. "Make him jealous. But there isn't anybody. Everyone at the office has girlfriends or is married. Except the nerds."

"Nerds aren't so bad. Look at Bill Gates. I think he's kind of cute."

"Matt wouldn't feel threatened by a Bill Gates."

"Well, I don't know what to tell you," said Mom. "You'll probably have to settle for letting Matt cool off and then see what happens."

"No, that's too chancy. We must be able to come up with some other ideas for how to make him jealous."

"I think you'd better forget playing these silly games

and let things develop honestly between you. Anything else makes a poor foundation for a lasting relationship."

"We haven't played any games in this relationship and look where it's gotten me," said Shelby. "I really do need to do something to open Matt's eyes. Come on, help me brainstorm."

"Well, okay. You could . . . tie yourself on the Monorail tracks. Make sure you have your cell phone with you, then you can call him to come rescue you."

"Thanks. That was real helpful."

"Okay," said Mom. "You might try sending flowers to yourself."

"Cute," said Shelby. "You are so not helpful." She suddenly remembered an old movie she and her mother had watched on TV a couple of years back. "Wait a minute. Are you thinking of that old Sandra Dee movie?"

"Oh, my gosh, no. I was just joking," said Mom, her voice threaded with panic.

"I remember that movie," said Shelby. "Sandra Dee wanted to make her husband jealous, so she sent flowers to herself. Wait, there was something more. What was it?"

"She said she bought them for herself, but when she went to the florist, she pretended to be a secretary ordering for her boss."

"Oh, yeah. Mr. Snow. No, wait. That's *Carousel*."

"Never mind his name," said Mom. "This is not a good idea."

Shelby ignored her. "And when Bobby Darin went to the florist and learned about the phony boss, he got jealous. Of course, it wasn't Sandra's fault he jumped to conclusions. She was telling the truth. She did buy them for herself." Shelby chortled. "Oh, I like this!"

"It was great fun on film," agreed Mom, "but you know perfectly well that things don't work in real life the way they do in movies. If you were to try something like that, chances are it would all blow up in your face."

"I don't see how," said Shelby. "What's Matt going to do, go beat up my imaginary lover?"

"I still think you'd do better to wait and see if Matt comes around on his own," Mom cautioned.

"That could take a long time, and somebody else might move in on him in the meantime. No, I like this. Let's see. What can we call him?"

"Shelby, I don't mind giving you an occasional piece of advice, but this has all the makings of a Lucille Ball fiasco and I don't want to get pulled into the middle of it."

"Come on. I need your help."

"I think you can handle thinking up a name on your own," said Mom. "But I will caution you, if you're going to do this, make sure you pick a name that is pretty common, like Smith or Jones. That way Matt can't possibly look it up in the phone book and find a real person to confront."

"Oh, yeah. Good idea."

Shelby hung up and began to think. What could she name her fictitious admirer?

She turned on her television for companionship. A local newscaster was looking at her sternly, informing her of a fire in an apartment building on the south end of Seattle. Oh, that was comforting.

She aimed the remote control and zapped him in favor of the rerun station. And, suddenly, there stood the Monkees, singing about taking the last train to Clarksville.

Shelby smiled. That show had been a rerun when she was twelve. She'd thought she was seeing it for the first time and had fallen madly in love with Davy Jones. Until her mother informed her that she, herself, had watched it as a teenager, which meant he was old, old, old. That had been a shock. Even now, looking at the image of her childhood heartthrob, Shelby found it hard to imagine how ancient the guy really was. Good old Davy Jones.

Davy Jones. David Jones. The name had a ring to it. The kind of ring to make a certain boyfriend jealous, perhaps?

# Four

*Diana hung up* the phone, wishing she had never answered. Shelby's current situation had "Danger—Explosives" written all over it. Of course, this latest ploy would result in more emotional chaos. Why on earth was Shelby trying so hard to keep a man who was looking less and less like a keeper?

Barrymore stalked into the kitchen in search of food and Diana picked him up and scratched his head. He endured her affection for three seconds, then began squirming to get free. She dropped him back to the floor in disgust. "You are the last male cat I'm ever getting," she informed him. "You men are all alike, no matter what your species."

Well, that wasn't fair. John had had his flaws, but he hadn't been afraid of commitment. He'd stayed with her in sickness and in health, reminding her after both of her miscarriages that they still had each other. He should have added, "to drive crazy for the rest of our lives."

She and John had discovered after living together over many years that opposites not only attract, they irritate.

He had been a neatnick, which, she supposed went hand in hand with being an accountant and liking everything in neat columns. She had been, well, not so neat. She had liked to spend money, he preferred to save it. Pinch it, actually. She loved to dance, he insisted he had two left feet and, after their first anniversary, could never again be lured onto a dance floor. She loved to explore romantic little towns, European capitals, and take cruises, while his idea of travel was to go in to Seattle for the University of Washington Huskies's football games. And he had never, in twenty-four years of marriage, stopped to ask directions! Good Lord, how had they survived so many years together? Stubbornness, she supposed.

The phone rang again. It was probably Shelby with a new trauma. Diana picked up the receiver reluctantly and was pleasantly surprised to hear Suzanne Goodman's voice.

"Hi! I had company for lunch today, and I've got to find someone to help me get rid of this temptation sitting in my fridge. Could you fall off your diet for a piece of chocolate cheesecake?"

Diana's taste buds sprang to attention. "Definitely. And I've got dinner to go with it. I just came in with Chinese take-out."

"Great. I'll be right over."

Diana had met Suzanne at a writers' conference. Both clueless, they had wandered from class to class, trying to make sense of the publishing business. They had shared dreams and phone numbers, and over the years they had read each other's work, watched each other's kids, and cried over each other's losses. Suzanne had divorced her husband a couple of years before John died, and although she dated now, there was no one special in her life other than the heroes she created for her books. And no wonder. Who could compete with the men Suzanne dreamed up? Diana had come to her senses about love long ago, but

Suzanne was still a believer, still waiting for Mr. Wonderful.

Which was probably why she pounced on the card Diana had tossed on her kitchen counter. "Lance Gregory. The diamond king? What's this all about?"

"Just a little present he left on my windshield," said Diana, opening a carton of noodles.

"Oh? Tell me more."

"Read the back."

Suzanne turned the card over and scanned the message. Her eyes widened. "Whoa. I think you might have hit the jackpot."

Diana plucked the card from her friend's fingers and tossed it in the garbage, saying, "Well, I'm not going to find out."

Suzanne gaped at her. "Are you certifiable? This man sounds fabulous."

Diana shrugged. "Then you call him. You're more the Lance Gregory sort of woman than I am."

It was true. Suzanne could have been an escapee from the old TV series *Dynasty*. She and Diana wore the same classic style of clothes with one big difference: Suzanne, with her height, her delicate features, and her frosted blonde hair, looked like she belonged in them.

"That card is a gift from the gods and you're scorning it," said Suzanne.

"Isn't that what they said about the Trojan Horse? Anyway, those whom the gods love, they make mad."

"Well, you're already crazy, so what could this hurt?" retorted Suzanne.

"Suz, you have been reading too many of your own books. Look at us and tell me if either of us should be in the market for a man. Your husband was a power-hungry skirt chaser and mine was the reincarnation of Jack Benny."

"You loved John," accused Suzanne.

"Yes, I did, but not enough to want to repeat history," Diana said firmly. "That was then. This is now. Other than an occasional spurt of sentimental loneliness, I do just fine on my own. I have a financial manager who actually encourages me to enjoy spending some of what I earn, a lawn service to mow my lawn, and a garage to put on my snow tires every winter. All those things John did, I can hire done. What do I need a man for?"

"Sex."

"I have no libido left, remember?"

"Oh, nonsense. I once read that our biggest sex organ is in our head," countered Suzanne.

"Well, it's not. It's in our glands. Early menopause stole my estrogen and killed my libido, and I really don't need a man in my life."

Suzanne looked at her through narrowed eyes. "Liar."

Diana turned her back on her friend and busied herself with pulling dishes from the cupboard. "It's true," she insisted.

"You are such a liar. I saw that longing expression on your face when we were watching *Romancing the Stone* on New Year's Eve. Remember the scene? Michael Douglas dancing with Kathleen Turner."

"Just remembering the past."

Suzanne gave a snort of disgust. "As if you and John ever danced like that. As if you and John ever danced at all."

That had always been the biggest sore spot in her marriage, but Diana refused to rise to the bait.

"And how about the hero in *Hope Floats*?" Suzanne persisted.

"Now, that movie made me want to run right out and find a man. Remember how many tissues we all used? The husband was a walking public service announcement for women. Beware. Men are hazardous to your health."

"What kind of a romance writer are you, anyway?"

"A realistic one."

"Oh, is that what you call it?"

"Come on, Suz. No more grief about *Dreams*, okay? I'd been writing the same thing for fifteen years. I needed a change."

"I wonder how many of your fans were ready for that change."

"The number of readers I've gained who prefer to look at life through a wider lens more than make up for any I've lost."

Suzanne's expression showed what she thought of traitors to the genre, but she let the subject drop. "You know that not all men are like the husband in *Hope Floats*," she pointed out, returning the conversation to Diana's love life. "And sometimes there is a great consolation prize out there, like Harry Connick, Jr."

Diana sighed. "I know. But the truth is, there aren't enough Harry Connicks to go around anymore."

"There might be one or two left. That might be one over there in the garbage."

Diana shook her head. "Probably not."

"You won't know if you don't call," said Suzanne softly.

"Thanks but no thanks."

"He sounds incredibly charming."

"Actually, I've done charming, and it's not all it's cracked up to be," said Diana.

Even now, years later, she could still feel the power surge of rage at the thought of the smooth-tongued user who had been her first love. She had been young: barely nineteen. He had been older, in his late twenties, and she had thought he was so exciting, so sophisticated. But his sophistication had been nothing more than a veneer of smooth moves and pat lines, all designed to help a woman out of her clothes. And he had tired of her quickly enough, dumping her for some bimbo he worked with and leaving her bleeding internally. She still hated him for it. No, she didn't want to go down that road again. Ever. Charming men were always charming for a reason, and it was never a good one.

"Come on," she said, "let's eat."

Lance laid aside his mystery novel and went to the bar to pour himself another Scotch. Speaking of mysteries, why hadn't Ms. Valentine called?

She probably didn't want to appear too eager. That was it. She'd call. Curiosity would get her in the end.

He settled himself back in his chair and looked again at the phone. She really should have called by now. He just couldn't understand it.

On the first Tuesday morning in January, a delivery person from Hearts and Flowers Florists arrived at Mutual Care, bearing a gargantuan bouquet of red and white roses and carnations, set off with ferns and baby's breath. It landed on Shelby's desk and drew the other women like the smell of chocolate.

"Who is that from?" demanded Jackie.

"Me," said Shelby. "I sent it to myself."

"Right." Jackie snatched the florist card from its holder, and Greta peered over her shoulder.

"You're wonderful," read Jackie. "David."

"David," echoed Greta. "David who?"

"David Jones. May I have that back?" said Shelby, holding out her hand.

Jackie handed it over. "Since when is your name David?"

"Since yesterday. I think I look like a David, don't you?"

"Sure," said Jackie.

"Oops, here comes the boss," said someone, and the women scattered back to their cubicles.

Shelby cast a quick glance across the room to see how Matt was reacting to her performance and caught him scowling at her. It looked like she would be getting an E-mail any minute.

He didn't disappoint her. "Who is that from?" he demanded.

She typed back. "Myself."

"What is that supposed to mean?"

"I sent them to myself," she typed.

"I'M NOT STUPID!!!" screamed her computer screen.

"Are you sure?" she replied, then added. "Quit bugging me, I'm trying to work."

One final E-mail came, warning, "I'll find out."

Oh, yes. This was working like a charm. Just like in the movie.

Matt sat at his desk, trying to think of his next move. But he couldn't seem to get beyond wondering where Shel had found a replacement for him in one day. Of course, she was cute enough to have no problem doing that, and the thought of some drooling creep hanging around her made his blood sizzle. She was his, damn it!

He caught sight of Jackie and another woman at the watercooler and decided he was suddenly thirsty. Their backs were turned to him, and he kept his approach quiet.

"It said 'You're wonderful'," Jackie was saying. "I wonder what she did to make David Jones think she's wonderful."

The other woman happened to turn just then and see Matt looming behind them. She looked like she'd just seen the headless horseman. "Oh, hi Matt," she said, her face turning red.

Jackie gave a start, sloshing water on herself.

"Be careful, Jackie. You're spilling," said Matt.

She gave him a nervous smile and he strolled off, doing

his best to look nonchalant and forcing his hands not to curl into fists.

David Jones, huh. What kind of dull lump was named David Jones, anyway? And who the hell was he? Whoever he was, it didn't matter. Matt would find him, they'd have a little talk, and the guy would be history.

Now all he had to do was figure out how he was going to do that. It shouldn't be too hard. He'd watched enough detective shows growing up, and he knew he had to start by getting the name of the florist who had delivered that showy mess on Shel's desk.

His opportunity to learn the name of the florist came when Greta strolled by his desk. Greta was a little too shopworn for Matt's taste. But she did have great legs, and today she was wearing a skirt short enough to make every man in the office happy when she bent over. It wasn't her skirt length that Matt was interested in, though; it was the information she had.

"Hi Matt," she said. "Are you doing okay?"

Translation: *Are you available?*

Matt nodded. "Yeah, I'm all right. Hey, who's the florist responsible for cluttering up Shel's desk?"

"Hearts and Flowers."

"The one right down in the lobby?"

Greta nodded.

*Oh, piece of cake. Way to go, Armstrong!* Now, all he had to do was saunter on down to Hearts and Flowers and . . .

Greta interrupted his thoughts. "I know this has got to be hard for you. If you want to go out for coffee and talk about it, I'd be happy to listen."

"Thanks, Greta. I'll keep that in mind."

As far as Matt was concerned, that finished the conversation, but Greta didn't go away. She just stood there, looking sympathetically at him, the little horsefly.

"Well, I guess I'd better get back to work," he said.

She took the hint. "Sure. See ya."

Even though he had no desire to become another trophy in Greta's case, Matt couldn't resist watching her backside as she walked away. Now, there was a sight to behold.

*Never mind her. Concentrate on Shel.*

During the morning coffee break, he slipped down to the florist's. He'd been in there a couple of times in the last year to buy flowers for Shel. They hadn't been as ostentatious as that allergy special all the women were talking about, but nice enough. The clerk smiled like she remembered him.

"Hi," she said. "Can I help you?"

"I was hoping you could give me some information on a bouquet you guys sent up to Mutual Care this morning."

"Oh, wasn't that gorgeous?" she gushed.

"Yeah, it was nice," agreed Matt. *If you like overkill.*

"Did you want to order some flowers for . . . someone?"

She was smiling at him and playing with her necklace. So, she was fishing, ready to flirt. Ready to give him any information he might want. Good.

He flashed her his killer smile. "Actually, no. It's about that bouquet. My co-worker lost the card and she wants to thank the man who sent it. She did him a favor." That sounded like Shel had had sex with the guy or something. "A business favor," he added.

"Oh, sure," said the girl, nodding. She looked around as if wondering where Shel was.

"She couldn't come down. She's swamped with work," Matt improvised. "I told her I'd stop by for her. You wouldn't happen to remember the customer's name?"

"Actually, I do remember that order. I took it myself right before we closed. A woman came in and paid cash for it. She said she was ordering the bouquet for her boss, who had just met someone and wanted to make an impression."

Ah-ha! He knew it. "Did she mention her boss's name?"

"Yeah, but I don't remember. Let me look it up." She went to her computer and started tapping keys. "Here it is. The boss's name was David Jones."

So Shelby sent those flowers to herself, did she? Like hell. Matt clamped down on the angry roar barreling up his throat and forced a polite smile. "Thanks."

For nothing. The guy had sent his secretary with cash. How was Matt going to find him? *Think like Magnum P.I.*

"You know," he said, "I think she knows more than one David Jones. I'd better make sure I get the right address. Ever done business with this guy before?"

The woman chewed her lip for a moment. "Boy, that name sounds familiar."

"Does he work around here?"

"Well, let me see." Again, she did some searching. "Ah ha," she crowed. "I knew I remembered that name. He ordered a bouquet for his mom at Christmas. Oh, yes, and flowers for his secretary."

"Nice boss," said Matt. *Jerk.*

"He's just down a couple blocks, in the SeaNet building. Harper Financial Counseling, Inc."

"Great," said Matt. "Thanks a lot."

"You're welcome. Did your co-worker like the bouquet?"

Matt forced the pleasant expression to stay on his face. "Oh, yeah."

The girl nodded. "Well, anytime you want something, I'm here."

Matt thanked her again, then left. Shel was probably waiting for him to come charging back to the office and act like a jealous idiot. But he was too smart for that. Let her think her evil, little plot had worked. It would all blow up in her face after Matt paid a visit to David Jones. No man liked being used, and once he opened this guy's eyes to what Shel was up to, he'd disappear faster than David Copperfield from a Vegas stage. So much for that little ploy, Shel. You lose. Point. Game. Set.

Whistling, Matt headed down the street to pay a little visit to David Jones at Harper Financial Counseling, Inc.

The office was nearly as large as Mutual Care, but more dignified, with discreetly closed office doors and a reception area lush with potted vegetation and dark mahogany furniture that looked like it had cost a bundle. The receptionist was just as dignified as the setting: a middle-aged woman in a black silk suit with ash blonde hair swept up into some sort of roll at the back of her head. She smiled at Matt and asked, "May I help you?"

He cleared his throat. "Yes, I'd like to see David Jones."

"Did you have an appointment?"

"No, but I only need to see him for a minute, if he's in."

She smiled and nodded. "Who may I say is calling?"

"Matt Armstrong. I'm here on personal business."

She picked up the phone on her desk, punched the intercom button and a number. "Mr. Jones, a Mr. Armstrong is here to see you—a personal matter." She smiled at Matt again. "You can go on in. His office is right there," she said, pointing to the door off to her right.

Matt thanked her and headed for it. The guy had his own office. Great. Just great. That meant he was older, and probably bringing in twice Matt's salary. Where had Shel found such a big dog so quick? And how was he going to convince this power broker to stay away from her?

David Jones stood up from his desk as Matt entered, and then his worries dissolved into contempt. The guy wasn't older. And he was a shrimp. He couldn't be more than two or three inches taller than Shel. He had curly, brown hair and eyes that made Matt think of a basset hound, and he looked like he was coming to the end of his twenties. What a loser. Matt supposed this was the best Shel could come up with on the spur of the moment, but if she wanted to make him jealous she was going to have to try harder.

David Jones did dress well, Matt would give him that, and he looked like he was in pretty good shape. But he was still a shrimp.

He came forward, holding out his hand. "Hi. I'm David Jones. What can I do for you?"

Matt took it and gripped it a little harder than necessary. "I'm Matt Armstrong."

The shrimp nodded, pretending Matt's name didn't mean anything to him.

Matt squeezed a little harder and Jones's eyebrows dropped to a suspicious angle.

He squeezed back. "Nice to meet you."

"Does my name sound familiar?" asked Matt tightening the vise grip one more notch before releasing Jones's hand.

He pulled it away, frowning. "No. Should it?"

So this was the way he was going to play it. "Well, let me put it another way. I'm Shelby Barrett's boyfriend. Now does the name ring a bell?"

The shrimp's look turned wary. He shook his head slowly. "No. I'm sorry, but I don't know anyone by that name."

No stunned look. No apology for moving in on another man's woman. That did it! Matt grabbed a fistful of shirt and yanked, pulling David weenie-boy Jones's face close to his. "Do you always send flowers to women you don't know?" he snarled.

Jones's eyes bugged out. Caption this expression "What?" The shrimp was in the wrong business. He should be in Hollywood.

"I know you sent her those flowers." Matt gave the little jerk's shirt another yank.

Jones's face was beginning to turn red, and his eyes were shrinking to slits. "I don't know who you are, but unless you want this Shelly Bartlett to have to come bail you out of jail, you'd better let go of my shirt."

Matt released it, shoving Jones in the process. "It's Shelby Barrett and you know it."

"I don't know any Shelby Barrett, and if she's as crazy as you, I don't want to."

"You always send flowers to women you don't know?" demanded Matt.

The shrimp didn't answer. Instead, he walked over to his desk and picked up his phone. "Alice, call security."

First round to Jones. Matt held up a hand. "Okay, I'm going. But just don't forget, Shelby's already taken."

"Yeah, by a nut," said David as the door shut on his strange visitor.

He fell onto his chair, took a deep breath and straightened his tie while he waited for his pulse to settle. That encounter had to have been the weirdest thing that had ever happened to him.

Not that anything weird ever did. His life was too well ordered to allow much room for the unpredictable. As for women, he'd had girlfriends, but they weren't the type to drive him to the kind of wild, antisocial behavior he had just witnessed. In fact, none of them had driven him to much of any behavior. Well, other than normal male responses. He was still waiting for that perfect woman who would walk into his life and turn it into a Bogie-Bacall movie.

He wondered what this Shelby person was like. She had to be something to inspire a man to make a complete fool of himself like that. Well, maybe not. Maybe that guy had just been a macho psycho nut, the type who had too much testosterone and not enough brain to balance it.

David attempted to turn his attention back to the investment portfolio of his newest client, but his thoughts were still running wild, chasing the elusive image of Shelby

Barrett. First he tried imagining her as an Ingrid Bergman type, complete with German accent. He loved women with European accents; they were so mysterious. But her name didn't fit the Ingrid image, so Ingrid was probably out. It was still a great name, though. And, judging from her boyfriend's behavior, she must have the body and face to match it. Sandra Bullock. She probably looked like Sandra Bullock. Or maybe Drew Barrymore.

"Like you're ever going to get a chance to find out what she looks like," he muttered, shaking his head.

And what good would it do if he did meet her? She obviously preferred jock dufuses like his brainless visitor. A vision of himself strolling off with the highly-valued Shelby on his arm leaving Matt Armstrong standing dumbstruck brought a smile to his face. In a fair world that was how it would be. The David Jones's of the world would triumph over the Matt Armstrongs.

But life wasn't fair, and Shelby Barrett was probably an airhead. They just didn't make women like Ingrid Bergman anymore, and the Sandra Bullocks didn't want regular guys.

Well, there was more to life than beautiful women, and if he could just think of it, then he might possibly be able to get back to work.

Shelby blinked. "You what?"

"You heard me," said Matt. "I went to Harper Financial Counseling and saw the poor schmuck you're using. I left his teeth in his mouth, but you probably won't be hearing from him again. The guy was too scared to even admit he knew you."

"Are you insane?" she cried. "How could you go to someone's business and . . . and . . . attack him?"

They were in the sandwich shop, and he nodded in the direction of two men lounging at a nearby table. "Do you think you can keep from turning this into something people will buy tickets to? Not that you haven't already," he added.

Shelby lowered her voice. "I told you I sent those flowers to myself. And how could you have met someone I made up!"

Matt wasn't listening. "I can't believe you would replace me in just a day with another man," he said.

"I didn't replace you," said Shelby between gritted teeth. "What is wrong with you? Why won't you believe me?" *How could this be happening?*

"What is wrong with me? What's wrong with you?" countered Matt. "How stupid do you think I am? Geez, Shel." He threw a five-dollar bill on the table and stood. "I've got to get back to work."

He started for the door and Shelby ran after him. "Don't you just walk out and leave me!"

Matt kept walking, looking straight ahead. "You missed your chance. There were two guys right there. You could have gotten one of them to send you flowers."

"That is not funny," said Shelby.

And it wasn't. She wanted to cry. Nothing was going according to plan. And now, on top of being about to lose Matt, she had some poor man in an office two buildings down who was walking around fearing for his life.

They reached the bank of elevators and she grabbed Matt's arm. "Matt, I really don't know any David Jones."

"Yeah, right," he scoffed. The elevator door opened and he stepped inside.

Shelby stepped right along with him and squeezed into the last available space. "You are so dense! And now I'm going to have to find that poor man and try to explain to him that I just borrowed his name to send myself flowers."

Matt rolled his eyes. "Do you have any idea how lame that sounds?"

Shelby heard a snicker escape someone in back of her

and felt her cheeks warming. She lowered her voice. "I did it to make you jealous. I just made him up."

"If you made him up how could I have talked to him this afternoon?" hissed Matt.

"I guess because he really exists."

"No. Do you think so?" Matt made a face and shook his head.

"We wouldn't even be having this conversation if commitment wasn't a dirty word to you," fired Shelby.

"Me! Oh, that's fine coming from Miss Keep-another-man-on-the-side. What was he, insurance?"

"I don't have to take that from you," said Shelby. The elevator doors opened and two people got out. Head held high, she marched out after them and heard the doors swoosh closed behind her.

The that-showed-him feeling lasted only an instant. She stood for a moment, reliving the whole ridiculous argument, wishing she hadn't let it get so out of hand. Why did every discussion she and Matt have always escalate into something stupid like this? Why didn't they just talk things out like two reasonable adults? And why had she gotten out on the eighth floor?

# *Five*

*Shelby punched the* up button for the next elevator to the eleventh floor.

Wait a minute. What was she doing? Did she really want to trail Matt into the office like a puppy hoping to get its ears scratched?

She moved away from the elevators. She'd just stay down here for a few minutes. She'd never seen what was on the eighth floor, anyway. Maybe she'd find something really interesting.

She didn't. She strolled by a dentist's office, a suite occupied by a commercial real estate company, and a psychiatrist's office. Maybe she should step in there and get some help, she thought bitterly.

But she wasn't the one who needed help. It was Matt. She could easily tell this David Jones that her boyfriend was emotionally unstable. After what Matt had pulled, that wouldn't be hard to believe. She was beginning to believe it herself.

With a long-suffering sigh, she returned to the elevators and pushed the button. Time to go make a phone call.

But once back at her desk, she couldn't bring herself to pick up the phone and call David Jones. What could she say? I'm the woman who almost got you assaulted. Hope you don't mind. Or how about, pay no attention to the man wringing your neck. He doesn't realize you're a figment of my imagination.

Oh, boy. Maybe she should just let the whole thing blow over. David Jones would be perfectly safe as long as she didn't send herself any more flowers.

That was cowardly. She owed the man an explanation and an apology.

She pulled out a phone book and looked up the number for Harper Financial Counseling, the name Matt had spat at her like it was a dirty word. She dialed it reluctantly. Maybe David Jones would be out to lunch or in a meeting.

No such luck. Mr. Jones was in and took her call. "Hello." His voice was a little lower than Matt's.

"Hi," she stammered. *What now?* "My name is Shelby Barrett and I owe you an apology." The silence on the other end of the line made her feel like a murderer waiting for her lethal injection. She hurried on, "I feel so terrible about what happened. You see, I didn't dream my boyfriend would find you." That wasn't quite right. "That is, you weren't supposed to be real. Oh, boy." How she wished she had a script in front of her!

"That's okay," said Mr. Jones in the tone of voice he might use with a dangerous lunatic.

"Look, I know you must think I'm crazy, that my boyfriend's crazy. There really is a logical explanation for all this. I'm just finding it a little hard to talk over the phone." So, what should she do? "Could I buy you a cup of coffee?"

A cup of coffee. A harmless enough offer.

David's common sense trotted out the memory of his

recent assault and warned, "Don't do it." Probably good advice. This was a volatile situation. Suppose the boyfriend spotted them sharing lattes. David could kiss his life good-bye. And it was such a pleasant, well-ordered life, too.

"Okay." The word came out slowly, wrestled away from his common sense.

"Great."

She sounded relieved, almost happy. She should be. A cup of coffee was pretty cheap penance for almost getting a man killed.

"How about the Starbucks Cafe in Pacific Place at quarter after five?" she said.

"Okay. What do you look like?"

"I'm short and I've got long, curly hair. Red. And I'm wearing a teal-colored suit. You won't be able to miss me. I'll be the sorriest-looking woman there."

"Okay," said David. "I'll see you at five-fifteen."

"Wait," she said. "What do you look like? How will I know you?"

After seeing her boyfriend, David had no desire to describe himself. But what did it matter? This wasn't a date. Anyway, better to be honest. That way she wouldn't be expecting some stud, and he wouldn't have to see the disappointment in her eyes. He suddenly wished he was six-foot-two and built like Schwartzenegger.

"Well," he said. "I'm not real tall, myself. About five-six." Five-five and a half was almost five-six. "Not much to look at," he added reluctantly.

"What color hair do you have?" she asked.

"Brown. It's curly, too."

"Really."

The tone in her voice made it sound like they had, somehow, bonded. All curly-haired, short people should stick together?

"What color eyes do you have?" she asked.

"Well, let's see. Hazel I guess you'd call 'em."

"Mmm," she said, and he couldn't tell what that meant. "Well, great. I'll be looking for you."

"Okay," said David and hung up.

He realized he was smiling. Great, Jones. You're going out with a woman whose boyfriend is a homicidal maniac and you're smiling. Not going out, he corrected himself. Just meeting her for coffee. And she was probably some kind of nut. This was dumb. Well, he just wouldn't go. And if she had the nerve to call and ask why he never showed, he'd tell her something important came up. Like a need for self-preservation.

Matt watched Shelby slip out the door. Five minutes early. Where was she going? He ground his teeth and grabbed his phone and dialed his uncle's cell phone.

Uncle Lance answered and Matt felt like a war-weary soldier seeing reinforcements arrive. He took a quick glance around to make sure no one was loitering within hearing distance. His coworkers were all busy shutting down computers, packing up briefcases and visiting. Good.

"It's Matt." He lowered his voice, just in case someone might pass by. "Things aren't going so good. She's getting flowers."

"Competition, huh?" guessed Uncle Lance.

"She claimed she sent them to herself. That was probably her mom's idea. I don't suppose you've made any progress with her mom?" Matt asked hopefully.

"I'm working on it," said Uncle Lance. "Meanwhile, if she's reduced to sending flowers to herself, it doesn't look like you've got much to worry about."

"Well, actually, I do. It turns out she didn't send them to herself. I met the guy. She claims it's all a mistake. Of course, she's just using him," Matt added.

"Probably," agreed his uncle.

"But things could heat up."

"She's upping the ante. But you don't want to pay. Right?"

"Not yet. There must be something I can do."

"Hmm."

Good. His uncle was thinking. That meant a brilliant strategy would be forthcoming.

"Okay, kid. Here's what you do."

*All right Uncle Lance! Way to come through.*

"Come on down to the store."

*What kind of help was this?* "What?"

"And get her a diamond."

"A diamond!"

"Not an engagement ring," said Uncle Lance, and Matt's heart settled back down. "We've got some nice earrings in right now, or you can get her a necklace with a diamond in it. A piece of fine jewelry should make a perfect pacifier. It says commitment, but not engagement."

"I don't know," said Matt. "She wants a ring."

"She'll settle for something that's close. This will give her hope, and proof that you care, which is all she really wants. She'll be happy, and you'll still be free."

"Hmm," said Matt.

Shelby headed for Pacific Place, Seattle's latest mall. This temple of commerce wasn't just any mall. Pacific Place was the crème de la crème of malls, bringing shops to Seattle that had, before this, been nothing more than distant elegant names to most of the populace. It was huge, but it didn't sprawl. Instead it climbed, seeming to go on for stories. Shelby loved it. She often strolled through Tiffany's on the ground floor to catch the sparkle from the rows of cases filled with diamond jewelry.

Today she headed straight for the escalators and the

third level, which housed the Starbucks Cafe. If she got there first, she'd have a chance to check out David Jones, her imaginary suitor come to life, before he ever got a glimpse of her.

No one fitting the description he'd given was sitting in the cafe yet, so she positioned herself near the escalator and leaned on the railing to look down at the anthill below. The place wasn't as busy as it was during lunch hour, but it still had plenty of people walking around, heading into Tiffany's, Cartier, or Restoration Hardware, the upscale home-decorating store. Many were riding the escalators, headed for J. Crew or to Papyrus for unique stationery, or the cinema to catch a movie.

After a while Shelby checked her watch. Five twenty-five. Maybe David Jones was running late. Maybe he'd stood her up. She searched the crowd again and saw mostly women. She sighed, feeling inexplicably disappointed.

Suddenly she caught sight of a head with curly, brown hair. It must be him. He separated from the group of people he'd been behind and she saw a short man in an overcoat. That had to be him. Now he was getting on the escalator, heading up.

Her pulse rate quickened. What was she doing here? What was she going to say? She watched the man round the bend and step onto the next escalator, heading to the third floor, and felt suddenly overwhelmed with dread.

She moved away from her post, smoothing the wrinkles from her skirt, then dug in her purse and spritzed on more perfume. He'd be getting off any minute!

She juggled the perfume back into her purse. *Go inside. Sit down. Act calm!* She hurried to one of the modern easy chairs arranged on a carpeted area just off the entrance and tried not to look like a crazy woman.

There he stood, in the doorway, looking around. He wasn't a heart-stopper like Matt, but he did have a sort of compact masculinity that was attractive: broad shoulders and a nice, square chin. There was something about his face that said, give this sweet boy a hug. *It must be the eyes,* she thought, *he has darling eyes.*

*Never mind his eyes. You're not here looking for a man. You're just here cleaning up a mess.*

He caught sight of her and his eyes widened into an expression that was definitely appreciative.

Good. That would make this whole thing easier. She smiled and gave a tiny wave.

He nodded and walked briskly toward her, his overcoat fluttering behind him like Superman's cape. Underneath he was wearing a very nice, dark suit. David Jones sure knew how to dress. And he wasn't all that short.

He came to her. "Shelby Barrett?"

She nodded.

"The face that launched a thousand ships," he murmured. "Or should I say fists?"

"I think I'm about nine-hundred and ninety-nine short," said Shelby.

He smiled. "It's only a matter of time."

Shelby was used to male admiration, but not such polished flattery. This was a far cry from, "Hey, gorgeous," or "What are you doing outside my dreams?" David Jones was no dummy. Which was going to make explaining her idiotic plan all the more embarrassing.

"I hope I haven't started a war," she said. "I'm just so sorry about what happened today."

"Nobody got hurt," said David.

"But somebody could have, and it would have been my fault."

He sat down opposite her. "And why would it have been your fault?"

"Because I made you up."

His eyebrows shot up. "You mean I'm not really real? Does Mom know?"

She needed coffee. "Here, let me get you some coffee first," she offered, sliding out of her seat. "What do you like?"

He stood up again and waved her back down. "Plain and strong, and I'm buying."

"Oh, no," said Shelby. "You've got to let me pay. It's the least I can do."

"Relax," he said. "What's your poison? Probably something with chocolate."

She nodded. "A double mocha."

"I'll be right back."

He went to the counter and ordered. Shelby crossed her legs and took a couple of deep breaths, reminding herself that there was nothing to be nervous about. This was all a simple misunderstanding, and could be easily cleared up. She'd look like a bimbo, of course, but that couldn't be helped.

David Jones returned with two large cups as well as a plate of biscotti dipped in white chocolate. The man had excellent taste.

"You didn't have to get biscotti," she said, eyeing the treat.

He set it down in front of her. "Chocolate, the way to a woman's heart."

"Are you sure about that?"

He shook his head. "When it comes to women, no man is ever sure about anything. But chocolate is one of the few facts I've mastered."

Shelby smiled. David Jones was a very smart man. And gracious, which made Matt's behavior all the more embarrassing, and her part in it all the more awful. She took a fortifying sip of coffee, then began her explanation. "Mr. Jones . . ."

"Call me David."

"David, I . . ." She stumbled to a stop. "Oh, gosh. I really don't know how to explain this."

"Try pretending I'm your best girlfriend."

That was not easy to do. And that, Shelby realized, was exactly why she was having trouble explaining. If David Jones had been ugly and rude, she'd have no trouble. But he was neither, and the words were jamming up in her throat.

She cleared it and plunged in. "I wanted an engagement ring for New Year's, well Christmas, actually, but New Year's would have worked."

"There's a nice store down below for that," David observed.

"Yes, I've been there. But my boyfriend, who you, er, met, well, he's not, that is." She sighed. This was like trying to pull out a tooth one jiggle at a time. *Just say it fast and get it over with.* "I wanted him to realize that there are other men out there who will marry me if he won't. So, I just made up a boyfriend—David Jones, like the one from the Monkees—and sent myself flowers from him to make Matt jealous. I never dreamed he'd find a real David Jones working right here downtown."

David nodded thoughtfully, as if he could see the logic. "So your boyfriend did some detective work and found me."

"You must use the same florist as I did," said Shelby. "I am so sorry."

"Don't be," he said. "I'm not."

"He could have broken your nose."

David shrugged. "He didn't. But if you're feeling guilty for putting my life in danger . . ." He nodded in the direction of the theater. "How about an early movie and dinner afterward?"

Go out with David Jones? That would definitely make Matt jealous. And he, in turn, would make David mush. She shook her head.

"I thought you wanted to make your boyfriend jealous," said David.

"I don't mind using figments of my imagination, but I draw the line at real people."

"It doesn't count as being used if I volunteer for the job," said David.

Shelby hesitated.

He reached across the table and lifted her hand. Little sparks raced up her arm.

"You know, until you have that ring on your finger, you're still available."

"Not really. Matt's got my heart."

"For the moment," agreed David. "But some guys can be real clumsy with the hearts they're given."

Shelby had to admit that Butterfingers Armstrong hadn't been handling hers very carefully lately, but she still loved him.

"I'm not asking you to go to Tahiti with me," pressed David. "Only a movie."

Well, it was a cinch she wouldn't be hearing from Matt tonight. If she went home she'd just mope around the apartment and be miserable. She chewed her lip.

"There's a new romantic comedy playing," he added.

Shelby loved romantic comedies. And since no one would be getting blown up, she could be certain she wouldn't find Matt there.

"Okay," she said. "But only if you let me pay."

He looked pained.

"That's the deal. Take it or leave it."

"Okay, I'll take it, but only if you let me buy dinner after."

"Deal," said Shelby, and told herself she wasn't being disloyal to Matt. In fact, this was all for Matt. She was cleaning up the mess he made.

"I'll bet if you were here by yourself you wouldn't be going to see this," she said as they entered the theater lobby.

"Oh? What would I be going to see?"

She pointed to a poster that looked like one gigantic explosion. "That."

He nodded. "You're right. But after I'd seen that I'd go see this. I like funny movies. In fact, I like all kinds of movies, even the old black-and-white ones they show on the A&E channel."

"I love old movies," said Shelby. "Especially ones with Cary Grant."

"Oh, yeah? What's your favorite?"

"The one where he and Grace Kelly got chased across Mount Rushmore."

"That was a great movie," agreed David, "But it wasn't Grace Kelly. It was Eva Marie Saint."

"No, I'm sure it was Grace Kelly."

"I'll bet you another date it was Eva Marie," said David.

His offer was more tempting than it should have been. Disgusted by her momentary lapse in loyalty, Shelby said, "I'll take your word for it." But she couldn't help adding, "Even though I think you're wrong."

David snapped his fingers. "I've got it. If I'm right, we go climb Mount Rushmore together."

Shelby caught a vision of herself clinging to a sheer wall of stone, inching along a narrow ledge next to a virile leading man: Matt, of course. "Actually, I think it would be exciting to be chased around Mount Rushmore."

"Only if you were with the right man," said David.

"Like Cary Grant?"

"Like someone who wouldn't be so busy saving his own skin that he forgot about yours. Not every man is a hero."

"Not every man gets chased around Mount Rushmore, so it's a little hard to tell these days."

"Not necessarily. Popcorn?"

• • •

Shelby enjoyed the movie. And she enjoyed the pizza they had at the trendy Gordon Biersch brewery and restaurant afterward.

And she enjoyed David Jones. He liked to laugh, and he liked to talk. And not just about himself. He wanted to know about her.

"Oh, let's see," she said. "I like to go to parties, and I love garage sales. And I hate camping."

He chuckled at that. "Don't like sleeping on the ground and cooking over an open fire, huh?"

"No, thanks," said Shelby. "I prefer a nice soft bed, a stove and a microwave."

"Which one do you use the most? The stove or the microwave," he added hastily.

Shelby looked at him, pretending to be wary. "Are you asking me if I can cook?"

"Just curious," he said.

"I'm a great cook."

"So, you're domesticated."

"Not really. I'm an actress. Well, right now I'm working as a temp, just until I can get a job acting."

David cocked his head and studied her. He nodded slowly. "You look like an actress. Like Julia Ormond, only cuter." He nodded. "Yeah, I could definitely see you on the big screen. So, why aren't you off in L.A., working as a waitress and waiting for your big break?"

"Because Hollywood doesn't make musicals anymore. Well, they do once in a while, but not enough for someone who wants to eat regularly."

"So you're going to head for New York."

"Probably not. But I am hoping to get hired for the ensemble for *Camelot* at the Fifth Avenue."

"No kidding? I've got season tickets. I always take my sister. So, we might see you?"

"You just might. I hope."

"But you don't know yet."

She shook her head. "I just had my callback on Sunday."

David shook his head. "I'm out with a real, live actress. Who'd have thought it? So, how come you're not living in New York?"

The words of Shelby's prof came back to haunt her. *You've got talent, Shelby, but it takes more than talent to make it. You need drive and incredible focus. I don't think you've got it. You may as well marry that party boyfriend of yours and settle for community theater.*

"I thought it would be easier to start here," she said, not wanting to share the painful words that had burrowed so deeply into her mind. David was studying her intently. She pretended she didn't notice and helped herself to another piece of pizza.

"So you're going to stay here because it's safe?"

"I don't want to move to New York and get knifed."

"I wasn't talking about that kind of safety," said David.

"I don't want to leave my home, my friends. Anyway, it will work out better for Matt and me if we're both working in Seattle."

"Well, working at the Fifth Avenue is nothing to sneeze at. Although if I were an actor and I had any talent I think I'd head for the Big Apple."

"You're a braver man than I, Gunga Din," said Shelby. "Maybe you're more of a risk taker."

His smile turned rueful. "No. I'm a wimp with the dull life to prove it. So I guess I can't say anything about taking chances and going to New York, can I?"

"I guess not."

"Well, I'll get my vicarious thrills by coming to see you," he said.

"And bringing your sister. That's really sweet."

"Nah. Just an easy way of making up for all those years I drove her nuts when we were kids. And it gets her away from dishes and diapers."

"I wish I had a sister," said Shelby wistfully. Well, she had Leeza, which was the next best thing.

"Got any brothers to scare away the guys?"

"No. My parents had enough trouble just producing me."

"Well, you didn't miss that much," said David. "Siblings just beat you up and borrow your stuff and don't return it."

"Oh, so you had a brother, too?"

"Nope, just an older sister."

"Then who beat you up?"

"My sister. She was one mean little kid."

Shelby chuckled. "You don't look like she scarred you too bad."

"Well, I did fight back when I got a little bigger," David admitted. "But that didn't last long. My mom caught me in the act one day. She told me that men don't hit women, then gave me a good thrashing to make sure I'd remember. So I got more subtle in my tortures. Every time Cassie got a new boyfriend I scared him away by threatening to beat *him* up. That got her twice as mad, so it was even better," he added.

Shelby smiled. "For a moment there I thought you were going to try and convince me you were being the noble, protective brother."

"At the time I probably thought I was, but my sister didn't appreciate it. And, anyway, that only worked until the boyfriends started getting bigger than me. But that's enough about my past. We're not done with your future yet. So, you'll become a local celebrity, get that ring you want from Mark . . ."

"Matt," corrected Shelby.

"Matt. And in between starring roles you'll have a kid or two and live happily ever after."

"Something like that," she said.

"Well, your boyfriend must be nuts not to have put a

ring on your finger yet. If I were him, I'd be driving you around in an armored car."

David's words were balm to Shelby's hurting pride. *Take that, Matt Armstrong. Somebody does value me.* "Thanks," she murmured. The hungry edge to David's smile made her suddenly self-conscious. She looked at her watch and was surprised to see it had taken them two hours to consume half a pizza. "It's getting late. I should get home."

"Okay. Do you have your car or can I give you a lift?"

"I'm not far, just north of Bell Town. And the buses are still running."

"You sure you want to wait for one this time of night, and risk some drunk cracking a bottle over your head? Let me give you a lift."

She might feel like she'd known David Jones forever, but she hadn't. And she sure didn't know him well enough to want to get in a car with him. "I'll be all right."

He didn't press her further. "Okay, then. How about if I wait at the bus stop with you?"

That sounded safe enough. If David proved to be a dangerous lunatic, then maybe a drunk would come to her rescue and crack him over the head with a bottle.

She nodded. He paid the tab, and they left the restaurant.

Seattle was dark and rainy. Traffic was light, both on the street and the sidewalk. Most of the working people had left for the suburbs, and the panhandlers had packed it in for the night. Shelby would probably have been perfectly safe waiting all by herself. Still, David was good company.

After a few minutes, her bus rumbled up and she turned to him. "I had a wonderful time. Thanks for being so understanding."

"Any time you want to use me," he said.

David Jones was an amazingly sweet man, Shelby decided as she got on the bus.

"Shelby," he called.

She turned.

"Where do you work?"

"Mutual Care," she answered. "Why?"

The bus doors shut before he could answer.

# Six

David drove to Seattle's Green Lake neighborhood, singing along with the radio at the top of his lungs. Shelby Barrett wasn't as taken as her boyfriend thought. No ring yet. All's fair in love and war.

It was still early by city standards, and the many small restaurants facing the lake were doing a brisk business. David allowed himself a moment to let his attention stray from the traffic to the lake's night-inked waters. What a view! But then, this city was littered with great views. He loved Seattle, especially his corner of it. Come summer, this neighborhood would be a madhouse, with people everywhere, either swimming in the lake or biking, skating, or walking their dogs around it. He could see Shelby Barrett skating next to him along the pedestrian path.

Or better yet, he could see her perched on the bow of that sailboat he was saving for, a summer breeze playing with those long, red curls of hers as they glided out onto Elliot Bay.

And to think he almost hadn't gone to meet her. What a fool!

Shelby was easily the most beautiful woman he'd ever met. And short enough that he almost towered over her. That felt good. Life felt good. He was on top of the world.

*Yeah,* said his saner self, *until Matt what's-his-name comes back for another visit and punches your lights out.*

Well, let him try.

Shelby entered the apartment humming a song from the movie she'd just seen.

Leeza was stretched out on the love seat in her sweats, a Diet Pepsi can and a couple of candy wrappers on the floor next to her. "Well," she said, looking up from her paperback, "You sure are happy for a woman who's got man trouble."

"Actually, I am," said Shelby. "I took my mom's advice and sent myself flowers today."

"Yeah?" Leeza threw down her book and bounded from the love seat. "And Matt fell for it, got insanely jealous and gave you a ring. Let's see." She grabbed Shelby's hand, then dropped it in disgust. "There's nothing there."

"Not yet."

Leeza went back to her book. "Then why are you so happy?"

"I just had a good time tonight, that's all," said Shelby, falling into the old armchair that had been one of Leeza's contributions to their furnishings.

"With Matt?"

"No, with David."

"David! Who's David?"

"My imaginary friend."

Leeza stared at her. "Was I supposed to follow that?"

"You are not going to believe this," said Shelby eagerly. "It's like something out of one of my mom's books. And it all started when I sent myself flowers and signed them from David Jones."

"Your imaginary friend."

"That I made up to make Matt jealous. But it turns out there is a David Jones who works in the SeaNet building. Matt tracked him down and went to his office and threatened to beat him up."

"Oh, my God," said Leeza. "That is just too strange."

"I know. Here I thought I was choosing such a common name that even if Matt looked in the phone book he'd never be able to pick anyone in particular to blame, and then it turns out there's a man right within walking distance of Mutual Care with that very name."

"So, after Matt threatened to beat him up?"

"I called to apologize. We met for coffee and wound up going to a movie and out to dinner."

"That is amazing. And you're right. It is like something out of a book. So, is he cute?"

"Yeah, he is. And he's really nice, too. And smart."

"And it sounds like Matt has some competition," said Leeza.

"No, not really."

"So you're not going to go out with this guy again?"

"Of course not. It wouldn't be right. I'd just be using him."

Leeza nodded. "True." Her expression turned thoughtful. "I wonder if he likes dancers."

Shelby had no intention of hurting David, and to turn him over to Leeza, who changed the men in her life every time she shaved her legs, would be cruel and inhumane. "There's no way I'm introducing you to him. You'd break his heart."

Leeza looked insulted. "How do you know that?"

"Because I know you."

"Well, I think it's pretty hoggy of you to be hoarding two men when I don't have anyone."

"For the moment," added Shelby.

Leeza grinned. "We're going dancing on Friday. I

should have someone by Saturday. You can come with and get yourself a third man."

"Two is enough," said Shelby.

Not two, she corrected herself. She wasn't going to see David Jones again.

On Wednesday afternoon, Shelby Barrett made history at Mutual Care by being the first female employee ever to receive flowers two days in a row. The other women swarmed her desk.

Jackie fished out a videocassette from the arrangement and examined it. "What's this?"

Shelby handed her the card and she read, "So when would you like to get chased across Mount Rushmore? David." She looked at Shelby. "I still don't get it. I thought you said there wasn't a David."

"It turns out there is," said Shelby.

"And he wants to chase you across Mount Rushmore?"

"We had a bet last night about what actress starred in *North By Northwest*. I said it was Grace Kelly and he said Eva Marie Saint. If I lost I was supposed to go with him and climb Mount Rushmore. So, here's the video to prove I lost."

Jackie shook her head, then read on. " 'P.S. Thanks for a wonderful evening.' So, was it?"

Shelby was aware of Greta standing at the edge of the group, anxiously awaiting her answer. The little spider! Well, it would be one way for Matt to hear he had competition, not that she was really using David. One evening out didn't constitute using. "We did have a nice time," she admitted.

"Mmm," said Greta. "Matt better look out. It sounds like he's got competition. Oh! Hi, Matt."

The women parted to make room for a grumpy looking Matt, then drifted away, smiling, as he picked up the videocassette.

"I suppose you sent this stuff to yourself," he said.

"No. These are from David. I met him last night to apologize for your behavior."

"That must have been some apology," said Matt snidely.

"What's that supposed to mean?" demanded Shelby.

"Nothing. I hope you're having a good time with this guy."

"It was kind of nice to be out with someone who appreciates me."

"Hey, I appreciate you." Matt lowered his voice. "Damn it, Shel, I love you and you know it. Let's quit playing these stupid games."

"Is that what you call me wanting you to commit to me—a game?"

He looked over his shoulder. "Keep it down, will ya? We're supposed to be working here."

"That's right, we are. So why don't you go back to your desk so I can get on with mine," Shelby suggested.

He glared. "All right, I will. But we need to talk about this. Tonight."

His tone was anything but romantic and she matched it. "Okay, fine."

"I'll take you to dinner. We'll go to that Thai place you love. How's that sound?"

*Like a general mobilizing his troops.* "Great," said Shelby, her words clipped.

His voice softened. "I've missed you, baby. You've gotta know that. It's been torture."

Right now he was looking at her like she was a ticket to the Super Bowl. How could a man look at you like that and not love you?

"I've missed you, too," she said.

He nodded in the direction of his desk. "I'm going to go try and get some work done and not think about you."

She watched him walk across the office, then turned

back to her computer wearing a triumphant smile. Tonight Matt would come around. Thank you, David Jones.

Her phone rang and she picked it up and sang a cheery hello.

"Hi there," said David.

"Oh, David." *Oh, dear.*

"So, when are we going to Mount Rushmore?"

She shouldn't have gone out with him. Now she was about to patch things up with Matt and she was going to hurt David's feelings. "You shouldn't have sent those flowers," she said. Something more to feel guilty over.

"I thought maybe they'd help the cause."

"Actually, they have. Matt and I are going out tonight to talk things out."

There was a moment's silence, then, "Well, good. I'm glad I could be of service. And if you have any more troubles, just holler."

"I think you've gotten dragged into my troubles enough," said Shelby.

"Nobody's dragging now," said David.

"You're an awfully nice man."

"Yeah, I know." He sounded sorry about it. "Good luck, Shelby."

"Thanks," she said. "For everything," and hung up the phone feeling like a dark cloud had swallowed her sun. *Don't be ridiculous,* she told herself. *You only went out with David Jones once, just to be polite. You don't owe him anything.*

So why did she feel so awful?

Shelby completely forgot the miserable mess with David Jones when Matt reached across the table at the restaurant that evening and took her hand.

"This is how it's supposed to be," he said. "I've missed you."

"And I've missed you. Oh, Matt. Let's not fight again."

"Okay, it's a deal."

The waiter showed up and they pulled apart long enough to order. Then Matt reached in his pocket and brought out a long, thin, black velvet box. "Happy New Year. Belated," he said, and slid it across the table.

This was not the right-sized box for a ring. Shelby opened it. There, resting on white satin lay a necklace—a fine gold chain with a heart-shaped pendant. And at the center of the heart, glinted a diamond. It wasn't a huge rock, but it was a lot more than a chip.

"Do you like it?" asked Matt.

It was tasteful and expensive looking, but it wasn't a ring. "It's beautiful," said Shelby, trying to sound properly appreciative.

"Put it on."

She lifted the necklace from its satin bed and held it up. The gold heart dangled and the diamond gave her a fiery wink. She put on the necklace.

Matt reached across the table and adjusted it. His fingers brushed her collarbone, making her skin tingle. "It looks good on you," he murmured.

"But why?" she asked.

"Because I love you, stupid."

"Is this supposed to be some sort of pre-engagement present?"

"It's to show you I'm committed, just not ready."

Just not ready. What did that mean? "Matt, I . . . ."

He laid a hand on her arm and stopped her. "I really do love you, Shel," he said softly.

Okay, so it wasn't a ring. It was still a diamond, which was Matt's way of saying that they would get engaged eventually.

"It's lovely," said Shelby. "Thank you."

Their dinner arrived: platters of spicy vegetables, chicken in exotic sauce, shrimp, Pad Thai noodles.

"Smells great," said Matt. He lifted his glass of Thai iced tea. "To the future."

She picked up her glass, touched it to his, and echoed, "To the future."

As the dinner progressed, Matt kept her entertained by detailing Greta's attempt to console him during their brief period of estrangement. But that wasn't half as entertaining as the plans he had for the future they had toasted, starting with a trip to San Francisco in the spring.

"We'll do Fisherman's Wharf, get Ghirardelli chocolates, have dinner at the Cliff House, the whole nine yards," he finished.

"It sounds wonderful," breathed Shelby.

"And this summer Ben and Shauna want us to go camping with them."

"Camping?" said Shelby weakly. And with another couple? How romantic was that?

"Yeah, it'll be great."

"You know I hate camping," she moaned.

"But you'll love this. We're gonna do the rainforest. Man, it is beautiful. You've never seen anything like it."

Camping in the rain? Suddenly Shelby wasn't quite so happy. She managed a ghost of a smile.

"It'll be good for us," said Matt. "If a couple can survive camping, they can survive anything."

"Oh, kind of like a pre-marriage test?"

Had Matt's smile shrunk just a tad? "Well, yeah. I guess."

"That might be fun," said Shelby.

"Yeah," said Matt a little less enthusiastically.

His conversational style lost some of its liveliness after that, and Shelby tried to revitalize it by commenting on the food, then on work. But neither subject seemed to provide a very deep conversational well.

She tried another tack. "That new movie with Megan Thomas and Ryan Hanks is cute."

Dumb idea. Matt looked at her suspiciously. "Did you go see that with David Jones?"

"No," she lied. "I went with Leeza."

"Oh, well. What's it about?"

"It's about this couple who each think they're in love with someone else when they first meet."

Matt rolled his eyes. "Kind of like every other Megan Thomas/Ryan Hanks movie?" he interrupted, "Only they're older."

"No," said Shelby, defending her taste in movies.

"Sounds like a chick flick to me," said Matt dismissively.

"Well, maybe if you went to a chick flick once in a while you'd see that there's something for men in them, too. I saw lots of men there." *And one of them was with me.*

"Yeah, all of 'em there with their girlfriends. I'll bet you didn't see any guy there by himself or with another guy."

"What should it matter if they were there with their girlfriends?" argued Shelby. "You see women with their boyfriends at most of those action-blow-people-apart movies that you like."

"That's different," said Matt.

"How?"

He shrugged. "I don't know. It just is. Are you going to finish that shrimp?"

Shelby had suddenly lost her appetite. "No," she said, and shoved her plate toward him.

Matt speared a shrimp and she sat and fingered the gold heart. It really was a beautiful necklace, and he'd probably paid plenty for it. He wouldn't have bought her such an expensive present if he wasn't committed to her. And he wouldn't be making all these plans for their future, either.

*Camping.* She cringed inwardly.

No, camping would be fun. She liked Matt's friend's wife. She liked trail mix. Everything was fine again, and she was happy. She watched Matt down the last of her shrimp and tried to look as happy as she knew she felt.

After he'd popped the last one in his mouth, he signaled

for the check, then said, "You know, if you want to go see that movie again, I'll go with you."

It was a nice gesture, but probably a bad idea. "No," she said. "You'd fidget and yawn all the way through it."

"But I'd be there, and that's what counts, isn't it?" he argued.

She supposed so. After all, wasn't that what love was all about, being there for the other person even when you didn't want to?

"Yeah, I guess you're right," she said.

They paid their bill and drove back to Shelby's apartment. Matt fiddled with the radio the whole way, surfing to a new channel just when she would start to get into a song, stirring up a vague, unreasonable discontent in her.

"Do you have to do that?" she complained.

"What?" He gave her a look that said, Now what is your problem?

"I don't get why you have to switch stations in the middle of a song. Don't you like to listen to it all the way through?"

"There might be something better on another station," said Matt.

They got to the apartment and she pulled out her key, but before she could insert it, he turned her around. He tucked a finger under her chin and raised her face up to look at him. "You know, we forgot the most important part of making up."

"What's that?"

"The kiss."

He leaned over and brushed his lips against hers, making every nerve in her body vibrate. She kissed him back, and after that the communication going on between them was strictly hormonal. He backed her up against the door, slipping his hands inside her coat, murmuring, "Baby, I love you so much," and her discontent trailed away like the last ghosts of fog on a sunny morning.

The door suddenly swung open, toppling them both into the apartment to the accompaniment of raucous laughter. Matt pushed himself off her and Shelby looked up to see that the place was packed.

"Oops," said a red-faced Leeza. "I thought I heard knocking."

Shelby was sure her face matched her roommate's. It felt like a three-alarm fire under her cheeks. She stole a glance at Matt, who was looking a little sheepish, but already recovering and laughing. He got to his feet, then took her hand and pulled her up.

"You're just in time," said Leeza, closing the door behind them. "We're celebrating."

Leeza certainly was dressed for it. She was wearing the black satin pants she'd gotten at a nearby consignment store and a slinky black top, and had sprayed glitter over every available bit of skin.

Matt eyed her with distaste. "What are we celebrating? Did you get a gig with Barnum and Bailey?"

"We're celebrating an engagement," retorted Leeza. "You have heard of that custom, haven't you?"

She pointed across the room full of people, all holding plastic cups of champagne, to the couple wedged together into her ancient armchair: Bette and Andrew, fellow actors. Bette was practically anorexic, with straight, dark hair, and a face that would never allow her a starring role. Andrew had a receding hairline. They smiled at each other as if they were the two most beautiful people in the world, then Bette held out a hand and displayed a thin band of gold with a tiny diamond Shelby had to squint to see.

Jealousy swelled her heart, but she forced a smile. "Congratulations."

"Here." Leeza shoved a plastic glass in her hand. "We were just about to make a toast."

"Whoa. What's this?" She zeroed in on the gold heart

dangling above Shelby's collarbone, lifting it for closer examination. A little pre-engagement present?"

"No," said Matt quickly. "Just something to show Shel I love her."

"That's quite a something," said Leeza, handing Matt a glass. She sloshed champagne into their glasses, then raised hers, saying, "Well, then. To love."

"To love," chimed in the others.

Shelby drank. The champagne was sour. And now, so was her evening. She drained the glass and went looking for more.

Much later that night, as she lay on her spinning bed, she toyed with the necklace Matt had given her and wondered if she really was getting any closer to an engagement. She had a diamond necklace. Did that mean she should start having sex with Matt again? After all, he had said he was committed. But if he was so committed, why couldn't he commit to getting a ring? She knew he wasn't ready, and she didn't mind waiting if she could just be sure what she was waiting for. What did Matt have against long engagements, anyway?

When she lifted her head to check her clock in the morning, it felt as if she had an axe embedded in it. She managed to roll one eye the direction of her bedside table and saw she'd overslept. Great.

She fumbled for the phone receiver, left an almost coherent message at Mutual Care that she was near death, then, oh, so slowly, got out of bed and went in search of aspirin.

Leeza was gone, probably already off to the gym or the dance studio, working on keeping her perfect dancer's legs in top condition. The place was a mess, with scraps of paper from their charades game scattered around the floor and plastic cups perched all about the room. Her electric keyboard was buried under open sheet music and song books and crumpled napkins.

Shelby decided to ignore it until the aspirin kicked in. She wrapped a blanket around her shoulders and settled in the old armchair.

She liked this chair of Leeza's. Even though it was old, its soft cream color went well with her love seat, which she had bought on sale at the Bon Marche's January sale a year ago. She looked around, enjoying the space she and Leeza had created. Her mom had given her some money to decorate, and she and Leeza had painted the walls a delicate yellow and the ceiling navy. She had draped black sheer fabric at the windows, and stuffed a couple of old, wooden fruit crates with orange and yellow dried flowers, and set them in strategic corners. All in all, they had designed a great living area.

Surveying her domain, she told herself she should not be feeling this vague discontent when she had so many good things in her life: a nice apartment, a great roommate, a future at the Fifth Avenue.

And a boyfriend who had just given her a necklace instead of a ring.

But it had a diamond, and diamonds are forever, right?

She shuffled to the kitchen, grabbed the phone, and called her mom to tell her the good news.

Mom answered on the third ring.

"I got a diamond," Shelby announced.

"Darling, that's wonderful!"

"It's not a ring, though,"

"Oh?"

"It's a necklace with a diamond in it."

"I suppose that's a first step," said Mom in her diplomatic mother voice.

"Matt says it means he's committed, just not ready," Shelby continued.

"What does that mean?" asked Mom.

"Well, I think it means it's a pre-preengagement present."

"I see," said her mother politely.

Shelby hurried on. "He's talking about all the things we're going to do together this year. He wants to take me to San Francisco this spring, and he wants to go camping this summer with Ben and his wife."

"You hate camping," said Mom.

"I know. Matt thinks it will be a good test."

"Oh. He's going to slip a pea under your sleeping bag and see if you sleep or not?"

"Funny, Mom. Anyway, the fact that he's making all these plans for the future says something."

"Yes, it does," agreed her mother. "So, how did Matt get so inspired? Did you send yourself flowers?"

"I did," said Shelby. "In fact, you'll never believe what happened."

"So tell me," said Mom.

Shelby spent the next half hour recounting how her imaginary lover came to life.

"David Jones sounds like a nice guy," said Mom when Shelby had finally run out of steam. "Maybe you should go out with him again."

"I couldn't do that to Matt," said Shelby, shocked. "Not after he went to all the trouble to get me this necklace."

"Well," said Mom, "if I were you, I'm not sure I would be committing myself to Matt at this point. I think I'd go out with this other man for a while and see what happens."

"You mean make Matt jealous?"

"I mean lose Matt," said Mom. "Haven't you figured it out yet? You ask for a ring, he gives you a necklace. He isn't going to be ready to get married for a long time. If that's what you're waiting for, you are at the wrong bus stop."

"But I don't think he'd spend all that money on a necklace if he wasn't serious," said Shelby.

"You're probably right," said Mom, sounding resigned. "Look, I've got to go. I'm right in the middle of a murder scene."

Shelby hung up, the same unreasonable discontent nibbling at her that she'd felt the night before. She wasn't sure what the cure for it was, but she knew what it wasn't. How could Mom even suggest seeing another man? It wouldn't be right. Her heart belonged to Matt. She, at least, understood the meaning of commitment.

Matt called her that afternoon to see how she was feeling.

"Are you going to be up for going out tomorrow night?" he asked.

"Oh, yeah," she said.

"Good, because Shauna and Ben are having a party."

"Leeza and the gang are going dancing and wanted us to come."

Shelby supposed Matt would insist on going to Ben's, arguing that they could go dancing any time. Well, they could. They didn't always have to do what she wanted to do.

But he surprised her. "Okay," he said, "how about we go to Ben's for a while, then meet up with Leeza later?"

"That's a good idea," she said.

"Great. Get well, babe, and I'll see you tomorrow."

Shelby hung up the phone. There. See how easily they had come to a compromise? If that wasn't proof they were a great match, she didn't know what was.

She wrapped her blanket more tightly around her and stared around the room. Her headache was subsiding, but she still felt listless. Too much champagne last night, that was all.

The events of the evening began to replay themselves. She was happy for Bette and Andrew. Really. And she was happy with the way her life was going. It was probably just as well she and Matt weren't engaged yet. She had her career to think of, and planning a wedding would definitely make her lose her focus. Anyway, Matt had proved his love with this necklace.

And she owed it all to David Jones. She really should call and thank him again.

She got up and fished the phone book from under a pile of paper plates encrusted with dried veggie dip and looked up the number of Harper Financial Counseling, Inc.

David Jones was all business when he answered, but his voice softened at the sound of hers.

"I just called to thank you again for your part in my evil plot," said Shelby.

"It was my pleasure," he said. "I take it things are going well."

"I think so," she said.

"Is he making eyes at you from across the office even as we speak?"

"That would be a little difficult since I'm home."

"Sick, huh. What have you got?"

"A hangover. Too much champagne."

"Too much celebrating with Mike?" guessed David.

"Matt."

"Oh, yeah. I don't know why I have so much trouble with that guy's name. So, how did your dinner go?"

"He gave me a diamond," said Shelby.

"Well, congratulations," said David politely. "That was what you wanted."

"Almost. The diamond is in a necklace."

"Oh, as in a pre-engagement present?"

"No, just sort of a commitment present."

"Sort of a commitment present. Uh-huh. Is that anything like being a little bit pregnant?"

"I wouldn't know." Shelby sighed. "I really don't feel very good."

"What you need is chicken soup," said David. "How

about I bring you some after work? And some French bread to go with it?"

"Actually soup and French bread sounds good," said Shelby. Suddenly she didn't feel quite so listless.

"Okay," he said. He sounded like a man at a ball game who had just seen his favorite player get a hit. Not a home run, but something that had at least taken the man as far as second base.

"All right," said Shelby, her own voice taking on new energy.

She hung up and hugged her blanket tightly around her, then went back to sit in the armchair. Wait, what was she doing sitting down? She needed to clean this place, get a shower, wash her hair. The phone rang and she raced to get it, catching herself in the blanket and stumbling across the room.

"Hello," she said breathlessly.

"It's David. Boy, I'm glad you're listed in the phone book. I don't want to spend an hour driving around looking for you. Can you tell me how to get to your place?"

Shelby obliged, then hung up, feeling giddy with excitement. But she wasn't excited because she was going to see David, she told herself. She just had cabin fever, and she was looking forward to having company. And she needed to wash her hair, anyway.

Lance Gregory tooled his Mercedes to the Washington Athletic Club. If it wasn't for the fact that he was due to meet a business acquaintance there for tennis and then dinner, he'd be tailing Diana Barrett and trying to arrange an accidental meeting.

He still hadn't heard from her and it was beginning to irritate him. Not in a big way, like a troublesome business deal, but more like having a raspberry seed stuck between his back molars. What kind of woman was this Diana Barrett that she could receive a mysterious note from a stranger and not have even the tiniest bit of curiosity? Was he losing his touch?

No. Impossible. He just needed to try a new tactic, that was all. Tomorrow he and Diana Barrett would meet.

# Seven

*The doorbell rang,* startling a million butterflies in Shelby's stomach. She checked her reflection one more time in the bathroom mirror, then hurried to the door.

There stood David, dressed in his business suit and overcoat, a briefcase in one hand and a plastic grocery bag in the other.

"You look like some poor, henpecked husband whose wife ordered him to pick up a few things at the store on the way home," Shelby observed.

"Gee thanks."

He entered, bringing into the room an interesting new fragrance: wet wool mixed with a trace of men's cologne. He set down his bag and briefcase and shrugged out of his overcoat, and Shelby took it and hung it in the entryway closet. It was as if they had done the routine for years. She turned around, took a step and almost bumped into him. The near contact set the butterflies rioting.

"Sorry," she said.

"I'm not," he said with a grin.

Trying to appear calm, she reached for the grocery bag.

David swooped down on it first. "Oh, no. You're sick. That means I'm the cook."

"But I'm not really sick," Shelby protested.

"And I'm not really a cook. I'll keep your dirty little secret if you'll keep mine." He stepped into the kitchen and set his bag on the counter. "So, where's the can opener?"

"Top drawer on your right." She leaned against the door-jamb, watching as he pulled a giant-sized can of soup from his bag. "And do you really think I'm going to eat all that?"

"I'll help," he said.

He looked so cute standing there at the counter opening the can—like he fit, somehow.

Of course, he fit. He was shorter than Matt. Matt was just too big to look right in such a small space.

"Actually," David was saying, "I'm not a total kitchen liability. I do a great omelette, and I can make salad and broil steak."

"That's not bad," agreed Shelby. "What else?"

"That's about it," he admitted. "The rest of my diet is made up of canned cuisine and deli delight." He opened a cupboard, saying, "Pot, where would I be if I were a pot?"

"The drawer under the stove. You really didn't have to do this, you know."

He pulled out a saucepan and dumped the contents of the can into it, then pulled a loaf of French bread out of the bag. "I know. I wanted an excuse to see you again."

Shelby felt herself blushing. She rubbed her finger over the gold heart dangling at the base of her throat. "I shouldn't be seeing you. I'm as good as engaged."

"Are you, really?"

His probing gaze made her snatch the bread and turn her attention to cutting it. "I know I don't have a ring," she said, sawing the loaf with more energy than the task demanded, "but we really are serious."

"Well, until you have a ring, I figure I can buy you coffee and bring you chicken soup with a clear conscience."

"I don't know if I can let you."

"Oh, sure you can," said David. "Never discourage a man from doing a good deed. Look, I know we've just met, but I can already tell you're a really nice woman. I think you deserve to be happy."

"So do you. And spending time with a woman who is involved with another man probably isn't the secret to happiness."

"Now, there's an interesting Freudian slip."

Shelby looked at him questioningly.

"You didn't say 'in love,'" said David.

"What?"

"You said 'involved with another man.' Interesting terminology, don't you think?"

Before Shelby could even open her mouth to explain that she was involved with Matt because she loved him, David changed tacks. "When we were having dinner, you said your mom was a writer. Do you believe in living happily ever after?"

"Of course," said Shelby.

"Me, too," he said. "Sometimes that can be hard to find, though. I don't think you should stop searching until you get yours. I mean, who wants to live *almost* happily ever after?"

His quip made her smile, but it also made her uncomfortable. She shouldn't have called him. He shouldn't be here.

As if knowing he'd made a misstep, David changed the topic completely. He pointed to her drama professor dart board decorating the far wall. "A friend of yours?"

"Just an old professor who didn't recognize greatness when he saw it."

David nodded. "Great inspiration."

"How about this?" he asked, indicating the framed pen and ink caricature hanging next to the stove. It was captioned "Shelby the Great," and showed an ecstatic Shelby, with her hair even more wild than in real life, wearing clown shoes under an evening gown and grasping a Tony. "Is that you?"

She nodded.

"What's with the clown feet?"

"That's supposed to represent the me of the present. The Tony and gown represent the future."

"So, you're a clown right now, but someday you'll take yourself seriously?"

"Well, I'm not always a clown. Just sometimes."

"Aren't we all?"

Shelby shook her head. "I'm a volunteer clown. I started something called Klowns for Kids, where we go to kids' birthday parties, juggle a little, make balloon animals, and generally make fools of ourselves. Then we donate the money the parents pay us to Children's Hospital."

"No kidding."

The admiration in David's eyes was embarrassing. "It's not that big a deal," said Shelby.

"I think it's pretty cool."

"Well, it's fun. If I get on at the Fifth Avenue and can free up my mornings, I'm going to try to join the Big Apple Circus Clown Care Unit the hospital started recently. I'd like to be able to go and visit the sick kids and give them something to laugh about in between getting stuck with needles and cut open." He was still looking at her like she was Joan of Arc, and she felt her cheeks heating.

Like what was on the stove. "Looks like the soup is hot," she said, directing his attention to the erupting pot.

"Whoa," he said, and pulled it off the burner, spilling soup in the process.

Shelby laughed and felt comfortable once more.

• • •

Canned soup had never tasted so good. And time had never gone by so quickly. David did no more probing near her heart, talking instead about the house he owned across from Green Lake, which had once been his grandmother's, regaling her with tales of his adventures in renovating and giving vivid descriptions of his eccentric neighbors.

It was pushing close to seven when Leeza sailed in, bearing a huge grocery sack brimming with food, calling, "I went by Mom's this afternoon, and she sent us a care package." She stopped at the sight of David sprawled at the dinette table and eyed him speculatively. "You didn't tell me we were having company tonight." A hand went up to her hair, which looked like it hadn't been brushed in a week. She was wearing her favorite black sweats and an old, green army jacket that was too big for her and looked fabulous. To be that big a mess and look that good—it was a gift.

"This is David Jones," said Shelby. "My roommate, Leeza."

"Hi," said Leeza, her voice turning syrupy.

"Hi," said David. He glanced at his watch and said, "I should be going."

"Don't hurry away on my account," said Leeza. "I love company. And I clean up well."

"I really do have to go." David turned to Shelby. "Think you'll be up for something more than soup by tomorrow? I do a great steak."

Shelby was surprised to find how disappointed she was that her Friday was already filled. "I can't. I have plans."

"Hey, bring him along," suggested Leeza. "A bunch of us are doing the TGIF thing and going dancing," she explained to David.

He brightened. "Yeah?"

"We can't do that. Matt's coming," said Shelby.

That drained the sunshine from his face.

"Oh," said Leeza, sobering. "Well, maybe another time."

"Sure," said David. The smile he gave Shelby looked like something left over from a funeral. "I had a good time. Thanks for letting me stop by."

"Thanks for coming."

"No problem," he said, and headed for the door.

Shelby followed him, casting about her mind for the right line to deliver.

He picked up his briefcase and turned, forcing another one of those joyless smiles. "Good night, Shelby."

Her vocal cords were suddenly out of service. She managed a nod. She should say something, do something, but she'd never been good at improv.

David didn't wait for a response. He slipped out the door and was gone, leaving her standing there, hugging herself.

"What on earth is going on?" demanded Leeza. "Are you using this guy or not?"

"I'm not," said Shelby, finding her voice.

"Well, then what was he doing over here?"

"Bringing me chicken soup. I'm sick."

"You can say that again. First you don't want to use him, then he's over here. What's the point? And he's cute. If you don't want him, give him to me. Don't just throw him back."

"You'd break his heart," said Shelby.

"Oh, and you're not?"

"I haven't known him long enough."

"It didn't look that way to me," said Leeza. She shook her head. "I need a shower."

The next morning Shelby went to grab her coat out of the entryway closet and discovered David's overcoat. It looked like she'd have to pay a call at Harper Financial Counseling, Inc. today.

At work, Matt stopped by her desk to say hi and firm up their plans for the night. "I'll see you at break," he added.

"I have to run an errand. Why don't you go hang out with the guys," she suggested.

"Okay," said Matt. "Then I'll take you to lunch."

"That's a deal. But not at that stupid cafeteria where you guys go."

"Red Robin, okay?"

"Okay."

She watched him leave, then grabbed her phone and dialed David's office. Funny, she didn't have to look the number up this time. It was now embedded in her brain.

The secretary put her through to David.

"Hi. It's Shelby. I've got something of yours."

"I know," he said.

"Did you miss it this morning?"

"It has been a little hard to keep breathing without it."

"Excuse me?"

"My heart," he said. "Isn't that what you were talking about?"

The butterflies from the day before started stirring again. "Funny. You don't look like the type who always says sweet things like that to women."

"I'm not."

Feelings kaleidoscoped through Shelby. Excitement, guilt, happiness, then more guilt. What was she doing?

"I meant your overcoat," she said. "You left it in my closet."

"I was a little distracted," he said.

"I could bring it over on my break," she offered.

"Why don't you bring it over at noon instead, and I'll take you to lunch."

Matt. She was going to Red Robin with Matt. But she had to return David's coat. "Okay."

"Where would you like to go?"

"Anywhere but Red Robin."

"All right. How about that Italian deli with the great prosciutto sandwiches?"

"That'll work fine."

"Okay," said David. "I'll pick you up."

*Matt might see! And he certainly wouldn't understand.* "No. I'll come to your office," she said quickly.

"Okay. See you at noon."

"Noon," repeated Shelby. What was she doing, anyway?

Nothing. She was just returning a friend's overcoat. That was all.

She sauntered by Matt's desk at eleven-thirty.

He looked up from his work and grinned. "Couldn't wait until noon to see me, huh?"

"That must be it," she said. "That and to tell you that we need to go shopping."

His expression sobered. "Shopping?"

"I need a new dress for tonight."

"Wear that tight-fitting black one. You look hot in that."

"I gained five pounds over Christmas. I look awful in it."

"Well, how about the maroon one? You know, the one that's really soft?"

"The velveteen dress?"

"Yeah. That's cool. It looks like the sixties."

"No, I got it at a consignment store, and I just wore it that one time to be different."

Matt sighed heavily. "I really don't want to go dress shopping with you, Shel."

She patted his arm. "I know, which is why I'm letting you off the hook. And you can buy me lunch on Monday."

Matt looked relieved and Shelby felt guilty. It was wrong to lie to your boyfriend. Sick and wrong.

• • •

An angry January wind howled at her as she made her way down the street to David's office. It tugged strands of her hair from its clip and boxed her nose till it turned red.

Her disheveled appearance didn't seem to bother David. His face lit up like New Year's Eve at the sight of her.

She held up his coat. "I've got what you were looking for," she said.

"I know," he replied, and the look he gave her quickened her pulse and warmed her cheeks.

He slipped it on, then put a hand on the small of her back and guided her out of the office, saying, "Let's go. I'm starving."

"I broke a date to be here," she said once they had sampled their sandwiches.

"Uh-oh. I see guilt settling in."

She nodded. "I lied. Matt thinks I'm shopping. I've never lied to him before." And that was a lie, too, since it wasn't Leeza with whom she'd gone to see that Megan Thomas–Ryan Hanks movie. She scratched at the label on her bottle of overpriced sparkling water. "I feel like I'm having an affair."

"If bringing a guy his overcoat qualifies as having an affair, somebody's getting ripped off here."

"We're practically engaged," said Shelby, "and I'm out having lunch with another man. It's not right."

David didn't try to convince her that it was. Instead, he looked at her steadily. "What are you going to do about it?"

She chewed her lip and studied his face. It one of those interesting faces you found yourself wanting to look at for a long time. If they'd both been waiting at a bus stop or a train station, Shelby knew she would be constantly stealing peeks at him from behind her magazine.

What was going on here? How could she love Matt and

still be so attracted to David? "I'm confused," she confessed.

"How can you be confused if the guy you're with is the right man for you?"

Good question. Shelby sat, trying to think of an equally good answer.

"Maybe it's because, deep down, you're not sure about Mark."

She didn't bother to correct David about Matt's name. She just continued to sit there, looking at him, wondering where her sure answer was when she needed it.

"I wish I could make up your mind for you," said David softly. "I'd decide in favor of me."

She leaned forward. "Why? Why would you decide in favor of you?"

"Partly because I'm as selfish as the next man. I think you're fabulous, and I want you for myself, not someone else. But it's more than that. I felt our hearts connect the first time I saw you sitting at that table at Starbucks. You looked so darned cute, like a pixie. You waved at me, and you must have had fairy dust in your hand, because I just . . . fell. There was something about you that, I don't know. I can't put it into words very well."

"You're doing fine," said Shelby.

He shook his head. "I don't know. Maybe you're not the sexiest woman in the world, but you're right up there in the top ten. Sandra Bullock has got nothing on you. And as for this"—he held up his overcoat—"let me tell you, I don't need it when I'm with you. I'm hot enough. If it was just attraction, you'd be nothing more than a poster girl, and it would be easier to forget you. But you're kind and fun to be with and . . ."

"Unprincipled and heartless," interrupted Shelby, feeling uncomfortable with her goddess status. "Here I am, having lunch with another man while my boyfriend thinks I'm shopping."

"And you feel awful about it. You're torn. A woman with no heart wouldn't feel a thing."

"I shouldn't be here. It's not fair to Matt or you."

"What's fair to you, Shelby?"

She wasn't sure she knew how to answer that, so she sat silent, shaking her head.

"Before you decide who you want to spend the rest of your life with, you might want to figure that out."

She nodded. "Meanwhile, I think I'd better get back to work."

David pointed to her barely touched sandwich. "You're not done."

"I am for today."

Diana knocked off work early and headed for the video store in search of the perfect treatment for a fried brain. Suzanne would be coming over for their usual Friday movie mania night, which meant she'd have to pick something romantic, but she had every intention of getting a movie with some punch to it, too. She wandered up and down the aisles, looking for just the right movie to suit her mood. *Conspiracy Theory*. That was a good one. She pulled the case off the shelf and moved on. Now, to find something that Suzanne would enjoy and she could tolerate. She moved to the classic movie section and stood there, chewing her lip.

"This is a good one," said a deep voice, and she turned to see a breathtakingly handsome man with dark hair tinged gray at the temples leaning forward to pluck a case from the row.

He was so tall. No, that wasn't what struck her; it was his presence. He was so very male, he seemed to fill the room. She blinked stupidly.

He smiled and she had to force her eyes away from his face to look at what he was holding: *Charade*, the old classic with Audrey Hepburn and Cary Grant.

She took it and switched her brain on again. "That is a good movie, and I haven't seen it in years. Thanks."

He was blindingly beautiful when he worked those sensuous lips into a smile. With teeth like that, he could be in a toothpaste commercial. And she'd always been a sucker for a man in a nice suit. This suit was a heck of a lot more than just nice. Her helper had to make some good money to afford it.

He nodded at the videos. "I hope you're not going to watch those all alone."

She shook her head. *Say something, stupid. You look like a junior high girl!* "I have a friend coming over," she managed, trying to sound like the mature and unflappable woman she was.

"Lucky friend."

He nodded politely, then left the store before she could gather her wits enough to introduce herself.

Just as well, she decided as she headed for the Safeway. Men her age were all divorced, and for good reason. Anyway, she'd done the man thing already and she didn't need to repeat history. She was perfectly happy just as she was.

But that particular specimen had been awfully good-looking. She could have at least gotten his name and passed it on to Suzanne, who was always in the market.

Inside the grocery store, she commandeered a cart and headed for the produce section. She'd gotten past the bananas and was inspecting the fresh ginger when she heard the plop of falling fruit. She whirled around and saw a pile of grapefruit emptying itself onto the floor. And there next to it . . .

Tall, dark, and handsome was rebalancing the remaining fruit. He bent to round up the escapees, and Diana went to help.

"It looks like someone sabotaged you," she commented.

"No," he said. "I did that on purpose."

She looked up, shocked.

He shrugged. "I wanted to meet you."

That made her smile. "You could have, in the video store."

"I was going to introduce myself, but, somehow, it lacked imagination."

She patted his arm and said confidentially, "So does this."

She stood and he mirrored the action, saying, "I know, but I wasn't sure I'd get a third chance. A man has to work with the materials at hand. Of course, I would have preferred to rescue you from a charging grocery cart."

Diana realized she was feeling like she'd had too much caffeine. She crossed her arms in front of her, anchoring them securely in an effort to ward off the jittery feeling. "Oh, so you're a knight in shining wool?"

He looked down at his suit in mock horror. "I hope not."

Diana grinned. Yes, this was a man that wouldn't be caught dead in a worn suit. Probably even his underwear were in mint condition.

"Well," she said, "I'd say you're a pretty daring man. My husband would have never knocked over a pile of grapefruit in a store full of people."

"Oh. You're married?" He sounded disappointed.

"Well, actually, I'm widowed. We were together a long time, though, and sometimes it just slips out."

"Understandable. I'm Lance Gregory," he said.

Lance Gregory? This was the man who went with the business card? Lordy.

He held out his hand. Diana put hers into it and was immediately aware of its warmth and strength. It did nothing for her imitation caffeine jitters.

"Diana Barrett," she said.

He smiled. "I know."

She withdrew her hand. He had watched her the other day in the parking lot, and now he'd been tailing her from store to store. The jitters now sprang from an entirely different source. "How do you know my name?" she demanded.

"My nephew gave me your name and address. You see, I'm from the enemy camp."

Was this some new pickup approach? Be an enigma, arouse her curiosity. It was working. "I'm afraid I don't understand."

"My nephew and your daughter seem to be at war. He thought if you and I met that maybe we could help negotiate a surrender."

Red flags went up. A smooth operator, this one. Smooth and slimy. Diana's eyes narrowed. "So, that business card on my car was just a cheap trick."

"Oh, no. That business card on your car was put there out of purely selfish motives. I had planned to be altruistic and do my duty. Until I saw you. Then I decided to let Matt fend for himself."

Diana nodded. "A good idea. And, if I might add, I hope he fends poorly."

"Maybe you could explain why over drinks," suggested Lance.

"Sorry, I really do have company coming over tonight," Diana said brusquely.

"You're probably taken tomorrow night, too. In fact, a woman as beautiful as you is probably booked weeks in advance. How about Valentine's Day? Could we meet then, at the top of the Empire State Building?"

Lance Gregory specialized in malarkey. The obvious reference to the meeting place in *Sleepless in Seattle* and *An Affair to Remember*, two female movie favorites, marked him as a man who had spent a good deal of time studying women. Matt had wanted him to talk to her. Was he acting as Matt's mentor?

He was looking at her expectantly. "I'll bet you've got a Ph.D. in flattery," she said.

"Only a Master's, and I don't use it unless I'm sincere."

"If you're sincere, it's not flattery. It's a compliment."

"You're right. I meant what I said. Will you meet me for drinks tomorrow night?"

She didn't want a man in her life, especially a smooth operator like this one. But it was only drinks. Anyway, she should find out a little more about his level of involvement in her daughter's affairs.

"All right," she said. "Where?"

"Canlis. Will seven o'clock work for you?"

"I suppose."

Lance Gregory smiled, that same gorgeous smile he'd showed her earlier, and her silly heart started pumping out a disco beat. She handed him the grapefruit she'd been holding. "This one looks ripe."

"Good. I like ripe fruit."

She made no comment, just turned and went back to the ginger. She broke off a piece with more force than necessary. She didn't like being made a fool of. Whatever Lance Gregory was up to, he'd learn that soon enough.

As they drove to Ben and Shauna's, Shelby kept wanting to ask Matt if Sandra Bullock had nothing on her. But then, she already knew what his answer to that question would be, didn't she? According to Matt, she'd be lucky to get on at the Fifth.

"You're sure quiet," he observed. "What's wrong?"

She turned to look at him. "Why do you think something's wrong?"

"I just told you, you're quiet."

The last thing she wanted to do right before having to spend an evening together being sociable was to get in a heated argument. "I'm fine," she said, forcing herself into the role of contented girlfriend.

"Okay," said Matt. "If that's the way you want to play it."

That was the way she wanted to play it. She turned her

head and looked out the car window at the charming array of brick Tudor and Dutch colonial houses they were passing in the Queen Anne Hill neighborhood. Temperatures had dropped and there was talk of snow, but so far the streets were clear. Snow would have made the houses even more charming, but they still looked pretty, with many of them still wearing their glowing Christmas lights. Most had their drapes pulled to shield the light inside from the surrounding darkness. They reminded her of giant cocoons, protecting the occupants from the cold, outside world. She wanted a house like that.

Matt parked the car and they walked in silence up the walk to his friend Ben Hargrove's front door.

He had barely finished knocking before Ben was swinging the door open wide. "Hey guys! Glad you could make it."

"We're only here for a couple hours," said Matt, herding Shelby through the door. "We've got to go dancing with Shel's dingy roommate and her friends."

Dingy roommate? He'd never called Leeza dingy before. And since when did flamboyant qualify as a synonym for dingy?

Ben frowned. "That stinks. Oh, well, you won't be missing much. Shauna's making us play this Mars and Venus game after dinner that she got for Christmas. We'll probably be ready for divorce court by the time it's done. Here, give me your coats."

They shed their coats and entered the living room. Two other couples were there, squeezed onto a couch that looked like it had come from a furniture warehouse. Married couples.

Shelby and Matt were the only two who weren't married. She had to force herself to shake off the feeling that she was walking into the room in her bra and panties.

Shauna came in from the kitchen. "Hi, guys. Hey there,

fellow camper," she said to Shelby. "Are you ready for adventure this summer?"

"I hope so," said Shelby.

Shauna caught sight of Shelby's new necklace. "Oh! Look at that diamond. Did you get this for Christmas?"

"No. Matt just gave it to me," said Shelby.

"Mr. Generous," cooed Shauna. "I can hardly wait to see what you get for Valentine's Day."

So could Shelby. One thing she knew it wouldn't be: a ring.

At dinner the other women shared recipes while the guys compared heating bills. She felt like a foreigner. Then the talk turned to sports and Matt, who had been more interested in his food than the conversation, came to life and joined the party. They talked about the Rose Bowl, they talked about the Huskies going to the Aloha Bowl, they talked about the Super Bowl. Shelby yawned.

"Me, I like the Salad Bowl," said Shauna, picking up the teakwood bowl and helping herself to more. "And if you don't quit talking about football, I'm going to dump it on your head," she threatened her husband.

"Okay, okay," said Ben. "I suppose we have to talk about woman stuff." He turned to Matt, and with a flopping hand and a falsetto voice, proclaimed, "I fell off my diet again this Christmas. I know I've gained at least five pounds. I need a new dress."

Matt guffawed. "Hey, that sounds just like you, Shel."

The other guys laughed, too, and agreed that it could have been their wives speaking.

Shelby sat there in her black dress and glared daggers at Matt. Of course, he hadn't noticed that she didn't get a new dress after all, hadn't noticed that she still looked fine in this one. She hoped he choked on that wine he was drinking.

Dessert was served: chocolate mousse and shortbread.

Shelby ate half her chocolate mousse and passed on the shortbread.

"Hey," said Matt, pointing to the unfinished dessert. "Aren't you going to finish that?"

"I'm not hungry," she said stiffly.

The women began to clear the table, and the men wandered out to the living room to return the conversation to football.

"Is everything okay with you and Matt?" asked Shauna in a low voice as Shelby picked up the dessert tray.

She nodded. "We're just going through some kind of phase, that's all. Did you ever have that with Ben?"

"Yeah. After we were married he started taking me for granted. I just didn't have sex with him for a week. He got over it real fast."

*Took me for granted.* The words struck a chord and reverberated. She and Matt weren't even engaged yet, and Matt had already settled in and started taking her for granted. It had taken sending herself flowers to wake him up. But even now, he was threatening to drift off again. She felt suddenly glad that crowd in her apartment the other night had saved her from falling into bed with him.

She cast a glance to the living room where he was lounging on the couch, laughing at something Ben had said. He was perfectly happy without her by his side. She was an ornament, something he enjoyed, but could live without just fine.

Shauna came out of the kitchen, followed by the other two women. "Okay," she said, "are you guys ready to play?"

"Can't we just play Trivial Pursuit or watch a movie?" complained Ben.

"No," said his wife, "we want to play this. It'll be fun."

He made a face. "You know we're going to be sorry. Somebody is bound to get mad at somebody." He turned to

the other men. "And you know what that means. Somebody's not gonna get his tonight."

His wife ignored him and pulled out the game box.

Shelby went to sit next to Matt and he put an arm
around her. "You want to do this?" he whispered.

Actually, she didn't. She felt like a powder keg just
waiting for a match. But she didn't see any polite way of
getting out of it. It would be rude to eat and run. She
shrugged.

Now Shauna had the game set up and was explaining
the rules. "And you guys have to guess how we would answer. And we have to do the same when you're asked a
question."

"That sounds easy enough," said one of the men. "I
know exactly how Carrie thinks, so we'll have no problem."

"Yeah? We'll see," said Ben skeptically.

The game began. The questions seemed innocuous
enough. And easy.

It came to Matt's turn to answer and Shauna read his
question. "When a woman asks, 'Do you love me?' a man
should say: A.) 'Of course I love you,' B.) 'Why else
would I be with you?' or C.) 'What do you think?'" She
looked expectantly at Matt.

Shelby watched him fondly. She knew what he would
say: "Of course I love you."

He picked his answer.

"Okay, Shelby," said Shauna. "What did he say?"

"He said, 'Of course I love you.'"

Shauna looked to Matt who was shaking his head.

"What did you say?" asked Ben.

"What do you think?" replied Matt.

"I don't know. That's why I'm asking?"

"What do you think?" Matt repeated.

"I don't have to guess," said Ben. "I'm not your
woman."

One of the guys laughed. "Just like 'Who's on first?' "

"Oh, that was your answer," said Ben, and all the men guffawed.

One of the women shook her head and smiled indulgently. Shauna scowled. Another looked disgusted. Just like Shelby felt.

She turned to Matt. "That was your answer? You wouldn't say something so rude."

"I might if you asked me such a dumb question," said Matt. "You should know how I feel by now."

"Besides, we need the point," said Ben. "Okay, next question."

The game continued, but Shelby was barely aware of it. She was too busy thinking about Matt's answer.

Time dragged and she thought they'd never finish the silly game.

At last they were done. Matt turned to her. "We'd probably better go, huh?" She could tell by the gentleness in his voice that he was feeling contrite.

Too little, too late. She nodded, barely able to be civil to him.

"Already?" said their hostess.

"Yeah," said Matt. "We're meeting some of Shelby's friends."

"Some of my dingy friends," added Shelby, and Matt's jaw clenched.

"I'll get your coats," offered Ben.

They said their good-byes and walked back to the car in the same silence they'd shared on their way up the walk earlier, only this time it was highly charged.

The car was barely moving when she turned to him and demanded, "Why did you say that?"

"It was just a game, Shel," said Matt. "And I was just kidding!"

"You could have answered another way."

"I wanted to win. Okay?"

"You wanted to win, so you acted like a jerk."

"It was a game."

"You were a jerk."

The corners of Matt's mouth pulled down. "Well, I probably don't have to tell you what you've been lately," he shot back. "You haven't exactly been fun to be with."

"Then why don't you just take me home," suggested Shelby.

"Good idea," growled Matt, and turned up the radio to fill the silence.

By the time they had pulled up in front of her apartment, Shelby had made up her mind. She unhooked the necklace and set it on the dashboard just as he turned to face her.

Matt regarded it with the expression of a sorely tried saint. "Now what are you doing?"

"I'm giving you back your necklace," said Shelby. "Maybe you can get a refund."

"I don't want a refund. I want you."

She started to open the door and Matt caught her arm. "What's this really about, Shel?"

"It's not working between us anymore."

"It was working fine up until we went over to your mom's place Christmas Eve."

"My mom has nothing to do with this," said Shelby stiffly. Just because she called her mom for advice occasionally didn't mean she was incapable of seeing for herself when she was being taken for granted.

"Then it's that guy, that David Jones," accused Matt.

Maybe it was. David had certainly opened her eyes to some unpleasant realities in regard to her life with Matt.

"I guess I'm more like you than I thought," she said. "I'm not ready to be committed yet."

Matt glared at her. "You were before you met him. If you're trying to use this guy, it won't work," he cautioned.

"It's not working now," she said. She opened the door and got out. "Good night, Matt. I'm sorry."

"Shelby!" he shouted.

She shut the car door, muffling his voice, and ran up the walk.

He got out of the car and called after her, and she kept running. She was at the apartment entrance now, and half expected him to come chasing after her.

The half that didn't expect it proved to be right. His car door slammed, the engined roared, and he screeched off down the street.

Her heart was hammering, but she didn't feel bad. Instead, she felt . . . relieved? What kind of way was that to feel when you'd just broken up with the man you loved? The words from the game they'd played came back and danced around her. *What do you think? What do you think?*

# *Eight*

*Shelby's phone rang.* It was probably Matt, calling from his cell phone to apologize. But at this point their relationship needed more than apologies. She let the answering machine pick up.

"I know you're out dancing," said David, "and this is just plain dumb to be calling . . ."

Shelby dove for the phone. "Don't hang up."

"Shelby?"

He sounded surprised, and she wondered if he would have called if he thought she was going to be home. "I didn't go dancing," she said, stating the obvious.

"Why not?"

"We didn't get that far. I gave back the necklace."

She could almost hear him grinning. "Really?"

"I'm not sure where Matt and I are going from here. In fact, I don't know if we're going anywhere." And more alarming than her uncertainty about her future with Matt was the ambivalence she held toward that uncertainty.

"Better to be safe than sorry," said David.

Shelby sighed. "I suppose. You know, it's crazy. Part of me feels like I've thrown away a winning Lotto ticket, but I also feel a little like I've just widened the window on my future, somehow."

"Maybe you have," said David. "I think you should celebrate."

"I'm not in the mood for crowds," said Shelby. "I don't feel that good."

"How about dancing? Are you in the mood for dancing?"

Shelby's chest tightened. "Maybe."

"Don't take your shoes off," he said, then hung up.

She stared at the phone receiver, blaring a dial tone at her. This was nuts.

Twenty minutes later her intercom buzzed. She punched it. "Who is it?"

"Fred Astaire. I'm looking for Ginger Rogers."

"Sorry," said Shelby, "there's nobody here by that name."

"Any Ginger Wanna-be's?"

"Come on up."

In a matter of moments, David was knocking at the door.

She opened it and he stepped in. He was wearing faded jeans and a pale yellow sweater that looked like it would be very soft to the touch. He nodded a greeting and walked past her to her CD player, and the fragrance of his musky aftershave tickled her nose and quickened her pulse.

He opened the CD, then turned and looked her up and down appreciatively. He nudged an invisible friend and said, "That woman standing over there is something incredible. And she's just the right height, too. She looks like she was designed to be a perfect fit in my arms. I'd better talk to the band. I need the perfect song for our first dance."

Shelby waited as he bent and inserted the CD, feeling like an astronaut hanging in space. Then the music started: a soft piano melody, tiptoeing into the room like a benevolent ghost.

David straightened and held out a hand. "Dance with me?"

How could she not? She moved toward him and he gently towed her into his embrace.

"Why did you call?" she asked.

"Maybe I'm a masochist, or else I've gotten hopelessly addicted to the sound of your voice." His own voice dropped to a murmur as he pulled her a little closer. "Thanks for letting me get my fix."

Shelby closed her eyes and indulged her senses in the sweetness of the music, the scent and feel of him. "My pleasure."

A male voice began to croon as David swayed them back and forth in sync with the bass and drums. She felt his breath ruffling her hair as he sang along with the artist, " 'When the stars fall and the sun goes out, and you find yourself alone with doubt, all you have to do is just reach out, cause I'll be there for you.' "

David and the CD sang on. " 'You may not need me now, but that's okay. I'll stick around until you do. I've waited forever at your heart's door. I'll wait forever more for you.' "

David pulled her closer to him, making them one silhouette. She'd been right about the sweater. It was soft, an intriguing contrast to the body beneath. She let her hand move up his shoulder and curl around his neck, and she thought she felt the touch of his lips on her hair.

The song whispered to an end and they stopped dancing. Still caught in the spell, Shelby stood with her eyes closed, waiting for the logical conclusion to such a perfect scene. Instead of kissing her, David pulled gently away, and she heard him moving across the floor. She turned to see him slipping out the door just as the singer was starting another song.

Suzanne stretched luxuriously. "That was a great movie. Where are men like Mel Gibson when you want them?"

"There are no men like Mel Gibson," said Diana. "Even Mel Gibson isn't like Mel Gibson."

"What's that supposed to mean?"

"You should know. You're a writer. We're all in love with the characters he plays, not with Mel, himself."

"Who said anything about love?" retorted Suzanne. "I'm just in lust. Mmm, those eyes, that dark hair. There is no other man on the planet as handsome as that."

"Maybe," said Diana.

"Oh? Name me one man who can even come close."

Diana shut her eyes and saw a strong chin, eyes as blue as Mel Gibson's, and dark hair, dusted with gray at the temples. "Lance Gregory."

Suzanne sat at attention. "You called him!"

"No. He chased me down. In fact, he knocked over a whole pile of grapefruit in the grocery store to get my attention."

Suzanne nodded. "The old meet 'em in the produce department ploy. I've got to admit, knocking fruit everywhere is a new twist. So, he's good looking?"

"Good looking is a gross understatement. He's a god."

"A god, huh? That statement does not sound like a woman with no libido."

"I can still appreciate beauty," said Diana.

"Are you going to go out with him?"

"We're meeting for drinks at Canlis tomorrow night."

"Well, isn't this an interesting development? Diana Barrett, confirmed monkette, is going out."

"For drinks. That's all."

"Yeah? We'll see," said Suzanne. "Anyway, there's nothing wrong with drinks evolving into something else."

"I don't know why I'm wasting my time doing this," said Diana. "I don't want a man. They're more trouble than dogs." She reached to pet Barrymore, who was stretched out on the couch at her feet. At her touch, he got up and jumped to the floor and sat with his haunches to her. "Or male cats," she added, frowning at him.

"Good comparison," observed Suzanne. She joined Barrymore on the floor and scratched behind his ear. He rubbed against her hand appreciatively.

"Traitor," muttered Diana.

"You just have to know how to treat him," said Suzanne. "So," she continued, returning to the subject of Lance Gregory, "deep down in your psyche, you must have a reason for agreeing to meet this guy for drinks."

"Yes, my daughter," said Diana, and proceeded to explain the connection between Lance Gregory and her daughter's boyfriend.

"It certainly made the perfect excuse for him to ask you out," said Suzanne. "But you don't think for a minute that's all there is to it, do you?" Diana didn't answer, and Suzanne continued, "And that's not the only reason you're going out with him."

"Actually, it is," said Diana. "This man strikes me as a lady-killer, and if he's doling out advice on women to his nephew it's no wonder Matt is balking at marriage."

"So you'll set him in his place and never see him again," said Suzanne, her voice heavy with cynicism.

"Exactly," said Diana.

"Very big of you, especially considering the fact you could have set him in his place in the grocery store."

Of course, that was what she should have done. "You're right," Diana admitted. "I should have told him to take a hike."

"Not if he looks like Mel Gibson," said Suzanne. "And for heaven's sake, if you decide you don't want him, give him to me. I'm not a misogamist."

"Hey, don't use those big words on me," Diana joked. "What do you think you are, a writer?"

"Yes, and a believer," said Suzanne. "Which is more than I can say for you. Maybe that's why this dream man dropped on you. Maybe the universe knows you need to become a believer again."

"It wasn't the universe who sent him, just a discontented, spoiled young man. And Lance Gregory is probably the older version of Matt. The part of my brain that's still working says I should leave him sitting alone in the lounge."

"My mother always told me to finish what I start," said Suzanne. "You already started this course. Don't back out now. Besides, it will be good for you to spend some time with someone who's got a voice lower than yours."

"So you say, but you're forgetting that my libido is dead."

"No. I'm remembering, and hoping that this guy might be able to resurrect it."

"That would be a miracle," said Diana.

Suzanne's expression turned puckish. "I believe in miracles."

What man in his right mind left a beautiful woman right after they had just shared the most romantic dance of his lifetime? thought David in disgust as he let himself back into his house.

But he'd had to. There they were, alone in her place. If he'd stayed, he'd have been lost, and things would have quickly gotten out of hand. He'd have become nothing more than a shorter version of what Shelby already had. Even if she hadn't slapped his face, but had gone along for the ride, how would she have felt about him afterward? How would she have felt about herself?

No, he had done the right thing. If he was going to

woo Shelby in a way she deserved and he could live with, he'd have to go slowly, wade into the water one inch at a time until he got accustomed to the high temperatures.

But he should have stayed for just one kiss. One kiss, for crying out loud. He wasn't seventeen anymore. He could have managed that. And she would have welcomed it. He was just being skittish.

Well, hopefully Shelby would view his quick exit as the noble romantic gesture it was meant to be. Hopefully.

Leeza came home at one in the morning and found Shelby curled up in the armchair, listening to a CD.

"You look like you just made love with Batman."

Shelby sighed. "Close."

"So, did Matt propose after all?"

Shelby shook her head. "I gave back the necklace."

"What?"

"I'm not sure I want to marry Matt."

Leeza sniffed the air. "But I smell man. Who was here?"

"David."

"That explains a lot. Have you got a thing going with David now?"

"He came over here and danced with me. And sang to me. It was so," Shelby shut her eyes and savored the memory, "romantic."

"Is that all you did?" pried Leeza.

"Yes. We danced one dance. I think he kissed the top of my head, but I'm not sure. And then he just slipped away," she added dreamily.

"My God," said Leeza, sinking into a chair. "Matt will never be able to compete with this."

Shelby set aside the vision of David and opened her eyes. "If Matt is so right for me, why am I attracted to David?"

"Sex," said Leeza. "You're in the throes of wanting.

Believe me, I know. I just met the most gorgeous thing named Horst, and I'm wanting pretty bad already. You should feel his arms. Mmm, baby."

Shelby shook her head in disgust. "This from the woman who told me not to get involved with a civilian."

"He's not a civilian. He's one of us, just serving the arts in a different branch. He's a sculptor."

"You are so fickle," said Shelby, shaking her head.

"No more fickle than you," retorted Leeza.

"I'm not trying to be fickle," Shelby protested. "But I do want to be sure. And I've got to admit that, although it's seemed so right with Matt, I really like spending time with David. But, you know, I could be feeling like that because right now I'm not happy with Matt. He's not doing what I want him to, so I decide I must not love him. And if that's the case, this David thing is not very noble on my part, is it?"

"Well," said Leeza, "lets test your theory. What if Matt showed up right now with a ring? Would you pick him or David?"

"Matt," said Shelby decidedly, and then wondered again what he would say if she asked him if he thought Sandra Bullock had nothing on her. "I think."

Leeza lifted an eyebrow.

"Oh, well, what does it matter, anyway?" said Shelby irritably. "Matt has his necklace back and we are no longer a couple."

"We'll see," said Leeza. "I don't think you could give up Matt any more than you could swear off Starbucks mochas."

Shelby groaned. "I'm a mess."

"You're an actress. It goes with the territory."

Saturday afternoon David sat looking at the football game on TV, not knowing if it was the first down or the third. He didn't know the score, either. Although he normally would care, today the only score he was interested in was the one he was trying to make with Shelby Barrett. If he and Matt What's-his-name were opposing teams, David knew who the money would be riding on, but he was pretty sure he was gaining yardage.

Good thing, because he wanted Shelby more than he had ever wanted anything in his life. She was perfect. He loved her looks, her laugh, and her impulsiveness. And he was impressed by her sense of misplaced loyalty. Like she needed to be loyal to a guy who had no desire to marry her. Good grief, what was wrong with women, anyway?

Not for the first time, David's glance shot to the phone. He really wanted to call her, but he sensed that would be a tactical error. If he appeared over-eager he'd send out needy nerd signals, and he didn't want to do that—not with the competition he had. He wanted to romance Shelby right out from under the jerk's nose, and the best way to do that was to give her what her heart wanted—a little romance coupled with a little mystery. Today was mystery day.

But what if Matt called her today, brought over a diamond ring? David watched a big bruiser from the Minnesota Vikings take down the Kansas City quarterback. The ball jumped out of the running back's arms and he went skidding along the field on his chin, his attacker holding on to his legs like a pit bull. David winced and hoped what he was watching wasn't symbolic. The phone seemed to cry to him to come pick it up. He folded his arms across his chest, dug his hands into his armpits, and forced himself to stay seated.

"May, me, ma, mo, moo," warbled Shelby, then moved her fingers up the keyboard half a step to play the next chord in the scale. "May, me, ma, mo, moo."

With the vocal volume turned up, she didn't realize the

phone had rung until she heard Leeza saying a hopeful hello. That one word was enough to make her stop vocalizing and turn to scan Leeza's face for any indication that they might be hearing from the theater.

Leeza shook her head, then cooed, "No, I wasn't busy. Just listening to my roommate screeching through her vocal exercises."

Shelby scowled, moved the pitch up another notch, and belted another of Leeza's favorite drills, "I loooove thee not."

"Yeah, well, the landlord's not going to love thee, either, if thou shatterest a window," said Leeza. "I can always go for a cup of coffee," she told the caller. "When? Sure, that works for me. Okay. Bye."

"Don't tell me, let me guess," said Shelby. "That was your newest acquisition."

"Yes. God's way of rewarding me for the suffering I endure when you vocalize."

"Hey, vocal cords can get just as out of shape as legs," said Shelby, pretending to be insulted.

"So, what are you going to do once you get your golden throat in shape?" asked Leeza.

"Oh, I don't know," said Shelby. "Probably read. Or go into Martha Stewart mode and bake."

"No baking," said Leeza firmly. "You have a tapeworm, but every time I even look at what you're whipping up in the kitchen I get fat. Why don't you get out of the apartment for a while?"

"No, I think I'll hang around," said Shelby. "Just in case someone from the Fifth Avenue calls."

"We have an answering machine," Leeza reminded her. "We're not going to miss hearing from the theater." Her expression turned sly, telegraphing what she was going to say as if they were running lines and Shelby had a script right in front of her. "You could call David, get another dancing lesson."

"I knew you were going to say that."

"Yeah, and I know what you're going to say, too, you idiot. It's not like Matt has called and asked you to save space on your calendar for him. You just broke up with him. You don't have to be loyal anymore. Anyway, I think you should spend some time with David. If you don't, how are you going to know whether he or Matt is the right one for you?"

Good point, thought Shelby. Still, it seemed somehow wrong to call one man the day after you'd broken up with another.

"I'll find something to do," she said, then, to make sure the subject stayed closed, she turned her attention back to the keyboard. "I looove thee not."

"Yooooou are a dope," came the echoing serenade.

Well, maybe she was a dope, but at least she was a principled one. Sort of.

Shelby closed her Nora Roberts novel. She always hated to come to the end of a good story. It was a little like having a friend move away just as you were getting close.

She checked her watch. Not even two o'clock yet. There was still a lot of afternoon left, and she suddenly felt restless. She looked out her window. Rare Seattle sunshine beckoned. Leeza was right, she should get out.

She had half expected Matt to call, but the phone had remained mute. Maybe he was up on the slopes, putting all thought of her aside as he risked life and limb on a snowboard. And David Jones, what would he be doing right about now?

Her gaze fell on the CD player. She still had his CD. She couldn't just keep it, that wouldn't be right. He was probably wishing he had it back. She'd better call and offer to get it to him.

David answered his phone on the first ring.

"You left your CD behind," said Shelby. "I thought you might want it in case you feel the overpowering urge to imitate Fred Astaire again."

"It's Saturday," said David. "I'd be John Travolta."

"I guess you don't need this CD then."

"Nope. I've got my *Saturday Night Fever* soundtrack. But, you know," he added thoughtfully, "I might want to be Fred Astaire again tomorrow. Would you meet me some place and give it to me?"

"Okay. Where?"

"Well, the sun is out and it's actually not too cold. I think I've got the perfect spot."

An hour later Shelby found herself strolling down a walk at Seattle's Woodland Park Zoo. They had seen the primates and the otters, and now they were headed for the lions and tigers. In typical Seattle style, the weather had climbed from the mid-thirties to a practically balmy fifty-one overnight, and the sun and the various strategically planted perennial bushes helped hide the fact that it was January.

A mother with a little girl in tow passed them. The child was following reluctantly. Like Lot's wife, her attention was turned in the direction they had come, and her pudgy little hand was stretched out toward the refreshment stand. "I want animal cookies," she sobbed.

"Good idea," said David. He turned to Shelby. "Want something to eat?"

"Sure."

He headed them for the refreshment stand, saying, "I think that lady should have bought her kid the cookies. Don't you?"

"Obviously, you would have," said Shelby. "Do you like kids?"

"All the ones I know. My nephew is great. Of course, he's still pretty young and he's got that cute factor going for him. If you're asking me whether I want some of my own someday, the answer is yes."

They bought hot dogs and ate them in front of the tigers. Watching the captive animals pace, Shelby decided this was as good a time as any to see how David Jones stood on that subject Matt hated.

"Usually, you get a wife before you get kids. How do you feel about marriage?" she asked, and hazarded a sidelong glance his direction.

He remained leaning on the railing, his gaze fixed on the big cats. "I'd take a life sentence in a heartbeat, if it was with the right person." He shifted his weight and turned to study her. "Is that the answer you were looking for?"

"All I was looking for was an honest answer."

"You got one."

Shelby studied the big tigress sunning herself. "How do you feel about having your heart broken?"

"It's yours to break," he said simply.

She turned to face him. "I could end up smashing it to smithereens. I've been with Matt for a long time, and I honestly don't know if this breakup is permanent. I'm going to hate myself if I hurt you."

"Well, I won't hate you," said David. "But I will be really mad at you if you stay with Matt just because he's become a habit. You weren't married to him, Shelby. You don't owe him forever. You don't owe that to a man who's not willing to give it."

"I can't blame him for being scared," said Shelby. "Forever can be a long time."

"No," said David. "With the right woman, it's not long enough."

Diana tucked her hair behind her ears and inserted her pearl earrings. Her dress was a cream-colored light wool with a squared neckline. She'd donned a simple, gold chain with a single, large freshwater pearl dropping from it, and it dangled above her breasts like a tiny arrow pointing directions.

She inspected herself. The first impression was good. She leaned closer to the mirror, and the fine lines around her eyes came into focus. She had a tiny wrinkle carving into each lid now, too, and although the makeup hid them, she still knew they were there. She backed away again and told her reflection, "Well, you're not twenty anymore. But neither is he, so who cares?"

Anyone seeing her getting ready might have thought she did. She'd done the bubble bath thing, the leg shaving, and had tried on three different outfits before finally settling on what to wear.

She made a face at herself. What was the matter with her, anyway? She was just meeting someone for drinks.

The handsome, chiseled face of that someone came to mind, making her heart skitter nervously. She should have told him no. Well, she'd stay for one drink, say her piece, then get out of there. She dabbed some perfume behind her ears and on her wrists, then slipped into her coat and headed for the car.

Canlis was a Seattle landmark. The restaurant had been around since nineteen fifty. Its recent one-point-five-million-dollar remodel had given it a new burnish, but hadn't changed its original Frank Lloyd Wright look. The view remained the same: priceless. From its high perch on Aurora Avenue, the restaurant's windows framed Lake Union and the Cascade Mountains for its guests to admire.

Diana passed through the foyer and went straight to the bar to find Lance Gregory already there and waiting at a table. At the sight of her he rose, an appreciative smile on his face. He held out his hand and took hers, handing her into her seat as if she were a royal princess, and saying, "And I thought you were stunning in your civvies. Look at you in dress uniform! You take my breath away."

Diana detested smooth talkers. She wondered what mind-bending drug she had accidentally taken that had influenced her to make this date.

"Obviously, I didn't take it all," she said. "That's quite a welcome speech."

"You think I was only flattering you? I wasn't, believe me."

Diana gave him a frosted smile. "I'm afraid I don't know you well enough to believe you about anything, Mr. Gregory."

"Lance," he corrected. "And let's see if we can change that."

The cocktail waitress was at the table now, and he turned to Diana. "What would you like?"

"Vodka gimlet, please," she said to the woman. "And a separate tab."

He leaned back in his seat. "I don't think so. The one who does the inviting gets to do the paying."

There was no sense making an issue out of it. "All right."

"Another Scotch and water, please," he told the waitress, then flashed his perfect smile at her.

She nodded and left them, looking as pleased as if he'd just slipped her a twenty-dollar tip.

Lance returned his attention to Diana, studying her like a police inspector trying to decide how best to intimidate a suspect. She cocked her head at him and raised an eyebrow.

"You've been having second thoughts, haven't you?" he guessed.

"Frankly, yes," said Diana. "There is really no need for this meeting. I'm afraid you're wasting your time."

"How could having drinks with such a beautiful woman possibly be a waste of time?"

"Because, if your intention is to win me over on your nephew's behalf, it's a misplaced effort. What I think about Matt has nothing to do with what's going on between Shelby and him. My daughter has a mind of her own."

"So she's never come to you for advice?" Now he sounded like Perry Mason, trying to trap her.

"No more than your nephew has come to you," she retorted.

He acknowledged the hit with a smile. "But this is all a moot point. I told you I started out as an emissary, but changed my purpose once I saw you."

"If you're hoping to start something between us, I'm sorry, I'm not in the market," said Diana.

"Now I am intrigued," said Lance.

"I wasn't trying to intrigue you. I was trying to discourage you.

"No attraction, hmm?"

The betraying warmth on her cheeks made Diana feel foolish. Her drink arrived and she took a sip. "A woman can walk past a case of diamond jewelry and be attracted. It doesn't mean she's going to buy."

"And why wouldn't she?"

His voice was light and teasing, and it goosed up her heart rate, making her irritated with herself.

She refused to match his bantering tone. This was no sexual dance they were doing, and she would show him that. "Because the cost is too high."

And the tag on this particular man was looking higher by the minute. She was having drinks with the middle-aged version of her charming, black-hearted first love.

He raised his glass and drank, eyeing her over its rim. Then he said, "Maybe I can convince you otherwise."

"I doubt it," said Diana.

"Well, let's start with the purported reason we're here:

my nephew. Then I can at least tell him I tried. What, exactly, have you got against him?"

"Other than the fact that he's stringing my daughter along, nothing."

Lance Gregory looked flabbergasted. "You interpret his concern that he's not ready for marriage as stringing her along?"

"Not ready—a euphemism for 'won't commit,'" scoffed Diana. "Any man who won't commit himself to the woman he claims to love isn't worth space on her calendar or in her heart. Unfortunately, Shelby has given Matt both for far too long, and I think she's going to get hurt."

"My nephew loves your daughter," said Lance, sounding hurt on behalf of his nephew.

"Then he should prove it," she said.

"I believe he just bought her an expensive necklace."

Diana's smile was cynical. "He bought her a pacifier."

That made him sit up and blink.

Diana hid her smile behind her glass. Time to go. She took one last sip of her drink, then picked up her purse. "Thanks for the drink."

He reached across the table and caught her arm. "Don't leave yet. Stay and have dinner with me."

"I don't think so," said Diana.

"You are hungry, aren't you?"

Was she?

"I won't eat you," he teased. "The food here is too good."

He released her arm, then lounged back in his chair and studied her. His scrutiny brought back her jitters.

"You know," he drawled, "I almost suspect that under that cool exterior hides a nervous woman. Is there something about me that makes you uncomfortable?"

Uncomfortable? There was an understatement. He smacked of danger and loss of control. If she were able to look down the road to his past, she'd probably see it littered with broken hearts.

"Surely you trust yourself enough to stay for dinner," he goaded.

Trust herself? As if she had no self-control, as if she couldn't control him? She was no little thirteen-year-old on a runaway horse. And she was no naive nineteen-year-old anymore, either.

"All right. Dinner," she said, taking the dare. Why not? She had to eat, and she was fond of the way Canlis prepared salmon.

He flashed a triumphant smile.

Another spoiled boy gets his way, thought Diana, sure her first impression of Lance had been correct.

But at dinner, she found him an interesting companion, and the more they talked, the more comfortable she felt. She learned that, like herself, he was fond of travel. He enjoyed Andrew Lloyd Webber musicals and liked to read mysteries, and he was intrigued when she mentioned that she was writing one.

"And how will Diana Valentine fans react to her switching from writing about the *petit mort* to murder?"

"I'm hoping they'll want to get to the know the new me."

"The old you looks pretty intriguing," said Lance. "But tell me about the new you. Will you be writing under a pen name?"

Diana nodded. "Amy Stery."

His brow puckered. "Not glamorous like Dorothy L. Sayers. Why did you pick it?"

"To give my readers a little something more to puzzle out."

He fished a gold pen and a small tablet from his inside jacket pocket and began to doodle. "Ah," he said after a moment. "A mystery. Very clever." He raised his glass of wine in salute. "Here's to you, Amy Stery. If your plots match your pen name in brilliance, I predict for you a stellar career as a mystery writer."

"Thank you. I hope your prediction comes true."

"So, if I promise to buy the book when it comes out, will you give me a preview tonight? Just something to whet my appetite."

Well, they had to talk about something. Diana decided to tell him just a little.

Before she knew it, he'd encouraged her to spin out most of the plot.

"I know who did it," he said, pointing his fork at her.

"You can't."

He nodded. "It was the mother's cousin." Diana sat back against her chair, nonplused, and he nodded sagely. "I'm right, aren't I."

"How did you know that?"

"Go out with me and I'll tell you."

"I'm already out with you."

"Go out with me again. Do you like to dance?"

The vision of herself dancing with Lance Gregory brought with it temporary amnesia regarding the fact that she'd gone through the tunnel of menopause and come out the other end with no libido. "Yes," she said slowly.

"Let's see what kind of partners we make."

Diana shook her head. "I don't think there's any purpose in our seeing each other again."

"Oh?" He ran his fingers around the rim of his wineglass. "Because we had such a terrible time tonight?"

"Because we didn't."

He chuckled. "Look, let's let the younger generation fend for themselves. Shall we?"

"A good idea," said Diana.

"Good. Then that's settled. So, about going out . . ."

She cut him off. "I don't think so. I'm really not in the market for a man. I prefer being single."

"What a coincidence! So do I. So how about it? What do you say we go out for the fun of it?"

How had he found her Achilles' heel so quickly? She shouldn't do this. Putting herself in Lance Gregory's arms would be like exposing her neck to a vampire. "Just dancing," she said, using her words as a talisman. "No strings, no dating, no wanting more."

He held up both hands. "Just the pleasure of your company."

As long as Lance knew the ground rules and was okay with them, what could it hurt to go out just once? "All right."

"Great! Now. What kind of dancing do you like? Salsa, swing, country? No, not country. You don't look the type."

"I haven't danced in years," said Diana.

"I bet you'll pick it up right away. What's your pleasure?"

He was right about the country music. She wasn't fond of it. And Salsa would be too sensual. "Swing," she pronounced.

"I know the perfect place," he said. "The Seattle Swing Club meets at the Mountaineers Club on Sunday evenings, from five till nine. Dance lessons at four. Would you like to take a lesson?"

"I'd better," said Diana.

"Okay, great. I'll pick you up at three-thirty."

"I suppose you already have my address."

He gave her an apologetic shrug. "My nephew gave it to me."

She shook her head at him. "I have a feeling I'll live to regret this."

"I'll try to make sure you don't," he said.

They ordered dessert and lingered over their coffee a little longer. By the time Diana reached her car, she realized that her jitters had completely gone, and a feeling of anticipation had taken their place. She felt like a high school freshman who had captured the attention of the cutest boy in school. This was silly, ridiculous.

She didn't have a thing to wear. She would have to run to the mall tomorrow.

Lance drove home, his car reverberating to Stravinsky's *Firebird Suite*. Appropriate. He felt on fire.

Diana Barrett was something else. Not only was she a fine-looking woman, but she was intelligent to boot. He had almost fallen off his chair when she made her comment about the necklace he'd advised Matt to give her daughter. It was uncanny, and more than a little unnerving to have a woman see through his strategy so easily, to use the same cynical word to describe that necklace that Lance had. It had made him feel like a miser brought face-to-face with the poor he refused to help, and he'd been determined to prove the feeling wrong. And as he had turned on the charm, Diana had warmed, showing traces of a sense of humor.

Of course, he'd already seen evidence of a keen wit in the book he was now reading. He'd picked up half a dozen Diana Valentine novels the day before: a mix of some of her earlier efforts and her latest releases. He had decided to read them in chronological order, starting with a reissue of her first effort and, surprisingly, had gotten sucked into the thing. He was already two-thirds through it, and the further he got, the more he saw of the author. This was a woman who loved romance. In spite of that cool facade she kept trying to maintain, she had to be a smoldering fire, waiting for someone to breathe on her. And Lance wanted to be the one to do it.

He could imagine the intoxicating pleasure of moving Diana around the dance floor, catching a whiff of her perfume every time they came into close contact. Swing dancing had been the perfect choice. It wasn't as in-your-face sexual as Latin or Salsa dancing, but the message was still undeniable. West Coast Swing was a dance of brushing bodies, sexy blues with a blood-pulsing beat, and a million ways to tease and provoke. And Lance intended to use as many of them as he could to lose Diana Barrett, Ice Queen, and bring out Diana Valentine, passionate woman.

He smiled. This was a favor he would definitely enjoy doing for his nephew.

Shelby and David had not only visited Seattle's zoo, they had stopped at the landmark Zesto's Drive-In for a milk shake on the way home. They had nursed their shakes for an hour, debating the year and make of the old fifties car that sat on its roof, then ordered hamburgers and monopolized the same table for another two hours. From there they had gone to the Shilshole Marina and braved the now icy night air to walk around and look at the sailboats and cabin cruisers nesting on the water. That was when Shelby learned David was saving to buy himself a sailboat. Listening to him talk, she could envision them ploughing through the choppy waters of Puget Sound on a windy day. It made for a very romantic vision.

After David had finally dropped her off, she'd tried to call her mom, but Mom hadn't been home, which had seemed odd, because ever since Daddy's death, Mom had spent most of her Friday and Saturday nights camped out in the family room, watching movies, either by herself or with a friend. Where could she be?

Shelby left a message on the machine and asked her mom to call her, then waited, reliving the day. It had truly been wonderful. David was wonderful. She wished he would kiss her. It would be so much easier to compare him to Matt if he would just kiss her. What was he waiting for, anyway? Maybe she should ask him.

Mom finally called back a little before nine.

"Where have you been?" asked Shelby.

"I went out for drinks," said Mom."

"Oh, fun. Who'd you go out with? Suzanne?"

"No."

"Well, who?" probed Shelby.

"Just someone I met."

Someone she met. Mom was sure being mysterious. Hmmm. "A man?"

"Yes, as a matter of fact."

"You're kidding! I thought you didn't want another man in your life. I remember you telling me that just this last summer when we saw that old lech staring at you in the gift shop in Port Townsend."

"This was drinks, Shelby, not marriage."

"Well, that's how it starts. First drinks. Next it will be going out to dinner, then a movie, then dancing, and then . . ."

"Nothing," interrupted Mom. "This is just the possible beginnings of friendship. That's it. And an odd friendship at that," she muttered.

Shelby pounced on the word. "Odd. What do you mean?" There was a long pause. "Mom," she prodded.

"I mean odd because this man is Matt's uncle." Mom's words came out in a guilty rush.

Shelby could hardly believe her ears. "His uncle Lance?"

"Yes."

This was not good. "Mom, trust me, you don't want to go out with him. Do you know what his family calls him? Lance Romance. He's had more girlfriends than a rock star."

"Well, don't worry," said Mom. "I'm not planning on becoming one of them."

What was Mom doing with Matt's uncle, anyway? It all sounded strange and contrived.

"Did you guys talk about us?" asked Shelby suspiciously.

"Only in that we agreed you two need to handle your own affairs," said Mom.

"Good idea," said Shelby, relieved.

"Speaking of which, how is it going with Matt?" asked Mom.

"Well, at the moment, I'm not with Matt. I gave the necklace back."

"That doesn't look good for our hero," quipped Mom.

"I don't know what it looks like," said Shelby, and sighed. "But maybe it's a good thing we're backing off, if you're going to be going out with his uncle. I mean, that would be just too strange."

"Probably," agreed Mom.

"I did have an interesting day, though," said Shelby, and proceeded to tell her mother about the time she spent with David.

"He sounds wonderful," said Mom. "I think it's definitely a good thing you returned Matt's necklace."

"Maybe," said Shelby, "I just wish I knew what I was doing."

"You'll figure it out sooner or later," said Mom encouragingly.

"Yeah? Well, if I could put in my order I'd rather know sooner."

Mom didn't offer any more pearls of wisdom, just chuckled.

"So, I guess I'll see you tomorrow?"

"Oh," said Mom, in a tone of voice that implied she'd rather not have her daughter hanging around.

Curiouser and curiouser. "Aren't you going to be home?" asked Shelby.

"Well, I have to run an errand, and then I'm going out. But you're still welcome to come over and do your laundry."

When the quarter gobbler the landlord provided had broken down in October, Shelby had started going to her mom's to do her laundry. The washing machine was fixed now, but it was more fun, not to mention cheaper, to go to Mom's. So Shelby went over almost every Sunday afternoon, hauling her dirty clothes, her latest culinary triumph, and whatever exotic new tea she had discovered earlier in the week at the Pike Place Market. While the clothes washed they would have tea and play Scrabble.

Shelby told herself it was about time her mother got a life. She was happy for Mom. But she had to admit, she wished that new life wasn't happening on what she had come to think of as their time together.

"Where are you going?" she asked, schooling her voice to hide her hurt feelings.

"Well, I'm going dancing," said Mom. It sounded more like a confession than an announcement.

"Don't tell me, let me guess," said Shelby. "With Matt's uncle?"

"Yes, as a matter of fact."

"Again? So soon?"

"Is there something wrong with that?"

Mom sounded just a little bit defensive. "No, no," said Shelby quickly. "Have fun." She couldn't help adding, "But be careful."

"I will," said Mom, amusement at their reversed roles plain in her voice. "And I'm glad you had a good time today."

They said their good-byes and Shelby hung up. She nuked herself a mug of hot water and dropped a tea bag in it, then went to the love seat to cogitate.

It really did seem odd that Mom and Matt's uncle were going out. Mom never did say exactly how they met. Shelby took a deep drink of tea and thought further, and came to a conclusion: something was definitely rotten in the state of Denmark. And she intended to find out what.

# *Nine*

*Lance was still* reading the Sunday paper when his nephew called, hoping for good news.

"Yes, I met Shelby's mom," said Lance.

"And did you guys hit it off?"

"We did. She's a very interesting woman."

"Great. So, do you think you can help me?"

"I think I can keep her distracted from your love life long enough to give you a clear shot at fixing things between you and Shelby."

"Well, that's one good thing, anyway," said Matt, his voice tired.

This did not sound like a man in control of his destiny. "What's the problem now?" asked Lance.

Matt sighed heavily. "Well, I did what you suggested and bought Shelby that necklace with the diamond in it."

"So what's the problem?"

"You know, I don't know. She liked it. I gave it to her at her favorite restaurant, and we had a great time, made all these plans for the future. Then, when we went out last night, she picked a fight and gave it back."

Lance thought a moment. "Did you say you've got competition?"

Matt gave a derisive snort. "You could hardly call the guy that."

So, Mama wasn't the only fly in the ointment now. Lance understood how the kid felt. No man's pride was fond of admitting the possibility that a rival could be giving his woman something he wasn't. Still, it was obvious.

"Then why did your present come bouncing back?" he asked.

"I don't know," said Matt. "None of this is making any sense. One minute she's wanting to get married, the next she's saying *she's* not sure she's ready."

"That is a switch," agreed Lance. "And it probably has something to do with the other man you think is so insignificant. If you've got competition, you'd better step up the romance, or it's going to be so long, Sam."

"You mean flowers and candy?"

"Maybe not something so obvious."

"You want obvious, you should have seen what this guy sent her. It was ridiculous. He even included a video of some dippy, old movie."

"Maybe they're finding a connection that you've lost with her," suggested Lance.

Matt gave a snort of disgust. "He's trying to find a connection, all right, and it ain't as soul mates."

"Well, you've known her longer. That gives you the inside track. Outdo him. Don't try to do the bigger and better thing," Lance advised. "That just looks like it's a competition and all you care about is winning. Think sentiment. Bring her a single white rose. Take her dancing." Lance had seen his nephew in action at a family wedding a couple years back and knew the kid was not a chip off the old block. Stepbrother Danny had two left feet, but Matt had taken after his old uncle Lance, and the sweet young things had practically lined up for a chance to dance with him. Yeah, the kid was all right.

"I don't think Shel would go with me right now," Matt was saying in discouraged tones.

"Well, then, ambush her. Happen to be there when she's out with her girlfriends and sweep her off her feet. Women love that sort of thing. Maybe that's why this other guy has the edge on you. Maybe he's more romantic."

Matt sighed. "This is getting to be a damned lot of work."

"Women are a lot of work," said Lance. "They're people, not pet rocks. If you don't like it, give 'em up."

"Thanks a lot."

"Just telling it like it is."

"Okay," said Matt, put in his place. "I'll give it a try. Thanks for the advice."

"You're welcome," said Lance.

After he hung up, he poured himself another cup of coffee. He suspected his nephew was in more trouble than he realized. If Shelby could be so quickly distracted by a rival, she probably wasn't as crazy about the kid as he liked to think. Women in love were loyal, and this one's loyalty was headed out the window.

Which probably meant that Lance didn't even need to bother with Mama anymore. But what the hell? He'd buzz around her for a while and see what happened. He could afford to step off the business treadmill for a few days.

He shook his head. He never thought he'd go out with a woman who had a grown child, but Diana Barrett was too interesting not to pursue. Of course, the prospect of sensual pleasure gave the usual fillip to the chase, but Lance knew his attraction for her functioned on a deeper level. Of all the women he'd dated in the last year, Diana was the only one whose conversation interested him as much as her body.

Yes, there was no sense packing it in so early.

• • •

Diana returned from the mall at two-fifty-five, lugging two shopping bags stuffed with everything from shoes to panty hose. She'd found just what she needed for dancing: new shoes, and a plain, black dress with some flare in the skirt that would swing when she moved. And moving was exactly what she was doing now, fast. She still had to take a shower, do her make-up, and get into her new clothes, and Lance would be arriving in thirty-five minutes.

As she had pulled up, she'd noted, with a slight sinking sensation, the presence of Shelby's car parked alongside the curb. Now she hurried through the garage to the kitchen door entrance, past the sloshing washing machine and wondered what phony errand she could send her nosy daughter on to get her out of the house for the next hour.

Shelby sat at the kitchen table, a plate of nachos in front of her, halfway into the paperback Diana had barely cracked.

"Hi," she called.

Diana forced a Mom-is-happy-to-see-you look onto her face and gave her daughter a hello and a kiss. "Say, I'm out of a few things. If I turned you loose with some money, would you be interested in making a run to the store for me?"

"Sure," said Shelby. "I'll go as soon as this load is done."

"I can put it in the dryer for you," offered Diana.

"Oh, that's okay. I'm not in a hurry. Leeza is flying today and I don't have anything to do."

*Except poke your nose into your mother's business,* thought Diana.

"Okay, great," she lied, then hurried to the bedroom, hoping that Shelby wouldn't follow her.

Vain hope.

"What'd you get?" asked Shelby, flopping onto the bed and digging into the first shopping bag.

"Just a few things," said Diana lightly, moving the bag with her new dress and panty hose to the bathroom and out of reach.

Shelby had already found the shoe box and had it open. She lifted out one of Diana's new, black dancing shoes. "These are cute. Can I borrow them?"

"You don't mind if I wear them once first, do you?" called Diana, stepping out of her slacks.

"Ha, ha," said Shelby. She came to stand in the bathroom doorway. "What's the hurry?"

"I'm going out. Remember? I bet your laundry's done. You might want to check it," Diana added, and peeled off her sweater.

"Are you trying to get rid of me?"

"No, just trying to get into the shower."

"Maybe it's just my imagination, but I get the impression you don't want to talk about Uncle Lance."

"He's not my uncle," said Diana.

"Well, he's Matt's," said Shelby.

"I know, dear. You told me."

"What if he's just using you?"

Diana turned and gave Shelby a look that would have shut her up only a few years ago.

"I mean it, Mom. Something is weird here."

So now the young woman who, only a few days ago, was ready to check into the Heartbreak Hotel was an expert on relationships?

"Shelby, for what possible purpose could he be using me?"

"To get to me."

"Do you have any idea how ridiculous and egotistical that sounds?" If anything, it had been just the opposite. Lance Gregory had used Shelby as an excuse to meet her.

"I know," said Shelby. "But look at the evidence. Matt and I are having difficulties. Matt is Uncle Lance's favorite nephew. Suddenly Uncle Lance shows up on your doorstep. That's a lot of coincidence."

"So, Lance Gregory is taking me dancing solely in the hopes that I'll put in a good word for his nephew with you?"

"That does sound dumb," admitted Shelby

"Just a little," agreed Diana. "And you can't convict a person on circumstantial evidence. Anyway, if Matt were going to sic his uncle on anyone, don't you think the logical person to butter up would be you, not me?"

"I guess you're right. But I still think you should be careful. You know, they say that people, after they've lost someone they love, get lonely. They rush into relationships that turn out to be terrible," said Doctor Shelby.

"Right now the only thing I'm trying to rush into is the shower," said Diana. "So, why don't you go check your laundry."

"Okay, fine," said Shelby. "And I wasn't trying to insult you or anything, just trying to help."

"I know," said Diana. "But I really am old enough to take care of myself." The same words her daughter had been saying to her for the last six years.

Shelby didn't say any more on the subject, only hung around to watch Diana get ready and offer unasked-for advice on everything from Diana's make-up to what earrings she should wear. It was a nuisance, but it was also sweet, and Diana even let herself be persuaded into wearing her antique onyx earrings with the diamond chips instead of the gold ones she had chosen.

"There," she said at last. "How do I look?"

"Fabulous," said Shelby. The doorbell rang and she hopped off Diana's bed, saying, "I'll get it."

Diana grabbed her arm. "I can do that myself, thank you."

Diana hurried through the living room and opened the door. Lance's good looks hit her like a blast. He was simply dressed: a white polo shirt tucked into crisply pressed, black slacks, his feet slipped into Italian loafers. An unbuttoned, black wool sports coat molded to his broad shoulders and set off the silvery accents in his hair.

He looked her up and down appreciatively. "I don't know how I'm going to be able to concentrate on my dance steps."

More malarkey, but this time it pleased her. "I was thinking the same thing myself," she said.

He grinned. "Flattery?"

"It's not flattery if you mean it," she retorted, quoting his own words back to him. "I'll just get my coat."

She reached into the hall closet and brought out her favorite long, camel hair coat. He took it from her and helped her into it.

That was when Shelby happened to saunter by. "Oh, hi," she said as if Lance's presence were a complete surprise.

Great. What was she up to now? Diana vowed to strangle her daughter as soon as there were no witnesses.

"Lance, I believe you know my daughter, Shelby."

"Sure. Good to see you, Shelby. How's my nephew these days?"

"He's fine," said Shelby politely.

"Glad to hear it," said Lance. He smiled down at Diana. "Shall we go?"

"Good idea."

"Have fun," said Shelby. "Say, would you like me to make dinner when you come back?"

"No, don't bother," said Diana. "I don't know what time we'll return."

"I don't mind waiting," offered Shelby.

Diana was sure she didn't. There was probably nothing

her daughter would like better than to stand sentinel over her mother and her date.

"We'll be fine," she said firmly.

Shelby gave up. "All right. I guess I'll just finish my laundry and take off."

"Good idea," said Diana.

"I'm glad you passed on the offer of dinner," said Lance, as they headed down the front walk, "since I was hoping you'd let me take you out."

"That sounds like a much better idea than what I'm sure my daughter had in mind."

"And what do you think she had planned, to see if I'm a real man and will eat quiche?"

"Whatever she would concoct, I can guarantee she would make sure it required her presence the whole time."

Lance opened the car door for her, and the conversation was broken while he went around to the driver's side and got settled.

He picked up the threads again as he put the car in motion, saying, "So, you have a guardian angel."

"I'm afraid so," said Diana. "She thinks it strange that I'm fraternizing with the enemy, I guess."

"I told you," said Lance, "I'm a defector from the enemy camp. And now, just to prove I mean it, I'm going to change the subject. Tell me your favorite kind of food."

"I love Thai," said Diana.

"I know the perfect restaurant where we can rest our feet later."

They chatted for a while, then Diana said, "You know, we talked so much about me last night I never did get a chance to find out much about you."

"What do you want to know?"

"More than I learned from reading your business card. What made you decide to become a jeweler?"

"I like nice things," he said simply.

"Even *Reader's Digest* would give me a little more than that," said Diana. "How did you get into the business?"

He shrugged. "I fell into it years ago, when I was young. I spent my youth working on a cruise ship in the Caribbean. Back then you could pick up some pretty unique stones for a song."

"And look at you now," said Diana. "Smart man."

"I'd say smart is what you've accomplished, Miss Bestseller," he countered.

"How'd you know that?"

"I visited your web site."

Diana hadn't mentioned her web site the night before, and she felt pleased that he'd been interested enough in her to search her out.

"And I just finished one of your books," he added. "*Promise Me Tomorrow*."

The reissue of the sappiest book she ever wrote. Diana cringed inwardly.

"Pretty impressive," said Lance, "and with the kind of heroes you imagine, I can see why you don't need a man."

She had said that, hadn't she? "Well, you men are good for some things," she admitted. The look he gave her made her cheeks burn. "Like dancing," she added.

He nodded. "Oh, yes. Dancing. Speaking of which, here we are: the Mountaineers Club."

He parked the car, then said, "Don't touch your door. I've had it wired to give goddesses who refuse worship a shock every time they try to open it unassisted."

She watched as he walked around the front of the car and came to open her door. "We goddesses are liberated now, or didn't anybody tell you that?" she said as he helped her out.

"Lots of bodies have told me that," he replied. "But I always figure good manners are timeless. Anyway, this gives me an excuse to hold your hand."

John had never said things like that to her. She knew it was only flattery that Lance Gregory was pouring out, but she found herself lapping it up like a thirsty cat.

The Mountaineers Club was a much larger building than it appeared from the outside—a three-storied affair with a ballroom that occupied most of its ground floor, and carpeted steps leading up to the next level, which offered many smaller conference and party rooms.

"It's not the most glamorous atmosphere, but it's a good place to come to keep up on your steps," said Lance.

After handing money over to a hefty matron presiding over a long table littered with brochures and name tags, Lance led Diana to an upstairs ballroom, saying, "I think the beginning West Coast Swing lessons are given here."

He slipped off his coat, giving Diana a better look at his physique. And it was a look well worth taking. Lance Gregory could have modeled for Michelangelo's David. He was all leanness and muscles and hard lines. The white of the shirt fabric contrasted with the swarthy skin and dark hair on his forearms, and looking at him, Diana realized he reminded her of Sean Connery in the old James Bond movies.

Not wanting to get caught staring, she forced her eyes away and studied her fellow dance pupils. Forty-some people milled around the room. Most of the women wore dresses meant to impress and dance shoes. The men ranged in size and appearance from portly and dumpy to tall and well-dressed. Some looked comfortable in their surroundings, and others, obviously coerced into coming by their significant others, were glancing around them like rookie convicts in a prison yard.

A new arrival created a stir. She was a small-boned woman, somewhere in her thirties, with tiny hips and ash blonde hair done at the Dolly Parton look-a-like salon. She was poured into black dress pants, topped with a silver metallic top that molded lovingly around full breasts, and she walked on black shoes with what looked like six-inch heels. The heels were not an impediment. She moved as if every step had been choreographed.

She went up to her assistant, a tall man with wavy, brown hair, wearing slacks and a black shirt that could have been stolen from Captain Kidd, and took the cordless mike he was holding out to her. The class held their collective breath.

She spoke into the microphone. "Hello. Are you all here for the beginner's class?"

The group nodded and mumbled and she beamed on them. "I'm Anna Deale," she informed them, "and I'll be introducing you to the West Coast Swing."

Diana did a quick sweep of the room, and noticed that the men who had previously looked unenthused had suddenly come to life. She was willing to bet that the West Coast Swing wasn't all they were in hopes of getting introduced to.

Having gotten their attention, their instructor proceeded to divide the group, moving the women to one side of the room and the men to the other.

"Good," she said when they were finished, as if they had already accomplished something. "Now, ladies, let's start with your steps."

Anna Deale spent a few moments going over the basic steps of the dance with the ladies, then turned her attention on the men. When they had all performed to her satisfaction, she re-formed the group into two circles, with the men on the outside and the women on the inside.

Diana found herself once more facing Lance.

"Now," said their instructor. "I want you to take the hand of the person opposite you."

Lance held out his hand. Diana put hers in it and felt

like she'd just touched a live wire. He smiled at her and her heart did another flip. What little estrogen she had left was obviously very aware of Lance Gregory.

"Before we walk through our steps, let's spend a moment talking about frame," said Anna.

She talked and Diana tried hard to listen, but she kept getting distracted by other thoughts, other feelings. So far, Lance was only holding her hand and they were standing an arm's length away from each other. What would happen when they came into closer contact?

She soon found out.

The music started. "Ready, begin," said Anna.

Lance gave Diana a gentle tug and she started moving toward him. Even with her eyes closed, she would have been aware of the moment she passed his body. It was as if she'd walked by a force field, and every part of her started humming.

"Good," said their teacher. "Now, ladies, let's have you move one partner to the right."

Diana left Lance regretfully, politely stepping in front of the man next to him, a short, husky specimen, who leered at her. They walked through the steps again, the man pulling Diana past him, first one way, then another, and she found she was better able to concentrate on her footwork without Lance in such close proximity.

"All right," said their teacher. "Now, let's try an underarm pass. Lance, would you help me demonstrate?"

Somehow, Diana wasn't surprised to learn that her date knew the pretty instructor. Diana could just imagine any number of women coming up to him and asking him if he would save them a dance. She watched him walk onto the center of the floor and put Anna Deale through her paces. He was sexy and graceful, and she realized her mouth was watering.

*Cut it out, Barrett. What's the matter with you, anyway?*

She knew what was the matter with her. She'd imagined

it and written about it for long enough. But she hadn't experienced it in years.

They continued the lesson, with the women working their way around the circle to a new dance partner every few steps, until they finally came full circle, back to their original partners.

Lance smiled at Diana and asked, "How are you doing?"

"Great," she said. And she was. It had been so long since she'd danced. It was like getting off a desert island and being offered chocolate.

"Now, let's put together everything we've learned today," said Anna Deale. "Okay, here's the music."

A bluesy piece started playing. Lance tugged Diana gently and she started toward him, her feet moving in time to the music, her heart fluttering to some primitive tempo of its own. She moved down the line of dance past him, every atom of her being aware of his height and strength. She did her little in-place steps on counts five and six and realized she was feeling sexier than she had in years. Lance pulled her back, and as she pranced toward him she was aware of her panty hose shimmering, and her dress swishing around her legs. He pulled her again, this time helping her turn with a warm hand pressed intimately on her side. Her dress twirled around her, mimicking her movement and showing a good expanse of thigh. She felt twenty.

Before she knew it, he was moving her into a turn they hadn't learned, something far beyond the scope of a beginner's class. It brought her close to him for one teasing moment, letting her feel his body against her backside, his arms around her middle. Her insides spasmed and her mouth went dry. He spun her away, then pulled her back to walk past him again. The scent of his aftershave tickled her nose.

The song ended and he grinned down at her. "I knew you'd be a great dancer."

"You didn't tell me Gene Kelly was your grandfather," said Diana.

"I worked on a cruise ship. Dancing was part of the job description."

Diana could imagine a younger Lance dancing under a warm Caribbean sky with a succession of pretty women, returning them all to the mainland minus their hearts.

The class was over. The pupils disseminated in the general direction of the grand ballroom.

"So, do you think you're going to enjoy West Coast Swing?" asked Lance as they headed back down the carpeted stairs.

Dancing, and with a handsome man. What was there not to enjoy? "I think I could get used to it," she replied.

"I think I could get used to dancing with you," he said, his voice a caress.

Diana felt like she was on a roller coaster, heading uphill for the big plunge and picking up steam. She couldn't think of anything to say so she kept her mouth shut.

They entered the ballroom, and he guided her to one of many round tables set up around the edges of the hardwood dance floor. "Can I buy you a juice or a soft drink?" he offered, nodding toward the casual refreshment setup at the end of the room.

She nodded. "Seven-Up would be great."

He left her and headed off to get their drinks. She watched him go, stopping to greet one or two people along the way. Even when he was just walking, Lance Gregory moved with the grace of a movie star.

A light tap on her shoulder gave her a start, and she turned to see a man in his forties with dark brown hair leaning over her. He was shorter than Lance but equally well-toned, and he wore dockers and a short-sleeved shirt.

"Hi. I'm Jack Carter, president of the Swing Club," he said. "You're new, aren't you?"

"Yes, I am," she said.

"How'd you hear about us?"

"A friend told me."

"Great," said Jack, smiling. "Did you come alone?"

At that moment, Lance returned. "She's with me."

"I should've known." Jack reached out his hand and gripped Lance's. "Hey, man. Haven't seen you here in a couple of months."

"I've been busy," said Lance.

Jack looked appreciatively at Diana. "I can see that." To Diana he said, "You be sure and remind him that it's proper dance etiquette to share."

"Well, I'll be happy to share," said Lance, "when I break my leg."

"We'll have to see what we can do about that," teased Jack. "I hope you'll save me a dance," he said to Diana, then moved on to greet other people.

Lance sat down next to her. "That guy is such an arrogant ass."

"He seemed nice."

"He thinks he's hot stuff."

Diana hid a smile. Lance Gregory could have been talking about himself.

The place rapidly filled, and by the time the DJ started the first song at five o'clock, there was hardly a seat available. Couples swarmed onto the floor and began executing moves that looked like they'd been learned from a Broadway choreographer.

Lance rose and held out a hand. "Shall we?"

Diana suddenly felt intimidated. "Oh, I don't know."

"Come on. You've got to start sometime."

True. And wasn't this what she'd been wanting for so many years? It was time to go enjoy the dream come true. She took Lance's hand and let him lead her onto the floor.

The minute they began to dance, she forgot her reluctance. The pleasure of the experience was too great for her to care if she did look like a beginner. And with Lance she didn't feel like one. With every misstep he caught her, making her ever aware of his strength. He twirled and moved her and made her laugh from the sheer thrill of the experience. For the first time since John's death she felt truly, fully alive.

Halfway through the evening, the DJ put on a slow song, and Lance took her out onto the floor, put his hand on the small of her back and pulled her close to him. She had to look up to see his face. Closer to her line of vision was his chest with its well-developed pecs. What would they feel like under her fingers?

She didn't need to know. Not tonight, not ever. To give in to the impulses of mere attraction would be just plain stupid. She had done that once in her life, and once was enough. But it looked like the disease of female stupidity, like chicken pox, stayed buried in your body, waiting to flare up later in life like a bad case of shingles. There was only one way to be safe from such a dangerous flare-up, and that would be to not go out with this man again.

She forced herself to appear unaffected by his closeness, letting her gaze roam the room. This was just a dance, after all. She looked up to give Lance a friendly, but slightly distant smile, to remind him that they were only dance partners, nothing more.

The expression on his face was anything but distant. It spoke of champagne and rumpled sheets, and made her temperature rise. Lance wasn't the only one who needed reminding.

As the evening wore on, Diana found it increasingly hard to remember why, exactly, it was that she didn't want a man in her life. Everything about being with Lance made the experience of living seem more vivid. After four hours of dancing, her whole body thrummed from exercise and stimulation. And then it had been time to eat, and the conversation affected her mind similar to the way the dancing had her body.

They were the last to leave the restaurant, and when he pulled his car up in front of her house, Diana found herself reluctant to see the evening end.

"Since you paid for dinner, the least I can do is offer you a cup of coffee," she said, amnesia wiping out all memory of her earlier resolutions.

Lance switched off the engine and turned to face her, resting an arm on the back of the seat. "Is that the only reason you're asking me in?"

"No." Her first impulse was to look away before he could read some betraying weakness in her eyes, but then she realized she'd already betrayed herself, so she held his gaze. "I enjoy talking to you." That was true. She did.

He cocked an eyebrow. "Just talking?"

"That's what friends do, isn't it?"

"Yes, but after dancing with you, I might find I can't bring myself to leave once I come in."

"I'll help you," Diana assured him.

"Will you?"

His intense gaze set off a tremor in her. She felt vulnerable, and found she didn't enjoy the feeling. This was why she didn't want a man in her life.

"On second thought, it's too late at night to be drinking caffeine," she said, and reached for the door handle.

His hand on her arm stopped her. "Ah-ah," he said. She watched him get out and walk around the car. It was ridiculous to be feeling nervous at her age. Still, she couldn't seem to make those jitters stop.

He walked her to the front door. The house stood in darkness. *Thank you, daughter dear, for not even leaving the porch light on,* Diana thought as she fumbled with her house key, trying to fit it in the lock.

"Need help?" offered Lance, plucking it from her fingers.

He had a small flashlight attached to his key ring and shined it on the keyhole, easily inserting the key and turning it. He pulled it out and handed it back. Then, he leaned over and touched his lips to hers, setting off sparklers inside her.

He pulled away slowly, and gave her a mischievous grin. "Don't worry. I know you don't want a man in your life. That was just a friendly kiss."

Needing to show him—and herself—that she was not a vulnerable little fool, she arched an eyebrow, then turned her back on him, stepping inside the house. As she shut the door in his face, she said, "We're not that good of friends."

She heard him chuckle, and it made her scowl. Lance Gregory fancied himself entirely too much in control of this relationship. *There is no relationship,* she reminded herself.

She stood, listening to his footsteps retreat down the walk. She heard his car door shut and the engine start.

Suddenly she realized she had heard another noise, too, one coming from right here in the house. A chill skipped up her spine, freezing her hot blood.

What was that? A door opening. She listened again. Movement, and from the general direction of the family room. Then, a low voice.

Shelby's car had been gone when Diana and Lance pulled up. There shouldn't be anyone in this house.

Fear jolted through Diana, and an instant regret that she hadn't gotten that alarm system she'd checked into after John's death. She opened the door and bolted out of the house.

She raced to the end of the front walk, hoping to flag Lance down, but all that was left of him was the glow of taillights at the end of the street. She did a quick scan to see who was home. Thank God, the Amundsens's porch light was on! Heart banging painfully against her rib cage, she began to run for their front door.

She was halfway across the lawn when a voice she hadn't heard since Thanksgiving called, "Diana, is that you?"

# *Ten*

*The porch light* came on and a head with hair the color of pink lemonade poked around the corner of Diana's front door. Diana would have known that lacquer helmet hairstyle anywhere.

"Mom!"

Her mother stepped out onto the porch. She was wearing her favorite gray wool slacks and a navy blue cardigan sweater over a white cotton turtleneck. She pulled the sweater more tightly around her as if she were an orphan caught in a blizzard.

"What are you doing running around on your front lawn?" she called.

Diana let out her breath and headed back for the house. She'd been so preoccupied with Lance she hadn't noticed the slightly battered Toyota. Now the thing stuck out like a cowlick. It would make the neighbors happy when they woke up in the morning and saw that new presence in the neighborhood. And there was no sense getting her mom anything new, because with the way Flo Bunt drove, it would look like garbage within six months.

"Honestly, Mother," scolded Diana, coming to give Flo a hug. "You nearly scared the skin off me. I thought you were a burglar. Why didn't you tell me you were coming?"

"I wanted to surprise you," said Flo.

"Well, you almost surprised me into a heart attack."

"If your heart is so weak, then you really should stop leaving that extra key in the flower pot on the back porch," retorted Flo. "Anyway, I thought you'd see my car."

"I didn't." Diana had reached the porch now, and she followed her mother back into the house, adding, "And why didn't you at least leave on a light?"

"I thought, perhaps, you'd gone away for a day or two, since no lights were on when I arrived. So what would be the sense? Really, Diana. You are so wasteful."

"I can afford to be wasteful. And, anyway, it's cheaper than keeling over from fear and having to take a ride in an ambulance." Her mother was looking perturbed, so Diana stopped the harangue and gave her another hug. "But it's good to see you."

"Thank you," said Flo regally, returning the hug and accepting these last words as if they were some form of apology.

"When did you get back from Ginny's?" asked Diana.

"Just Friday. But I missed seeing my baby girl so much, I did a quick load of laundry, straightened up the house, and headed on out the door. And here I am. Anyway, Ocean Shores is so blowy and unfriendly this time of year."

Diana smiled fondly. Her mother was a real gadabout. She usually spent Christmas and New Year's in Arizona with Diana's older sister, Virginia, and her husband, and then moved on to stay in California with Diana's brother and his wife. There she would spend the month of January, poking her nose into her grandsons' lives and insisting on helping her daughter-in-law with the housework, which usually meant rearranging her cupboards. But Diana's brother, the science professor (probably prompted by his wife), had just taken a teaching position at Alaska Pacific University in Anchorage, leaving Flo high and dry for a sunny spot to camp during January. Diana hoped her sweet, loving, busybody mother wasn't planning on spending the whole month with her baby girl.

"I don't know why you won't let me buy you a place in Arizona," she said.

"Because I don't need a place in Arizona," replied Flo. "If I lived down there all winter your sister would feel she had to entertain me, and I certainly don't want that. Besides, what would poor Harry Emerson do if I left him all winter long? Who would play chess with him?"

"In Ocean Shores? He could probably find plenty of older women . . ."

"Mature," interrupted Flo.

". . . mature women to play chess with him, among other things."

"Which is another reason I don't need to be away from home for months at a time." said Flo.

"I thought you always said absence makes the heart grow fonder," teased Diana.

"That's abstinence, dear," corrected her mother with a wink. She strolled off toward the family room again. "I found a cute movie on the A&E channel with Loretta Young. Want to join me?"

"Why not?" said Diana. She hung up her coat, then followed her little, pink-haired pixie of a mother down the hall, hoping for an opportunity to pump her about the proposed length of her visit.

It wasn't that she didn't want to see Flo. Diana loved her mother's visits. They had the same taste in books and movies, and enjoyed the same food. Flo was fond of Diana's friends and was always ready to try anything, from roller skating to karate. But the last thing Diana needed right now was to have her mother hovering over her like Cupid in drag, wanting to know every detail about Lance Gregory.

Well, if Mom was planning to dig in for more than a couple of days, Diana would put her to work cleaning her cupboards. She'd never be able to find anything again, but that was better than having her mother on hand to coach her through every phone conversation with Lance. How she would keep Flo from cornering him if he came to the house and telling him how pretty her daughter had been as a teenager was another matter. The only way Diana could prevent that would be to stuff her mother in one of the freshly cleaned cupboards.

Flo had staked out the huge couch in the family room, so Diana took a seat in the recliner and kicked off her shoes.

She was barely settled before her mother's interest in the movie waned. Flo cocked her head to one side and studied her daughter.

"You're all dressed up. Where have you been?"

"Just out with a friend," said Diana, keeping her voice casual. "Oh, I've seen this movie. It's great."

Her mother aimed the remote control and killed the power on the television. "Actually, I've seen it, too. Let's talk."

Diana braced herself.

"So, which of your friends were you out with? Suzanne?"

"No."

"Elise?"

"No."

Flo's eyes narrowed. "You are being very evasive."

"No. You're being very nosy. Good grief. You just got here and already we're starting the Spanish Inquisition."

"It's a man!" cried Flo. "Thank God, you've decided to live again."

"Oh, for heaven's sake, Mother," said Diana in disgust.

"Well, is it?" persisted Flo.

"Yes, it is," said Diana irritably. "But it's nothing romantic," she insisted. "We're just seeing each other as friends."

"And how long have you been seeing each other as friends?" asked Flo.

"This was only the second time we've been out."

Flo waved a hand. "Well, it's too early to tell, then, isn't it?"

"Yes, it is," agreed Diana.

"But you find him attractive?"

*Who wouldn't?* "Yes, he's nice looking," Diana admitted.

"Hmmm," said her mother thoughtfully.

"Mother."

Flo's eyes opened wide at the warning tone in her daughter's voice. "Really, dear. I don't know why you're being so defensive. I mean, I was just asking. What kind of mother would I be if I didn't care about what happened to my own daughter?"

"A less irritating one," muttered Diana.

"What?"

Diana smiled. "Never mind. For how long are you here?"

"Oh, I don't know," said Flo. "I do have to get back in time to plan the decorations and refreshments for the Valentine's Day party at the Senior Center. I suppose I won't be able to stay more than a couple of weeks."

Diana breathed an inward sigh of relief. Her mother couldn't cause too much mischief in that short a time.

"And how's our Shelby doing?" asked Flo. "Is she still going out with that nice young man?"

"Well, I'm not so sure that he's such a nice young man," said Diana. "He's balking at getting engaged."

Flo pursed her lips and shook her head. "Not a good

sign," she agreed. "Of course, in my day we weren't doing all this living together nonsense."

"No, in your day, everyone was just frantically having sex in the backseats of cars because they were sure their boyfriends would be killed in World War Two, and if they didn't have it then, they never would."

"Well I wasn't one of them," said Flo haughtily. "I was much too young for that anyway. And your father couldn't serve in the war, remember? He had flat feet."

Diana just shook her head.

"So," said her mother, returning them to the subject, "are Shelby and this boy living together?"

"No, Mother, they're not," said Diana, deciding they didn't need yet one more mother worrying about Shelby's sex life. Anyway, the kids each had separate places, so technically they weren't and she wasn't lying to her mom.

"Then what's the problem?" persisted Flo. "Is there something wrong with the boy? Doesn't he love her?"

"Actually, I don't think he does," said Diana.

"Oh, dear. What a shame," said Flo. "And I suppose she's still madly in love with him."

Diana thought about the new man on Shelby's horizon. "I'm not sure," she said thoughtfully. "I think Matt has got some competition."

"Well, there's nothing like a rival to motivate a man to propose," said Flo cheerfully.

And if Matt proposed would Shelby accept? Probably, thought Diana. It was what she had wanted all along.

"Oh, I almost forgot to tell you," said Flo, interrupting her daughter's musings, "Suzanne called for you earlier. She wanted to know where you were. I told her I didn't know," she added innocently.

Fishing again. Well, she wouldn't catch anything.

"That's okay," said Diana. "I'll call her tomorrow. I think I'm going to head off to bed. You've got all your things stowed away in the guest room?"

Flo nodded. "I'm all set." She picked up the remote and turned the television back on. "I guess I'll watch the rest of this movie, since my own daughter isn't going to tell me any more about her evening."

•Diana grinned. "Good idea," she said. "But I'll make it up to you tomorrow by making you French toast." She kissed her mother and headed off to her bedroom.

Once there, she decided to call Suzanne.

"Well, it's about time," said her friend. "I've been dying to know how things went with Mr. Wonderful."

Diana heard the faintest click on the line. "Mother, I'm on the phone," she said sternly.

"Oh, excuse me," said Flo. "I was just going to call Harry."

She hung up and Suzanne snickered. "Your mom's back, I see. With everything that's going on in your life right now, she's going to have a great time."

"If I don't murder her first."

"So tell me about Lance Gregory before she comes on the line again," demanded Suzanne.

"Well, he is pretty wonderful. We met for drinks last night, and that turned into dinner. And you'll never guess what we did tonight."

"Went to his house and made love in front of a roaring fire."

"Better than that. We went dancing."

"Dancing," breathed Suzanne. "He went voluntarily?"

"He suggested it."

"A man who dances. Oh, you lucky woman. And is he good?"

"He's incredible," said Diana, reliving their close encounters on the dance floor.

"I'm jealous," said Suzanne.

"Want me to ask if he's got a younger brother?" Diana offered.

"Don't bother. He sounds like one of a kind. I'll just live vicariously through you."

"You'll have to stand in line behind my mother," said Diana.

He had to win. He had to get Shelby back. Matt rubbed his aching forehead and glared at his phone. He had left two messages on her answering machine. She should have been home from her mom's by now. Where was she? And, more to the point, who was she with?

As if he couldn't guess. She was probably out with that wimp, David Jones. Matt swore and slammed his hand on the apartment wall, producing a howl of protest from his neighbor.

The adrenaline surge sapped his energy. He swallowed, trying to wash away the scratchy feeling spreading up his throat. Of all the times to start getting sick, this was not it, not when he needed all his strength to win Shelby back.

He really was feeling rotten. Maybe he'd just lie down on the couch, catch the last of the Sunday night movie. He'd hear the phone if it rang.

He grabbed the remote from the coffee table and punched the television to life. A grenade exploded on the screen, sending dirt shooting into the air like a fountain, scattering the running soldiers like bowling pins. Cool, a war movie. That should keep him awake.

He flopped on the couch and moaned. Geez, he was tired. And everything ached; his muscles, his bones, even the fillings in his teeth seemed to hurt. He tried to concentrate on the jungle war scene in front of him, but his eyelids keep distracting him. They felt like they weighed a hundred pounds each. Finally he found he hadn't the strength to keep them up. He'd just shut his eyes for a minute. There, that was better.

His body began to settle into the soft nothingness of

sleep. Now he was drifting, the boom and whine of war a distant rumble. Out there in the far distance something rang. And rang. And rang. Then stopped. And Matt drifted on, his subconscious heading deep into steamy jungles to save the world.

As he drove home, Lance realized that he had, once again, found himself as interested in Diana Barrett's mind as her body. Although, heaven knew coming into such teasingly close contact with that tempting little body had not left him unaffected. Still, he had simply enjoyed being with her, and when they were together, he actually forgot he had any ulterior motive at all for seeing her.

All in all, he couldn't remember when he had felt so compelled to be around a woman. Well, there was that one time, but she had been no Diana Barrett. Of course, he'd been infatuated many times before, and even just plain greedy to test his skills on any number of feminine curves. The parade of willing women he had romanced in his youth while working as a purser on the *Caribbean Star* had given him a taste for flings and flirtations. As long as he was the one in control. And that didn't change after he returned to the life of a landlubber with his fat savings account and his cache of Caribbean jewels.

There had been that one time, though, when he imagined he had found true love. He had met Allison Swain at a five-hundred-dollar-a-plate fund-raiser. She had been tall and elegant and well-mannered, and he had imagined she was interested in sharing his life. But when he came home early from a business trip and stopped by her place to surprise her and take her out to dinner, it was he who got the surprise. Allison had another man on the side, a distant cousin who already had lodged himself in the center of her heart. All she had really wanted to share with Lance was his bank account.

After that, he'd retreated to the safety of his old behavior patterns, spending the next ten years indulging himself in romances that went nowhere. Even after deciding he was ready to change from Don Juan to Ward Cleaver, he found himself always tiring of what he caught once the chase was over and moving on to someone new.

But Diana Barrett appeared to be a different animal than the ones he usually hunted. She stood alone, completely self-sufficient and successful in her own right. From that first verbal sparring match at Canlis, he'd known she was his equal, both in age and intellect, which made dating her an intriguing novelty. Of course, the sexual attraction was there, too. Dancing with her had been sweet torture: every time her dress had swirled around her thighs he'd had to fight the urge to reach out and run his hand along the expanse of shining leg. But Diana promised to be more than a bed partner; certainly more than a casual companion.

Lance frowned. What kind of sentimental claptrap was this? He needed to remember that he was just playing an agreeable game. And when the game was over, he'd move on.

Matt wasn't at work on Monday, and Shelby looked over to his vacant desk with mixed feelings. She had been perturbed when she called him back and got only his recorded voice, telling her to leave a message. Another time she would have given a syrupy effusion telling him how she missed him. Last night she'd gotten right to the point and asked him what he knew about his uncle and her mother, then demanded he call her back. And now, today, she wasn't looking at his empty desk with the same longing she would have felt only a few days ago. Instead, she found herself wondering what David Jones was doing.

Her phone rang. It was David, and the sound of his

voice made her feel like she'd eaten Mexican jumping beans for breakfast.

"What are you doing tonight?" he asked.

"Watching Monday night football," she joked.

"Really?"

He sounded so eager, so pleased, she didn't have the heart to tell him she thought football was the stupidest game ever invented. All those men, scrabbling around in the mud, falling on each other. Ugh!

"I've got an idea," he said. "I had to tape one of the playoff games this weekend. Why don't you come over to my place and watch it."

What should she do now, fess up or go over and pretend to have a clue? No, pretending wasn't an option. She was too clueless.

"Actually, I was just kidding," she said. "I don't understand the first thing about football. I never can find the person who has the ball until right before everybody makes a big pile on top of him."

"Well, football is like chess. It's only fun if you understand the strategy."

"I guess," said Shelby dubiously.

"In honor of Super Bowl Sunday, which is right around the corner, I think you should come over to my place and let me give you a crash course," said David.

"Football for dummies?"

"Football for the uninformed," he corrected. "I'll even throw in dinner. Good, hearty football food."

She could just imagine. Pretzels and Bud Light.

"Okay," she said, vowing to make herself a salad before heading in his direction.

She ran a couple of errands after work, then went home to make her salad. She entered the apartment to find a party in full swing.

"Shelby! Come on in. Have a drink," called James, her fellow actor from the Civic Light Opera.

"Sure. What are we celebrating this time?"

"My call from the Fifth Avenue."

"You got called?"

He nodded. "Just this afternoon. Isn't that incredible? I'm so glad I didn't take the Burien Little Theater offer, although that would have been a plum role. But this. The Fifth! I'm in heaven."

Shelby's pulse rate was dancing. That meant they had to have heard. She'd known she'd done well! She turned expectantly to Leeza, who was sitting crossed-legged on the floor. "Did we get a call?"

Leeza looked as if she was screwing up her courage to tell Shelby about a death in the family. "Um. I did."

"Yeah?"

"I'm in."

"Great! How about me?" Even as she asked the question, Shelby knew the answer wasn't going to be good. She'd known it from the moment James had shared his good news. Something dark and heavy settled in her stomach, making her feel queasy.

Leeza lowered her gaze to her plastic cup of champagne. "There weren't any calls for you."

"That doesn't mean you won't," said James quickly.

*Smile. Not that fakey thing beauty pageant losers wear. Dig deep. Find your joy for your friends' happiness.* Shelby dug clear down to her toenails and came up with a small but sincere smile.

"I'm happy for you guys," she said.

"Hey, don't panic yet," said Leeza, getting up and crossing the room to give her a hug.

"Yeah. I didn't get called yet, either," piped Anne Marie from her corner of the couch.

As the freckle-faced Anne Marie was as close to no talent as an actress could get and still have the nerve to call herself an actress, Shelby found it hard to find consolation in her words.

"I'm not panicking," she said.

"Of course, you are," said James. "My God. I was a nervous wreck when I heard Lee had gotten called."

"Lee heard, too?" squeaked Shelby.

"They haven't called everyone yet," said James. "Cindy hasn't heard anything yet, neither has Vic. And you know they'll call Vic because he's the best dancer on the planet."

Shelby nodded. James was right. There wasn't any need to panic just yet. She took a deep drink of the cheap champagne Leeza had stuck in her hand. "You know, even if I didn't have the look they wanted for Nimue, wouldn't you think I'd still make it into the chorus?"

"Of course," said the other three.

Shelby looked at James's dark hair and brown eyes and perfect jawline, at Leeza's brown hair and statuesque figure. That had to be it. Her look was wrong. She was too short. Her hair was too red. Oh, geez. Had Bernadette Peters ever gone through this?

"Oh well, it's not the end of the world," she said brightly. "There's always next season." Why, oh why hadn't she'd gone to the general audition at the Burien Little Theater with James in December? Surely she would have gotten a part there.

Because she'd been stupid and put all her eggs in this one basket, that was why. What had she been thinking of, anyway?

Nothing. She hadn't been thinking, and that was the problem. She'd been so busy with her love life that she'd let her acting life unravel. *Fool. Stupid fool!*

"Some food will make you feel better," said Leeza. "We're going to Benahani's to meet Horst for sushi."

"I can't. I'm supposed to go over to David's." *And lose my focus even more than I already have.* She had already allowed one man to mess up her life. Now she was starting in on a new one. The Mad Hatter had nothing on her.

"Okay," said Leeza. "We'll all go out and party again when you get your call."

"Sure," said Shelby brightly.

She watched as her friends donned coats and scarves and headed for the door. For a moment, she was tempted to go with them. After all, no one understood the misery of not getting that all-important call for a part better than another actor. But there was also no one worse to be around when you were the one on the outside looking in. Shelby knew she'd only be miserable, and she'd be a wet blanket on their celebration, too, as the role of selfless friend was not one she could sustain all evening. She'd master it eventually, but it would take a while. She waved them out the door, then went to change and freshen up, dragging along her heavy heart.

She slipped into jeans and a black cotton turtleneck, even got as far as putting on her favorite old loafers. But at the door, she turned herself back. This was ridiculous. She wasn't even good company for herself, let alone someone else. Especially not another man. She needed to put herself on a strict no male regimen and pull her acting life together, and she might as well start tonight.

She dialed David. He answered on the first ring, as though he'd been sitting by the phone, waiting for her to call.

"I'm going to pass on the football game," she said.

"No problem. Wanna tell why?"

"I wouldn't be good company tonight."

"And why is that?"

"Because I'm mildly suicidal."

"Interesting. How are you going to do it?"

"I don't know yet. Nothing messy."

"That's good to know. I think it's a shame to desecrate works of art."

He was so sweet. His words made her voice tremble. "I wish you were a director."

"Oh. Now I get it. No news from the Fifth Avenue yet, huh?"

"Three of my friends have heard." She rubbed her head as if the pressure of her hand on her forehead would turn the tide of escaping tears back behind her eyes.

"If you're feeling suicidal you definitely shouldn't be alone."

"I'm just not up to coming over," said Shelby. In fact, she wasn't up to much of anything other than sitting on the couch, reliving her callback audition and trying to figure out where she went wrong.

"You shouldn't be on the streets in your present condition, anyway," said David. "You might do something crazy, like drive off an embankment. Stay put. I've got just what you need."

What she needed was no men in her life, but before she could get out the words he'd already hung up.

Half an hour later, David was buzzing to be let in, and Shelby found herself unable to be so ungracious as to turn him away after he'd gone to the trouble of coming over to comfort her.

She pointed to the video tucked under his arm as he walked through the door. "I need to watch a movie?"

He turned the video to show her the cover. There stood Dustin Hoffman in a red sequined evening gown and a wig. "*Tootsie*."

She shook her head in amazement. "You are incredible."

"I was a shrink in another life. Now. You will watch other struggling actors and remember why you do this," he said with a Freudian accent. "You'll laugh a little, get inspired, and then you'll feel better."

He pulled a bag of microwave popcorn out of his jacket pocket. "Everything we need, except the pop." He looked around the room at the plastic glasses and the empty champagne bottle and shrugged. "Maybe you're not thirsty anymore."

"We were celebrating," said Shelby.

David smiled at her. "I'd say if you could toast your friends' success, you're Academy Award material."

"I'd rather have a Tony."

"It's yours," he said. He scooped up the champagne bottle and presented it to her. "And the winner is . . . Shelby Barrett."

She lost her smile. Her lower lip wobbled with the strain of holding back the tears. "They all went out to dinner. I couldn't go. I . . . couldn't . . ." Tears choked off the sentence and she sank onto the love seat.

David joined her and wrapped his arms around her. "Hey, now. What's this?"

"I never thought I could make it on Broadway, but I'd hoped I could at least manage the Fifth Avenue. Now it looks like I can't even do that. It's a good thing I got my Master's. Those who can't teach."

"You won't be teaching," said David firmly.

"How do you know?" demanded Shelby, pulling away. "You've never seen me act."

"I feel it. There's something about you that's . . . I don't know . . . magical."

Shelby gave a snort and rolled her eyes. "Oh, please."

"No. it's true. I can't describe it. It's like an aura. Audrey Hepburn had it, Julia Roberts has it. You've got it. I don't know what it is, but I can see it in the great ones. And I think you've got it."

"Yeah, I know. Sandra Bullock has got nothing on me."

David grinned. "Whoever said that was a very smart man."

Shelby lifted the champagne bottle and examined it. "Were you here drinking this stuff and I didn't notice? How much did you have, anyway?"

"Go ahead, laugh. But one day you'll see I'm right."

Shelby wasn't up for laughing, but thanks to David, she managed to achieve a smile. "You should rent yourself out for pep talks to struggling actors," she said. "You could make a fortune."

David got off the couch, carrying his popcorn to the microwave, saying, "Nah, I have to mean what I say, and I'm sure there are plenty of people out there I couldn't make that comment to with any conviction."

"You don't think, perhaps, you're just a little biased?"

"No."

He stood guard at the microwave until the popcorn had popped, then returned, inserted his rental tape in the VCR, and joined Shelby on the couch.

"Okay, now watch this," he commanded.

She did. And Dustin Hoffman's character spoke to her, reminding her that she was an actress and she had to work, that there was no excuse for not acting.

He was right. And if she didn't get on at the Fifth Avenue, so what? She would get a part somewhere, because she had to act. It was what made her soul sing.

She turned to David after Tootsie Dustin and Jessica Lange had walked off down the New York sidewalk, dragging the ending credits behind them. "Thanks for bringing that over. You were right, doc. It was just what I needed."

"Anything else I can get you?"

"I don't think so," she said. "I'm fine."

"That you are," he agreed, moving closer to her.

Shelby's insides twitched and she held her breath. Big love scene coming up.

He tucked her under his arm and it felt so natural. She exhaled.

"Why don't you forget the stage?" he murmured. "You should do movies."

"And why is that?"

"Because you have the kind of face that is perfect for close-ups.

He was looking at her lips like a thirsty man would look at a tall glass of ice water. Then he was lowering his head, and Shelby found she was holding her breath once more.

# *Eleven*

*David's lips touched* Shelby's, lightly at first, starting a slow warmth spreading through her body. Then the pressure increased, the kiss deepened, and the big fireworks started, and they weren't going off in her head. The next thing she knew, she was slipping her arms around his neck, diving her fingers into his curls, and he was pulling her closer. When he finally released her, her lips were tingling with the memory of his touch.

"That was incredible," he murmured. "You're incredible." He moved aside her hair and kissed her neck, shooting electric volts down her chest. Then he took her chin in his hand and turned her face back to his. "One more for the road," he said, and covered her lips again.

She would have kept the kiss going indefinitely, but he stopped it, pulling away and saying, "I think that's all I can take for a while."

She looked at him, puzzled. He was going to stop with two kisses? What was wrong with him?

As if reading her thoughts, he said, "We'd better stop before I get completely wild and crazy."

"I like wild and crazy," said Shelby, pulling close again.

He set her firmly away. "I'm not just after your body, Shelby. I want the whole package. I want your heart, too. Right now, part of it still belongs to Matt, doesn't it?"

From the way she had just kissed David, it would seem that Matt's share was shrinking rapidly. She sat back and fell silent, wondering what was going on in her own head. It seemed like lately her thoughts chased each other around her brain like horses on a carousel.

"I don't know," she admitted.

"I'm willing to wait until you do. You're worth waiting for."

That was downright heroic. David obviously watched too many old movies. Or else he was a time traveler from a more chivalrous era, trying to pretend he fit in with modern life. Or maybe he was just an amazingly romantic and sweet man.

And maybe he was a man who deserved a woman who had her act together, one who could separate stage roles from reality, and who really was as ready to settle down as she claimed.

She shook her head. "I'm a flake. You should get while the getting's good."

"I thought all actresses were flaky," said David. "That's why they need someone stable in their life. And when it comes to stable, they don't come any better than me."

His smile reminded her of Hugh Grant, and the way he was looking at her made her want to grab him and kiss him again. She reminded herself she wasn't Julia Roberts, and this wasn't a scene from *Notting Hill*.

"You're right," she said. "We'd better stop."

She walked him to the door and he turned in the doorway and tapped her nose. "Good night, star."

Star. The way he said it made Shelby determined to believe in herself again. She shut the door and leaned against it. Life wasn't as bleak as she had thought just a few short hours ago. She began to dance her way through the apartment, collecting plastic cups and belting out the words from her favorite song in the musical *Funny Girl*. David was right. She was by far the greatest star.

And David Jones knew it. He was better than motivational tapes.

When he was pursuing a woman, Lance followed certain rules. Rule number one was to wait a week after a first date to call her. That waiting period kept her wondering, built excitement. This time, however, he was finding it difficult to hold to his rule. He'd already made an exception by taking Diana dancing the same weekend they'd met for drinks. But surely drinks didn't count as a date, even if they had evolved into dinner. Anyway, he was on a mission to help his favorite nephew, and they were fighting the clock, after all.

He closed the book Diana had authored and sat contemplating its cover. It showed a wall hung with portraits symbolizing three generations of the family chronicled within. *If Walls Could Talk*, read the title. This book preceded Diana's latest, which he had already devoured, and now he was two-thirds through this one and trying to prolong the pleasure. He ran his fingers over the embossed gold letters of her name. Diana Valentine. Great pen name. If things kept progressing this rapidly between them, it wouldn't be long before he found out if it fit the woman as well as he suspected. Did he really want to wait a week to talk to her?

"Are you going to lay down any time soon?" demanded Flo.

Diana captured her wandering thoughts and discarded. Dumb. Why had she parted with the ace of hearts when she needed it for a run?

Her mother gleefully snatched it up, then proceeded to spread her hand on the kitchen table. "Gin."

"Great," said Diana. "You caught me with at least fifty." She counted out the points represented by the cards she was holding and added them to her already high score. "I hate this game," she groused, shoving the cards toward her mother.

Flo picked them up and began to shuffle. "You never used to," she said. "But then you've never played this badly. I think you're just a little distracted tonight."

"I'm still working out my murder scene," said Diana.

Her mother smiled slyly. "I think it's a love scene you're working on."

"Really, Mother," Diana said in disgust.

"Yes, really," said Flo. "So, are you going to tell me about this man or not?"

"There's not much to tell. We've only gone out a couple of times."

"Well, after two dates you should have something to say."

"He's incredibly good-looking," said Diana.

"That's nice, but what is he like?"

"Sophisticated, intelligent."

"Smooth?"

Diana nodded.

"Humph," grunted Flo. "Shades of Dan Sterling. I never liked that boy."

"He's not quite like Dan. He does have quite a line, but I think he's deeper."

"So, after two dates there's not much to tell except that you've discerned he's a deep thinker?" scoffed Flo.

"That's about the sum of it."

Her mother stopped shuffling and slapped the deck of cards on the table. "Diana, do you know what you're doing?"

"Of course," lied Diana. "I am seeing this man as friends."

Her mother lowered her glasses down her nose and surveyed Diana with an expression that made her feel fourteen all over again.

"Good grief, Mother," said Diana. "Give me credit for having developed some sense in the last twenty-five years."

"When it comes to men, even the most sensible woman can get stupid in a big hurry," said Flo. "I'd just hate to see you hurt."

Diana's lips tugged up at that. Her mother's statement so echoed her own feelings in regard to Shelby she could be listening to herself.

"It never changes, does it?" she mused. "That whole mother-daughter thing. No matter what your age, you're still a mother, and no matter what your daughter's age, she's still your child."

"And you worry," added Flo. "I want to see you happy, dear. And really happy this time."

"I was happy with John," protested Diana.

"Yes. Mildly so."

"He was a good man," Diana insisted.

"Yes, he was," agreed her mother. "A good, sweet, boring specimen of manhood. You've had a sleeze and a slug. I'd love to see you find something in between the two extremes."

"I don't want to find anyone," said Diana. "I'm perfectly content as I am."

"That's what every pauper says until she wins the lottery."

"Well, you know what the odds are against that," said Diana. "Are you going to talk or deal?"

Flo dealt, and the next hand was a worse mess than the first. Diana was just tallying the damage when the phone on the kitchen wall rang. She reached up behind her and lifted the receiver then said a grumpy hello.

"Hello. Diana?"

Lance Gregory's rich baritone voice thrummed in her ear and set off tremors in her stomach. Good vibrations. They pulled a smile out of her, which made her mother lay down her cards and narrow her eyes.

"I was just sitting here reading another one of your books," said Lance.

"Who is it?" hissed Flo.

Diana ignored her. "Oh, which one?"

"*If Walls Could Talk*. Great title. You should have saved it for a mystery."

"It fits that plot," said Diana.

"Yes, actually, it does. I'm enjoying the book."

"I'm glad to hear it."

"It's a little edgier than your earlier efforts, but I like it. Will you autograph it for me?"

"Is it Lance?" demanded Flo.

Diana stood up and turned her back on her mother. Barrymore entered the room and, seeing her turn toward the counter, stalked up and rubbed against her, making his own bid for attention or, rather, food. She moved him away with her foot and he took a swipe at her calf.

"I want to meet him," said Flo, the decibel of her voice rising.

"I hear a voice. Do you have company?"

"Only my cat and my mother, who are both pestering me at the moment," said Diana, trying to shame Flo into silence.

"I can call back," Lance offered.

"Please don't leave me. She's torturing me."

"Very funny," muttered Flo.

Lance chuckled. "Isn't that what mothers are for?"

"Mine seems to think so."

"So, when can I get my autograph?" he asked.

"When would you like it?"

"Right now."

"How about tomorrow?"

"All right. You can give it to me over dinner. How about if I pick you up at seven?"

"Okay," said Diana. "But don't expect more than an autograph. I meant what I said when we first met."

"I know. Just for fun," said Lance.

"That's right."

"You drive a hard bargain, Ms. Valentine. I'll see you tomorrow."

Diana hung up, wondering who needed reminding the most, Lance or herself. She came out of her trance to see her mother, arms crossed over her chest, studying her and wearing a frown.

"I'm not sure I like this," said Flo.

"Don't worry," said Diana. "I really can handle myself."

Flo sighed heavily.

Diana picked up the deck of cards and began to deal a new hand, saying, "I have a feeling the tide of this game is going to turn."

"Oh? And why is that?"

"Because worry has reared its ugly head to break your concentration," teased Diana.

"I hope the only thing that gets broken around here is my concentration," retorted her mother.

Lance called Avenue One, a popular nineteen-thirties-Parisian-style cafe, and made a dinner reservation, specifying that he wanted a quiet corner table. The place had a unique decor, featuring a thirty-foot coved ceiling and a chandelier of Marano glass, as well as a stunning mural that took up almost an entire wall. The food was equally excellent, winning the restaurant a place in the December 1999 issue of *Bon Appétit* magazine. Fine food, vintage wine, a romantic setting, and a beautiful woman: the perfect combination. And, maybe, somewhere along the way, he could persuade Diana Barrett that their relationship wouldn't suffer for having a few strings attached to it.

On Wednesday Shelby went to lunch with David. In spite of his obvious motivational gifts, she had intended not to see him for a while, to give herself time to concentrate on her career, to come up with a plan B in case the Fifth Avenue didn't call, but, like he'd said when he suggested they meet, she had to eat.

"There's nothing wrong with having friends," he'd added, "and going out to lunch with one won't get you kicked out of the Actors' Guild."

"Yes, but that's not all you want to be."

"Of course not," he had replied. "Didn't you ever see *When Harry Met Sally*? So, how about it? Lunch at Palomino's?"

"I'll meet you at twelve-fifteen," said Shelby.

"This is great," David said, as soon as they'd fought the crowd and found a table. "Maybe I'll luck out and Matt will stay sick all month."

"Oh, nice guy," said Shelby.

"Well, you'd know him better than I would," said David.

"I meant you, and you know it."

David grinned. He lifted his glass of Italian soda. "Here's to nice guys. May they learn to finish first."

"I guess I can drink to that with a clear conscience," said Shelby.

And she did. She and Matt were still a non-couple, and if he didn't want her to have lunch with other men he could get her an engagement ring. Because right now that was the only thing that would stop her.

● ● ●

She popped in at her mom's that evening to discuss the current state of her love life, but found her mother gone and her grandmother home.

"Gram!" she cried, giving the older woman a hug. "Mom didn't tell me you were here."

"Oh, I haven't been here that long," said Gram, leading the way into the living room. "Just long enough to hear that you now have two young men after you."

"Well, I have one after me, anyway," said Shelby, curling herself into a corner of the couch. "The other just takes me for granted."

Flo's lips pursed in disapproval at that. "Well, I can't imagine any young man so foolish as to take my favorite granddaughter for granted."

"Also your only granddaughter," pointed out Shelby.

"That, too."

She looked at her grandmother with mock sternness. "And when were you going to get around to calling and telling me you were here?"

"Oh, just as soon as I'd finished meddling in your mother's life," replied Gram airily. "You were next on the list."

"Where is Mom, by the way?"

"She's having dinner with Lance Gregory."

"Hmmm," said Shelby.

"What is this Lance Gregory like? I can't get much out of your mother."

"He's a wolf. He's Matt's uncle, and the whole family calls him Lance Romance."

"Lance Romance." Gram nodded her head. "I thought he sounded like a smoothie."

"I'm not sure I like the idea of Mom going out with him," said Shelby. "I think Matt put him up to it, although I'm not sure why."

"Well, your mother is normally a bright woman. Hopefully, if there is an ulterior motive to Mr. Gregory's courtship, she'll find it."

"She says she's not interested in him," said Shelby.

"She's lying."

Shelby chewed her lower lip. "I don't want her to get hurt, Gram."

"Don't worry, dear," said Gram. "Your mother has been around long enough to learn her lessons in love. In the end, she'll know how to take care of herself."

"Do you really believe that?"

"I think so."

Diana and Lance had gotten to dessert when he handed over her book, along with his gold pen. "Just write something simple, like, 'To Lance, the most wonderful and inspiring man I know.' "

Diana cocked an eyebrow, then took the pen and wrote. She finished with a flourish and pushed the book back at him.

He read, "To Lance. If the walls could talk about you, would we all be blushing?" He pulled a face. "Cute. Now, how can I show that to my friends?"

"With perverse pleasure?"

He grimaced. "I suppose that's the best you're going to do for me."

"You suppose correctly," Diana agreed.

"I guess we can be thankful walls can't talk," he said. "What, by the way, are the walls saying about my nephew and your daughter these days?"

A tiny warning bell went off in Diana's head. Could Shelby's far-fetched theory be correct? Was Matt Armstrong really using his uncle to influence her so that she, in turn, would influence Shelby?

"I thought you'd pulled out of the battle," she countered.

"I have. I'm neutral, but still curious."

"If you must know, I think your nephew has some competition."

Lance nodded. "Ah, the eternal triangle: two men do battle for the lady's heart."

"I'd be surprised if Matt came out of it a winner," said Diana. "He isn't willing to make the kind of investment he needs to win this war. No woman wants a man who can't commit."

"Yourself excepted," said Lance.

"Been there. Done that."

"Didn't like it enough to do it again?"

"Just don't need it," said Diana. "I have other things to occupy my time."

Lance leaned across the table and ran a finger up her arm, making the sensitive nerves under her skin sizzle. "Surely, even a woman as busy as yourself could find time for a little romance with the right man."

Diana pulled her arm away and took a sip of coffee. "You seem to have a faulty memory chip, Mr. Gregory."

"There's nothing wrong with my memory," said Lance, leaning back in his seat. "There's nothing wrong with my eyesight or my perception, either."

Diana began to feel nervous, but she put on a good face. "Oh? And just what is it you perceive about me?"

"The obvious fact that you're a woman who has too much fire left in her to remain alone for the next thirty years of her life. But you're afraid of it."

"Oh, please," drawled Diana.

Lance ignored her and continued with his assessment. "I think Diana Barrett may not have had the kind of perfect relationship she writes about in books and it's colored her thinking. She loves to invent men who are vigorous and interesting, heroes who eventually manage to act heroically, but she believes that in real life all men are either boring or selfish."

"And she's wrong?" challenged Diana.

"I think so," said Lance. "But it's hard to admit when you're wrong about the opposite sex, because if you do that, then you have to give them a chance. Give a guy a chance and he'll slip right past your armor."

"Well, then," said Diana, "let's see if I'm wrong. Let's talk about Lance Gregory for a minute and see what category of man he fits into. He is well-educated, suave, has a variety of interests. And probably has known many women. Am I correct?"

Lance tried to look modest.

"So he certainly can't be boring. What category does that leave us?" Diana continued, and the smile that had been playing on Lance's lips suddenly went away. "Why, exactly, haven't you married?" she pressed.

He shrugged. "I never found the right woman."

"Oh, come now. I find that hard to believe. As many women as you have to have known, surely there was one somewhere along the way who met your exacting standards."

She saw his lips tighten, saw the hard line of his jaw come into relief against muscles suddenly gone rigid with anger. She had definitely hit a nerve. She raised both eyebrows, daring him to prove her wrong.

He took a sudden interest in studying the fusion painting of Paris in the thirties that ran along the wall.

"There was a Miss Right once," he said at last. "At least that was what I thought. But it turned out she wasn't in love with me, only my bank account. She had another man on the side."

Each word came out tersely, as if snipped short by pain still very much alive. Diana felt like she had just trampled on something sacred. And she had: the man's pride.

He turned back to face her and his eyes were hard.

She lowered her gaze, unable to meet them. "I'm sorry."

"Don't be," he said, his poise returning. "I'm not. It was a narrow escape. I'm smart enough to realize that all women aren't like that, and open-minded enough to give your sex another chance. I wonder, Diana. Can you say the same thing?"

"Why should I have to? There's nothing wrong with choosing to live the rest of my life alone," countered Diana.

He nodded. "No, as long as you're choosing for the right reasons."

Diana gave him a cynical smile. "It's very noble of you to want to help me sort out my feelings and save me from myself."

"Save you for myself, you mean. I guess we both know what category of man I fall into. But maybe I don't want to be selfish all my life."

"And maybe I misjudged you."

"I guess you'll just have to spend more time with me so you can find out."

More time feeling unsettled and nervous and out of control. She looked at her watch. "I should get home."

"Yes, your mother might be worried," teased Lance. Diana looked pained and he chuckled. "How about if we take the long way home? No freeway. If we dawdle long enough, she'll be in bed by the time you get in."

Diana shook her head. "Probably not. If only I'd had the foresight to break a sleeping pill into her afternoon tea."

Lance took the scenic route back to Edmonds and, somehow, they wound up parked in front of the beach instead of Diana's house. To the north, they could see a ferry slipping up to the dock, coming in from nearby Kingston.

"How about a ferry ride to top off the night?" he suggested.

Diana slanted him a look. "More trying to save me from myself?"

"Can't friends ride the ferry together?" He got out of the car before she could answer.

"I guess they can," she said, watching him come around to open her door.

Lance purchased two walk-on tickets for them, and they followed the string of foot passengers down the dock and onto the ferry.

Once on the boat they went outside to the upper deck railing to watch the cars load onto the car deck beneath. Diana had her camel hair coat buttoned and her gloves on, but no hat. A nippy gust mussed her hair and sent a shiver slipping down her neck. Or was it Lance's close proximity?

The last of the cars rolled on and the ferry workers pulled away the heavy ropes that moored the boat to the dock, then set about securing the back end of the boat against rolling automobiles. The water beneath churned as the boat began to pull slowly away.

The breeze grew icy and gained strength, wrapping around Diana's legs and making her wish she'd worn slacks to dinner instead of a dress and panty hose. It pulled harder at her coat and sent her short curls flying in all directions. She clutched her coat collar tight to her neck and pushed a strand of hair out of her eyes with her free hand. The wind blew on her cheeks, making them tingle.

Lance laid an arm on the rail and turned to regard her. "You look beautiful," he murmured. "Friends can tell each other that, can't they?"

"I suppose so," said Diana. Still holding her collar close, she propped her elbows on the rail and watched the Edmonds waterfront begin to diminish as the boat pulled farther out into Puget Sound.

Now the wind grew furious, and Diana shivered and rubbed her arms.

"You're cold," said Lance, and before she could suggest they go inside, he'd moved in back of her, pulled her against him, and wrapped his arms around her. "There. Is that better?"

"The front of me is still cold," she said.

He turned her around and nestled her close to him, and her blood began to churn like the waters beneath the boat.

"How's that?" he asked.

She smiled up at him. "Better." *What was she doing? What was she thinking?*

His head lowered and she shut her eyes as his hand slipped to the back of her skull, cradling it with warmth. Then his lips touched hers and she forgot that she had ever been cold.

By the time the boat docked in Kingston, Diana's lips were swollen and she felt like a river at flood season. She turned out of Lance's embrace and let the wind chill her flushed cheeks.

"Diana," he said gently.

She shook her head. "This really isn't a good idea."

"What are you so afraid of?"

She turned again to face him. "You. I think you're heartbreak in a suit, and I don't want to be hurt. It's not fun."

"I know," he said softly.

"Then let's not go there. Let's go dancing and discuss mysteries. Let's not mess this relationship up with chemistry. I don't want to have to clean up the mess."

Before he could say anything, she walked back inside the boat, leaving him to follow if he wished.

She settled onto a seat by the window and looked out at nothing. Lance's reflection walked past. Well, that settled that.

Ten minutes later, the boat was pulling away for its return trip and he was back with two cups of coffee. He handed one to her. The smile he was wearing wasn't his usual charming number. It was simple, sweet, with nothing to sell.

"Are we friends again?"

"Friendships take a long time to develop," said Diana.

"I've got time."

"I wonder," she mused.

How long before he realized she meant what she said and tired of the chase? She had been enjoying spending time with Lance Gregory and she hated to give that up. But he would eventually lose interest in doing things with a woman when there was no payoff in sight and drift out of her life. The thought saddened her.

"What are you thinking?" he asked.

"That this probably won't last," she answered honestly. "You'll either want to conquer me or you'll move on to find a woman you can."

"How did such a beautiful woman get so cynical?"

"Realistic," she corrected.

He sighed and shook his head. "I hope you're wrong about me."

"So do I," said Diana.

# Twelve

As *Lance drove* away from Diana's house, he caught sight of his reflection in the rearview mirror. And for the first time in more years than he could remember, he didn't like what he saw. Heartbreak in a suit, conqueror.

*Don't hold anything back. Ms. Valentine. Tell me how you really feel.*

All right. So he'd been using women for years, just like they'd been using him. Women enjoyed his company, they wore the jewelry he bought them to the nice places he took them and loved every minute of it. He always did his part in a relationship. How many hearts really got broken?

He frowned. Suddenly the pleasant game he'd been playing with Diana Barrett, a.k.a. Valentine, wasn't so pleasant anymore. And he wasn't so sure it was still a game, either.

Diana was glad to find that her mother had, indeed, given up on her and turned in for the night. She went to her bedroom, shed her clothes and slipped into bed. Loneliness climbed in next to her.

It wasn't the same kind of feeling she had experienced after John's death. That sad emptiness had known no hope, but neither had it known uncertainty. She had loss, but she also had the security of a life with no one in it who could break her heart. This new loneliness saw the equal possibility of gain and hurt, and it yearned for the feel of a hard body next to hers, of strong arms wrapped around her middle, for legs tangled with hers in the sheets. She bunched up her pillow and buried her face in it, and felt the sting of hot, salty tears. Hope and fear hugged each side of her. There wasn't room for three in this bed. Someone would have to go.

Lance walked unseeingly past the credenza in the entryway that held the twenty-five-thousand-dollar piece of Chilhuly glasswork which normally gave him such a surge of accomplishment and pleasure. He shot a glance at the living room off to the left. It looked like something out of a magazine, with its buttery leather couch and matching love seat, its pristine glass coffee table. The whole room looked sterile and cold, like his life.

The answering machine on the kitchen counter flashed him a welcome home. He pressed the play button.

"Hey, Uncle Lance. It's Matt. I'm home sicker than a dog. I have a feeling that shrimp Jones is moving in on Shelby. Has her mom said anything about him to you? Can you call me when you get in?"

The next voice that came on was female. "Hey Lancer," it said in sultry tones. "Haven't heard from you in a while. Call me."

Lance sighed and made the call.

"Well, it's about time I heard from you," said Adele Bertelli. "I was beginning to think you died."

"No, I'm still alive and kicking. Just busy. Can you get away from work to meet me for lunch on Friday?"

"Lunch, not dinner?" she chided, showing that she well

understood the difference on a romantic scale between the two.

"Let's do lunch," said Lance.

"Okay," she said, her voice less enthusiastic than it had been when they started their conversation.

Lance could almost feel a small demon that looked a lot like Diana Barrett jumping up and down on his shoulder, screaming, "User, user!"

He gave it a mental swat, and said, "I'll make reservations for noon at Cutters."

"All right," said Adele. "See you then."

Lance hung up and punched in his nephew's phone number. The kid picked up on the second ring, croaking a weak hello.

"You could have trouble," said Lance. "I was just out with Shelby's mom, and it looks like you're losing the race." Lance waited for his nephew to finish swearing, then continued. "I don't know what else to tell you, kid. You win some, you lose some. Why don't you move on and let Shelby get on with her life?"

"I don't want to lose Shelby," protested Matt.

Lance sighed. He really had no desire to be his nephew's love coach anymore.

"Look, kid. I think you're stuck on your own on this. We've given it a good shot, but the bottom line is, Shelby wants to be married. Now, you can buy her presents and romance the hell out of her, but it's going to keep coming back to that."

"I don't mind it coming back to that eventually," said Matt. "Just not yet. And I can't even talk to her when I'm out sick."

"That's what florists are for," said Lance. "Look, I wish I could help you more, but I think I've done about all I can."

"You're still going out with her mom, aren't you?" asked Matt.

"Yeah," said Lance warily.

"Well, can't you put in a good word for me?"

Lance was having a hard enough time just putting in a good word for himself. "Right now there is no good word for you," he said, "and the only way to change that is to cough up a ring."

He could almost feel the waves of stubbornness coming off his nephew. It was hopeless. The kid was going to lose his girl, and that would be that. Maybe he'd learn something from the situation. Probably not, though. When it came right down to it, Matt was selfish, just like his uncle Lance.

"Get some sleep, kid," said Lance, and hung up. He knew he wouldn't be sleeping much tonight with all he had to think about. "Get some for both of us," he added.

Matt felt like dirt, but he still hauled himself out of bed at ten A.M. to call Hearts and Flowers and order a dozen long-stemmed white roses sent to Shelby at work. He had finally maxed out his Visa when he'd gotten her the necklace, so he put the flowers on his MasterCard. He had to get things settled between Shel and himself pretty soon. He couldn't afford to keep up this present buying much longer.

Of course, he couldn't afford a lot of things. Shelby could get by on next to nothing; her dumpy place was just north of Bell Town. But he was right in it, and it was not a cheap neighborhood. And while women seemed to like having roommates, that arrangement didn't work well for most guys. Roommates cramped your style. So, housing wasn't a place where he could cut corners. Neither was transportation. He needed a good car, and, heck, everybody had car payments. Then there was work. He had to have a decent wardrobe for that. Where did that leave him any pennies to pinch? He certainly wasn't going to let up on his aggressive investment plan, although he could use the extra cash. Money was just tight now, that was all there was to it. And that was why he couldn't get married yet. He wasn't going to be dumb like his dad and get tied down before he had his fortune built, then spend the next thirty years listening to his wife complain that they couldn't afford a new car or that Disneyland vacation.

But that didn't mean he couldn't plan for the future, think about being married a few years down the road. Say, five years. In five years he'd be a lot better off, Shel would have gotten this acting bug out of her system, and they'd both be ready for marriage.

He'd had the florist sign the card, "We need to talk about the future." Hopefully, that would hold off Shel from doing something stupid until he got well and he could really explain all this to her. And once the doc gave him some drugs for this creeping crud, he'd be back on his feet in no time.

Shelby read Matt's message on the floral card and wondered what sort of new stalling tactic this might be. Or had he finally come to his senses and realized he wanted to get married? Well, she supposed she should give him a fair chance. After three years together, she probably owed that to both of them. She'd call him when she got home from work.

And what about David? She owed it to him to stop things before they went any further, so when he called later in the afternoon to see if she wanted to go out on Friday, she declined.

"I'm going to take a few days and see if I can sort out my feelings," she said.

"Okay," he said, disappointment plain in his voice. "I don't want to push you. I hope you won't let anybody push you," he added, and she knew he meant Matt.

"Don't worry. I won't."

• • •

Matt was in no position to push anyone. He barely had the energy to sigh as he parked his car in the underground garage of his apartment house and dragged himself to the elevator. He felt like crap.

Stupid doctor! There must have been something the guy could prescribe that could knock this bug. If we could send a man to the moon, couldn't somebody discover something to kill a virus? He thought of the work piling up on his desk and ground his teeth with frustration.

The only bright spot on his horizon was that Shel was waiting for him to get better. They had talked after she got the flowers. She'd even offered to come over with soup. But he'd told her to stay away. This thing was nasty, and she didn't need it, especially if she got on at the Fifth.

He had his doubts that was going to happen. After all, most of her friends had heard by now, so she should have, too.

Once they had made up, she'd have other things to think about. Meanwhile, the flowers had worked like a deposit, putting a hold on Shel's heart until Matt could return to personally take possession. He'd have to be content with that for now.

As for work, at the rate he was recovering it looked like he'd be putting in some late hours when he did get finally back. Right now he couldn't think about that. He trudged down the hall to his apartment, opened the door and got as far as the couch, where he flopped facedown and fell instantly asleep.

Diana and Flo had spent an enjoyable Friday morning in downtown Seattle, but Diana could tell her mother was getting tired.

"Ready for lunch?" she asked.

"More than ready; I'm starving. And my feet hurt."

"They should," said Diana, "after everywhere we've been."

"We should have quit after Nordstrom's Rack," said Flo. "I think the Market might have been too much for my little piggies. Is there someplace nice nearby? I'll treat."

"Cutters isn't far," said Diana, "and they have a lovely view of the sound."

"Perfect. Lead on."

By the time they got to the restaurant it was quarter to one. As Diana had hoped, some of the lunch crowd had cleared out to get back to the office and finish up their week's work. Although the restaurant still had plenty of customers, she saw a few empty tables. She quickly scanned the large expanse of floor, looking for a window seat where they could watch the ferries running back and forth from Seattle to Bainbridge Island and Bremerton.

Her gaze stopped when she came to a profile she instantly recognized as Lance's. He was seated across from a woman who looked to be somewhere in her thirties—dark-haired, slim and fit looking, and wearing business attire.

But they weren't doing business. Diana watched as Lance slid a long, slim, jeweler's box across the table to her, felt her heart constrict as the woman flashed him a sexy smile and opened it.

She turned quickly, not wanting to see what was inside. "Let's try someplace else."

Flo craned her neck around her daughter. "But there are plenty of tables."

"This is not going to work," said Diana, ushering her out the door.

"What on earth was that all about?" demanded Flo, as they trudged back down the street.

"I saw someone I didn't want to run into," said Diana. "I'm sorry, Mom. I know your feet hurt. There's a little cafe not far from here you'll love."

"Oh, for heaven's sake, Diana," said Flo grumpily. "I

can't imagine . . ." She broke off her sentence. "That man giving the young woman a present. Do you know him?"

"It's not important," said Diana. "I just didn't want an awkward scene." She didn't turn to look at her mother, but she could feel Flo's intense scrutiny.

"That wasn't, perhaps, your Mr. Gregory, was it?"

"Let's not talk about this, okay?"

They walked half a block in silence before Flo broke it. "Maybe you shouldn't jump to conclusions, dear. That might have been his sister."

"Oh, yes, that looked like exactly the sort of present Andy would give me," said Diana. "Anyway, it doesn't matter. I told you we were just going out as friends. We laid those ground rules down at the very beginning."

*And I was foolish enough to break them and let him kiss me.* Lance Gregory and his handy dandy jewelry store— how many women's hearts had he purchased wholesale?

"Lance, it's lovely," breathed Adele.

"I wanted you to have something to remember all the good times."

It took a moment for her to look up from the bracelet, and when she did, she wasn't smiling. "I see," she said slowly, and shut the case.

"You're a wonderful woman," said Lance, "but I don't think, that is . . ."

"Is there someone else?"

Did Diana Barrett technically count as "someone else"? She wasn't exactly falling all over herself to impress him. Every muscle in his neck suddenly felt tight and angry. He rubbed the back of it, desperately searching his mental file of soothing flatteries for something Adele would appreciate. The file came up empty.

"Well," she said shortly. "I think it's time I went back to work. It's been fun, Lancer. Don't call me again."

She left the bracelet sitting on the table and walked away.

Lance wished she'd have taken it, but he supposed he didn't deserve to have his conscience eased.

It was ten-thirty by the time Diana got out of bed Saturday morning, but she felt like she hadn't slept at all. What a coincidence. She hadn't.

She wandered out to the kitchen, thinking to see her mother there, sipping coffee. She found the coffee, but no Flo. Diana went to the guest room, and that, too, was empty. She discovered her mother tucked into a corner of the sofa in her office, mug of coffee in hand, perusing the manuscript for Diana's mystery.

Flo looked up and smiled. "Good morning, sleepy-head."

Diana found herself wishing she'd thought to hide that hard copy. Not that she wasn't proud of her work, but sometimes she and her mother didn't agree on what was proper for a lady to write, and her mother's unrequested critiques had a way of stirring up otherwise calm waters, both in her inner self and in a normally good mother-daughter relationship.

"I see you found something to read," she said.

"This is really quite good," said Flo. "Although it does seem excessively gory. Must you go into so much detail? How can anyone read this sort of thing and keep their breakfast down?"

"I don't know. You tell me."

"I can't. I haven't had my breakfast yet."

"Well, come have some. I'll make us waffles."

"You look like you didn't sleep a wink," said Flo as they made their way to the kitchen.

"Oh, I slept a wink."

"And did you come to any conclusion in regards to Lance Gregory?"

"Please, let's not spoil my appetite by talking about him," protested Diana.

"Don't pretend you don't want to," said Flo. "I know better."

"And speaking of knowing better, so do I now. I'm not going to see Lance again. I don't need new jewelry that badly."

"A wise decision," said Flo. "Unless, of course, Mr. Gregory is changing his wicked ways. Perhaps he was saying good-bye to that young woman."

"That doesn't mean he's changing, and it doesn't mean I should line up to be the next one who gets bought off with a string of pearls."

"You do have a point," admitted Flo. She was silent a moment, then asked, "You're not heartbroken, are you, darling?"

Although she'd felt better, Diana had certainly gone through worse than this. She shrugged. "Maybe a little bruised, but not broken."

Flo sighed. "You know the last thing I want is to see you get hurt, but I also hope this one disappointing incident isn't going to make you take a seat on the side of the road and watch life pass you by."

"That was very poetic," said Diana, giving her mother's cheek a pat. "Don't worry. I'm not going to turn into a modern day Miss Haversham and board myself up in my house."

"I hope not. I hate cobwebs."

"I've got an idea. Why don't you see if your friend Harry Emerson has a single son. We could double date."

"You can fish all you want, but I'm not going to be lured into talking about Harry," said Flo.

"And why is that, I wonder? Are you embarrassed to admit you've got the hots for him?"

"Phht." Her mother waved away Diana's teasing with a flick of her hand. "That silly, old coot."

But Diana had seen the pink blooming on her mother's cheeks. "As Shelby would say, 'Me thinks the lady doth protest too much.'"

"You can think what you like," said Flo brusquely.

"I suppose that new dress you bought when we were out shopping yesterday was just to impress the ladies at the Rhododendron Club."

"That's right," said Flo, taking a sudden interest in pouring herself more coffee.

"And the new lipstick?"

"I needed something with sun protection." said Flo.

"Of course," agreed Diana. "And what was the SPF?"

"How on earth should I know what the ingredients are?"

"Let's see," said Diana. "She doesn't know the SPF but she bought that lipstick for UV protection. I think the one who needs protection is old Harry."

Her mother shook a finger at Diana. "If you're going to be this obnoxious, then you can just pay for it and take me to lunch."

"It will have to be a quick one," said Diana. "I promised Shelby I'd help her with a birthday party this afternoon."

"I'll try to eat fast," promised Flo.

By the time they got home, Diana barely had time to climb into the red clown suit with white polka dots that Shelby had given her for those rare occasions when she needed a quick fill-in for a Klowns for Kids party.

Klowns for Kids had been Shelby's brain baby, her way of encouraging her friends to get involved with charities, and Diana was proud of her daughter's selflessness. Shelby and her clowns weren't Ringling Brothers, but they offered enough excitement to keep the young guests entertained and help the mothers in charge of the pandemonium stay sane. And when it came time to pay up, the grateful moms wrote out a check, not to Shelby, but to the Children's Hospital.

Shelby had lost one of her clowns to New York, another was down with the flu, and the third, her roommate, was flying the friendly skies. So she was down to Diana, who couldn't do much more than paint faces and look silly. Still, Diana supposed having her for backup was better than having to face thirty first-graders alone.

By ten after two, she was riding shotgun in Shelby's ancient Toyota on what Seattle area people called the East Side, in a posh Bellevue neighborhood. Diana could imagine what kind of a sight they made as they rumbled down the streets in Shelby's beater, wearing their matching clown suits and orange fright wigs: the white trash clown patrol.

"Okay, we should be getting close," said Shelby.

Diana scanned the street for house numbers. "I see it," she said. "It's that white colonial on the corner."

"Good, and we're only ten minutes late."

Shelby turned off the engine and the car shuddered to a stop.

"We're lucky we made it at all. We could have taken my car, you know," said Diana.

"This one's fine," said Shelby. "It got us here, didn't it?"

"Yes, but will it get us home?"

"Of course," said Shelby, climbing out. She opened the backseat door and hauled out her two shopping bags of goodies.

Diana climbed out her side and promptly tripped over her clown shoes. It had been a while since she'd done this and she'd forgotten that walking in the things was an art.

Shelby laughed. "Save that for the party."

"I'll try," retorted Diana as she stomped up the sidewalk after her daughter.

They weren't even to the door when a frazzled-looking

woman in designer jeans and a long-sleeved, silk blouse opened it and stepped out onto the porch.

"Thank God you're here," she breathed.

As if on cue, a roar of childish noise whooshed out at the newcomers.

I'm getting too old for this, thought Diana.

"Don't worry, Mrs. Lister," said Shelby. "You can breathe easy now. Klowns for Kids is here."

They followed Mrs. Lister through the house to the basement, where the chaos was in full swing. Fearless, Shelby stepped into the heart of the hurricane and pronounced, "Let the games begin!"

Diana watched, amazed, as her daughter went into a frenzied routine Robin Williams would have envied. In a two-minute span she became every animal known to zoo-keepers. The kids loved it and joined in the mayhem. Once she had them bouncing off the ceiling, she brought them back down by juggling for them.

Diana set up her face-painting station at one corner of the long table laid out with paper plates and party favors, and one by one, Shelby sent the kids over to her to get their transformations.

"I want you to make a rhinoceros," ordered one little boy, pointing to a plump, freckled cheek just begging to be kissed.

Rhinoceros. Diana gulped inwardly. She did her best and the child whooped off to join a circle game Shelby was conducting involving a beach ball and a great amount of shrieks.

One child wanted the Little Mermaid on her cheek, while another wanted to look like Cinderella. Diana obliged each customer, gritting her teeth as she worked. The children were adorable individually, but as a herd the noise and chaos they produced was enough to inspire madness.

She stole a peek at her watch. They had another forty

minutes to go. Where were those cowardly moms? Wasn't it time for birthday cake yet? Remembering the zippy effects of sugar, Diana decided maybe not. *Grit your teeth and remember you will never do this again as long as you live.*

Diana was just glittering a child's face when Shelby's beach ball came at her like a stealth bomb and whapped her on the side of the head.

Shelby loped over to retrieve it. "Sorry. Are you okay?"

"Don't have grandchildren," said Diana between gritted teeth.

The party finally ended, the children got taken away by their parents, and Shelby left with a sizable check and a very tired mother drooping along behind her.

Diana almost made it back to the car without tripping over her clown shoes, but she was just so tired she could barely put one foot in front of the other. The toe of her right shoe caught on the pavement and next thing she knew she'd gone down and skinned both her palms.

"Mom!"

Shelby came flopping over to her while the two remaining children, who were capering on the front lawn, burst into enthusiastic laughter. "That was funny," said one.

"Are you all right?" asked Shelby, helping her up.

"Oh, yes. Just wanted to make sure the customer got her money's worth," muttered Diana, examining her shredded flesh. "I think next time, I'll just write you a check."

"Oh, now, it wasn't that bad," said Shelby.

"No. It was worse."

"Let's go see if Mrs. Lister has some hydrogen peroxide," suggested Shelby.

"Let's just get out of here," said Diana, and led the way to the car.

She collapsed on the seat, thankful she had nothing more planned for the night than to watch a video with her mother and eat whatever Flo had concocted in her absence. She could hardly wait to get home, tear off this ridiculous outfit, and put salve on her stinging hands.

They rumbled across the floating bridge and hit the freeway, and Diana fantasized about the big tub of bubbles she was going to sink into the minute she got in the door. They were just exiting when she smelled the distinct fragrance of overheated car.

"Shelby, is this thing overheating?"

"I don't see how it could be," said Shelby. "I put water in it before I left."

Diana stole a glance at the temperature gauge. Hot.

"Maybe we should pull off the road," she suggested.

Shelby set her chin in determination and pushed down on the gas pedal. "We can make it."

"Shelby, stop this thing before it blows up," cried Diana.

"It won't blow up," said Shelby, and bit down on her lower lip.

Little feathers of steam began to escape from under the hood.

"I think you've got a radiator problem," said Diana, ace mechanic.

Shelby scowled. "Why couldn't this stupid thing have held until payday," she growled.

"Why couldn't you have told me you needed a new radiator?" suggested Diana.

"Because I had everything under control. I was going to take it in this week. I'd put sealant in it and it was just fine."

"Well, it's not fine now," said Diana. "Stop this tin can before it blows up in our faces."

Now they were three blocks from home and the feathers of steam had gathered into huge plumes. Shelby would probably have pressed on if not for the mention of possible body damage, which was enough to make any actress see the light. She gave up the fight and pulled up alongside the parking strip.

"We could have taken my car, you know," said Diana in disgust. She climbed out of the car, and her daughter followed suit.

I'll just call Big Tow from your house and have them tow it back to my place," said Shelby humbly.

"Meanwhile, we can both stroll down the sidewalk singing 'Send in the Clowns,'" snapped Diana, flapping off down the street.

Shelby caught up to her. "Mom, I'm sorry. The guy at the station was pretty sure that some sealant would hold me until I could get the car in."

"Was that before or after you told him how many miles you were going to put on it? Honestly, Shelby. What if you'd been on the freeway, or some nasty part of town late at night?" scolded Diana.

"Then I'd have gotten mugged and you could have said 'I told you so,'" said Shelby cheerfully.

Diana shook her head and clomped on.

Shelby caught up with her. "Come on, don't be mad. You remember what it was like being on a budget."

"Yes," said Diana. "It was the pits. So, why don't you let me help you more?"

"Because you've helped me enough already and I don't want to have to change my middle name to leech. I'll get the radiator fixed and it will all be okay. Okay?"

"Okay," said Diana, pulling off the boxing gloves and giving her daughter a kiss. "Unless someone I know sees me walking down the street looking like this, then I'm afraid I'll just have to kill you."

They were within half a block of the house when she spotted Lance's car and froze in her tracks.

"What's the matter?" asked Shelby. She caught sight of the car and said, "Uh-oh. Is this where I play my big death scene?"

Diana could already feel her cheeks heating up in attempt to match her lovely polka dot outfit. Maybe she could . . . No, she couldn't slip around the back, because there he was, standing on the front porch with her mother, observing her with a cocked head and an amused smile.

Great. The perfect ending to a perfect day.

# *Thirteen*

♡

*Now here was* an interesting sight, thought Lance, grinning—sophisticate Diana Barrett clumping down the street in a clown suit. She had looked better. Still, there was something oddly appealing about seeing her like this. The getup lent her a certain vulnerability. No, the clothes and fright wig didn't *lend* vulnerability, they *exposed* it, brought out another facet of the real woman.

Lance had seen her stop in her tracks at the sight of him and had been pleased with her reaction. Clearly, she hadn't wanted to be caught looking her worst—a sure sign of a woman in the early throes of infatuation. If this were some kind of battle, he would definitely say that he had just been given the upper hand. He waited until she reached the porch to speak.

"This is a side of you I haven't yet seen."

Diana stopped trying to maneuver her clown shoes up the stairs. With a growl, she pulled them off.

"I hope, under the circumstances, you're not expecting me to say it's nice to see you."

"I find the present circumstance very interesting," he responded. "It shows you have a playful side."

Diana pulled a frown. "This is not my idea of playful," she said, yanking off the fright wig and shaking out her curls.

"How did it go?" asked her mom.

"Mom was a hit as usual," said Shelby cheerfully.

"This is the last time she's roping me into this," Diana vowed, continuing on up the stairs.

Flo looked past them down the street. "But where's the car?"

"Three blocks down. We had radiator problems," said Diana in a voice that spoke volumes.

"Mom," said Shelby sternly, following her mother inside, "I said I'd take care of it. Why are you bringing this up again?"

"Oh, dear," said Flo as they walked past her. Left in charge of the door, she hovered there as if uncertain whether to extend hospitality to a relative stranger or allow her family privacy in which to bicker.

She appeared to come to a sudden decision. "May I offer you a ringside seat?"

Lance thanked her and stepped inside. He could hear female voices sniping down the hall. Flo blithely covered the sound with comments on the weather, and led him into the living room.

As on Lance's first time inside Diana's house, he got the impression of soft, restful colors and well-maintained elegance. But what immediately arrested his attention now that she wasn't present to distract him, was the glass sculpture perched on her coffee table. It was small, and deep pink, and it looked like a May basket without the handle. The piece wasn't Chilhuly, but it had obviously been done by one of the artists from the same school, possibly Bergsma. Funny, not only did Diana Barrett enjoy the same music he did and the same type of book, she appeared to have a similar fondness for art glass.

"Make yourself at home," said Flo, and Lance parked himself on the couch. "How do you take your coffee?" she asked.

"Black," said Lance.

She left and he let his gaze roam the room, taking in the dried hydrangeas blooming out of an antique jardienierre in one corner, the watercolor garden scene hanging over the fireplace, and the delicate Dresden knickknacks on display in the curio cabinet. The room had a definite feminine touch, but that wasn't the main difference he noticed between his house and Diana's: hers felt lived in.

The sound of laughter echoed out to him, announcing that mother and daughter had made up. Laughter, that was another thing lacking in his oh-so-perfect house.

His surrogate hostess returned with the coffee and he thanked her.

She perched on the opposite end of the couch and smiled at him. "Tell me a little about yourself, Lance."

Although they had already gotten on a first-name basis when they were visiting on the front porch, it obviously didn't make him exempt from the parental third degree—something he hadn't gone through in at least twenty years.

"There's really not much to tell," he said with false modesty. "I sell jewelry."

"That much I know. In fact, Diana and I were in Cutters yesterday and saw you peddling some."

Lance's coffee suddenly tasted bitter. He nodded slowly. "Actually, I was saying good-bye to an old friend."

"Um-hmm," said Flo thoughtfully. "I see."

"I hope you do," said Lance.

"Well, it probably doesn't matter what I do or don't see, does it?"

"Mothers don't count?"

She smiled at that. "Tell me about yourself."

Cutting right to the chase. Next she'd want to know his intentions toward her daughter.

"I enjoy dancing and tennis," said Lance. "I travel frequently and have a weakness for musicals. I'm also fond of mysteries."

"I suppose my daughter looks like an interesting mystery to you," said Flo.

"I find her very intriguing," said Lance.

"And when you've solved the mystery, then what?"

He'd had root canals that were easier to endure than this conversation. How on earth did he answer that question when he wasn't sure of the answer?

Lance was spared by the arrival of Shelby. She held a pot of some sort of grease and a gloppy-looking tissue, and most of her face had already emerged from under the clown white. Even devoid of makeup she was a very pretty girl.

Her grandmother looked less than pleased to see her.

She said hi to Lance, then announced, "I guess I'll call Big Tow."

"Oh, dear," said Flo. "How will you get home, dear?"

"In the tow truck," said Shelby nonchalantly. "I'm sure the experience will teach me some sort of life lesson," she added snidely, tempering the remark with a wink.

Her grandmother followed, asking her if she wanted to stay for dinner, and Lance breathed an inward sigh of relief. For the moment, Flo Bunt, Inquisitor, had been diverted from the subject of Diana and Lance.

He wished he could as easily divert himself. What was he doing, anyway? Where was this relationship headed? Well, he knew where it was headed, but beyond that, what?

Diana sank into the tub of bubbles with a sigh. Maybe if she stayed in here long enough Lance Gregory would give up and go away. Maybe they'd all go away. Well, Lance and Shelby, anyway. Her mother had dug in like a hibernating bear, and there would be no shooing her off.

Diana suspected there would be no getting rid of Lance, either. He wasn't going to leave her life until he'd gotten what he wanted: her heart. She felt like a woman dangling from a cliff of wet clay. In spite of her white knuckles, she was losing her grip.

She sank deeper into the tub. She had to scramble up that cliff, tell Lance in no uncertain terms to take a hike, especially in light of what she had seen yesterday.

She heard a knock on her bedroom door, followed by Flo's voice, calling, "Diana?"

For a moment she considered sinking under the water and hiding beneath the bubbles. As if that would stop her mother from finding her.

Sure enough. Next thing she knew, Flo was hovering next to the tub. Diana sighed.

"Don't tell me you're already running out of cute stories about my childhood," she said.

"There's no one out there to tell them to," replied Flo.

Disappointment crept up on Diana and surprised her. "Lance left?"

"Are you sorry?"

"It would be nice if just one of us asked the questions here."

"Okay," agreed Flo. "So, are you sorry?"

"Mother!"

"Big Tow can't come for at least an hour. Your friend went out with Shelby to look at her radiator," said Flo, capitulating. "He offered after that to run her down the hill to the store to get some kind of sealant. I must admit, that was very gentlemanly of him."

"Surprisingly so," said Diana. "He doesn't strike me as the type of man who normally puts himself out for someone else."

"Maybe you've misjudged him."

"Isn't it time for you to go clean another cupboard?"

Flo opened the medicine cabinet and began rearranging its contents. "I'm in no hurry."

"And I want no privacy."

Flo ignored her daughter's sarcasm. "Would you like to know about the young lady we saw him with yesterday?"

"Oh, no. Tell me you didn't ask him."

"Not directly," Flo replied comfortingly. "He said he was saying good-bye to an old friend."

"And that means he's suddenly a safe romantic bet for your daughter?"

Flo tossed a near-empty deodorant stick into the wastebasket. "It means you should invite him to stay for dinner so we can find out."

"With me, my mother and my daughter. Oh, what a wonderful idea!"

"I thought so. Let's see what sort of family man he is."

"He's not, Mother, and I'm not going to see him anymore."

Flo wasn't fooled. "Baloney. I'm already thawing another chicken breast in the microwave."

Diana moaned and submerged herself. But she didn't stay down for long. The thought of remaining in the tub and allowing her mother further unsupervised access to Lance brought her out in a hurry.

By the time Lance and Shelby had returned, she had slipped into slacks and a sweater, and had on her real makeup. Judging from the condition of Lance's hands, he had not only played the role of Shelby's chauffeur, but had taken a hand at car repair, too.

"So, you moonlight as a mechanic?"

"You wouldn't want your daughter to have to deal with engine troubles when there was a perfectly able-bodied man around, would you?" he answered.

"Yes."

"Child abuse," muttered Shelby, and he smiled.

"My mother is already killing the fatted calf on your behalf," said Diana, "so I hope your stomach can accommodate an early dinner."

"I don't get much home cooking. It sounds great. If you can tell me where I can wash up?"

Diana pointed him to the bathroom.

As soon as he was out of earshot, Shelby turned to her. "Is this getting serious?"

Never. "No, we're just friends," said Diana. The memory of their hot encounter on the ferry returned to taunt her, and she turned so her daughter couldn't see the rising tide of color she felt burning its way across her face.

She headed for the kitchen, calling over her shoulder, "I guess I'd better see what Gram is cooking up for us."

Shelby refused to be thrown off the scent. She dogged her mother into the kitchen, saying, "For just friends, you seem to be spending a lot of time together."

"Well, we won't be in the future."

Shelby rolled her eyes. "Right. Do you want to know what he said about you when we were out looking at my car?" Without waiting for an answer, she continued, "He said he thinks you are the most charming woman he's ever met."

Typical Lance Gregory malarkey. "What else did he say?"

"That perfection runs in our family and good taste obviously runs in his. How's that for a line?"

"So, he asked you about Matt?"

"Not directly. Just hinted at it. He was more interested in getting the lowdown on you."

"What kind of lowdown?"

"Like if he had competition."

"He said that?"

"Not in so many words. Just hinted at it."

"Well, I hope you didn't say anything," said Diana.

"No offense, Mom, but there's nothing to say," said

Shelby. "Your life has been positively boring since Daddy died. Actually," she amended, "it was kind of boring before that, so I guess it's been more like dead."

Diana looked at her daughter aghast. "You didn't say that, did you?"

"Not in so many words." Shelby grinned and added, "Just . . ."

". . . hinted at it," Diana finished with her. "Thanks."

"What do you care if you're not interested?"

"Simple pride. Now, subject closed."

"Okay, so you're not willing to admit you're attracted to him," Shelby continued as if Diana had never spoken. "That's fine, and I respect your right to hide things from your only child, although it's obvious he makes your motor race. But remember, his family doesn't call him Lance Romance for nothing."

Diana had already seen enough at Cutters to convince her that her earliest opinion of Lance Gregory was correct. She didn't need confirmation. "Shelby. I'm done discussing this with you," she said firmly.

"Okay, okay," said Shelby. "Just trying to help as one grown woman to another."

"I appreciate the thought," lied Diana, and gave her a quick pat on the cheek. "But as I've been a grown woman a lot longer than you, I think you can trust me to be able to handle my own love life."

"As you've done so beautifully in the past," muttered Flo from the counter, where she was busy putting the finishing touches on a side dish of wild rice and Portobello mushrooms.

Diana grimaced and went to the fridge to pull out salad makings.

"Diana, Shelby and I can manage in here just fine," said Flo. "You go on out and visit with your friend."

Diana got the underlying message. But what did her mother think Lance Gregory would tell her if she confronted him about the skinny brunette other than what he thought she wanted to hear?

She found him ensconced on the couch, and she took a seat on a chair a careful distance away. He raised a mocking eyebrow, but made no comment. Instead, he turned the conversation into safe waters, nodding at her glass sculpture and saying, "I see we have the same taste in art. I have a Chilhuly."

Somehow, that didn't surprise her. Lance Gregory would want only the best.

"I'm sure you can tell this isn't one," she said. "I found I couldn't rationalize indulging myself quite that much."

"It's nice, though," said Lance. "Same school. You have good taste, and a lovely house. But then, I'm not surprised."

More flattery. It was like a well that never ran dry. Diana leaned back in her chair and studied him.

"What? You don't think I'm sincere in what I'm saying?"

"Rarely."

He shrugged. "Well, I guess this is one of those rare occasions."

Diana made a little noise of disgust and left her chair to go pretend to look out the window at a sky turning winter dark. He followed her and came to stand in back of her. She could smell his spicy aftershave, and his close presence at her back was making her skin tingle.

"Your mother tells me that you ladies saw me at Cutters."

"We did."

"And you didn't come over to say hello?"

"You looked a little busy."

"I wasn't busy for long. The lady left rather quickly."

"And did she take your present with her?" asked Diana, still not turning to look at him.

"No, she left it. But I wish she had taken it. I meant it as a kind gesture."

"In the tradition of an aristocrat paying off his mistress?"

"No, in the tradition of a man trying not to feel like a heel. I know you think I have a ready supply of appropriate phrases, Diana, but you're wrong. There are times when words aren't enough. Jewelry is my business, and sometimes I can say what I want better with a gift than a word."

"And what, exactly, did you want to say to that woman?"

"That I couldn't string her along."

What was she was supposed to say to that, and what did it mean, really?

"Do you believe that people can change, Diana?" he asked softly.

"I'm not sure," she said. "It seems to me that once people reach our age they're pretty well set in stone."

"I hope I'm not. How about you? Is your heart set in stone?"

He leaned in close and slipped his arms around her, and the contact made her heart stitch. No stone there.

"You know, you looked terribly cute as a clown," he whispered.

The sound of a throat clearing pushed Diana away from Lance as though they were two polarized magnets.

"Gram wants to know if you want something to drink," said Shelby, doing a convincing portrayal of a woman who had seen nothing.

Diana knew she was blushing like a guilty teenager. She stole a look at Lance, and saw that he appeared a little rattled, himself.

"White wine will be fine," he said.

"Mom?"

"Nothing for me," said Diana. She was already off balance enough.

Shelby disappeared and they stood there, looking at each other.

"I don't know what to make of you," said Diana.

"Yes, you do. You've already told me. But maybe what I'm trying to conquer has changed since you first met me."

"What are you trying to conquer now?"

"My past."

Not surprisingly, Lance was the perfect dinner guest: witty and urbane and, of course, appreciative of the cook's talents.

"Does this run in the family?" he asked.

"It skips a generation," said Shelby. "Mom is a terrible cook."

"I am not," protested Diana.

"Well, not when she's paying attention to what she's doing," Shelby conceded. "But if she's talking while she's cooking, look out. You're as likely to get a tablespoon of salt in the cake batter as a teaspoon. And she's been known to get sucked into what's on her computer screen and leave eggs boiling dry on the stove. She's gone through two teapots. We finally decided to get her the kind that whistles so she won't burn down the house."

"I haven't burned down the house yet," said Diana in her own defense.

"Thank God for smoke alarms," joked Shelby.

Diana rolled her eyes and shook her head. And caught sight of the expression on Lance's face. She knew that look. It was the teasing, intimate smile of a lover. The room felt suddenly warm. Hot flash, she told herself. *Liar.*

She grabbed her plate and stood up. "Dessert, anyone?"

"Not me, I'm stuffed," said Shelby. "Anyway, I'd better get my car home." She kissed her mother and grandmother, then sailed off in the direction of the front door.

"I should be leaving, too," said Lance.

"Oh, stay and have some pie," urged Flo. "The night is young."

*Translation: I'm not done questioning you,* thought Diana. But enough was enough.

"Mother, the man does have a life," she said, squelching any more chumminess. "It was nice of you to stop by," she said, leaving the dining room.

He followed her lead, and together they walked to the front door. She had handed him his jacket and opened the door, ready to send him into the darkness when he caught her arm and drew her close.

"The Swing Dancers will be meeting tomorrow. Come with me?"

She had to stop this right now, before it was absolutely too late. She started to shake her head.

"Come on," urged Lance. "You had a wonderful time last week."

Which was why she needed to not go with him again. Ever.

He leaned down and touched his forehead to hers. "Come on, Diana. Put me to the test. Anyway, what can happen to you on the dance floor?"

More than had happened to her in bed with John in years. Diana could already feel her adrenaline moving up to the starting gate for the race to come.

She hung for a moment, undecided, then jumped. "All right."

The current was too swift. Why keep fighting it? If she drowned, she drowned.

Lance had never wanted a woman as much as he now wanted Diana Barrett. Even that near disaster with Allison Swain ten years ago, which had put his feelings at high tide, couldn't compare to what Diana was doing to him now. He didn't just want Diana Barrett anymore. He needed her.

But if he was going to get her he'd have to handle her gently, like a trainer coaxing a skittish horse to trust him. He'd have to give her a little room to run.

True to his resolution, he kept their time together the following evening light and nonthreatening, and his banter free of sexual innuendo. But on the dance floor, as their bodies brushed so temptingly close, he wondered how much of this he could take. At one point, she flashed him a smile that made him ask himself what he was waiting for.

Now, at her doorstep, it was all he could do not to grab her and kiss her like a demon. Instead, he settled for running his fingers along her jawline.

"Good night, goddess," he murmured, then turned and ran lightly down her front steps, carrying with him the memory of how, in the soft glow of the porch light, he had seen her eyes darken at his touch.

It took every ounce of strength he possessed to get himself into his car and leave her. The best things in life are worth waiting for, he reminded himself. And Diana Barrett was definitely the best thing that had ever come into his life.

Diana shut her door feeling like a cat who had sniffed too much catnip.

"Did you have a nice time?" called her mother from the couch.

Like a teenager trying to hide mussed clothes, Diana made a quick mental adjustment. "I certainly got my exercise," she said.

"So, has he asked you to go to bed with him yet?" Flo probed.

"Really, Mother. I told you, we're just friends."

"No man can be just friends with a pretty woman. They simply are not wired that way," said Flo.

Diana cocked her head. "Um-hmm. So, where does that leave you and Harry?"

Flo's face pinkened. "In the forbidden topic category."

"Oh, I see. It's open hunting on my love life but no trespassing on yours," said Diana.

"That's right," said Flo.

Diana just shook her head. She slipped off her shoes, and fell onto the couch. "I'll tell you one thing. That man has got the moves."

"Just don't let him use them on you," cautioned Flo.

"I was speaking about the dance floor," said Diana.

"I wasn't," said Flo. "I suspect there might actually be a real man behind that suave facade of Lance Gregory's. But it's early days yet, and remember daughter, it's a lot easier to jump out of a slow-moving car than one speeding down the freeway. So take your time, don't let him rush you."

Diana combed her fingers through her hair and sighed. "I think I'll go work on my mystery."

Lecza was still winging her way back home from a San Francisco run, which left Shelby to face the blinking answering machine all alone when she got in from work on Tuesday. It was the Fifth Avenue, she knew it. Her stomach began to roil and she had to force herself to walk to the answering machine and push the play button.

"This is Michael Burke looking for Shelby Barrett," said a male voice.

Shelby's heart stood at attention and she held her breath.

"Our orchestra manager, Sterling Tinsley, missed your callback and would like to meet with you. Could you give us a call and set up a time to come in as soon as possible?"

"Could I?" cried Shelby. This had to mean they wanted her. She went into a frenzy, dancing around the room and whooping. "I'm in, I'm in!" she sang to the empty room.

Well, not officially. But close. Surely close enough to celebrate. She checked her watch. It was nearly a quarter after five, and only the ticket office would be open. She wouldn't find the person she needed to talk to now. How would she ever wait until tomorrow?

And, meanwhile, who could she tell? She called Matt and only got his answering service. Of course, sick as he was, he wouldn't be picking up. She left a message anyway, because she knew he'd want to know. "Matt, I got a call from the Fifth Avenue! Isn't that exciting?"

Of course, she got no feedback. Why did Matt have to pick now, of all times, to get sick?

She tried her mother. Mom's line was busy. Shelby scowled and wished that just this once her mother would actually use her call waiting.

The excitement in Shelby's chest was a ticking bomb. She had to tell someone.

She hadn't planned on seeing David anymore, at least, not for a long time, not until she really knew what she was doing with Matt. But David had been such a good friend to her, he would want to hear about her success. There was nothing wrong with just giving him a quick call. She checked her watch. It was pushing twenty after now. He might still be at work. She called his private line, assuring herself that she wasn't really abandoning her earlier resolution. She wasn't being unkind or leading him on. She was just sharing some good news.

"This is David," he said.

Did he sound a little depressed? If he was, it was her fault, so she hoped she was imagining his lackluster tone.

"It's Shelby."

If he had any hard feelings about the way she'd treated him, he did a great job of hiding them. "Well, hello," he said, his voice taking on energy.

"I shouldn't be bothering you at work," Shelby began.

Actually, she shouldn't be bothering him at all. "But I just wanted to tell you I got a call from the Fifth Avenue."

"Hey, that's great! So, it looks like I'll be seeing you again soon after all."

"I don't officially have the part yet. I have to call tomorrow and go in to meet with the orchestra manager."

"You don't sound too worried," said David.

"Actually, I'm not," said Shelby. "I don't think I'd be meeting with him if they didn't want me. I could be wrong, though," she added, and the thought sent a nervous spasm rippling through her.

"You're not," David assured her. "And I hope Matt is taking you someplace fabulous tonight to celebrate."

"He probably would if he wasn't still sick."

"Still? That's too bad," said David, sounding anything but sorry. "So, what are you going to do to make this moment last?"

"Well, I just told you about it," said Shelby.

"You have to do better than that. Look. I'm almost done here. Why don't I take you out? Just as friends," he added quickly. "We have to do something in honor of your achievement."

He was right. She had to celebrate. There was nothing wrong with celebrating your success. With a friend. A friend who knew he was only a friend.

David took her hesitation for acceptance, saying, "I'll come by and get you in an hour."

An hour later, he led her out the front door of the apartment building and up to a gleaming, black limo. She blinked in surprise, then looked at him questioningly.

"I thought you should get used to riding in one of these," he said simply.

"Oh, my God, David. This must have cost you a fortune."

He shrugged. "I figured it was a good investment in my

future. When you're a big star on Broadway, I expect free tickets."

He bowed and motioned her in. She slid onto the seat and made contact with soft leather. She took in the dark red carpet, the drink bar, the tinted windows that shut her off from the hoi poloi.

"Ah, the life of a star," said David, sliding in next to her. He produced a bottle of champagne—not the cheap stuff she and Leeza were used to—and poured them each a glass. "Here's looking at you, kid," he said. "Something I never seem to get tired of doing."

Dear God, what had she done?

Fresh guilt attacked her when the limo pulled in at the Seattle Center and parked in the shadow of the city's favorite tourist attraction. "Oh, please tell me we're not going to the Space Needle."

"Feeling unworthy?" teased David. "I thought you had more self-esteem than this."

"I have enough self-esteem for either the limo or the Space Needle, but not enough for both. David, this is too much."

"What? None of your friends ever do nice things for you?"

"Of course they do, but they can't afford to be this nice."

"Well, I can."

While they waited for a window table, David led Shelby out onto the observation deck. It circled the Needle, and offered an incomparable view of all of Seattle, as well as the surrounding bodies of water and distant snowfrosted mountain ranges that made the Emerald City so beautiful.

They huddled close for warmth and David's breath tickled her ear as he spoke. "There it is, all of Seattle, waiting to lay herself at your feet."

Shelby looked at him in amazement. "Where do you come up with these great lines?"

"You inspire me," he said. "It should be New York we're looking down on, you know."

New York? No. She didn't have what it took to make it in New York. "I'm happy enough with Seattle," she said.

"Are you?"

This was a subject she really didn't need to explore right now. "I wonder if our table's ready."

He took the hint and led them back inside.

The last time Shelby had been to the Space Needle was when her parents had taken her and her best friend to celebrate their high school graduation. And then she hadn't paid much attention to the numbers printed next to the glowing entree descriptions. Guilt perched on her shoulder and directed her attention to them now. The prices were nearly as incomparable as the view.

She tried not to order extravagantly, but David seemed determined to thwart her, talking her into an appetizer, and ordering still more champagne. At this rate, he'd have to carry her back to the apartment. Why did the thought of him carrying her up her stairs Rhett Butler–style send a zing through her? This had not been a good idea. She should never have called him.

"We didn't have to come here, you know," she said.

"Of course, we did," said David. "This is the most perfect place to celebrate your success."

"Prematurely," she reminded him.

"No, we're making a self-fulfilling prophecy," he corrected her.

"Is this what you would counsel your clients to do with their hard-earned money?" she chided.

"Absolutely," replied David. He held up a finger and intoned, "Never take out a loan for something that will depreciate, never touch your principal, and never undervalue accomplishment. And you have accomplished something,

Shelby. Do you know how few people manage to achieve what you have?"

"You are an amazing motivator," Shelby observed.

"Am I? Maybe I should write a book."

"Write it on how to be a great friend, because you're an expert on that."

For an instant she caught a flash of something in his eyes that made her insides quiver, but he tamped it down so quickly she found herself questioning whether she had really seen anything at all.

The waiter arrived with their champagne. David tested and approved it, and they watched in silence while the man poured golden bubbles into their wineglasses.

David lifted his and extended it to her. "Well, here's to friendship," he said. "And to comedy and tragedy. May your roles in real life be full of the first and lacking in the second."

They clinked glasses, then drank. It was so intimate. Too intimate. She should be doing this with Matt.

She suddenly felt awkward and slipped into babbling. "You should definitely write a book. You have got a way with words."

"If I really had a way with words, we'd be celebrating something besides your acting success."

The light banter, the smiling face wiped clean of longing: Shelby realized that, of the two of them, David had the stronger acting talent. He made a great Cyrano de Bergerac to her Roxanne, hiding his hurt every time she chose Matt over him.

She should have stuck with her resolution to leave him alone. "Why do you let me keep doing this?" she blurted.

"Doing what?"

"Going out with you when I still don't know for sure how I feel about Matt."

David was silent a moment. "Therapy," he said at last.

"Therapy? Haven't we used that excuse before?"

"Therapy takes a long time," David argued. "Right now you're confused. You see," he said, donning his mock Viennese accent, "You thought you knew what you wanted until you met me, then you weren't sure. Back there somewhere in your Id, you're only pretty sure you know what you want. And that is bothering you because you don't want to make a mistake. Maybe someone in your family married the wrong man and the fear that you would do the same thing has stuck in your subconscious."

An image of her parents standing in line for a movie, side by side but not touching, shot across her mind. She had seen more crackle on the pages of her mother's books than she'd seen between Mom and Dad. When mate shopping, her mother had obviously settled for a less than perfect match rather than end up with nothing.

David's words seemed psychic. He had stopped talking, and was smiling, waiting for her wandering attention to return.

Half afraid of what she'd hear next, she said, "Go on."

"Well, now that you're on the verge of choosing, you're pulling back, taking another look. You don't want to jump and have no one there to catch you. Of course, you feel guilty for that because your mother never told you it's a woman's prerogative to change her mind. So," he finished, "I am here to help you conquer the guilt and make the right choice."

"And the right choice would be?"

David held out his hands and tried to look humble.

"It's just not that easy," said Shelby with a sigh. "Matt and I have been together a long time."

"You sound like one of my clients trying to convince me he should hang onto stock in a failing company."

"Matt is not a failing company," protested Shelby.

"So you say, but where's the ring?"

Good question. And one she was getting pretty darned

tired of trying to answer. She drained her champagne glass and held it out. "Please, sir, I'd like some more."

David grinned. *"Oliver!"* he said. He pulled out the champagne bottle and refilled her glass, humming a song from the musical "As Long as He Needs Me."

The refrain about selfless dedication could be David's theme song. It made Shelby feel like a selfish bitch.

"Don't." It came out sharp. And bitchy.

He blinked.

"Sorry," she muttered. "Maybe I'd better lay off this stuff for a while."

But the slippery downhill slide had started. By the time they left the restaurant, Shelby's head was floating above the rest of her body like a balloon.

She lay back against the limo cushions and smiled up at David and announced, "My head is buzzing and my lips are numb."

"Numb, you say. This calls for further diagnostic treatment. Tell me if you feel this," he murmured, leaning over her.

His lips touched hers. They were not numb now. The kiss deepened, his hand slid across her midriff and spread fire through her body, and she slipped her arms around his neck. She felt his arm wrap around her and draw her closer.

What in the name of love were they doing!

She pulled away and swallowed hard. "We have to stop."

"I know," said David softly.

"It's not that . . . I just can't . . ." *finish this sentence without sounding like I need to see a shrink.* She bit her lip and shifted her brain cells into high gear, hoping they would come up with an explanation for her jumbled feelings that would satisfy both David and herself.

The look he was giving her burned like a laser. "Someone here is deceiving herself."

She shook her head and looked out the window.

"Shelby, Matt is a fantasy you've built up in your head," David continued. "Props are great for the stage, but you don't want that in real life, do you?"

"Don't. Let's not spoil everything."

He subsided against the seat with a sigh and Shelby kept looking out the window. What was wrong with her, anyway? Where was her sense of loyalty, and why was she torturing poor David like this? Why couldn't she just leave the man alone?

It was raining now, and the drops slid down the glass like tears.

The rest of their ride home was silent, and by the time the limo pulled to a stop, Shelby had kicked herself until her psyche was black and blue. She turned to David.

"I'm so sorry. I should never have called you."

He said nothing, just nodded.

"I won't do this to you again," she said. "I promise."

The promise didn't appear to cheer him.

The driver opened the door for them and David climbed out with one smooth motion. The unaccustomed amounts of alcohol she'd put in her system made Shelby a little less graceful, and she tripped making her exit. David caught her, and she felt that darned zing again. Matt needed to get well soon.

David escorted Shelby to the apartment to find Leeza back from flying, and ensconced on the love seat with Horst. The guy was a giant block of hard lines and sharp angles. Compared to him, David felt out of shape, and vowed to hit the gym one more day a week.

"You're back," said Shelby, stating the obvious.

Leeza disentangled herself from Mr. Muscle and brushed back a long strand of hair flopping over one eye, saying, "So are you. Darn."

"We've been out toasting Shelby's success," said David.

Horst was instantly forgotten and Leeza sat at attention. "Yeah?"

"I got the call," said Shelby, and David noticed the excitement was no longer bubbling in her voice.

He was responsible for that, dumb, selfish fool that he was. It had been wrong to try and parlay a kind gesture into something more, and he wished he could go back and do everything over.

Leeza bounded off the couch and loped across the room to hug her. "That's great!"

"Well, I have to go meet with Sterling Tinsley first."

"Oh, you're in," said Leeza. "They wouldn't have you meeting with him if they didn't want you. We need to celebrate."

"We just did," Shelby reminded her. "At the Space Needle."

Leeza eyed David speculatively, making his shirt collar suddenly feel too tight and his jacket stifling. *Sugar Daddy David, already gearing up for his role as a stage door Johnny.*

"Whoa," she said. "That's a few steps up from cheap champagne in plastic glasses." After braking long enough to make that observation, she barreled on. "We need a party. Tomorrow night. I'll start calling everybody right now. David, you can come, can't you?" she called over her shoulder.

"I guess," he said.

There was no way to tell for sure whether or not his presence was okay with Shelby, as she refused to look at him. That in itself spoke volumes, but David preferred to cultivate deafness.

Leeza was already punching numbers on the phone. "This is so great. We are on our way!"

*On our way.* As he made his way back to the limo, the words echoed painfully in David's mind. Shelby was on her way to becoming a star. What made him think she was ever going to have any interest in an average guy like him?

He answered his own question with a stubborn clenching of his jaw and the reasoning that people who made it big needed an inner circle who knew them when, friends they could count on to like them for themselves, not their fame and the perks that came with it. They needed people who, although lacking talent, still had the soul to appreciate it in others. Creative types had to have common sense people around to help them keep one toe anchored in the real world. He could do that for Shelby, could help her manage her money. All he had to do was make her realize she needed him.

Of course, she would never need him as much as he needed her. Before Shelby, his world had been black and white. She had brought it color. She was life, and when he was with her, he felt so much more, did so much more. With his common sense and her talent they could make a great team. He just had to convince her of that.

And how, exactly, did a harmonica convince a baby grand that they could make beautiful music together?

*I have the part. I have the part!* Shelby danced out of the Fifth Avenue. She could hardly believe it; the dream she had cherished as a girl was actually coming true. All those dance lessons and voice lessons, all those high school plays, classes at the U., and actor workshops had finally paid off.

As soon as she got in the door of the apartment she called Matt. She only got a recorded voice instructing her to leave a message. No surprise. It was beginning to feel like he had been sick forever. She was like Leslie Caron in the movie *Daddy Long Legs*, faithfully recounting the events of her life to an invisible man. Well, no matter. They wouldn't have much time to spend together for a while anyway.

The thought of starting rehearsals freshened her excitement. "It's final. I got the part," she bubbled. "Can you believe it?"

Nothing but stunned silence from the old answering service.

Next she called her mother and was thrilled to get a human voice. She barely gave Mom a chance to say hello before announcing, "It looks like you and Gram will be receiving tickets to *Camelot*. Your daughter got the part of Nimue."

"Sweetheart, that's wonderful!" exclaimed Mom. "And you're not only in the chorus, but you've got a part as well?"

"Yes. Isn't it amazing?"

"With your talent, not in the least. Oh, you'd better get a ticket for Suzanne. If we don't include her, she'll kill us."

"No problem," said Shelby. "It will be fun to have my own rooting section. Maybe I'll even get an extra in case we think of anyone else we want to come."

"Let me know how much it is," said Mom.

"No, this one's on me."

"Well, all right," said Mom dubiously.

"Don't worry," said Shelby blithely. "I'll put it on my plastic."

Mom obviously decided it was time to change the subject. "So," she said, "I imagine you're doing something to celebrate?"

"We're having a party."

"An excellent idea," said Mom. "And if you like, one day next week I'll take you out for dinner."

"Actually, I went out last night."

"Celebrating early?"

"More like a self-fulfilling prophecy," said Shelby, stealing David's words.

"That's what I like to see: confidence," said Mom. "Who'd you go out with?"

"David Jones."

"Oh?"

Shelby knew that tone of voice. It was a sure sign of a mother jumping to conclusions. "We just went as friends."

"Where did you go?"

"The Space Needle."

"Now that's what I call a friend," said Mom.

Shelby got the hidden message. She ignored it, simply saying, "Well, I'd better go," before Mom could ask her any questions she couldn't answer. "I've got to get this place cleaned up."

"Have fun," said Mom. "You deserve it. You've worked hard for this."

"Thanks," said Shelby.

Mom was right. She had worked hard for this moment. It was an important milestone, and she intended to celebrate it thoroughly.

The party was in full swing by the time David arrived, and it wasn't long before he was feeling fresh insecurity. It was like experiencing one of those parties of Judy Garland's that he'd once read about: beautiful, talented people everywhere, each one taking a turn at showing off their talent. Actors recited, dancers danced until neighbors came knocking at the door to complain. And when that happened, they were given a drink and drawn into the magic circle, and the enchantment continued.

Until Leeza said, "Okay, David, your turn." Then he suddenly felt like one of the rats that hauled Cinderella's coach after the spell was broken.

His mouth went dry and he shook his head. "Sorry, I left my dancing shoes at home."

Leeza came over and grabbed him by the arm. "Then you can sing," she retorted, hauling him to his feet.

"My pianist is on strike for higher wages," he protested.

"That's okay. Ours is non-union."

"Ha!" said a skinny guy seated at the small, electric keyboard set up in the corner of the room.

"I don't sing," David confessed.

Leeza squinted her eyes at him. "I know you do something well."

"I do, but please, not here, in front of everyone. What would Shelby's mother say?"

The guests laughed and Shelby's face pinkened.

"Do something," growled Leeza.

David sighed. Actually, he did have a skill he used to love to show off at frat parties, but it wasn't the sort of thing you did in front of the next generation of Broadway stars.

"Come on," goaded Leeza. "If you can't contribute, you're out of the show."

"Okay, okay," he said, and began to stretch his muscles. "Everyone back up, and move those chairs out of the way. I need space from here to that bedroom door."

This was ridiculous. What was he doing, anyway?

Dumb question. He knew exactly what he was doing— showing off for a pretty girl, like any adolescent idiot. No, it was more than that. He was the knight about to joust for the lady he loved. *So get it over with, Jones, and hope you remember how.*

He took a deep breath, stretched his arms in front of him, centering his weight. Then he bent his legs and pulled his arms back to give him momentum. He could feel his quads and calve muscles bunching, turning him into a powerful spring ready to uncoil. He threw up his arms and launched himself, and performed a perfect double back handspring.

The crowd went wild.

David's adrenaline hit overdrive and he did a roundhouse and a forward handspring that would have earned him a nine in competition.

"Whoa!" exclaimed James.

"Amazing," said Leeza.

Amazing. Yeah, come to think of it, once upon a time when he was in college and doing those gymnastics competitions he had thought he was pretty amazing. Not Olympics' material; he hadn't had the kind of obsessive dedication that required. But he had enjoyed the sport. He'd collected a fair share of second place, and even some first place ribbons, and had gotten pretty buff in the process. When he had abandoned gymnastics to give more time to his business classes, he had asked himself what he'd ever use it for, anyway. Now he knew, and he was glad he had something to show off. He was sure old Matt couldn't do a handspring.

"David, that was incredible," cried Shelby, as he took a seat on the floor next to her.

"Oh, I know where this is leading," put in Leeza. "All that flattery—she's just buttering you up so she can get you into a clown suit and let you make a fool of yourself for charity."

David knew he'd be more than happy to make a fool of himself for Shelby.

"Well, never mind that now," said Leeza. "It's time for a live interview with future star, Shelby Barrett. Will you come up here, please, Miss Barrett?"

Shelby obliged, and Leeza spoke into an imaginary microphone. "So, you had your meeting with Sterling Tinsley today. Correct?"

She extended the mike to Shelby, who nodded and answered, "On my lunch break."

"Tell us, Miss Barrett, what happened when you met with Mr. Tinsley?"

"He had me sing. He asked me if I could get a darker quality to my voice and I said I could."

Leeza spoke into her invisible mike. "And you demonstrated?"

"I did," said Shelby.

"And?"

"He showed me where he wanted me to crescendo. He actually gave me new insight into how to interpret the song. It was amazing."

"And when he was done?" asked Leeza.

"He said, 'Go see Michael Burke about your contract.'"

Here everyone broke into thunderous applause.

Leeza held up a hand for silence. "And now, the moment you've all been waiting for. Allow me to introduce the woman who is someday going to be the toast of New York, who will ride around in a limo, eating caviar and wearing clothes by Dolce and Gabbana. Here is Miss Shelby Barrett, soon to be Nimue, singing the song that began her stellar career. Maestro," she commanded, waving a hand at the guy seated at the keyboard.

He began to play, Shelby transformed into a wood nymph, and David knew what the sailors experienced when they heard the Loreli sing. Her voice was incredible, rich and full and vibrant. He watched as she moved her hands, and marveled at how exquisite they were.

Her voice shimmered as she commanded her audience to follow her.

Anywhere, thought David.

At last, she finished. At first, a reverential church silence hung over the room. Then someone started to clap, maybe it was him, and everyone went wild.

The room was thick with jubilation, and David felt choked. What was he doing here, anyway? A couple of circus flips and he thought he was in the same class as brilliance? Good God, what an idiot! What had made him think he could have a chance with Shelby, really? He was like a man trying to make love to a mermaid.

He didn't care. Like Don Quixote, every man needed an impossible dream to chase. Shelby was his and he'd keep chasing her until she told him to stop.

The ringing phone was hardly audible over the talk and

laughter, but Leeza finally grabbed it and sang, "Home of Seattle's best performers. Is this a talent agent?" She listened a moment, then called, "Shelby, it's Matt."

David's insides tensed. He kept the pleasant expression on his face, fighting back the raging jealousy inside him. *Please don't let him come over. Please.*

Shelby took the cordless phone into her room, covering her free ear as she went so as to hear better. She shut the door behind her and a rock landed in his belly. He knew that body language, had seen it in his sister when she was dating his brother-in-law. It was the posturing of a woman involved in an important conversation.

David felt a barely controllable urge to punch a wall.

Shelby didn't stay in the room long, though, and hope rose in him.

"So, is he coming over?" called Leeza.

"No, he doesn't feel good enough. He just called to say congrats."

Yes! There was a God. Now David felt so light he thought he might float to the top of the ceiling and get stuck there. Armstrong wasn't coming. The field was his. He thought of the movie *While You Were Sleeping*, where the stud lay in the hospital bed while his brother won the girl. *Stay there just a little longer, muscle boy. Take your time getting well, and while you do I'll take good care of Shelby.*

# *Fourteen*

*Matt was back* at work on Thursday, looking gaunt, and when he looked at Shelby, hungry. That didn't surprise her. How long had it been since they'd made love?

He took her to lunch, and they were barely seated before he was trying to parlay that into dinner.

"I can't," she said. "It's Mom's birthday and I'm bringing the cake."

"Okay, after," he urged, reaching across the table and taking her hand. "Stop by my place. I haven't been able to think of anything but you the whole time I've been sick. I even hallucinated once that you were there, right by my bed. Then you laid down next to me . . ."

Now his thumb was caressing the top of her hand and getting the rest of her all excited. She crossed her legs, trying to distract herself from her body's response, and slid her hand free. They needed to be talking about their future, not their sex drives.

Matt translated the body language correctly, and said, "Anyway, we need to talk about our future."

Yes, right away, once and for all, before she could waffle around anymore and drive herself—and poor David Jones—crazy. In fact, what was wrong with having that talk right here?

Matt had a ready answer for that question. "There's not enough time. No privacy."

And Shelby knew what they needed that for. Her heart rate picked up.

"So, will you come?" pressed Matt.

"Okay," she said. But they'd better get something settled. She only had so much patience.

Suzanne showed up at the house early, bringing with her the most decadent chocolate cake Diana had seen in some time.

"Vitamin C," she said, lifting it from the bakery box. "As you get older, your daily requirement for chocolate increases."

"Oh, Lord," moaned Diana. "What kind of a friend are you? I'll have to diet for a hundred years after eating just one piece."

"Eat it fast and it cuts the calories in half," said Suzanne.

"You'll have to eat it fast," said Flo. "It's either that or hide it, because Shelby's been working on your birthday cake for the last two days."

"Uh-oh. Get the plates, quick," said Suzanne. "We'll have to get rid of the evidence."

Diana looked longingly at the cake. "I'll end up wearing the evidence on my hips."

"You're not planning on having a man in your life, anyway, so what do you care?" taunted Suzanne, fishing Diana's cake cutter from her utensil drawer.

"Ha!" muttered Flo, from where she stood at the stove.

Suzanne shot up a questioning eyebrow and Diana just rolled her eyes.

"So, tell," said Suzanne. She sliced a generous piece of

cake and waved it under Diana's nose. "Spill your secrets and this can be yours."

Diana made a face at her friend, shoved the temptation aside and cut herself a thin serving of vitamin C.

Suzanne sighed heavily. "Your daughter has turned into a clam in her middle years," she complained to Flo.

"There's nothing to tell," said Diana.

"No, nothing at all," agreed Flo. "Just drop-in visits from Mr. Tall, Dark and Handsome, and late nights out dancing. Nothing going on here at all."

"For a girl with no libido, you get around," observed Suzanne. "Which reminds me." She reached into the shopping bag she was carrying and pulled out a present wrapped in silver foil and tied with a mauve ribbon. "I bought wrapping paper to match your roots."

"Cute," said Diana, then turned her attention to Suzanne's gift. "And what could it be, I wonder. A first edition, perhaps?"

Suzanne was looking very pleased with herself. Now Diana could hardly wait to see what fabulous find lay under the paper. She snapped off the ribbon and unfolded the wrapping to reveal . . . *The Estrogen Cookbook*? Oh, thrill. How can I ever thank you? Just wait till your birthday."

"I got you something else, don't worry," said Suzanne, producing a smaller package and handing it over. "But since you refuse to do the hormone replacement thing, I figured you could at least try some of those recipes."

"I think you're being silly, anyway," put in Flo, leaving her pot on the stove and coming over to thumb through the book. "I've done hormone replacement therapy for years. All that worry over cancer—your chances of getting osteoporosis are higher. And look how young-looking it's kept me." She turned to give them a view of her profile.

"You don't look a day over seventy-six," said Diana, draping a pretty cloisonne bracelet over her wrist.

"I'm not," snapped Flo, snatching the cake cutter and stabbing the cake.

"This is lovely, Suz," said Diana, and gave her friend a hug.

"My pleasure," said Suzanne, then bent to dig more goodies out of her bag, including a plastic container filled with a yellowish powder. "And now it's time for an age-appropriate toast."

"I hope that isn't what I think it is," said Diana.

"Just try it," urged Suzanne, who now had a banana in her hand and was peeling it. "Two tablespoons of soy powder for your phytoestrogen, a spoonful of sugar to make the medicine go down, a banana, a cup of skim milk . . ." She moved to the blender and began dumping things in.

"I'll get the milk," offered Flo.

"Oh, really. This is ridiculous," said Diana.

"There is nothing wrong with doing all you can to keep your body in shape," said Suzanne.

"And nothing wrong with living again," added Flo, handing over the milk carton.

"Thank you Ponce de Leon and Dorian Gray," said Diana.

"In drag and at your service," retorted Suzanne and flipped on the blender.

Diana watched the soy milk shake whirring in it. This was silly. She felt like a frontier sucker standing at the snake oil man's wagon. *Drink this magic drink. Be young and attractive again. Have a sex life. Have a life.* Ha!

Suzanne punched the blender into silence, then poured the drink. "Just try it," she coaxed.

Diana took the glass and suddenly thought of Jerry Lewis in the old movie *The Nutty Professor*. Would she swig this stuff and turn into the female equivalent of Buddy Love?

"Cheers," said Suzanne encouragingly.

Diana took a cautious sip. Actually, it wasn't bad. She took another.

Suzanne grinned smugly. "There, now that's not so bad, is it?"

"No, Mommy."

"Go ahead, mock me. And when your energy level rises and your libido returns, don't feel you need to go out and buy an expensive thank-you present. Lifelong gratitude will do."

"Libido?" Flo pounced on the word. "Let me try a little of that, Suz."

"Sure," said Suzanne, and did the honors.

Diana shook her head. "I can remember the days when we used this blender to whip up strawberry daiquiris."

Suzanne dug further into her grocery bag and out came the good stuff. "I haven't forgotten," she said, and popped a frozen strawberry in her mouth. "I intend to get the scoop on you and Lance Gregory, one way or the other."

They were still in the kitchen and just finishing their first drink when Shelby arrived, bearing a bottle of wine and the most beautiful fat bombe Diana had ever seen. Shelby had decorated both the cake and the antique glass plate with lace and ribbons and tiny silk flowers. The result was something worthy of a magazine cover. Thank God they had ditched the bakery cake five minutes earlier.

"That is truly beautiful," breathed Diana.

"Shelby, you are an artist," raved Suzanne.

"It would be a sin to eat it," Flo added.

"It would be a sin not to," said Shelby. "I got the recipe from the *Death By Chocolate* cookbook, and I've been working on this thing for the last two days. I am now the queen of ganache. Happy birthday, Mom," she added, hugging her mother. Then, looking around, she added, "Hey, no fair. You guys started without me."

"Barely," said Suzanne, and dumped more strawberries into the blender. "We'll have you caught up in no time.

Say, I hear congratulations are in order and you now belong to the world, or at least, Seattle."

"Yes, I'm so excited. We start rehearsals Monday. Tomorrow is my last day as an office slave."

"I can hardly wait to see you," said Suzanne.

"Us, too," added Diana.

"So, is Matt excited?" asked Suzanne.

Shelby looked surprised by the question. "Actually, we haven't had much chance to discuss it. He's been sick."

"And they've had other things to talk about," added Diana.

"Yeah, like whether we're going to be a couple or not."

"Oh, not good," said Suzanne.

Barrymore rubbed against her leg and she leaned over and petted him. He tolerated it for a moment, then strolled away to scratch on the wall.

"Matt's been a little gun-shy," added Flo, swatting at the cat.

Suzanne gave a knowing nod. "Afraid of the 'C' word?"

"A little," said Shelby, sarcasm heavy in her voice. "I'm beginning to think he was cloned from Barrymore."

"But she's found someone to console her," said Diana.

"Really?" Suzanne handed Shelby a daiquiri and poured fresh drinks all around. "Using another man to make him jealous? I thought we didn't do that sort of thing anymore."

"I never meant to use David," said Shelby. "It was an accident."

She went on to explain, and by the time she had finished her story, Suzanne's eyes had taken on a sparkle.

"So, while you're waiting for Mr. Right to get his act together, Mr. Right comes along."

"He is a sweet guy," said Diana. "He took Shelby to the Space Needle to celebrate her getting the part."

"He's not cheap, that's good."

Shelby shook her head. "No, he's generous and kind, and funny, too."

"So, what's wrong with that?" demanded Suzanne.

Shelby shook her head. "I don't know, exactly. It's . . . complicated."

"It usually is," agreed Suzanne.

"Well, it's just that Matt and I have been together three years."

Suzanne gave a snort. "I had this dress once. It never did fit right, but I kept hanging onto it, thinking eventually it would."

Shelby shook her head. "It's not the same."

"Probably not," agreed Suzanne. "I paid a fortune for that dress. Anyway, go on. You've been with Matt forever."

"And everything was perfect until the subject of getting officially engaged came up."

Suzanne and Diana exchanged looks.

Shelby didn't see. She was busy tracing the edge of her glass. In a way, Diana wished she had seen the look in Suzanne's eyes, because she might have questioned it. And, just possibly, she'd have taken a common-sense lecture from Suz.

"I don't know," continued Shelby. "David is wonderful, and he's so nice. I should be in love with him. Sometimes I think I am. But if there's a chance that Matt and . . ." She shook her head and let her sentence die half-formed. "I don't know. David would marry me in a heartbeat, I'm sure, but I don't want to marry someone just for love insurance."

"How do you know that's not what you'd be doing with Matt?" countered Suzanne.

"Good question," said Shelby. "I'll let you know as soon as I figure it out."

"You will," Suzanne predicted, and Diana hoped she

was right. "Meanwhile," Suzanne added, "hold your heart for the highest bidder and don't settle for less."

"I'll drink to that," said Diana. "Here's to learning how to protect our hearts," she added, hoisting her glass. "And to strawberry daiquiris, and friends."

"To friends with birthdays," said Suzanne. "May the wrinkles not keep pace with the laughs. And," she finished, turning to Shelby, "may true love reign."

"Hear, hear," said Flo in an overly hearty voice.

"Hear, hear," echoed Diana, and hoped her daughter had her mental hearing aid turned up and was doing just that.

"Yeah," said Shelby, her voice quiet.

Birthdays that dragged you ever closer to the big 5-0, daughters with tangled love lives. Ugh. Thank God for strawberry daiquiris and friends, thought Diana.

"And next year for your birthday," Suzanne was saying, "I'm going to get you some of that human growth hormone. Or maybe the new Viagra for women I hear they're working on."

"A few more doses of Lance Gregory and I doubt she'll need it," said Flo.

Diana tried to look aloof, but she knew the warmth on her face was giving her away.

"Well, well," said Suzanne. "So you *have* discovered the fountain of youth."

Shelby left shortly after the presents had been opened. Her mother had loved the peach-scented bubble bath and lotion. Hard to believe Mom was forty-eight now. She sure didn't look it.

Shelby almost envied her mom. She had her successful career, and now a love life she was in total control of.

Well, Shelby was going to take control of hers now, too. Tonight.

She parked on the street below Matt's window, then

hurried to the front door and pushed the buzzer to be let in. Nothing. She pushed again. And again. Great. He'd probably had a relapse and was now in bed, asleep. So, here she was with nothing resolved. How many more of her nights was Matt going to get, anyway?

She turned and marched back to her car, Suzanne Goodman's words flying around her head like so many hornets. Maybe Matt the low bidder had just had his last chance.

Suzanne was on her third drink and her second piece of cake, and had just decided to spend the night when Lance called.

Diana could barely hear him over the noise of her and Flo's laughter.

"It sounds like you're having a party," he said.

"Actually, we are," said Diana. "A birthday party."

"Yours?"

"Yes. I'm thirty-nine again."

"A good year," he agreed. "How would you like to do more celebrating this weekend?"

"With you?" *Of course, with him, stupid!* She shouldn't have had that last drink.

"Yes, I'm doing something tomorrow evening that I think you'll enjoy: getting a Friday night sneak preview of a couple of estate sales."

"That does sound like fun," Diana agreed.

"Good. I'll pick you up at five. We can go treasure hunting, then I'll take you out for dinner."

"With no strings," Diana reminded him.

"No strings, no ulterior motives," he assured her.

"Okay, great."

She hung up and Suzanne said, "No strings? Who on earth was that?"

"Mr. Lance Gregory," said Flo.

Suzanne nodded knowingly. "Ah, no strings, as in no sex."

"That's right," said Diana.

"Well, we'll see what you say after you've been on my speedo-libido cocktails for a while."

Diana shook her head. "No, no. I like things just the way they are."

She did. Really.

Shelby was getting ready for work when Matt called. His first words were, "Don't hang up."

"I wouldn't dream of it," she informed him. "I'm dying to hear your excuse for leaving me standing outside your apartment in the cold."

"I took some cough medicine and the damned stuff zonked me."

Shelby waited a moment, giving him a chance to add something romantic and sweet. Nothing came. The facts, ma'am, just the facts.

"Shel?" he prompted.

"I'm here."

"Look, I know you're ticked, and I don't blame you. But I'll make it up to you. I won't be in the office today. The boss is sending me to a training session. But we can go out tonight. I'll take you someplace special."

"I can't," said Shelby.

"What?"

He sounded so surprised. Did he think she had no life? "James and Horst are coming over for dinner."

"Still celebrating your role?"

His tone of voice sounded snide. "What's that supposed to mean?"

He backpedaled quickly enough, saying, "Nothing. It's just that you can see your friends any time."

"Well, if I'd known you were going to feel good enough and have time for me in your schedule I would never have planned this dinner party," snapped Shelby.

"Aw, Shel, come on. You know what I mean. I want to

see you, baby. I need you. I'm going through withdrawals. You have no idea how hard it's been."

Shelby sighed. All right, she had to give Matt a fair chance here.

"You can join us for dinner," she offered.

"That will be fun. Just the five of us," he groused.

"Well, I can't un-invite everyone."

"Yeah, I guess you're right. Okay. I'll come over. Then we can take a drive afterward. Or you can come to my place."

His place. She knew what that meant: his big, leather couch, a fire in the gas fireplace, and Matt kissing her. But not before they had had that serious talk about their future.

Flo caught Diana mixing up a mid-morning estrogen shake—came up behind her and made her jump, in fact.

"And I thought you weren't interested in that stuff," crowed Flo. "Nothing like starting the day with a little speedo-libido cocktail."

"I'm not taking this for the reasons you're thinking," said Diana. "But it's natural, and there's nothing wrong with trying something that's good for me."

"Absolutely not," agreed Flo.

"And now, if you'll excuse me, I need to do some writing," said Diana, and strolled out of the kitchen to prove she wasn't anxious to get away from her mother's knowing look.

Diana knew her mother was becoming increasingly biased toward Lance, however, and the fact that he brought Flo chocolates when he came to pick up Diana didn't do anything to hurt his cause.

"You really shouldn't feed the animals," she told him as they went down the walk to his car.

"She seems harmless enough."

"That shows how much you know."

He opened the car door and she slipped into the luxurious interior. Going places with Lance Gregory was a treat. John would have had both arms cut off rather than part with enough money to pay for a car like this. On the other hand, getting into a car with him had never made her insides shiver. Diana felt a sudden longing for her deceased husband, and the safety he represented.

The last time she had been out with Lance, he'd behaved like a brother instead of a suitor. His courtliness should have made her feel relaxed. It didn't. Instead, she sat stiffly in her seat, feeling like a string pulled too tightly on a violin. She tried to ignore the feeling now, concentrating instead on where they were heading.

"So, what exactly are you looking for?"

"Antique jewelry. Estate sales can be a good place to find it."

"I didn't know you sold antique jewelry in your stores."

"I don't. I buy the stuff for myself." He turned and flashed her a grin. "And my friends."

The first house they visited was old and large, and its garage was stuffed full of antique furniture, marked and ready for the next day's expected bargain hunters. Lance picked up a diamond brooch and a string of pearls. Diana fingered an opal ring, and he asked her if she liked it, but she resisted the temptation to say yes.

Temptation wasn't so easy to resist at the next stop. She found herself drawn to a necklace and earring set she'd found in a cardboard gift box full of costume jewelry.

"Art deco," murmured Lance at her elbow.

"How can you tell?"

"The materials: marcasite, very big in the twenties, and garnets."

"Those are garnets?"

"They come in more colors than red," said Lance. He continued to explain about the rest of the piece. "Silver was popular in art deco, too," he continued. "Then, there's the geometric design, which was everywhere." He picked up one of the earrings and held the dangling, green rectangle to her ear. "These are the perfect accent for your coloring."

"I think you're right," said Diana.

She reached for the set, but he beat her to it, saying, "Sorry, I have a hankering to buy it, myself."

He strolled away from her, leaving her frowning. Until she heard the numbers being bandied back and forth between him and the woman who had admitted them to the house. That was not the kind of money she was accustomed to spending at garage sales.

Feeling guilty for eavesdropping, Diana moved away to inspect some of the furniture marked for the sale that would be open to the public the following day.

Once Lance had completed his negotiations, he took her arm and escorted her back to the car, where he laid the jewelry in her lap. "Happy birthday, Diana Barrett. Put them on and let's see if you turn into a flapper."

Diana gasped. "I can't take this."

"Of course you can."

"No, they're too expensive."

"I give expensive gifts. Anyway, as I said before, jewelry is what I know. You express yourself with writing, I do it with jewelry."

"There's a big difference in price between a book and a piece of antique jewelry."

"Neither one of us needs to worry about money, so what does that matter? Come on, this isn't the fifties," he added, "and I promise your virtue won't be tarnished."

Diana chewed her lip, looking with longing at the baubles in her lap.

"Go ahead." Lance said. "You can accept them with a clear conscience, because I didn't pay anywhere near what they're worth."

Diana couldn't help herself. "What are they worth?"

"Probably around two thousand dollars."

"My God, I would never have guessed it." She held up the earring and examined it again. It was lovely. "You didn't pay for this, you stole it. Aren't you ashamed?"

He gave her a sly grin. "Never. Not in cases like this. The woman was more than happy with what I gave her. And, judging by the other articles she's got for sale, she'll do okay. As for the original owner, she's not around to protest. What's getting sold now is what nobody wants. The vultures have already swooped in to take all the things they've been eyeing for years. Now they'll sell off what's left so they can buy their own treasures. And someone else will, in turn, sell those when they're finally gone."

"How morbid!"

"Yes, isn't it?" he agreed, oblivious to the fact that her comment was more directed at his observations than the scenario he painted.

"Still, I can't take this."

"Don't be phony, Diana. You want it. Take it."

That was Lance Gregory's philosophy of life. He didn't fool her when he left her at her door wanting more after only one kiss. They were still negotiating, but he intended to get what he wanted. And she wasn't so sure anymore how she felt about that.

It had been Shelby's last day at work. Her coworkers had ordered a cake and chipped in on a scrapbook for her reviews and other career mementos.

A party in the afternoon, and now a dinner to celebrate her freedom from the constricting world of business. And Matt coming over so they could settle things once and for all. It should be a memorable evening, she thought as she hurried through the darkening drizzle to the Pike Place Market. She'd find the spices she needed for the Indian recipe she'd gotten from Martha Stewart's web site at that great store in the basement of the Market.

She was just at the main entrance when she heard someone call her name. She turned to see David running down
the street toward her.

He was still in his business clothes, and his overcoat
soared behind him like a giant cape as he ran. He looked
compact and graceful. Someone should film him running,
she thought. He's beautiful.

He bounded up to her. "Hi."

"What are you doing here?"

"Just running a quick errand. I promised my sister I'd
get her some Market Spice Tea."

"Really?"

He nodded. "Yeah. What are you doing here?"

"Heading for the spice shop that sells the Market Spice
Tea."

"What a coincidence," he said, taking her arm and
strolling them down the street.

"Is it, really?"

"What?" he said, playing dumb.

"You know. A coincidence?"

"Well, almost. I called your place and Leeza said you
were coming here to do some shopping. But I did tell my
sister I'd get her some tea. So, what are you doing
tonight?" he asked casually.

"Staying away from you just like I promised so I don't
break your heart."

"It's my heart. I guess if I want to get it broken that's
my business," he argued. "So, like I said, what are you
doing?"

"I'm surprised Leeza didn't tell you that. I'm cooking
dinner for Leeza and James and Horst. And Matt," she
added, feeling self-conscious even as she said it.

Which was stupid. Why on earth shouldn't she have her
boyfriend over for dinner? And why should she be embarrassed to tell David about it?

No reason. Only a shared moment of passion in the back of a limousine.

David played along as if the fact that she was going to spend the evening with Matt were no big thing. "What are you cooking?"

"Chicken Malai Kabob with Cashew Paste. I need the spices for the Garam Masala."

David nodded. "Ah. Garam Masala."

"You know what that is?"

"Of course, I do. It's something you say when somebody sneezes."

"Just what I suspected, you're ignorant."

"So, wise me up."

She stopped and looked at him seriously. "Okay. Matt is going to ask me to marry him tonight and I'm going to say yes. If I were you, I'd buy my Market Spice Tea some other time."

David stood there staring for a moment, then let out a whoosh of breath. "Well, that wasn't quite what I meant, but I'll consider myself wised up now." He started them walking again, saying, "I really need to get that tea tonight, so I may as well walk with you. You know, one last time, for old times' sake."

"I don't think we've known each other long enough to have an old times' sake," said Shelby.

"It feels like it to me," argued David.

It did to her, too, and that bothered her, almost as much as the fact that she knew she hadn't wanted to see him turn and walk away. Would a ring from Matt really make her feel different?

They went to the spice shop and David watched Shelby make the purchases for her Garam Masala: cardamom pods, coriander seeds and whole nutmeg.

"So that's what nutmeg looks like before they put it in that little jar," said David. "And you're going to use all that?"

Shelby nodded. "Along with black peppercorns, cumin seeds and dried bay leaf. Cinnamon, too. I've already got all of them at home."

"This is going to be some kind of meal," David predicted.

Shelby was sure he was fishing for an invitation, but she refused to bite. That was all she needed: David and Matt together at the dinner table.

David bought a bag of Market Spice Tea and snagged them each a sample cup of it on their way out. He downed his in two gulps and gave a satisfied sigh. "I love this place."

Shelby knew he didn't mean just the spice store. The whole market was something to fall in love with.

"So do I," she said. "Mom used to bring me down here all the time when I was a kid."

"Mine, too. I loved walking by all those produce stalls."

"I liked the flowers," said Shelby.

"Well then, let's go see what the flower ladies are selling today," he suggested.

"I need to get going," said Shelby, determined to quit dragging out this good-bye.

"Before you go, how about one final latte? You know, to kind of bring things full circle."

She should not do this. "I've got to get home and start cooking."

"Ease me out of your life gently," he said. "Don't you think you owe me that final kindness?"

She owed him more than that. "Okay."

He grinned like she'd just promised to go to bed with him and she felt like a heel. David Jones was just plain too good for her. That was the problem. He was such a sweet guy. She should match him up with someone. But right off the top of her head she couldn't think of anyone good enough for him.

•   •   •

That last ploy had been hitting below the belt, thought David as he and Shelby sat in a little cafe and sipped lattes. But desperate times called for desperate measures. Now, if he could just make her see how misplaced her loyalty was.

He knew he wasn't using his last opportunity very wisely, though. Instead of being brilliant and arguing his case convincingly, he was staring at her like an idiot. But she was so pretty. It was all he could do not to grab her right there in front of God and everyone and kiss her stupid.

Well, the jock jerk had obviously beaten him to it, and the stupid hangover had yet to wear off. She still thought she loved the guy.

She checked her watch. "I'd better get going."

David had hoped against hope that she'd invite him back to her place, ask him to stay and sample her cooking. Would seeing Matt the Meathead have spoiled his appetite? He'd never know, since she obviously had no intention of inviting him.

Still saving him from himself. Or herself. Whichever of them it was, he wished she'd stop it. He didn't press the issue, though. A gentleman didn't force himself on a woman. That was what his mother had always said. Sometimes he wondered if Mom knew as much about how to treat a woman as she claimed.

He got up and helped Shelby on with her coat. The close contact shot warmth to places the latte couldn't reach, and he almost felt sick with longing. Maybe Shelby had a point. Why was he doing this to himself? He should just go cold turkey and be done with it. Like she was giving him any choice.

They walked outside to find the drizzle turning to serious rain and the sky completely dark. The after-work crowd had begun to scurry as if everyone had remembered they had plans for the evening and they were late.

Shelby's pace picked up, too. She thanked him quickly

for the latte, then stepped into the street, smiling over her shoulder, saying, "This was fun. I'm glad I ran into . . ."

David never heard the rest of the sentence. His attention was claimed by the car shooting toward her.

# *Fifteen*

*Shelby heard the* squeal of brakes and swiveled her head to see a giant, red bullet bearing down on her. David jerked her arm, flying her off the street. The next thing she knew, she was back on the sidewalk, his arms wrapped around her in an armor of flesh. Inside that armor, she stood shaking, her heart hammering violently.

The driver of the car opened his door and stepped out to lean over his hood and shout over the thumping base of his radio, "You dumb bitch, watch where you're going!"

The man looked like a poster boy for the NFL. His angry words and menacing expression made Shelby's mouth go dry and sent her heart rate soaring even higher.

David's arms tightened around her and he yelled back, "Ask whoever you bribed into giving you a driver's license who has the right-of-way, a pedestrian or a car!"

The guy began to walk around the hood of his car. "You want to say that again?"

"You didn't understand it the first time?" David put Shelby behind him and strode to meet his opponent, jaw clenched, neck muscles bunched.

"David, no!" cried Shelby. She ran and inserted herself between him and the hostile driver. Out of the corner of her eye she could see a crowd growing. This was not the kind of audience she wanted to play to. "You're right," she told the stranger. "I wasn't looking where I was going."

"Don't apologize to this missing link," growled David, stepping back in front of her. "He almost squashed you like a pop can."

"And it would have been my fault," she said, tugging on David's arm. "I'm really sorry," she told the other man. "Um, have a nice day. Oh, and would you mind terribly backing up? I'm afraid I threw my cardamom under your right front tire."

The guy, obviously spoiling for a fight, ignored her and continued to glare at David. This was probably exactly his kind of audience.

"Come on, David," she said, tugging more urgently. She lowered her voice to a stage whisper. "You know how it upset the sensei when you broke that man's shoulder last month."

She stole a glance at Mr. No-Neck and saw fear flicker in his eyes. But he held his ground.

"Nobody got hurt, guys," Shelby continued. "Let's just forget it. Okay? You know, live and let live."

"Yeah, all right," snarled the stranger.

"Thank you," she said sweetly.

"Not so fast," said David, his voice still vibrating with anger. "You owe this woman an apology for insulting her."

"David, remember the sensei," pleaded Shelby.

"Hey, sorry," snapped the guy. "Next time just watch where you're going." He pushed past an onlooker, then got back in his car, wheeled to the side and drove away, sending pedestrians half a block farther down the street scattering like so many frightened chickens.

David swooped down on Shelby's crushed package, muttering, "I should have punched that twerp's face in."

Shelby refrained from pointing out that the twerp had been a good six inches and fifty pounds bigger than David.

"My God, Shelby. What if he'd broken your leg? You wouldn't have been out of a cast in time to go on at the Fifth."

Shelby felt suddenly weak. She reached out to take her crushed package from him and saw that her hand was shaking. And her knees had turned to rubber.

David wrapped an arm around her. "Are you okay?"

She nodded. "I think so." Then, to prove it, she burst into tears.

He hugged her until she got control of herself, then said, "Come on. I'll walk you home."

Outside her apartment door, she turned to him and said, "I don't know how to thank you. You know, that guy could have beaten you up, I've seen barrels smaller than his chest."

"And I've probably seen peanuts bigger than his brain," said David. "I wasn't too worried."

"You should have been."

She inserted the key in her apartment door and opened it, saying, "Since you just saved my life, the least I can do is feed you."

"I'm sure Matt will love that," said David.

He had a point there. But after what David had just done, how could she not ask him for dinner?

Leeza was in the kitchen, taking dishes out of the cupboard. "Hi David," she called. "Been busy rescuing Shelby, huh?"

Shelby pulled him inside, shutting the door behind him. She shrugged out of her coat, then began tugging on the sleeves of his overcoat. She noticed he didn't do much to resist.

"I'll just stay for a cup of coffee," he said.

Leeza leaned against the doorjamb. "So, what'd you do?" she asked David.

Afraid he'd blow the whole thing off as nothing, Shelby answered for him. "He pulled me from in front of a speeding car."

Leeza's eyes grew round. "What?"

"It's true," said Shelby. "I wasn't watching where I was going and I walked right in front of a car."

"And we almost lost the best Nimue the world has ever seen," added David.

"You could have broken a leg," gasped Leeza. "Oh, my God." She rushed to Shelby and began to examine her as if unable to believe she had actually escaped unscathed. "When I heard you talking about him saving your life a minute ago I thought you meant something like him having an extra dollar to pay for your spices. But this . . . oh, my God."

"It's okay," said Shelby, patting her friend's arm. "I'm all right. Although," she added, looking at David, "it's a wonder he survived."

"What? He almost got hit, too?"

"Not by the car, by the driver. The guy was ready to beat him up. And this man was huge. He had a chin like a block of ice."

"I could have handled him," said David stubbornly. "But I suppose my sensei, whoever he is, will be glad I chose the path of peace."

Leeza's features scrunched into an expression of complete confusion. "What?"

"Never mind," said Shelby. "Just get David something to drink while I wash up and begin to prepare heaven for our taste buds."

"Oh, by the way, Matt called," said Leeza.

Shelby stole a look at David. He stood there wearing a mask of nonchalance. But his body looked tense, as if he was steeling himself for a blow. She realized she was feeling the same way.

"He said he's pooped from his training session," Leeza

continued. "He's going to catch a nap and come in time for dessert."

David's posture relaxed and Shelby said, "Now there's no reason for you not to stay for dinner."

Anything Shelby made would have been heaven for David's taste buds, but he especially enjoyed the exotic Indian dish she put together for them. And he enjoyed her friends. Leeza, with her larger than life gestures balanced Horst, who sat like a slab of marble, and contributed little to the conversation but a nod and an occasional, "Ya." The man looked like he ate human bones for breakfast, but his face took on a warm glow every time he looked at Leeza, and when she said something funny, Horst's laugh shook the room. Then there was James, cultured, funny and subtly gay, which was fine with David, because if James had been straight David would have been very jealous of his closeness with Shelby.

She caught him watching her, and her cheeks pinkened. He couldn't tell if her embarrassed smile was because she was finally admitting to herself that she was falling for him and it still felt too new to be comfortable, or if she wished he hadn't fallen for her. He hoped it was the former.

The phone rang before they got to dessert. David immediately knew who it was, and his gut clenched.

Sure enough. Filtering out the voices around him, he could hear Shelby on the kitchen extension, saying. "Yeah, we're just finishing the main course."

David suddenly wasn't hungry for dessert.

Shelby returned to the table. "That was Matt," she announced, avoiding meeting David's eyes as if they were adulterers trying to pretend innocence. "He's on his way."

David felt like everyone was looking at him even though the other guests were studiously focusing on the empty plates. He wished the floor would swallow him.

Trying to sound casual, he said, "Well, I should get going."

"We haven't had dessert yet," protested Leeza.

"I'm full, anyway," said David, rising. "Great dinner, Shelby. Thanks."

"Oh, sit down. You have time for dessert," said Leeza, picking up Horst's dinner plate and shoving it at Shelby. "It's custard, and there's always room for custard. Or was that Jell-O? I don't remember."

David sat, all the while trying to figure out if he was staying out of determination to fight for Shelby or simply because he didn't want to make a scene over leaving.

Shelby just stood there, uncertain, and Leeza grabbed James's plate and gave that to her, too, saying, "Come on, let's get the table cleared." Shelby headed to the kitchen and Leeza walked around the table, and picked up David's plate. She bent over and whispered, "If you try to leave I will have Horst break both your legs. Don't be stupid," she added, then scooped up her own plate and followed Shelby to the kitchen.

"What are you doing?" hissed Shelby as soon as Leeza had gained the kitchen.

Leeza looked at her with wide, innocent eyes.

"Just being a good hostess," she hissed back.

"Well, stop it. Did you see the look on David's face? Do you know how awkward it will be for him with Matt here?"

"Well that didn't stop you from inviting him in the first place."

"He saved my life. What was I supposed to do?"

"Exactly what you did. And if you want to talk about awkward, let's talk about how awkward you've been making life for David ever since you met him," she finished, her volume level turning up.

"Ssh," commanded Shelby, glaring at her.

"What's the matter with you, anyway?" continued Leeza, her voice dripping with disgust. "You've got Godiva chocolates in one hand and Tootsie Rolls in the other and you can't seem to tell the difference."

At that moment James poked his head around the door. "Need help?"

Both women jumped. Both smiled and said, "No." Shelby pulled out dessert bowls and started slapping custard into them and Leeza began to whang plates into the dishwasher.

"Well, okay," he said. "If you're sure."

"We'll be out in a minute," said Leeza sweetly. James left and she added under her breath, "just as soon as I shove my stupid roommate's head in the dishwasher to clear it."

James returned to the table, smiling as if no one had heard the two women arguing in the kitchen. "They're just cleaning up."

David smiled weakly. He should have left. But he hadn't, and now he was making everyone uncomfortable. The three men were sitting at the table like rocks. He should say something, but he couldn't think of anything. Why hadn't he left?

"So," asked James cheerily, "anybody read any good books lately?"

"I should leave," said David.

"No, you shouldn't," said James, his voice turning to steel.

Leeza returned with Shelby close on her heels. The dessert was passed around, sampled, then properly praised. After that Leeza and James single-handedly kept the conversation going while Horst inhaled his custard and David and Shelby toyed with theirs.

Leeza was just fetching more for Horst when Matt arrived. David observed his self-satisfied smile as he sauntered into the room in Shelby's wake, and felt a deep longing to plant his fist in the guy's face. The smile slipped when he saw David.

"Jones. What are you doing here?"

"Eating," Leeza replied for Shelby. "He ran into her at the Market and saved her from a speeding car, and we're rewarding him with dinner."

"Whoa. Superman lives," mocked Matt, making David's jaw clench and his hands fist.

James jumped into the fray. "Oh, but that's your title, isn't it, Big Mattster?"

Matt threw a scowl in James's general direction.

"Come and sit down and have some custard," said Shelby quickly.

Matt found a seat at the table and Leeza introduced him to Horst.

"So, Horst, are you an actor, too?" asked Matt. With that condescending tone, David was surprised Horst didn't reach out one of his huge hands and pound Matt right through his chair.

Horst was no more affected than a boulder would be by the scrabbling of a lizard at its base. "No. I'm a sculptor," he said in his Schwarzenegger accent.

Matt nodded politely. "Cool."

"Ya," agreed Horst.

"Do you make any money at it?"

Leeza sprang to Horst's defense. "Of course not. He's a starving artist."

"Good thing your girlfriend's working, huh?"

Shelby gave him a look that should have killed him on the spot. He didn't see it, though. He was busy frowning at the custard she'd put in front of him.

"Matt, it looks like you've lost weight," sniped James.

Matt shifted in his chair. "Maybe a little. I haven't had much appetite since I've been sick." He shot a look at David. "Don't have much of one now, come to think of it."

"Well, eat your custard," said James. "It will make you big and strong like Horst."

Matt's eyes narrowed. He opened his mouth to speak, but Shelby cut in, saying in a chipper voice, "I hope you guys are in the mood for a movie, because Leeza has rented *Midsummer Night's Dream* and *Much Ado About Nothing*."

"Great idea!" James enthused. "Let's start 'em right now."

"Okay," said Leeza, springing from her seat.

She hurried over to the small, ancient television, and the others quickly followed her, vacating the table as if moving away from something contaminated—everyone but Matt and David, who sat glaring at each other.

"Don't you have some place you need to be?" asked Matt.

"No, as a matter of fact, I don't," David replied and left Matt sitting at the table with his untouched custard.

He saw that Shelby had avoided the love seat, which only sat two, opting instead to defuse the situation by sitting with James on the cushions on the floor. He would have loved to join them, but decided to follow her lead and not create more friction. Even though he wanted Shelby to see that Matt was all wrong for her, he didn't want to make her any more uncomfortable than she already was.

Of course, if he really didn't want her to be uncomfortable, he should leave. That would solve the problem. Part of him wanted to just get out of Dodge and never come back. But the part of him that couldn't, his pride, kept him pinned to that chair.

And he paid for his pride. Matt joined Shelby on the floor, sprawled out next to her, and put a hand on her back.

She didn't even look at him. Probably his punishment for acting like such a jerk and embarrassing her in front of her friends. David wished she could see that Matt hadn't been acting.

The movie started, and Matt pulled Shelby closer to him. David frowned at the TV.

Matt spent most of the night acting like a dog with a bone. Every time David glanced their direction he saw the cretin's paw on some part of Shelby's body, either caressing her back, playing with her hair, or resting on her shoulder. Once, he whispered something in her ear, then followed it with a kiss.

David knew his rival was grinding an oversized heel into his heart, and he wanted to stand up, throw back his head and scream from the pain. Instead, he kept his features set in granite while he bled internally. Once, it seemed to David that Shelby moved away from Matt's possessive paw, but he couldn't be sure. Maybe she was just shifting positions.

He wanted to leave after the first movie—he had watched it with blind eyes and hadn't a clue what had happened, anyway—but he stubbornly stayed on, torturing himself and probably Shelby, too, and feeling like a villain for doing it.

Finally, the second torture session ended. David forced himself to rise from his chair slowly. "That was great," he lied.

"You leaving already?" asked Leeza.

"Yeah, I'd better be going. I've got a busy day tomorrow." Another lie.

Shelby got up. "Let me get your coat."

Matt remained lounging on the floor and started talking to Horst as if David were invisible.

The guy's confidence made David's blood bubble, but he kept his civilized mask firmly in place, following Shelby to the coat closet.

She pulled out his overcoat—the same one he'd left in her closet a lifetime ago—and handed it to him. "Thanks again for rescuing me," she said softly.

Was her expression wistful, or was she just sad that

David had stayed and wrecked her evening? Probably the latter since she hadn't planned on inviting him for dinner until he'd put her in a position where politeness demanded it. He wished he could ask her.

Instead, he said, "It was my pleasure." And probably the last pleasure he'd ever have in her company.

James hung around a few more minutes, then he, too, decided the party was over.

Shelby had just seen him to the door when Matt joined her. "So, you ready to take a drive over to my place?"

She had lost all desire to join Matt on his leather couch.

"I don't think so," she said. "It's been a long day. Anyway, you look kind of tired."

"I'm not. I took a nap."

"Well, I didn't."

"What's going on, Shel?" he demanded in a low voice.

She glanced over her shoulder to see if Leeza was eavesdropping. Leeza was busy with Horst, but she was fully capable of doing two things at once. Shelby opened the door and moved them into the hallway.

"Okay," demanded Matt. "What's going on? And what was Jones doing here tonight?"

"We told you. I ran into him at the Market. He saved me from getting hit by a car. The least I could do was invite him back for dinner."

"You and this guy seem to be getting pretty chummy. Is that all it was?"

"What are you implying?"

"Maybe Jones didn't just happen to run into you at the Market."

"He did!"

Matt continued as if she hadn't said a thing. "Here I've been sicker than a dog, practically dying. And while I'm dying, what's my girlfriend doing? Hitting on some little pip-squeak!"

"That little pip-squeak saved my life, and instead of thanking him, you were rude to him. In fact you were rude to everyone. I don't know what's the matter with you these days, but I think my mom was right. I have been waiting at the wrong bus stop. In fact . . ."

Matt silenced her by grabbing her and kissing her fiercely. "I love you, Shel, and I'm not letting you go. Understand?"

That was pretty straightforward. She should have been thrilled to hear it.

"I don't know what that bus stop crap is all about—your mom can think what she likes—but I'm committed to you."

Shelby broke the contact. "Where's the proof? I don't see a ring."

"How am I supposed to get one when my Visa is maxed out!" shot back Matt, his voice as close to a shout as a man could get in an apartment hallway at almost midnight.

Yet another excuse, which meant all that talk about settling their future had been just another Matt Armstrong smoke screen. David had been right: Matt was nothing more than a stage prop.

"How convenient," she said.

He sidled up to her and put his hands on her waist. "Aw, baby. Can't you be patient? Give me a break here. Give me time to breathe, a chance to get my debts cleared up."

She removed his hands and stepped back. "The way you spend money that could be years from now."

"What are you afraid of, anyway, that I'm going to vanish in the night?"

"And what is so scary to you about living in one apartment instead of two?" she retorted.

He stood silent for a moment, then his face lit up, and he said, "Okay. We'll live in one apartment." He grabbed her arms again. "Move in with me, Shel," he urged, his voice charged with excitement.

Oh, this was incredible. "Just like that? Move in with you in the hope that someday you might just be in the mood to get engaged. I'm good enough to have sex with but not good enough to marry. Is that it?"

"I didn't say that."

"You didn't need to."

"Why are you making such a big deal about getting married all of a sudden? We love each other, so why worry about having a piece of paper?"

She drew herself up and gave him a frosty glare. "That piece of paper symbolizes something you're obviously not willing to give: yourself." How long had she known this and been unwilling to face it?

And there was something else she had to face. "Tell me, Matt. Do you think Sandra Bullock has got nothing on me?"

He stared at her in complete confusion. "I have no idea what in the hell you're talking about."

"I know," said Shelby. She stepped back into the apartment, shut the door and locked it. "Good-bye, Matt."

# Sixteen

*Shelby stood there* for a moment, watching the wood of the apartment door thump as Matt banged on it.

"Shelby! Open up."

Not this time. No more encores. Pull the curtain on this farce and send the audience home.

The wood jumped again. "Shelby!"

She turned and headed for her bedroom. As she passed Leeza and Horst, who sat entangled on the love seat, Leeza grinned at her and murmured, "She can be taught."

Matt gave up banging on the door and stormed off down the hall. Okay. Fine. If that was the way she wanted it, then it was over. He'd never asked her when her last day at the office was, but he imagined it would be soon. Maybe it had even been Friday. And that would suit him fine, because when he came back to work on Monday he wouldn't have to look at her. And if he couldn't see her he wouldn't want her. Out of sight, out of mind, that was it.

He fell into his car with a sigh. Damn it all, he didn't

want her out of sight or out of mind. He wanted her in his bed.

How bad did he want her? Bad enough to call Uncle Lance and wrangle a deal on a diamond? He started the car, then went on auto pilot, cruising back to his place while he turned the possibility over in his mind.

He shivered and turned on the heat. He wasn't ready for this, and if he allowed Shel to push him into it they'd probably both live to regret it.

For a moment, Matt thought of calling his uncle and getting some fresh advice. But, no. He could handle this. Last time he'd talked to Uncle Lance he had the distinct impression that old unc was getting a little tired of coaching his favorite nephew. He'd only call if he really ran into major trouble.

On the surface it looked like he was in major trouble now, but he knew he wasn't. Not really. Yes, Shelby was pissed at him. So pissed she was still using poor Jones. But she wouldn't stay mad forever. She'd come around.

Lance closed Diana's latest book, *Dreams*, and laid it on his nightstand. The last of the six he had purchased, it had been a satisfying read, more complex than any of her previous books. He was amazed she had been able to interweave the threads of three different love relationships so tightly, not to mention bringing alive all those secondary characters. But, in spite of that accomplishment, he wondered how well her readers liked it. Although beautifully written, the tale didn't end with wrapping each couple in a pink bow and stamping "happily ever after" on them. Somehow, for a love story, that didn't seem right. Her first two books, he'd noticed, had been insistently hopeful. But, over the years, subtly and slowly, Diana's writing voice had changed. Now, with this latest offering, although she had shot off some bright flares of humor, they hadn't been enough to hide the cynicism lurking beneath her story line.

Like the poison-packing villain in that murder mystery she was currently writing, Diana Barrett had been slowly and deliberately killing Diana Valentine. Why?

David was doing his usual Sunday afternoon puttering on the house. Today, he was sanding the wood windowsills and finding it almost comforting. He loved this old place of his grandmother's. It was a forties add-on, a shack originally built in 1903 as a summer home. His grandmother had let it get run-down the last few years before she moved into the nursing home, and he had had to cope with everything from peeling paint to dry rot, and a rockery bulkhead growing weeds instead flowers. But the place was looking good now. He'd painted the exterior a conservative beige, then splashed the trim yellow, and, thanks to some help from his sister, Cassie, the rockery now spilled over with all manner of flowers and herbs. When the tulip tree in the front was in bloom, it made passersby lust.

He'd had more than one person approach him when he was working in the yard last summer and ask if he wanted to sell. He always smiled and said, "Never," because someday he was going to raise a family here, let the kids romp in the fenced backyard on weekday afternoons and take them across the street to Green Lake on Saturdays to play.

He had spent the last two and a half weeks imagining those kids with red, curly hair. Dumb. He turned on the sander and ground the sandpaper into the wood in an attempt to grind away all memory of his recent imbecility.

"Hey!" hollered a female voice, making him start and nearly drop the sander. He turned to see Cassie standing in the middle of the living room, her kid slung over one hip.

"Who let you in?"

"Me. You weren't answering. We waved at you as we came up the walk, but you didn't see. We pounded on the door, rang the doorbell, but you were too busy playing Tim the Tool Man."

David set down his toy and came over to them, and the kid broke into a smile and began to bounce against his mother, chanting, "Unca, Unca."

"Hey there M.D.," said David. The baby leaned toward him and reached out. Taking the hint, David plucked him from his mother's arms. Michael David was soft and substantial, and smelled like baby powder. Holding him summoned ghosts from David's dead dream to taunt him. His chest suddenly felt constricted and his eyes started to sting. His throat was growing a lump and he cleared it and walked with the baby to the window to hide his moment of weakness from his sister.

The kid pointed a pudgy hand toward the lake and said, "Lake."

"Michael David wanted to come see his uncle," said Cassie.

"Right after he sees Green Lake," observed David.

"Have you noticed? The sun is actually almost out. We may not see it again until August," said Cassie. "We should take advantage of it." She looked at him critically. "Besides, you look like you could use some fresh air."

Right now the last thing David wanted was to stroll on the grassy banks of Green Lake with his eagle-eyed sister observing him.

"I really wanted to get these windows done today," he said.

"It's Sunday. You know, as in day of rest, time to see your family? Speaking of which, nobody's seen much of you lately."

"I've been busy," said David. He set his nephew down, and Michael David promptly went for the sander.

"Oh, no, you don't," said David and snatched it out of reach, making his nephew howl in protest.

Cassie crossed the room and scooped up the child. "Come on. He needs distraction."

Ten minutes later, David found himself standing on the

edge of the lake, hunched inside his bomber jacket. The sun had been swallowed by slate skies, bringing an instant drop in temperature. It was going to rain any second. He wished his sister had gone shopping.

"So, who is she?" asked Cassie.

"Who?"

"The woman you've been chasing the last couple of weeks."

He didn't say anything. Just stood there, looking across the lake.

"Nothing to say for yourself? That proves it's a woman. Come on, you may as well tell. You know I'll find out, anyway."

She was right. She'd pry it out of him eventually. He sighed. "There's nothing to tell now."

"Oh. Begun and ended that soon?"

"Something like that. She had a boyfriend, anyway. It was stupid to chase her."

"If she had a boyfriend, why was she going out with you?"

"Long story," said David.

"Okay, then we'll go back to the house and you can tell me."

An hour and two mugs of coffee later David had pretty much told all there was to tell.

"I don't think she really loves this guy," said Cassie.

"Me, either," said David. "But there's not much I can do until she realizes that. And she may not. A lot of people get married thinking they're in love."

"She won't. Not if she's as smart as you say she is."

"I don't know." He looked out the window. The rain had started and fat drops began to pock the window. He felt as gray as the sky. It shouldn't have turned out this way. "There was a connection there," he said at last. "I know she felt it."

"Then why are you giving up?"

"Because it's time. You don't keep picking up a hammer and hitting your thumb with it. There comes a point when it's time to lay the thing down."

"So you're going to let her go. Just like that?"

David nodded. "Just like that."

Cassie studied him a moment. He met her gaze with a steady one of his own, not letting on that her scrutiny was making him feel hot and squirmy.

At last she spoke. "Then I guess she wasn't the right woman for you, because I know you'd fight for her if she was."

Michael David, who had been getting a little squirmy himself, pushed away the baby cookie his mother was offering with a whimper and rubbed one eye with the back of his hand.

"Well," said Cassie. "Guess it's time to go home for a nap. Are you coming over to watch the Super Bowl next week?"

"Sure," said David.

Why not? He didn't have anything else going on now that the woman he didn't love and wouldn't fight for was out of his life. He wondered what she was doing right now.

Shelby sat in front of the TV and watched Julia Roberts gallop away from groom number three in *Runaway Bride*.

She wasn't as stupid as Julia's character. She at least knew who she was. Still, she could tell she was not going to see the humor in this movie today. She stopped the video and pulled it out. Maybe she could get into her library book enough to help herself forget about what a mess she'd made of her love life.

She had to stop wondering what poor David was doing. If the look she'd seen on his face Saturday night was any indication, he was probably thanking his lucky stars he was rid of her.

As for Matt, every time she thought of him she thanked

those same lucky stars she'd finally wised up. She hated to think how much more time she would have wasted on him if the lightbulb hadn't finally gone off in her head at that fateful dinner.

She thought back to the hours they'd spent rehearsing their scenes when they'd done that first college play together. They'd had everything possible in common then. Even when he'd gotten caught up in his business classes, he'd still enjoyed coming to see Shelby perform. But she'd gone further into the theater world and he'd stopped at some invisible gate. And, looking from the other side of that gate she saw with new clarity just how much they had in common now: dancing and hot sex. Hardly enough to build a lasting relationship on.

What an idiot she'd been! Matt Armstrong was the human equivalent of fools' gold. Because he was handsome and fun, she had stupidly convinced herself that he was perfect for her. In reality, he was only a habit, and that perfect future she'd imagined with him had been nothing more than a fantasy.

She thought of her mom, married to Daddy all those years and pretending even to herself that she was happy. These days Mom wasn't pretending.

Shelby didn't want to pretend either. Marriage to Matt was not the equivalent of a Tony, and it wasn't the best she could do.

And to think, in spite of all those darts she'd thrown at that picture in the kitchen, that she had almost settled for second best just so she could say to herself she'd accomplished something. To stay in Seattle going nowhere with Matt and not even try for Broadway—what a close call!

But no more. She was going to go for the whole enchilada, the best of everything in every aspect of her life.

If David were here right now, he'd applaud. He believed in her so strongly. He was a wonderful, sweet man, and a great kisser, but he was . . . nice.

And nice wasn't any better of a choice than safe.

She sighed. Forget about David. Life went on and so must the show. And rehearsals started tomorrow.

Swing dancing with Lance at the Mountaineers Club on Sundays was becoming a habit, and as he pulled her toward him to the beat of a sassy blues song, Diana realized it was a habit she didn't want to break.

The song was about to come to an end, and Lance said, "Okay, let's try a grand finale. On your next pass I'm going to turn you and we'll end in a dip. Lean back and I'll catch you."

And they did just that. The next thing she knew, Diana was falling backward, sure she would land on her head. But, instead, she landed in Lance's arms and found herself clutching his sleeve like a lifeline.

He smiled down at her. "You didn't really think I was going to let you fall, did you?"

He set her upright, still keeping an arm around her waist.

"I may have had a moment's doubt."

"No more doubts. Good dancers trust their partners to be there for them. It's a lot like life. You have to reach a point where you trust the person you're involved with. Once you do, you're a team, and you can do great things together."

The DJ put on a slow song, and Lance turned her to face him and began to move them into a nightclub two-step. By now their steps matched perfectly.

"We're good together, Diana. When are you going to admit that and quit playing games with me?"

"You knew the rules when we started," she said defensively.

"And can you honestly say you're still happy playing by them?"

"I don't know."

He smiled and pulled her closer. "That's the first honest thing I've heard you say."

He said no more on the subject of their relationship until he got her to her front porch. Then he gave her a kiss that set her on a slow burn and said, "Do us both a favor, Diana, and think about what I said. When you're ready to quit the sidelines and join the dance, call me. I'll be ready to catch you."

The chorus of the *Camelot* production would be practicing at the Masonic Temple until it was time to start blocking out their movements on the stage. Now, seated on folding chairs, the singers banged out their various parts. Shelby exulted in the feeling of accomplishment and camaraderie that came from working with a group of people to produce something beautiful. Although they had only had a few practices, the songs were taking shape, and listening to the blend of voices often gave her goose bumps.

She looked to where James sat with the tenors. He happened to glance her way and gave her a triumphant grin. They had made it. Now, here they sat, morphing a dream into reality.

And it felt so good to be here. In spite of her flakiness, the dire predictions of her prof, the distractions in her life, even the lack of emotional support from Matt, she had made it.

But she hadn't been entirely without support. Mom had believed in her. So had David.

There he was, haunting her thoughts again, after all the times she had shoved him away, throwing herself into rehearsing, exercising, vocalizing and learning her big scene with Arthur.

Matt had been haunting her, too, although his haunting had been considerably less subtle. His voice had begun to take up permanent residence in her answering machine. "Shel, we can't leave things like this . . . Shel, we have to talk . . . Shel, call me . . . Shel, I know you're there." She ignored each message. There was no point in calling him back.

David, however, had been conspicuous by his absence. No calls, no messages asking how she was doing. She could hardly blame him.

And even though she had often felt the illogical urge to call him and tell him how rehearsals were going, she resisted. It wouldn't be right to start stringing him along all over again.

"All right, sopranos. Let's try that section one more time."

Shelby jerked her thoughts back to the present. *Live the moment, stay focused. And don't be turning poor David into a stage prop like you did with Matt.*

"I think you're nuts," said Leeza, as they prowled the produce section in the Market the following day. She picked up a head of lettuce and examined it. "You know you're going to give in and call him eventually, so why not end his torture?"

"Because it wouldn't be right. It would be like a woman starting to date the day after she got divorced."

"You weren't married," pointed out Leeza, her voice rising in frustration. "You weren't even engaged."

"But you don't break up with someone you've been with for three years and jump right into another relationship," said Shelby, inspecting a tomato.

"Oh, for heaven's sake," said Leeza in disgust. "Why don't you just get real and admit you and David are both so attracted to each other you can hardly stand it."

"I am attracted to him, but that doesn't mean we're a match."

"Well, you won't know you're a match if you don't go out with him."

"I don't want to hurt him."

"You're already doing that," said Leeza.

"I don't want to do it more. I've already managed to confuse sex with love. I'm not going to be stupid again and confuse it with passion."

"That does not even make sense," said Leeza.

"Yes, it does," insisted Shelby. "I've been thinking about this a lot, and I know what I want now. I want more than sex, which is just bodies and chemistry. And I want more than friendship. I want passion, and that's souls."

"Well, if I've ever seen the perfect soul mate for you, it's David."

"Maybe, but I've got the show to concentrate on right now, and that's enough," said Shelby.

"'Till the curtain goes down and you're left alone," said Leeza.

"Oh, this from the woman who once told me I should concentrate on my career."

"So I've changed my philosophy, at least where you're concerned. Do you want to end up like Norma Desmond in *Sunset Boulevard*?"

"I think I have a few years before I have to worry about that," Shelby retorted. "Come on. Let's go get some fish."

Leeza dropped the subject, but it lived on in Shelby's mind. She wished her friend hadn't used that Norma Desmond analogy. She didn't want to shrivel into some faded, love-starved has-been. But just wanting love insurance wasn't a good enough reason to call David. She'd already treated him like a human yo-yo, and she wasn't going to take a chance on repeating history. He deserved better than that.

It would seem he agreed, since the only contact she had with him was when she closed her eyes and saw his face in those defenseless hours just before sleep.

David slouched in an armchair at his brother-in-law's house, his face pointed in the direction of the TV. On the tray next to his chair, a half-eaten hot dog sat abandoned on a paper plate, a can of barely sipped beer going flat next to it.

The other men were all so engrossed in the game, yelling at the players and slugging beer, that no one noticed David's lack of participation in this year's annual Super Bowl party. But his sister did.

She laid a hand on his shoulder, making him start. "You didn't try any of my potato salad."

"I'm not all that hungry. I ate before I came."

"You never eat before you come," she said.

"Well, I did this time."

"Touchdown!" whooped her husband as the other guests either cheered or moaned, depending on their team sympathies.

Cassie squatted next to the chair. "Why don't you call her?"

David picked up his plate. "If I eat some of your potato salad will you quit bugging me?"

"No," she said. "I'm determined not to be the only woman at this party next year."

"Okay, I'll bring Mom."

She stuck out her tongue at him, and headed for the kitchen.

He watched the players on the screen tackling and bruising each other and thought of the bruising his pride had taken from Matt Armstrong. He'd let the guy break bones if he thought there was a chance he could win Shelby, but the game had been fixed from the beginning.

And the best man hadn't won. David knew he wasn't good enough for Shelby. He could live with that. What was choking him was the knowledge that the selfish, blond mannequin in the Armani knockoff, who was even less deserving, was going to get her. And the mannequin wouldn't appreciate her, probably wouldn't even stick with her.

David watched his team's quarterback go down and ground his teeth. The fourth quarter had ended and Matt had won. That was that.

"She won't take my calls," Matt complained to his uncle.

It had been more than a week since their fight, and Matt had resolved not to bug Uncle Lance unless he was desperate. But now he was desperate.

"Got a ring yet?"

"A ring! I don't even have the woman now."

"You know, you're spending a lot of time and energy on a game you can't win," said Uncle Lance.

"I can win it," insisted Matt. "I just need to figure a way to make an end run."

"The only way you're going to do that is to catch her outside the apartment. Ambush her when she's out with her girlfriends. Act like a movie hero and sweep her off her feet."

"I don't know how I'm going to even know when she's out when nobody's answering the phone at her place," grumbled Matt.

"You don't have a lot of choice here, kid. It's either wait her out or go find someone who wants to play the game your way. And there are plenty who do. Frankly, I think you ought to throw in the towel."

"No. She wants me. She's just being stubborn."

"Suit yourself," said his uncle. "But I think you're being stupid, and at this point, there isn't any more I can do to help you."

That ended the conversation, and Matt hung up feeling even more frustrated than he had before he called. He wished he'd asked his uncle how things were going with Shelby's mom. Uncle Lance hadn't mentioned anything about her in a long time. Odd, his uncle usually had a way with women, and something should have happened on that end by now. As for the ambush thing, it was a great idea, but short of stalking Shel, he had no idea how he was going to pull off that game plan. And he hated waiting.

He consoled himself the next few days by continuing to work overtime, catching up on all the paperwork that had piled up on his desk when he was out. One night he went snowboarding at Snoqualmie with some friends, which effectively took his mind off Shel.

Until he got in bed and dreamed about her.

He called her the next day and got Leeza, who said Shel was at the gym, working out. He took his coffee break early and went to the gym only to learn from the guy at the sign-in desk that he'd missed her by five minutes. And when he phoned the apartment an hour later there was no answer. Leeza had probably told Shel he called and now they were hiding out again. He ground his teeth and hung up without leaving a message.

Tomorrow was Friday. He'd go to the apartment with a single rose and the necklace she'd returned, and he'd promise her a ring next Christmas. And if he still wasn't ready by then, well, they'd cross that bridge when they came to it.

Shelby was in the shower when Leeza picked up the phone in the kitchen and called David. He answered on the first ring, as if he'd been camped out by the phone. Yes, she was doing the right thing. This proved it.

"David, it's Leeza. Listen, this is our last weekend before we start rehearsing afternoons and nights at the theater, and some of us are going dancing tonight."

"Good idea," said David noncommittally.

"Well, it is, except Shelby doesn't seem to be in much of a mood for fun. I think she's been hoping you'd call."

"Right. "

"She broke up with Matt."

There was silence for a moment, followed by a cautious, "Oh?"

"The same night you were here. After you left she slammed the door in his face and told him to get lost."

"Oh?" David's voice was taking on new energy now.

"Look, the only thing keeping you out of the race is, well, how can I put this delicately?"

"What?"

"If you could show a little passion, a little sense of the dramatic. If you could find a way to be not quite so nice."

"What?"

He sounded like he thought she was nuts. Oh, boy. If she had to explain it, then David and Shelby really weren't a match.

"I can't draw you a map. That would be cheating. Just think about what I said a little. Something will come to you. Now, we're going to . . ."

"Did you remember to call James?"

Leeza jumped and turned to see Shelby strolling into the kitchen, toweling off her wet hair.

"That's who I'm talking to right now," lied Leeza. "So, see you there, James," she said and hung up on David.

David stared at the receiver. James? And she didn't even tell him where they were going. Well, that probably wouldn't be hard. Leeza was bound to leave him some kind of clue. He sat a moment, chewing his lip.

Why was Leeza playing matchmaker behind her friend's back? Maybe it was because she knew Shelby would feel awkward calling him. She shouldn't. In fact, she should realize he'd be thrilled to hear from her, deliriously happy to know she'd broken up with Matt the Meathead. So, maybe Shelby really didn't want to see him, but Leeza felt she should. Leeza was doing this for her friend's good even though her friend didn't want to see him at all. Not good.

And what did she mean by showing passion? Did she think he didn't have it in him? Of course he did. No one loved those old movie heroes more than he did. And just because he wasn't an actor didn't mean he didn't appreciate flair for the dramatic. His favorite musical character was *The Phantom of the Opera*, for crying out loud!

He scowled at the phone. What did Leeza expect him to do, anyway? Come riding into the dance club on a white horse and carry Shelby away?

As he continued to think, the mist of a wild idea began to swirl into shape in his brain. But it was too bizarre, too crazy. He'd feel like an idiot.

But who would know it was him? And wasn't Shelby worth making a fool of himself for?

He'd only done one play in his whole life, and that had been in high school. He'd forgotten his lines opening night and been mortified, and he'd graduated from memory loss to wooden self-consciousness with the following performances. He had welcomed closing night like a long lost lover, and after that had never walked on a stage again. Even the thought of making such a complete fool out of himself in front of a room full of strangers, not to mention Shelby, made him shrink back from the monstrous idea. But only for a moment. He'd willingly make a fool of himself for Shelby. And if he was going to get her attention, get her to really see him, he would have to do something over-the-top. As things stood right now, she was lost. If he tried this one last idea maybe, just maybe . . . What would it hurt to try?

Matt sat a block down from Shelby's apartment house, hunched behind the wheel of Ben's car, playing Magnum P.I. again. Slushy snowflakes flew at his windshield like a multitude of ghosts, making him shiver. He fiddled with the heater, even though he knew the effort was in vain. Ben had warned him that it wasn't working. Teeth chattering, he forced his gaze beyond the dizzying army of attacking snowflakes and onto the apartment house door and told himself for the fourth time that he was not acting like a stalker, that this was perfectly sane behavior.

Well, maybe it was a little insane, but he knew who to blame for that. He would never, in a million years, understand what had gotten into Shel lately. But he did know that all it would take was one great night to make it change back again.

The apartment door opened, and Shelby and Leeza emerged. Matt grinned when he saw Leeza tape some sort of note on the door. It would be a piece of cake to find Shel.

He waited a full ten minutes, just to make sure they were really gone, then moved the car down the street. He got out and ran up the steps to read the note.

"Horst," it began in Leeza's big scrawl. "Couldn't get ahold of you. We've all gone dancing. Join us."

Matt made a mental note of the familiar club name beneath the words, then headed for Pioneer Square to sweep Shelby off her feet.

# Seventeen

♡

*Shelby had just* collapsed at their table next to James to cool off and guzzle her tonic water when she looked across the crowd and spotted him. Great. This was all she needed. She ducked down under the table and pretended to search for some invisible, lost item.

A hand on her shoulder made her jump and bang her head. Rubbing it, she sat up to see Matt looking down at her. "Lose something?"

"Only a perfectly good evening now that you're here. Go away and leave me alone."

"What a wonderful suggestion," put in James.

Matt shot him a glare. "Get lost."

James gave Shelby a questioning look, and she nodded. "Okay," he said. "If Big Body Little Brain gives you any trouble, just call me and I'll sic the bouncers on him."

James exited and Matt slid into the seat next to Shelby, laying a single white rose on the table. "You don't really want me to leave, Shel."

"Oh, yes, I do."

"Don't you think we ought to at least try to fix this?"

"It can't be fixed," said Shelby. "It's taken me a long time to see that, but now I know it. We're not the same two people we were when we were in college."

"Of course we are," he insisted.

"Well, one of us is," she said sadly.

"Don't you think after three years you owe me more than a quick brush-off?" Matt stood up and took her hand. "Come on, dance with me. Let's talk. Please?" he added.

Reluctantly, she went with him onto the dance floor. This was such a waste of time.

The music was slow and sensual. He pulled her into his arms and she felt nothing.

He looked down at her, his face a picture of earnest contrition. "I don't understand how, overnight, you could suddenly not love me."

"It hasn't been overnight, Matt. It just seemed like it."

He shook his head, refusing her words. "Everything was fine until your mom started talking about weddings."

Shelby thought back to the day Professor Williams told her she didn't have the focus or the passion it took to make it on Broadway, that she'd better plan to teach drama or just marry her party boyfriend and do community theater. Leeza had insisted he said the same thing to everyone in the hopes of inspiring them to go out and prove him wrong, but the words had lodged in Shelby's heart over the past few months and grown into a dream almost as good as her original one of stellar achievement. Local theater would be good enough if she had a big wedding and a perfect marriage to balance it. Now she realized she'd been like a land rush pioneer, afraid to go beyond what she knew she could grab. And she'd almost settled for less.

"It may have been fine, but it was all wrong," she said.

"Three years together and, just like that, it was all wrong?"

Shelby shrugged helplessly. "You don't fit in my world

anymore, and I don't want to fit in yours. I hate camping, Matt, and I want to go to Broadway."

"Come on. You don't really want to move to New York. It's crowded and full of muggers."

"And you don't want to marry me. See? I told you, we're not a match."

She pulled away from him and began threading her way through the swaying couples.

He caught up with her at the edge of the floor. "You don't mean this, and we are, too, a match." His eyes suddenly opened wide. "What the hell?"

She was vaguely aware of movement at her side, and turned to see a man in a long black velvet cape, a wide-brimmed black felt hat, and *Phantom of the Opera*–style mask looming over her.

"Come with me, Shelby," the mystery man commanded her, his voice husky.

It could only be one person in that costume, but the mask and cape turned him into a stranger. "David?" she squeaked.

"Halloween's over," sneered Matt.

"Yes, it is," agreed the man. He stepped behind Shelby and wrapped a hard, muscled arm around her shoulders, and his cloak swallowed her. "So why don't you crawl back under your rock and leave this woman alone?"

Matt's eyes narrowed. "Let go of her."

"So you can harass her some more?"

A small crowd was collecting around them, and Shelby caught sight of two heavily tattooed goons in black jeans and matching T-shirts marching their direction. This scene was going to get ugly in a moment. She should stop it right now. All she had to do was step out of the Phantom's arms and walk away. But she couldn't bring herself to do it. She had to play the scene out and see where it led.

"At least I don't have to play dress up to get her attention," Matt retorted. "Now let her go or I'm going to rip your head off."

The Phantom seemed completely unruffled, either by the commotion he was causing or by Matt's threats. "I don't think so," he said calmly. To prove his lack of fear, he kissed Shelby's temple. The simple touch of his lips on her skin made her mouth go dry, and she had to remind herself to breathe.

Matt let out a growl and reached for him, and the Phantom pulled back a step, taking Shelby stumbling with him. His free hand shot up, and he hurled something to the floor. There was a pop, and then Shelby found herself cut off from Matt by a wall of smoke.

She barely had time to cough before the Phantom was hurrying her away from the startled screams and angry shouts, past chairs and tables, down the club's narrow back hallway and past the bathrooms, then out a small door.

He held her waist tightly, and rushed with her over the cobblestones of the narrow alley, running through the falling snow like some hunted thing. Her heart was pumping wildly now, and she couldn't be sure if it was from fear or excitement.

Halfway down the alley, he pulled her into a doorway and drew her against him. His breathing was coming hard, and she could feel his heart hammering inside his chest.

"David, what are you doing?"

The Phantom looked at her, no trace of David's easy smile visible on his face. "I'm not David," he said.

She almost believed him. The David she knew was kind and gentle, easygoing. He was pleasant, and warm; free of the kind of depth and darkness she was sensing in this man.

"I'm your angel of music, and the man who loves you," he said, pivoting her against the brick wall of the old building and looking down at her.

There they stood, his hard torso covering hers, his

stance of possession as old as the first man and woman. He propped an arm above her and his cape fell like a curtain, hiding her from the world. His free hand caressed her chin and slid down her neck, and she thought of the old vampire movies she'd watched on late night TV as a kid. Now she knew how those women felt, knew the seductive power of that mixture of fear and attraction.

Before she could say anything, his lips came down on hers, hot and demanding. This wasn't David, not the David she knew, anyway. She began to struggle.

He stopped the kiss. His eyes glinted from behind the mask. "Why are you fighting me?"

That sounded like something a rapist would say. Panic seized her and she pushed him, but he didn't budge. "Let me go," she cried frantically.

"You only had to ask," he said softly. He stepped back, and the cape fell around him. "Do you really want to go?"

She squinted into the darkness, studying the man in front of her. He stood there, regarding her from under the lowered brim of his hat, the black velvet cape swirling around his legs, and power radiating off him. She was sure she caught sight of a familiar curl of brown hair under that hat. Her head told her she knew the face behind the mask. But this man seemed taller than David. And the mask suddenly looked malevolent. Still, it beckoned her. She stood rooted and let her opportunity to run slip away.

He held out an arm, and the voluminous piece of black velvet unfolded like a giant wing. "Shelby, I love you," he whispered. "Let me help you catch your dreams and give you everything you secretly long for."

This was what she longed for: not just a man with hot hands, but one with a soul equally impassioned, a man who understood about dreams. She took a step, and with that step left reality behind. The Phantom caught her in his arms and his cape enfolded her. He pulled her tightly against him and ran his mouth along her chin, whispering, "You set me on fire, Shelby."

"You've gotten a pretty good blaze going yourself," she murmured.

"Bad dialogue," he whispered, and before she could utter any more, he kissed her.

She settled into the Phantom's embrace with a sigh, and slipped her arms up his back. From down the alley, she heard Matt calling her name. Her Phantom drew her farther into the dark doorway, his mouth growing more demanding and his embrace more possessive, and Shelby gave herself up to the possession. Soon Matt's angry calls ceased to exist.

As the car came to a stop in front of Lance's house, Diana asked herself what on earth she thought she was doing. Done would be a better word to use. She had fallen in love with Lance, and they both knew it. When she called him she'd waved the white flag and surrendered her heart. Although he had kept the conversation light during dinner, she had known she would soon be saying good-bye to the platonic stage of their relationship. She hadn't been surprised when he suggested they go to his place and discuss their future in private. Now here she was, about to entangle herself in all those strings she once insisted she didn't want. And once entangled, then what? Happiness and security or humiliation and misery? If only she were clairvoyant!

He smiled at her. "Here it is. Home, sweet home."

Sweet was not the word that came to mind when Diana looked at Lance's house. It was a light gray contemporary with bold lines, slick and good-looking, a reflection of the man who owned it.

He opened the car door and helped her out—right into his arms. The kiss he gave her made her forget about the nippy breeze and the wet flakes hoping to slip past the defenses of her coat, made her forget that she was a woman with no libido and no need for a man in her life.

She was being an idiot. She could still change her mind and say she only arranged this last date so she could tell Lance face to face that she preferred to sit out the dance rather than risk the fall. She broke the kiss.

If her lack of romantic enthusiasm bothered him, he didn't betray it. He merely smiled and said, "Let's go try that nineteen-eighty port I promised you."

They entered the house, and the magnificent piece of Chilhuly glass on the credenza immediately drew her attention. She walked over to it and stood taking in the color and shape.

Lance joined her. "As you can see, we have the same taste in art."

Art, dancing, books. She and Lance shared a world of common interests. She felt him moving closer and walked into the living-dining room area. The window pulled her like a magnet. She loved the view of water at night. The lights of houses across Lake Sammamish twinkled at her.

"You have a beautiful view."

She turned to see him leaning against the wall, hands in his pockets. "I certainly do."

The glint in his eyes brought that jittery feeling he was so good at triggering in her. She moved again, this time out to the kitchen, and was aware of him following her.

Here, too, the windows framed a view of the lake. The room was a gleaming white, the cupboards sleek and modern, the countertops marble.

She faced him, leaning against a counter, trying to look casual. "This is quite an impressive kitchen. Do you ever cook in it?"

"Does coffee count?"

He moved closer and she turned away, pretending great absorption with what she saw out the window. "I suppose every room in this house has a great view."

"The bedroom has the best."

He slipped off her coat and kissed her neck. "Are we done playing tag now?"

"What's that supposed to mean?" As if she didn't know.

He turned her to face him. "I've been chasing you all over the house. I've never met a grown woman as nervous as you."

"Why should I be nervous?" she hedged.

He tossed her coat over the work island. "That's what I'm wondering, especially since it was you who called me."

"I realize now I shouldn't have," said Diana. "It was a mistake."

"No," Lance corrected her. "It was a beginning. The direction we're going now is a mistake, especially in light of the fact that we've finally built up an element of trust."

"A woman can only build so far when she's dating a man whose nickname is Lance Romance," said Diana.

"That's an old family joke," protested Lance, his face coloring. "It has nothing to do with us."

"Are you sure?"

He shook his head in disbelief. "After all the time we've spent together, do you really think all you are to me is a sexual challenge? Tell me, Diana, who put that hard shell on you?"

"A man."

She hadn't meant to say that, and the bitter tone that had crept into her voice was an equal surprise. Now Lance was studying her through narrowed eyes.

"I thought you had been a happily married woman," he said.

"Of course I was." She turned away again.

"Don't do that," he commanded, making her face him. "Don't keep turning your back on me, putting up those walls. Talk to me, Diana. What was wrong with your marriage?"

"Nothing. I was married to a very nice man."

"Then why are you so mistrustful? Why not assume that there are other men out there who are equally nice?"

"I never said there weren't."

Lance looked like she'd just slapped him. He nodded slowly. "I get it. Old Lance Romance doesn't happen to be one of them."

"I told you before. I don't want to get hurt."

"All these circles we're going in are making me dizzy, so let's stop. Tell me, who is it that I remind you of?"

He just couldn't quit badgering, could he? All right. If he really wanted to know. "A lying bastard."

The color drained from his face, making her feel suddenly sick. She supposed she was, to let such ancient history still affect her. And that remark had been completely uncalled for.

"I'm sorry," she said quickly. *Sorry for a lot of things.*

"Well, at least the truth is out now," he said with forced lightness. He stood for a moment, regarding her. "Want to tell me about it?"

She felt a warning prickle in her eyes. She shook her head. "No."

"But you will." He took her by the waist and lifted her onto the kitchen counter. The marble felt cold beneath her. "Who burned you so badly, Diana?"

She looked at the floor and said nothing.

"Okay," said Lance, "I'll take a wild guess. He was a smooth talker; he told you he loved you just so he could get you into bed."

The hard edge to his voice made her look up, ready to defend herself. But she saw that he wasn't looking at her. He was staring out the window.

"Then what happened?" he asked, still not looking at her.

"Nothing."

"And therein lies the rub." He turned his gaze on her. "Did he get you pregnant?"

She nodded, and felt the pain of that time in her life as freshly as if it were brand new.

"What happened to the baby?"

An old ghost was suddenly in the room, one that had haunted Diana for years. She shook her head and pressed her lips tightly together. *Don't resurrect any more pain. Don't talk about the baby you wish you'd had.*

Lance's mouth settled into a hard line. At last he spoke. "So, Mr. Wonderful used you and left you."

She shrugged. "It took two to make that mess."

"And you didn't want any more messes, so the next time around you settled. I'm surprised you even let another man get close."

"John was a good man. "

"Unlike the one I remind you of." He went on before she could say anything. "So, because dear John was a nice guy, you married him, hoping something magic would grow out of that soil. But it didn't, did it? Instead of magic, you got . . ."

Diana cut him off. "A good life, and a wonderful daughter. I have no complaints."

"Oh, yes, you do, but you'd never voice them. I'm sure you never voiced them to anyone but yourself all the time you were married. And you fooled yourself into thinking you had everyone convinced you were happy. Maybe you even convinced yourself. Did you?"

This was too much. "I don't appreciate being psycho-analyzed." Strong words. They would have sounded stronger if her voice hadn't cracked.

"I'll just bet you don't," agreed Lance. "Why aren't you writing love stories anymore?"

"Because I'm sick of them," spat Diana. "I don't need the fantasy and I don't need the money. I can finally do what I want."

"That's not why. It's because you're shriveling up inside. So much so that you can't even bring love alive in your imagination anymore. You're lonely as hell, but you'd rather keep drying up than take another chance and be disappointed."

She was not shriveling up. And she'd been perfectly content until she met Lance Gregory!

"I've heard enough," she informed him, hopping off the counter.

Lance didn't move to let her by. "Every regret you've ever had you can trace back to him. And I'm him, aren't I? The older version." He blew out an angry hiss. "If this isn't poetic justice."

"What happened to just going out together to have fun, to having no strings?" cried Diana. "Why do you have to keep pushing for more?"

"Because it's what we both want. I want to be close to you. I love you," he added softly. "You were right about me. I've been a cad since the day I discovered girls. But I swear I'm shedding that old skin. You've stripped it right off me."

Diana studied his face. Could she believe him? "Oh, Lance, I want to believe that. I'm just afraid. I'm too old to fight the battle of the sexes. I want security."

"And I want to give it to you," he said. "Pretend we're on the dance floor. Trust me."

The phone rang, inserting its demanding presence between them.

"Your phone's ringing," she said.

"Like I care," he replied, and pulled her into his arms.

His kiss was hard and demanding. Inside, she felt like she was falling. She sighed and let him pull her closer.

At first she was barely aware of the voice coming through the answering machine on the opposite counter, but the vague familiarity of it finally seeped through the romantic fog surrounding her brain and caught her attention. "Things are a mess with Shel," said Matt. "I'm going to have to break down and at least give her a ring. The trouble is, I'm tapped out from that necklace you suggested I get her."

The words fell on Diana like ice water. She stiffened and Lance pulled away.

He moved to pick up the phone, but Diana caught his arm. "Let's listen to the rest of the message."

Lance obliged and stood, jaw clenched.

"Could you give me a deal?" continued Matt, "Let me take the ring now and make payments. I swear to God it's the last favor I'll ask." He sighed heavily. "I guess you're out with Shel's mom, so who knows when you'll get in. Not that it's done any good, anyway," he added sulkily. "But will you call me as soon as you get this? I'm desperate."

He hung up, and for a suspended moment Diana and Lance stood in the cold silence, regarding each other. Then Diana's anger seared through it. As she scooped up her coat she felt like an atom about to split.

She brushed past him, saying, "Call me a cab. I'll wait outside."

He grabbed her arm. "Oh, no. You don't get to leave like that without us talking."

Talking? As if she ever wanted to say anything to this man again other than I hate you? She looked down at his hand. "Be glad I don't know where you keep your meat cleaver. If I did I wouldn't simply ask you to take your hand off me."

"For crying out loud, Diana. Don't you hate books where the conflict arises from a simple misunderstanding that could be cleared up with one conversation?"

She couldn't believe the nerve he had. She gave him a look that should have flash frozen him. "A simple conversation will turn you from a snake into a saint? You must be a magician."

He took her coat from her. "No. Just a man who is in the middle of changing. And most people caught in that process come with a past."

Diana nodded at the blinking answering machine. "So I heard. Too bad you don't use an answering service. I could have missed that call."

"I do for my business."

"You have an answering machine at home so you can monitor your calls?" she guessed. "How fortunate for me."

"I've been a snake for years," he admitted. "But I told you, I'm shedding that old skin. And that wasn't a lie."

"You used me. You played head games with me and tried to interfere in my daughter's love life."

"Oh, come on, Diana," pleaded Lance. "Haven't you done your share of interfering in that relationship?"

"I didn't use and manipulate another human being. I didn't pretend to care." Diana's throat constricted, choking off the last word.

"You're right, of course. And don't you think I've already felt like the king of slime? I told Matt he's on his own with Shelby, but he obviously never heard."

"I guess you didn't tell him very loudly."

"I guess not. Frankly, I was a little distracted. I've been busy, myself, falling in love with Shelby's mother."

"Stop it!" she cried, shaking off his hand. "You don't need to keep up the deception anymore." She grabbed her coat again and started out of the room.

Once more, he prevented her. "You're angry. I don't blame you. But I can fix this with one phone call."

"Oh, please."

He towed her back into the kitchen, picked her up and set her back on the counter. He pointed a finger at her, saying, "Stay there."

She stayed, looking daggers at him as he picked up the phone and began punching in numbers. When he had finished, he returned her look with an expression that dared her to just try and leave.

She looked away and hoped her facade of righteous anger would stay in place until she could get out of this cold, hard house and salve her broken heart with salty tears.

"Matt. It's Uncle Lance. Yeah, I got your message. Now you need to get mine. I'm off your team. I'm not giving you a deal on a diamond because you're just going to use it to stall Shelby. There may have been a time when that wouldn't have bothered me, but it does now. If you want to marry the girl, hock something and go to Tiffany's." Diana could hear the faint squawk of a raised voice.

"That's the way it goes, kid. You're on your own. I'm through helping you turn into me."

He hung up and Diana said, "And that's supposed to prove . . . ?"

"That I was wrong and stupid, and that I don't want to be either anymore. That I meant it when I said I love you. Marry me."

His words left her reeling. "You're insane."

"Why, thank you. Your reaction certainly makes this proposal a memorable one. But you still haven't given me an answer."

"That would be a little silly, wouldn't it? You don't mean a word of what you just said. That was all for show."

"Just for show?" In two strides, Lance was in front of her, hauling her off the counter. He grabbed her coat and held it out, saying, "You want show? I'll give you show. Then you'll have to find some other excuse to turn me down."

"What are you doing?"

"Taking you ring shopping. Not every man in my family is afraid of commitment."

"This is crazy," she protested, even as she allowed him to slip her coat up her arms.

"I don't think so. In fact, I think I've never been saner, never done anything more smart, more right in my whole selfish, rotten life," he said, hurrying her out of the room.

"You're insane." Diana was half laughing, half crying now as they hurried down the hall to the front door. "We can't just run out in the middle of the night and get a ring."

"Why not? In case you've forgotten, I happen to own a jewelry store."

"This is too quick. I can't . . ."

"Yes, you can. And, anyway, don't you want a down-payment on that security I promised you?"

Lance had the front door open now, and was looking at her expectantly. She smiled at him and crossed the threshold.

Her common sense commanded her to stop, but her feet continued their mutiny, rushing her down the front walk alongside Lance.

She had never seen him drive so fast. And his speech matched his driving speed. "I have the perfect ring: a Colombian emerald. It has a minor blue secondary coloration and it's exquisite. Of course, if you want something more ornate, we can incorporate some diamonds into the design, but the emerald suits your coloring. Did you know, my love, that the Greeks dedicated the emerald to the goddess Aphrodite? That's the main reason you need one. You are a goddess."

"Oh, please," she protested halfheartedly.

"I think I should see what I can do about finding a matching necklace," Lance continued, "and earrings, too."

Diana felt nearly giddy from the carousel her feelings were riding. She laughed and said, "Stop already."

He reached across the seat and caught her hand. "I can't seem to help myself. I haven't felt like this in years." He grinned at her. "It's great."

It was, indeed. "But I can't believe we're doing this," said Diana.

"I hope you don't want to call off the engagement already."

She chuckled. "You should be so lucky."

They slipped into the store, and Lance flipped on the lights. While he disarmed the alarm system, Diana took in the opulent setting. With its chandeliers and thick carpet, it was an impressive store. The richly upholstered chairs beckoned her to come in, make herself at home and relieve herself of a small fortune while she was at it. Diamonds and other precious gems set in various pieces of jewelry sparkled at her from the display cases. In one corner, a fine piece of Chilhuly bloomed.

"It's lovely," she said, looking around.

"My kingdom," said Lance, slipping his arms around her. "I lay it at your feet, my lady."

"I'll take it," she said.

The light moment slipped into something more serious. Their embrace tightened, and the next thing Diana knew Lance was kissing her, sliding his hands down her back, and she was slipping her fingers into his hair.

She was sure she could have stayed that way all night, but she didn't object when he ended the kiss to nuzzle her hair.

"I suppose your scarred past is going to insist that I wait to show you the view from the bedroom until after we're married," he complained.

"That is a strong likelihood," Diana agreed.

"Which means that we will, of course, be married immediately."

"Valentine's Day," she murmured.

"Trite, but I suppose I can live with it."

"Good, because I think it's appropriate that Lance Romance, the cad, disappear from history on Valentine's Day."

"And who, exactly, will take his place?"

"Lance Gregory, family man."

Lance waggled his eyebrows at her. "And won't we have fun making that family?"

"Well, actually, it will be more like inheriting than making."

Lance looked puzzled by her remark. "You don't want kids?"

"In case you haven't noticed, I have a grown daughter."

"Well, yes, but you were obviously very young when you had her. Lots of people start another family later in life."

"Not this person," said Diana firmly. "Even if I were insane enough to want to do that, I couldn't."

Lance's brows knit together. "You mean you've had your tubes tied?"

"By nature. I've gone through menopause." He looked at her in shock, and she didn't know why, but she almost felt like she'd deceived him, somehow. "Lance, you know how old my daughter is. How old do you think I am?"

"Forty-one, maybe forty-two."

"I just turned forty-eight and I can't have any more children."

She watched the furrows form on his forehead, saw the stunned look turn to one of despair. "Oh," he said. "Well."

It was the first time she'd ever seen him at a loss for words.

"Lance?" she prompted. "Is that a problem?" Of course, it was, but she couldn't admit it, not yet, not until that last ember of hope had been extinguished.

"No, no, not really," he said, his voice growing faint. "It just came as a surprise, that's all. I always thought I'd have a son someday, you know, someone to leave the family business to."

Now he was finding it difficult to look at her. Watching his discomfort made her heart feel like it had been injected with lead. This was no simple misunderstanding to be cleared up with a heart-to-heart conversation. Lance

Gregory wanted a fertile woman and a child of his own. He didn't want to simply inherit what another man before him had made.

She couldn't give him what he wanted. They had nothing with which to weave a future.

She laid a hand on his arm. "I think we'd better wait on the ring. You need time to think about this."

His face had lost its color and his mouth looked pinched. He still couldn't seem to find his voice, so he just nodded.

"Where's the phone?" she said softly. "I think I'll call that cab now."

# *Eighteen*

*It was two* A.M. and Shelby was still awake, dreaming of her wild encounter with David. She touched her hand where he had kissed it before helping her into the cab he'd had waiting.

"When will I see you again?" she'd blurted.

"Soon, I hope," he'd answered. "In your dreams." Then he'd given the cabdriver her address and stepped away from the car.

As it squealed off, she'd watched out the window, unable to take her eyes off the sight of him standing there, looking like every romantic figure she'd ever dreamed of as a girl. And she hadn't stopped watching him until the cab turned a corner.

Now she understood firsthand the meaning of that old-fashioned word, ravished. She had, indeed, been carried away and overwhelmed with emotion. David the Phantom had carried her higher with his all-too-short session of passionate kisses and caresses than Matt had ever been able to using his whole arsenal of sexual tricks. Matt had turned

her on, but David had made her fly. Matt had played her
body, but David had claimed her soul.

So, that was passion.

She smiled as she remembered how she had resolved to
leave David alone. That would have been about as bright
as Cinderella passing on Prince Charming's proposal because she had soot under her fingernails. There was nobil-
ity and there was stupidity. She was so glad she now knew
the difference.


Diana didn't know her mother was in the kitchen until
Flo's hand on her shoulder made her start.

"What's happened?" she asked.

Diana propped her elbows on the oak table and let her
face fall into her hands. She thought she'd used up all her
tears, but they seemed to form out of nothing, making a
fresh assault on her tired eyes, rushing into her throat and
constricting it. She shook her head.

Flo sat down opposite her. "Things didn't work out with
Lance."

"No," said Diana, rubbing her aching forehead. She'd
been chewing aspirin like candy, but aspirin couldn't reach
the kind of pain she felt.

"What happened?" prompted Flo.

"We weren't a match," Diana managed.

"You looked like a match."

"He wants children."

"What? At his age?"

"He's not that old."

"For starting a family he is," insisted Flo. "He'd be on
social security when the child was in high school. I never
heard anything so silly in my life."

"Lot's of people start families later in life these days,
and he wants a son. He thought I was younger, thought I
could have children."

"Oh, my," said Flo, her voice heavy with sadness. "Oh, baby, I'm so sorry."

Sorry. What a pitiful, ineffectual word that was! It did nothing for the pain seething inside her. Diana laid her head on the table and brought up the agony with big, racking sobs. She felt her mother at her side, hugging her, and she turned and buried her face in Flo's old, terry cloth bathrobe and clung tightly. It was such small comfort, but it was all she had. She tightened her grip and cried harder.

The bedside clock told Lance it was now nearly three in the morning. He reached over and shut off the alarm. He wouldn't need it. He wasn't ever going to get to sleep tonight, so there was no need to worry about waking up. He got out of bed, slipped on his bathrobe and went to the library to search for a book. Diana's was the first one he saw, and he swore. To torture himself further, he went to his favorite chair where it lay, picked it up and turned to the back page. There was the same photo that had intrigued him when he first saw it on her web site.

Nature had played a damned dirty trick, making her look so young and sexy and fertile. Who would have guessed she couldn't have kids? Didn't women have periods clear up to their fifties? He supposed, after all the women he had used, that it was God's little joke to bring him one who was perfect except for the fact that she couldn't give him what he wanted.

Some joke. He threw the book across the room.

"So," said Leeza, peering over Shelby's shoulder to check the progress of the omelette she was cooking. "How are you feeling this morning, Christine Daaè?"

"Indescribably fabulous."

"That was truly amazing last night," said Leeza dreamily. "I've never seen anything like it off a stage. Oh, and you should have seen Matt's face when the smoke cleared.

He was so ticked I thought his head was going to pop off."
She pulled a pitcher of orange juice out of the refrigerator.
"I guess David isn't so normal and boring after all, huh?"

"I guess I didn't know him as well as I thought," Shelby
admitted.

"So, has he called yet?"

Shelby shook her head.

"Oh, well. He's probably giving you time to sleep in."

"Probably," agreed Shelby.

But the morning wore on with no call from David.

"It is the weekend. Maybe he had to go out of town,"
said Leeza.

"Maybe," said Shelby. "But doesn't it seem odd that he
hasn't called or sent flowers, or done something to follow
up last night?"

"A little. Still, after last night, a phone call would be a
real letdown. He's probably working on a sequel."

Just thinking about taking up where they left off made
Shelby go weak in the knees. Leeza was right, of course.

They were getting ready to leave for rehearsal when the
phone rang. Shelby jumped for it.

"It might be Matt," cautioned Leeza.

"Yeah, you're right." Shelby moved to the answering
machine, hand poised to pick up if it was David.

Matt's voice entered the room. "Shel, I'm calling to see
if you're all right. That guy didn't hurt you, did he?"

Both women guffawed.

"Baby, I know I've been wrong, and I want to prove it
to you. We can go to Tiffany's, put some money down on
a ring. Just call me back. I'm not giving up, Shel. I'm not
taking no for an answer."

There it was, the one thing she'd been waiting for, an-
gling for, and now she didn't want it. Matt would have to
take no for an answer. It was all she had to give.

"You know, I feel kind of sorry for him," said Leeza.

"Not half as sorry as he feels for himself," said Shelby,

"but he'll get over it." She sighed. "I sure almost blew it, didn't I? What a femalus stupidus!"

"Oh, well, we're all dumb when it comes to men. Look at poor, old Guenevere—all those years she spent with Arthur when she was longing for Lancelot."

The phone rang again.

"Speaking of Lancelot, it's probably David," said Leeza, and snatched up the receiver.

Shelby watched her hopefully.

"No, Matt," lied Leeza, "I just got in, myself, but Shel's not here. We've got rehearsals starting, so she probably won't be back till late. Yeah, I'll tell her, but don't hold your breath."

She hung up. "Boy, he doesn't give up."

Shelby frowned. "I thought for sure it would be David."

"You'll be hearing from him," predicted Leeza. "No man's going to go to all the trouble he went to last night and not follow up on it."

But there was no follow-up all weekend. No flowers arrived at the Fifth Avenue, and no Phantom lurked at the stage door.

By Monday morning Shelby couldn't stand it anymore. She called his office and got the receptionist, who politely asked who was calling. Shelby gave her name, then waited. The woman came back on a minute later to say he was in a meeting.

"Well, he could be," said Leeza, still optimistic.

Shelby called again right before noon, when David usually took his lunch break. This time he was out of the office, and now she knew for sure he was avoiding her. But why? It didn't make any sense.

Unless he was trying to punish her for the way she'd strung him along. That was it.

"Don't be stupid," scoffed Leeza after hearing Shelby's theory. "Guys don't do stuff like that."

"Didn't you ever read *The Count of Monte Cristo*?" challenged Shelby.

"David loves you," Leeza insisted.

"If he loves me so much, why hasn't he called me since Saturday? My God, I made such a fool of myself. I practically begged him to do it right there in that doorway."

"So, now that he has you panting for him, he just rides off into the sunset? He leaves out the slam bam and just says, 'Thank you, Ma'am?' What man thinks like that?"

"One who wants to get even," said Shelby dully. "And I deserved it."

"Oh, you did not. You couldn't help it if you didn't know who you loved."

"And now that I know who I do, it's the perfect time to dump me."

Leeza made a face. "You need to be locked up. You really do."

"I wish I could be locked up. With David. Right now."

"Well, that makes two of us," said Leeza. "Then you'd see how stupid you're being."

"I hope that's all it is," said Shelby wistfully.

Diana paused in the hallway. Her mother was talking on the guest room extension in the kind of hushed voice one used at funerals. Diana carefully turned the knob and cracked the door. Flo sat on the bed, hunched over the phone.

"You'll have to get someone else to do the decorating for the Valentine's party. Something has come up here and I need to stay with my daughter."

Diana pushed the door open and leaned against the doorjamb.

Her mother turned at the sound, and, seeing Diana, gave a start. "Oh, well, it was nice of you to call, Vi. You take care and I'll see you when I get back."

She hung up the phone and offered an innocent smile

that couldn't hope to stand up to Diana's accusatory raised eyebrow.

"What are you doing?" Diana demanded.

"Just talking with Vi Singleton. You remember Vi, the woman with the awful dye job."

As if her mother was one to talk, but that was beside the point.

"And what were you talking about?"

"She just called to see how I was doing."

"The phone hasn't rung," observed Diana. How she wished it would!

"Oh, well." Flo didn't finish her sentence. "Did you want something, dear?"

"Just to know why you're canceling going back to Ocean Shores."

Flo abandoned the pleasant mask. "Because I don't want to leave you like this."

"Are you planning on staying for the next six months?"

"I could," offered Flo.

"You'd run out of things to clean." Diana sat down on the bed and put an arm around her mother's shoulders. "I appreciate the thought, Mom, but there's no sense in neither of us having a life."

"I have a life," said Flo, "and you're the most important part of it. Darling, I know I can't even pretend to take the place of a lost love, but sometimes a limping heart just needs someone to lean on for a little while. This old crutch may not have many more years. You should use her while you can. Anyway," she added briskly, "there's no sense going home when I'd have to turn right around and come back to see my granddaughter starring at the Fifth Avenue, now, is there? And I have a lot of corners left to clean in this place. That woman you've been using does not do a thorough job."

Diana gave up the fight, and realized that she was glad she'd lost. No one in this world loved you as unconditionally as your mother. Gratefully, she hugged hers, buried her face against the soft, wrinkled skin, and smelled that peculiar mixture of Chanel No. 5 and mothballs that she'd come to associate with her mother. Once it had been Chanel and chocolate chip cookies.

"I think I need some chocolate," she murmured.

"It's a girl's best friend," said Flo. "I think I saw a package of chocolate chips in your cupboard."

Diana sighed deeply. Chocolate was a small consolation for what she had lost. Life would never be the same again. But then, life never was; days ebbed and flowed like the tide and the sand doing their dance, unearthing some treasures and burying others. Gain and loss both contributed to human existence, and she'd have to come to grips with that sooner or later.

Her treacherous heart suddenly conjured an image of Lance's face, and she knew it would be later. Much later.

Like a shipwreck survivor clinging to a piece of wood, Shelby continued to hang on to the hope that David would return her calls or come to the Fifth Avenue to see her, but when the second week of February began, she gave up and let herself sink into a sea of misery. She tried to stay focused on the play, tried to lose herself in the dialogue being exchanged on the stage between Noel Harrison and Lauri Landry, but it was hard. She'd forgotten what a boring play *Camelot* was for the chorus. Not enough to do, not enough to keep her from thinking about her own magical experience, and how it had turned out to be simply that: some enchanted evening.

She must have been enchanted, must have dreamed the whole thing. Except Leeza had seen it, too, so she couldn't have dreamed it.

As she blocked out her scene with Arthur and sang her seductive song, she wished it was David standing downstage from her. She called to Arthur to follow her and stretched her arms toward him, willing the image of herself into David's mind.

When she had finished, Mr. Harrison complimented her, and as she smiled and thanked him, she thought how happy David would have been to see her making such an impression on the star of the show. Maybe, after a couple of seasons at the Fifth, she'd work up her nerve and go to Broadway. After all, she had nothing to lose, and nothing to keep her in Seattle. Now.

She and Leeza came home to find the answering machine flashing with yet another message of love from Matt. Poor Matt. Would he ever give up? And why couldn't David have left even one word on there?

On the morning of February twelfth, Shelby started out to run some errands and opened her apartment door to find an envelope bearing her name taped to it.

"What's that?" asked Leeza.

"I have no idea," said Shelby, studying the printing. She ripped open the envelope to find an odd-looking missive: a series of words cut from newspapers and magazines, pasted on plain white printer paper. "Meet me tomorrow at eleven A.M. at Tiffany's," it commanded, and was signed, "the man who can't give up."

"Oh, great," she moaned. "Now he's trying to get tricky."

"You're going to have to go see him," said Leeza.

"I am not meeting Matt at Tiffany's," said Shelby firmly.

"It's the only way to get him out of your life for good. You're going to have to take the ring and throw it in his face before he can accept the fact that he's really lost you."

Why couldn't he just get it through his head they were through? This was so unfun, so irritating, so . . . Matt.

"What did I ever see in him?" Leeza opened her mouth to speak and Shelby cut her off. "That was a retorical question."

"Too bad," said Leeza. "I had a great answer."

"It should have been David sending that note," grumbled Shelby.

"Well, maybe you should have sent one to him."

It was a thought.

In fact, it was a good one. "You know, I think you've got something there. What could I do? What would impress someone like David?"

"You could write him a poem," suggested Leeza. "Roses are red, violets are blue. I never met a Phantom like you."

Shelby looked at her in disgust. "That was deep."

"Hey, I'm a dancer, not a writer. What do you expect?"

"It's got to be something that will really appeal to his sentimental side, something uniquely us," said Shelby, and began pacing the room, waiting for inspiration to strike.

"I've got it!" said Leeza, snapping her fingers. "What about the old movie thing? You could do like he did with you; send him some flowers and include a tape of some movie that symbolizes your relationship. Actually, you'd better make that a DVD since he's not broke like us, and, being a guy, he'll have the latest technology."

"Hmmm, not a bad idea," said Shelby thoughtfully. "What could I send him?"

"How about . . . *Cyrano de Bergerac*."

"He dies."

"Oh, yeah."

"I know," said Shelby. "*While You Were Sleeping*."

"Oooh, great idea. The woman who thinks she loves the hunk and then falls in love with a real man—that would be perfect."

"Come on," said Shelby, suddenly full of enthusiasm. She grabbed Leeza and began towing her toward the door. "Help me pick out something a man would like."

•  •  •

At two o'clock that afternoon a basket of cheeses and meats wrapped in red cellophane was delivered to Harper Investments, Inc. Nestled among them sat a DVD.

"I assume this is from the woman who was looking for you earlier this week," said Ruth, the receptionist. "You have obviously made an impression."

"It would appear I have," said David, plucking out the DVD. He looked at the cover and chuckled.

He could feel Ruth buzzing with curiosity next to him, so he turned it so she could see.

*"While You Were Sleeping?"*

David's chuckle grew to a laugh, and the laugh grew into something bigger, something that made him throw back his head and howl.

"Oh, I love it," he said at last. "Life is good."

"Well, I guess so," said Ruth, as he strolled away. "Wait a minute," she called. "You're forgetting the rest of your goodies."

"Take them home for your family," he said and shut himself back in his office.

He sat down at his desk, propped the DVD against his computer monitor, then tipped back in his chair and admired it. He felt so good he just had to chuckle again. This was perfect. Shelby finally, truly wanted him. She was the one doing the pursuing now. And, best of all, she had no idea what was going on in his head. She was worried and desperate. For him. It just didn't get any better than this.

Saturday the thirteenth, the day before Valentine's Day. Shelby burrowed farther under the covers. Maybe she could pay Leeza to go to Tiffany's for her.

Why was Matt torturing her like this, anyway? Why couldn't he just accept the fact that they were through? For the same reason she hadn't been able to accept it for so long: stubbornness. Only, unlike hers, which she now realized had been rooted in fear, Matt's tenaciousness grew out of pride. His ego never allowed him to lose at anything. That was probably doubly true when it came to women. She'd bet he hadn't heard the word "no" from anyone of the opposite sex since he was five years old. Well, it was time for him to expand his vocabulary.

And it was time for her to grow up and take responsibility for what she wanted in life. First she'd lose Matt, then she'd win David. Then, together, they would conquer New York.

Filled with determination, she threw off the covers, gathered her clothes, and headed for the shower.

Leeza wandered out of her bedroom just as Shelby was slipping into her jacket. "You look like a woman with a purpose," she observed.

"I am. I'm going to tell Matt off in a way even he can understand, and then I'm going to call David's answering machine and invite myself to his place for a nice, long chat. No begging or pleading, no manipulating. I'm done with that. I'm just going to put it to him straight: Are we soul mates or not?"

Leeza nodded her approval. "Just don't forget you have to be at the theater by noon."

"Well, it shouldn't take him too long to answer one question."

"No, but if he answers it right, it may take you guys a while to unglue yourselves."

The thought of being in David's arms again made Shelby feel like she was backstage on opening night. "Yeah," she said with a grin.

She marched out of the apartment with an air of confidence, but as she walked into Pacific Place she could feel it exiting stage right, while dread stepped in to take over, making her slightly nauseous. She should just not show. Matt would get the message. She turned and began her retreat.

No. She'd come all this way. It would be gutless to leave now. She pivoted and headed toward Tiffany's.

The wink of the diamonds was almost blinding as she entered the store, but not so blinding that she couldn't sec David standing by the counter, chatting with the sales clerk. David. Her heart bounced down to her toes and back again. It was a mirage, the jewelry store variety being experienced by a woman whose love life the last few days made the Sahara look like a rainforest. Shc blinked.

He was still there. And next to him, on top of the counter, sat two tall cups of Starbucks coffee and a platter overloaded with croissants, sliced melons, and grapes. The clerk saw her and nodded her direction.

David turned and flashed her a cocky grin. "Join me for breakfast?"

# Nineteen

*Shelby wanted to* laugh, cry, shout. "What are you doing?"

"Having breakfast at Tiffany's," said David. "And, I hope, buying a ring for the most beautiful woman on the planet." He picked up a cup and held it out to her. "Join me?"

She did. "Is that a mocha?"

"Of course."

"You are amazing."

"I have only begun to amaze you," he said, and slipped his arms around her.

He had done it to her again, made her feel like she had stepped through a mirror into a world of magic and wonder.

"Oh, David," she sighed and kissed him, heedless of their audience of one.

Clapping and some appreciative hoots made her realize that the audience had grown. Blushing, she pulled away from David to see that four other customers had entered the store and were enjoying the show.

He chuckled and tapped the tip of her nose. "We'll do

the curtain call later. Now, pick out the ring of your dreams."

And she did; a one-karat solitaire set in white gold. She left the shop wearing it, with David at her side, an arm possessively wrapped around her waist.

He escorted her to the Fifth Avenue, and there they found Leeza and James positioned at the backstage door, with the whole chorus waiting behind them.

"You knew," Shelby accused her friend.

"Of course. Who do you think taped that letter on the door for him?"

"So, show us the ring," James demanded.

Shelby held out her hand and everyone leaned forward to ooh and aah.

James let out a whistle. "Now, that is class. So, when are you going to get married?"

"Whenever Shelby wants," said David.

"You're going to spoil her so rotten," Leeza lamented.

"Impossible," said David.

"I agree," said James. "Now, we've talked with Michael, and he said it's okay for you to hang around and watch rehearsal. During dinner break we're taking you guys out to celebrate."

Shelby turned to David. "Did you have plans?"

"Yes. To see as much of you as possible."

That sounded good to her.

David hung out at the theater all afternoon and evening. It was a beautiful, old place, built in the twenties and designed with an elaborate Chinese motif. Its great domed ceiling, with its rich colors and designs looked fit for an Oriental palace, while elaborately carved dragons emerged from the supporting beams. The overall effect was stunning opulence.

Much as David admired the architecture and decor of the historic building, today he only had eyes for what was happening on stage. Sitting just in back of the orchestra pit and watching Shelby sing, he felt like he was seeing a young Judy Garland or a Sarah Brightman. No, better than Sarah Brightman, he decided. Shelby brought a fresh creativity to her small part when she sang that he was sure Sarah could never have had. He sat transfixed as she sang to King Arthur. She was a true wood nymph; sexy and alluring, yet playful. When the reviews came out, David knew it would be her praises the critics sang and not the stars'.

It was well after eleven when he finally took Shelby home, and they curled up together on her couch to share kisses and dreams.

"So, you really wouldn't mind living in New York?" she asked for the third time.

"I wouldn't mind living in Timbuktu, as long as I was with you. Look, Shelby, you've got talent, and we both know it. I can't be selfish and expect to get to keep that all to myself. It would be like a man buying stolen art and then hiding it away in some secret room where only he could enjoy it."

"But what about your job?"

"I can manage money anywhere. And, by the way, I intend to manage yours, so that when you start commanding those star salaries you won't end up squandering it all."

"Yessir," she said with mock humility.

"And one more thing."

"What?"

David ran his fingers along her jaw, settling them under her chin. "Remember, when you're singing opposite all those handsome men, you only have one real life leading man."

"I'll try," she said.

He tilted her chin and lowered his mouth to hers, murmuring, "Let me give you something to help you remember."

• • •

The first thing Shelby did when she awakened on Valentine's Day was to check her left hand. Yes, there really was a diamond sparkling on it. Yesterday hadn't been a dream and she was truly engaged. To the right man.

Time to call Mom.

Gram answered the phone.

"Hi Gram. Is Mom there? I've got some news for her."

"Oh?" prompted Gram

"I'm engaged. But you can't tell her."

"I wouldn't dream of it," said Gram. "Let me go see if she's awake."

What was that all about? It was almost ten, and Mom was always up by eight.

Mom came on the phone. Her voice held all the energy of overcooked spaghetti.

"You sound awful," said Shelby. "Are you okay?"

"I'm just tired," said Mom. "How are you doing?"

"I'm doing great. I'm engaged to David."

"Well, well," said Mom.

"He is truly the most amazing man on the entire planet. Do you know how he proposed?"

"No idea."

"We had breakfast at Tiffany's. How's that for impressive?"

"Pretty good. And did you dress like Audrey Hepburn?"

"I didn't even know he was going to be there. I got a note made of cut-out letters. I thought it was going to be Matt, making one last try. I am so glad now that Matt was such a jerk. If he hadn't been, I'd have never met David."

"Things have a way of working out," said Mom. But there was something in her tone of voice that made it sound like she didn't really believe it.

"Are you sure you're okay?" pressed Shelby.

"Of course. Now, when are you going to bring David over so we can get acquainted with him?"

"How about tomorrow? No rehearsals on Mondays."

"Tomorrow will be perfect. Bring him for dinner."

"Great," said Shelby. "I can hardly wait for you to meet him. He really is wonderful."

"He's willing to make a commitment. That already makes him wonderful in my book," said Mom.

Shelby got the underlying message. Mom had been skeptical of Matt all along. Mom had been right. "I know," said Shelby, acknowledging her mother's superior wisdom.

She sang David's praises for a few more minutes, then said good-bye to her mom. After she'd hung up, she realized she should have asked to talk to Gram again. Gram would have told her what was going on over there.

And something was. In spite of her warm wishes and kind words, Shelby could just tell that her mother wasn't her usual happy self. It probably had something to do with Matt's uncle Lance. Like uncle like nephew. If that had blown up it was just as well. Mom needed someone stable and together, an older version of David. Maybe David had an uncle.

Well, she'd think of someone. Meanwhile, she had to get in the shower. David would be over in less than an hour, and she was going to make crepes for him and Leeza before they all went to the theater.

Matt walked to his car, fingering the ring box in his overcoat pocket. Never had a day dragged by so slowly. He had been waiting for this since one, when he had called the theater to find out when the performers usually broke for dinner. It would be worth the wait, though, when he saw the look on Shel's face after he made his Valentine's Day ambush and stuck this ring under her nose. It wasn't the Hope diamond, but it was the thought that counted, and when Shel learned how much thought he'd put into swinging this financially, she'd be doubly impressed. He still couldn't believe he was about to become engaged. But it would be okay; they'd have a long engagement. Shel wouldn't care. All she really wanted was the symbol on her finger that said she'd won.

He left his car in a nearby parking lot and made the short hike to the Fifth Avenue, envisioning how it would all go down. He'd give her the ring, take her to dinner down at the Metropolitan Grill and ply her with champagne. Then, after rehearsal, he'd take her to his place and they'd celebrate between the sheets.

The alley behind the theater, with its uneven bricks and Dumpsters, had the feel of alleys everywhere. It spoke of neglect and loneliness. It was the holding pen for the unwanted, the unlovely, and the unpresentable. Dejection hung over it as palpably as the mist that was trying to slip cold droplets down his neck. He hunched inside his overcoat and wondered how long he'd have to lurk out here, waiting for Shel to come out.

He walked up to the stage door. Laughing, disembodied voices floated out from a small speaker mounted on the wall. Would this be how he would spend his life once he was married to Shel, holding up brick walls on damp, chilly nights, listening to her voice, waiting for her to come back into the real world?

A chorus of voices squawked out of the speaker, singing to him about the lusty month of May, and he turned the box in his pocket over and over and tried to sort Shel's voice out from the herd. He couldn't. It was one giant, warbling mass.

The singing stopped and was replaced by the buzz of several conversations and scattered laughter. "I'm starving," said someone.

This was it. They were starting their dinner break. Shel would be coming out any minute. He decided he didn't want to propose to her here in the alley, and knocked on the backstage door.

He had to knock again, harder, before a short guy with a battered beret pulled over shaggy, black hair opened it.

"Hi," said Matt. "I've got something for Shelby Barrett. Is it okay if I wait for her?"

"Sure," said the guy, swinging the door wide. "If she doesn't leave by the other door. "

*Great.* "Can you go get her and tell her someone's here to see her?"

"Okay. Wait here."

Matt waited. He tried to distract himself from his growing impatience by examining the bricks of the wall. Many of them had been painted with the titles from the various shows done at the Fifth Avenue over the last twenty years, and bore the signatures of all the cast members. He supposed after this show was over that somewhere there would be a brick sporting Shel's signature. Big deal. Your name on a brick.

Another moment and he heard her voice and Leeza's familiar laugh. And a lower voice. James? He'd be damned if he'd make his proposal in front of that idiot. He'd pull Shelby aside, have her tell them to go on without her.

They came down the backstage stairs, Leeza and James in the lead, Leeza looking back over her shoulder and laughing. Behind them came Shelby and . . . Matt's stomach felt like he'd just started a fifty-story elevator plunge. "Jones."

Shel looked surprised. Painfully so. Matt's armpits sprang a leak. Only determination kept him rooted where he stood.

She said his name, and he cringed at the unenthusiastic tone in her voice. "What are you doing here?"

"I need to talk to you," he said. "Alone."

"We'll wait outside," said Leeza, and she and James slipped by him like he had the plague.

Jones didn't move.

"Do you mind?" snapped Matt.

"Yes, actually, I do. Anything you have to say to Shelby you can say to me."

"I didn't come to propose to you."

Shelby's eyes filled with pity, and now Matt really didn't want to be here. "I'm sorry, Matt. I'm already engaged." She held out her hand and flashed a diamond ring at him.

He felt like he'd been snuck up on and hit alongside the head with a two-by-four. This couldn't be happening.

"I can't believe it," he stammered. "You barely know this guy."

"No, *you* barely know him. David and I are a match. You and I aren't. Maybe we were once, but not now. I'm sorry."

"Yeah, I can tell," snarled Matt. "Well, have a nice life."

He sounded like a junior high boy, but he couldn't help it. Pain was expanding inside his chest and his eyes were stinging, and all he could think about was getting to his car where he could bawl like a baby and no one would see. He pushed his way out of the door and went down the alley as fast as he could without looking like he was running. The mist had turned to sleet. And that was good, because no one he passed would be able to tell for sure what was putting the drops on his cheeks.

Shelby turned to David. "I feel terrible."

"Regrets?"

"About you? Never. I just feel bad that he feels so bad."

"He'll get over it. His pride took a hit and he's mad as hell. But the bottom line is, if he really loved you, really wanted you forever, he would have done what he needed to do to keep you."

"Are you saying Matt never really wanted me?"

"Of course he wanted you. On his terms. Maybe that's his definition of love. It's not mine."

Shelby smiled at him and put a hand to his cheek. "You

are truly wonderful. What would my life have been like if I hadn't met you?"

"Oh, you'd have gone through a string of brainless beefcakes who would have squandered your money. Come on, let's catch up with Leeza and James. I'm starving."

It had been the weekend from hell. Saturday his store had been overrun with babies too young to even be driving let alone marrying, all running up their charge cards and drooling over engagement rings, their happy faces mocking him. Lance finally escaped to the racquet club and duked it out with the ball machine. On Sunday afternoon he spent his Valentine's Day hiding in his perfect, sterile house, watching a football game on TV with only a bottle of Scotch for company.

Today his head hurt almost as much as his heart and it was all he could do to be civil to the other Rotarians mingling around him, enjoying their pre-lunch cocktail. Only one other businessman at the lunch seemed to be in as foul a mood as he was, and he wandered over to see what had happened to make his old pal, Harry Carlson, so miserable.

"What's the matter, Harry? Did they put dog shit in your glass?"

Harry glowered at his drink. "They may as well have. Nothing tastes good these days."

"Business bad?"

"Business is great. It's life that stinks." Harry let out a gigantic sigh. "I think you had the right idea, Gregory. Stay single. Don't have kids." He shook his head, and the loose skin at his neck wobbled with the motion. "You work all your life, slave to give them something to pass on, and why? Nobody wants it."

"You've got a son."

Harry's snort told Lance what he thought of his son. "Yeah. Well, he just told me this weekend that he doesn't want the business. He wants to be a clothing designer. He's got a lover in New York now, and he wants to move there to be with him. Wants to follow his bliss. What does that mean?"

"You have a daughter, don't you?"

"If I leave her the business, that creep she's married to will drink away all the profits. I tell you, it's a good thing Martha isn't alive to see this. It would kill her. Hell, it's killing me."

"I'm sorry," said Lance. Even as he said the words he felt like he'd just offered to attach a severed arm with masking tape. Sorry was a trite piece of nothing to offer a man whose children had refused his legacy.

"Yeah, well, so am I," said Harry. "I'm sorry I ever had kids. You know, you think after working your butt off for them and sacrificing that they're going to appreciate it. They don't. Kids are the worst investment you can ever make."

"That's easy for you to say, Harry. You've got some."

"You can have 'em," retorted Harry.

Regret seemed to be the main entree for lunch today, and Lance found he'd lost his appetite. He clapped Harry on the back and moved away. He kept moving until he found himself in his car and driving north, out of the city.

"I think we should have rib roast for dinner," said Flo. "All men love prime rib."

"Good idea," said Diana. "I'll pick up a cake at the bakery while I'm at it."

"You'll do no such thing. Cake is a woman's dessert. Get me a can of cherries and I'll make a pie. And pick up some vanilla ice cream to go with it."

"All right."

"And try to smile once in a while. I'd hate you to run into anyone we know and have them think I died."

Diana managed to lift the corners of her lips. "I know. I need to quit acting like a tragedy queen."

"Yes, you do," agreed your mother. "Let's spend today at least concentrating on what we can be happy about. Shelby has found a nice young man and you don't have to worry about her anymore."

"Really? You mean to tell me that once she's married I'll stop worrying about her?"

"I didn't say that. I just said you don't have to."

"Like you don't have to worry about me."

"Old habits die hard."

Diana hugged her mother, and Flo hugged back. She kissed Diana's cheek and said, "I wish I could make this easier for you, baby."

Diana gave Flo one final squeeze before pulling away. "Hugs help. Anyway, I guess life just wasn't meant to be easy."

"I'd say that's a good guess. But when the going gets tough, the tough go shopping. So get going."

"Yes, ma'am," said Diana, and made a sharp salute. "I'll be back in an hour. Try not to start any big cleaning projects."

"Just a little dusting," promised Flo.


Diana spent the next hour forcing herself to think only about Shelby and David and what she should have for dinner. She abandoned her mother's suggestion for rib roast in favor of salmon, then picked up fresh mushrooms for the tossed salad and some roses for the table.

She returned home to see a familiar car parked in front of the house, and her breathing stopped. Why was Lance here, and what could he possibly want? She gathered her bags and hurried into the house, hope and fear fighting for transcendence.

She found him seated at the kitchen table with her mother, nursing a cup of coffee. He stood the second she entered the room, and the look he gave her was one she had imagined on countless heros' faces as she wrote that all-important scene where conflicts were finally resolved.

"Diana."

Still looking at him, she set the bags on the counter.

"Well," said Flo. "Why don't you two take a drive, and I'll start working on the roast."

Lance already had Diana's arm and was urging her out of the room. "I got salmon," she called over her shoulder.

"I hope you got enough for an extra guest," said Lance.

"Why are you here? What are you doing?"

"Changing the plot of this story before it's too late," he said. "Come on. Let's go for a drive."

Once in the car, he headed downhill for the Edmonds waterfront. "I hear your daughter's engaged," he said casually, keeping his eyes on the traffic.

"She is, but not to your nephew."

"Good for her."

He found a parking spot with a view of the sound, then shut off the engine and turned to face her. "I've been miserable all weekend."

"What am I supposed to say to that?"

"Nothing. Let me finish telling you what a fool I've been and then please tell me I haven't blown it. Diana, I want to be with you for the rest of my life. I can't believe I almost threw that away on some pride-induced fantasy. I'm no medieval king and I don't need an heir. What I do need is a woman who loves me, warts and all, and who wants to be with me. I'm hoping you still do, because if you don't, I'm lost. I'll never find another woman like you."

"Oh, Lance, are you sure? Most people want children."

"Yeah, they do. And most children turn out to be a disappointment."

"Mine hasn't."

"So, maybe you'll share."

Diana indulged herself in a coy smile. "Maybe."

"And maybe you'll kiss me now."

"Definitely."


Diana wore green that night, to match her engagement ring. The dinner was delicious, and the only one who seemed to miss the rib roast was Flo. Barrymore showed his gratitude for the change of menu by tipping the salmon pan off the stove and scattering skin and fish bones all over Flo's newly mopped kitchen floor.

"That's it," growled Flo. "Let's skin him."

"No, let's send him home with Shelby," suggested Diana.

"Mom, you know I can't have pets." As Diana began thoughtfully regarding David, she added, "And don't even think of foisting him on David. I don't want my engagement broken before it's barely begun."

"I think we can deal with this," said Lance, and he and David managed a cleanup job that met Flo's standards. Then, to further impress her, they served dessert.

"Well, things are finally under control around here. I guess I can go home now," Flo said as Lance poured the dessert coffee.

"After opening night," Shelby reminded her.

"Oh, yes. I wouldn't want to miss that for the world."

"Now that you're going to be part of the family, I hope you'll be there, too, Lance," Shelby added. "We just happen to have an extra ticket."

Her words seemed to please him. "Absolutely."

"I can't remember when I've seen Mom this happy," she said to her grandmother later as they loaded the dishwasher. "She's practically giddy."

"It just goes to show you, if you wait long enough the right man does come along."

Shelby's expression turned dreamy. "He sure did."

• • •

Both David and Lance had sent Shelby flowers on opening night, making her feel like a star. Her song had gone beautifully, and the applause she got, both after the number and during the curtain call, still rang in her ears. Mom, Gram, David, Lance, and Suzanne had all come backstage to congratulate her after the performance, each predicting a successful Broadway career. She was still so excited, she was sure she would never sleep again as long as she lived. In fact, she didn't think she could ever feel any higher.

Until Norb turned to her at the cast party and said, "I'm going to be directing a revival of *Guys and Dolls* in New York this fall. How do you think you'd look in a Salvation Army suit?"

"You're kidding."

He shook his head. "I think you should come out and audition for the part of Sarah Brown."

"So what do you think, babe?" said David, giving her a squeeze.

Think? Who could think?

"She'll be there," said David.

Lance walked Diana and Flo up the walk to the house.

"I just can't get over how wonderful Shelby was," said Flo for the fourth time.

"She takes after her mother," said Lance, lifting the key from Diana's hand and opening the door for them.

"Well, I'm going right to bed," Flo announced, walking straight through the living room. "It's late and I need my beauty sleep."

Diana and Lance wished her good night, and as soon as she'd disappeared into the hallway, he pulled Diana into his arms. "Your daughter's on her way to becoming a star, your mother has your house in order. This would be the perfect time to elope."

"Oh? And where will we go for our honeymoon?"

"Niagara Falls, Paris, Rome. You name it."

Diana thought a moment. "You know, I've never been to the Caribbean. A cruise might be nice."

"It might at that," said Lance thoughtfully.

"And you can show me all the great romantic hide-aways."

"Absolutely."

"And shops."

Lance eyed her. "Oh, really?"

"Yes, really. I want to visit all those little-known places and get a steal on precious gems."

"You'll find a lot of them in the Caribbean, my love," said Lance, "but none as valuable as the one I'll be bringing with me."

"More flattery," said Diana in mock disgust.

"It's only flattery if you don't mean it," said Lance, and kissed her.

# Passionately Ever After

*The flight from* Seattle Tacoma International Airport to New York was now loading. It was a wonder, even with the use of a microphone, that the attendant was able to make that information heard over the noise of the crowd who had come to see off Mr. and Mrs. David Jones.

"Take care of my house," David said to his sister. "Shelby and I will be coming back to retire in it someday."

"I'll believe that when I see it," said Cassie. "And just remember, we expect the guest room to be ready when we come to see Shelby in *Guys and Dolls*."

"I don't have the part yet," said Shelby.

David just rolled his eyes. He kissed his mom, then turned to give his mother-in-law a hug and shake hands with his father-in-law.

"Take care," said Lance, "and keep us posted."

"We will," David promised.

"There's the last call," said Suzanne. "You'd better get going."

Shelby gave her mom one final hug, then she and David grabbed hands and headed for the gate. A voice that sounded like Leeza's off-pitch alto started singing the chorus of *There's No Business Like Show Business*.

David grinned at Shelby. "This is it: Act two. Are you ready?"

Ready or not, she was going.

Shelby nodded.

"Okay," said David. "Let's go knock 'em dead."

Dear Reader,

Hopefully, your search for the perfect soul mate has gone more smoothly than that of the characters who stumbled their way through these pages. And I'm sure you're all much wiser than Shelby, who probably ranks second only to Lois Lane in female stupidity. But, if you're wanting some advice on finding Mr. Perfect, I hope you'll check out my next book, titled *A Prince of a Guy*. There you'll meet Doctor Kate Stonewall, radio shrink and expert on how to tell the princes from the frogs. Kate has no trouble solving other people's problems, but when her competition, radio personality Jeff Hardin, moves in next door, it looks like it's the good doctor who will be needing advice. I hope you'll look for it this summer. Watch my web site, www.Sheilasplace.com for the upcoming sneak preview.